The 31 Days of May

Helen Aitchison

D1610680

Cahill Davis Publishing

Copyright © 2024 Helen Aitchison

The moral right of Helen Aitchison to be identified as the Author of the Work has been asserted by her in accordance with the Copyright, Designs and Patents Act 1988.

First published in Great Britain in 2024 by Cahill Davis Publishing Limited.

First published in paperback in Great Britain in 2024 by Cahill Davis Publishing Limited.

Printed and bound in Great Britain by Clays Ltd, Elcograf S.p.A

Apart from any use permitted under UK copyright law, this publication may only be reproduced, stored, or transmitted, in any form, or by any means, with prior permission in writing of the publishers or, in case of reprographic production, in accordance with the terms of licences issued by the Copyright Licencing Agency.

All characters in this publication are fictitious and any resemblance to real persons, living or dead, is purely coincidental.

ISBN 978-1-915307-08-8 (eBook)

ISBN 978-1-915307-07-1 (Paperback)

Cahill Davis Publishing Limited

www.cahilldavispublishing.co.uk

To Mam and Dad, for your eternal love and support (to us all).

Part One

The Past

Prologue

May had heard the story of how she came into the world countless times over the years by her parents. Repeated, like a CD skipping at the same part over and over again. She would roll her eyes, shake her head and smile faintly whilst it was retold at cousins' birthday parties, Christmas get-togethers, weddings, christenings and even funerals.

It made social situations, which could already be a challenge to May, more cringeworthy. She would squirm in her seat as the tale was told, hoping the engaged listeners would focus on the speakers and not the subject of the story. May would quickly get up at the end of the anecdote, making an excuse, such as needing the toilet or getting drinks, to simply escape any further focus on herself and dissolve the flashing Hollywood-style arrow she almost felt penetrating down from the ceiling in her direction. It had embarrassed her as an adolescent and became tedious as an adult.

But May never realised that one day she would give anything to hear her parents telling the tale.

Chapter 1

May had a loving childhood, with parents who wrapped her in a blanket of security and affection. Her childhood was nothing flashy, nothing extraordinary, but it was safe, happy and nurturing. Her mother, Fran, worked in office admin; her dad, Victor, was a mechanic. They had a comfortable life, holidaying every year to Greece and sometimes Spain. Fran and Victor were not lucky enough to conceive again after a seven-year battle to carry May. Although an only child, May didn't mind her own company; in fact, she often preferred it, finding making friends a challenge that sometimes felt like meeting the threshold to compete in the Olympic Games.

There had always been something 'different' about May. Nowadays, difference is celebrated and embraced in a way it should be, but it wasn't as much when May was at school. She was awkward in presence, looks and articulation. She struggled with friends, struggled with expression and struggled with her inner conflicts that seemed to be minuscule to others. May tried to blend in, like a new coat of paint on a stained part of the wall, but she never managed it, becoming accustomed to always being on her guard, as if waiting for a predator to swoop. From as early as she could remember, May thrived on routine and organisation. It kept her feeling useful, in control and content.

She would write lists and cross off items when complete. As a youngster, it would be lists of games, cartoons and names she could call her dolls. When she became

a little older, she taught herself how to use the computer one summer, and her lists evolved to spreadsheet
form and included food items for the weekly shop with
Fran. Fran would look at the print-off and smile at her
daughter, kiss her on the forehead and tell her she knew
what her baby wanted. May hated being called a baby and
wanted to grow up as quickly as she could, always feeling
she wasn't like her peers in maturity and interests.

At the weekly food shop, May would ask Fran to reach
any shelves above two in height. Her mam would look
lovingly down at her, hand her the smooth peanut butter
with the red lid or apricot jam, pat May's head and call
her 'my methodical May'. May liked being called this
much more than being called a baby.

Over the years, Fran became accustomed to May's
quirks. It was fine that May helped with the intricacies
of household budgeting at the age of eight, that they
watched documentaries in the evenings instead of soaps
and that they had to take an endless list of items on
holiday in fear she couldn't purchase them there.

School was difficult at times, especially as May wasn't
memorable. If she were ice cream, she would be vanilla,
without sprinkles or toffee sauce. Just vanilla. Plain, boring to many, predictable vanilla. May saw nothing wrong
with vanilla, but other people liked chocolate chip, pista-
chio or even mango sorbet. She didn't speak up in class,
never raised her hand and always tried to make herself
as small as possible to avoid being targeted by teachers.
The teachers knew she was clever and that she would
have the answers in a class full of uninterested children,
so they would ask her, wanting someone to engage with
learning, perhaps even innocently trying to include May,
using her as an example for the others to concentrate
and try. May at least hoped it was this and that they
didn't intentionally realise they were exposing her to
more mockery and exclusion. She would sit in the corner,
her palms sweaty, trying to shrink. Hard to do when she
was five-foot-ten by the age of thirteen. Her height was

an open door for name-calling—lanky, beanpole, streak of piss.

May had a saving grace at school in the form of Scarlett. A small number of other friends tiptoed on the periphery, but Scarlett was May's everything. They had become inseparable in primary school, when they were ten years old. Scarlett joined the school after her family moved to Newcastle from North Yorkshire. Scarlett wasn't anywhere near as awkward, quiet or tall as May, and May always felt she would have been a bigger target to some of the class cows had it not been for Scarlett. She was beautiful inside and out, naturally pretty without being showy. But the most stunning side of Scarlett was her personality. She was gentle, kind and funny, with wonderful dancing and singing talent.

May was logical and thrived in mathematics and science in particular, but every academic subject felt quite easy to her. Her lack of after-school activities, except running club each Tuesday and seeing Scarlett a few times a week, meant she had time to study. May was naturally gifted in the IQ department and knew she wanted to be a scientist, researching scientific phenomena to make medicine and the world a better place. She read books on her research heroes and watched documentary after documentary about science, evolution, medicine and breakthroughs.

After her high school exams, May moved on to college, where she studied physics, chemistry, biology and mathematics. People at college were less cliquey, less irritatingly giggly and immature. May felt more comfortable being vanilla in a more eclectic environment and with smaller classes. She didn't have to try to dissolve in the corner, frightened of being asked any questions. Scarlett attended the same college, studying performing arts. They often met during their lunch break, and May made a few other friends but always enjoyed a little time to herself. She would sit in the library, absorbed in books, soaking up knowledge like a parched plant with the summer rain.

After college, May went to university. She had never wanted to go to another part of the country to study. The thought of living in a box room whilst sharing a grubby bathroom and kitchen full of dirty pots and pans made her wriggle in disgust. She was happy living at home, where she felt comfortable and in control. It was also financially responsible, so why change a good thing?

University brought another layer of life to May's world. She relished in the structure of her semester lectures, seminars and library time. It allowed her to accommodate a part-time job working in a local estate agency, Lawson's, where she helped the director, Jack, with admin and small finance tasks. Lawson's was a productive team on the whole, and she enjoyed the work with minimal distractions. The team was pleasant, with a few louder members, but they never bothered with May. She just smiled and kept her head down, absorbing the tasks and taking delight in utilising her finely tuned organisational skills. Her hours were upped from an initial Saturday to additional Thursday evenings and a few hours on Tuesday afternoons, slotting in nicely with her university timetable. With work, university and a few new acquaintances she had made as well as remaining connected to Scarlett (albeit not seeing her as much as she would like), life was good. Perhaps even vanilla ice cream with a wafer and chocolate flake.

May graduated and decided to go on to study for her master's, where she was particularly interested in biochemistry and scientific research. She remained at Lawson's, with a view that she would look for a role in science that could become permanent after her studies in the second year of her master's. Over the years, she had become more comfortable and relaxed with her colleagues. She made excuses for most social events and didn't join in with all the banter, struggling with the sense of humour of some at times, but she knew they accepted her, and the smiles and offers of cups of tea and biscuits—especially from the receptionist, Trish—made May feel the team liked her. Lawson's was just like those comfortable pyjama bottoms, and she was a stickler for routine. But her dreams of science, the gravitational pull to advance medicine, was a drive she'd had for so long, and the right time would come, she was sure of that.

Then Thomas Graham arrived at Lawson's and life got very interesting.

Chapter 2

May would never forget the day she'd first seen Thomas. It was the summer break of the first year of her master's degree at university. She was twenty-two years old and had planned to look for and secure another job by winter, meanwhile working as many hours as she could get at Lawson's over the summer holiday. She had grabbed handfuls of extra shifts like an eager cinemagoer grabs at popcorn. After working there for almost three years, she knew the processes like the freckles on her face. She had implemented new ways of working, more efficient, methodical ways of working, and the owner, Jack, was delighted. The bonus for May was that she had her own small office, and although it was mainly taken up by filing cabinets, there was room for a desk. It meant some privacy from the noise of the rest of the team, but she wasn't cut off completely, as her office looked into the main office and Jack's office was next door.

May had made a friend in Trish, even looking forward to their chats after her coat of awkward anxiety had become lighter to wear. Trish would talk about mundane things, such as washing clothes or the journey to work, and May would always listen intently, as she had done all those years before while watching science documentaries. Trish now understood that May walking away blankly was her reflecting on something she had taken from a simple conversation. She was always telling May she was 'one of a kind'. May wasn't sure if that was a good or bad thing, but she did like to be around Trish, and her round cheeks and kind eyes made May content in her company.

That Tuesday morning, May had just finished her usual mid-morning snack of yoghurt-coated rice cakes. They were interviewing that day for a conveyancer. May had been asked to sit in on the interviews, along with the director, Jack, and the sales manager, Toni. She had organised all the paperwork, and it was methodically ready for the four candidates they were interviewing.

Thomas Graham was last in, by which time it was 3 p.m. All six-foot-two of him walked into the reception area like a swirl of rusty-coloured leaves in the autumn breeze, his hypnotic turquoise eyes framed by glasses that made him look handsome and intelligent. Thomas wasn't what you would call 'traditionally handsome' by most people's accounts, but he had a magnetic presence and an infectious lopsided smile.

May involuntarily exhaled loudly as she stood in the back-office doorway, a pile of papers threatening to fall to the floor out of her weakened grip as she stared at Thomas Graham. She blushed, knowing her neck and face would be a strong strawberry colour, unfaded by her lack of facial make-up, which immediately made her feel exposed.

Trish frowned in a puzzled manner at May, but May was too entranced to notice.

Trish quickly pushed her glasses to the bridge of her nose and rose from her seat. 'I'm Trish, and you must be Thomas Graham?' she asked, documents in one hand as she extended her other to Thomas.

'That's me. Nice to meet you,' he replied, shaking Trish's hand. Thomas had a confidence in his stance—shoulders back and chin tilted slightly to the ceiling—that gave him an assertive presence. 'Great place you have here.' He looked around the office, his palm turned up as his eyes scanned the clean white walls against the burgundy carpet and desk chairs.

Trish stood on the spot, a slow, unsure nod of her head before glancing in May's direction.

May thought it was a strange thing for someone to say—it wasn't as if he were viewing a house, just somewhere that sold them—but she'd never completely grasped small talk.

She cleared her throat, took a deep breath and shook her head from side to side slightly, as if to shake the nerves away. She hoped a confident, calm version of herself would appear as she walked over, smoothing down her long, brown hair. 'Hello, is it Thomas?' Her voice was shaky, and she felt her legs trembling. She could only inwardly wince and pray he hadn't noticed.

'Yes, hi, nice to meet you,' Thomas replied, advancing his hand. He smiled a nervous but trying-to-look-casual smile that made his presence brighter, like a lighthouse shining on a dark night.

May shook his hand lamely, as she imagined a 101-year-old would do a handshake. 'I'm May, May Mc-Clelland. If you would like to follow me,' she managed, swallowing afterwards and desperately trying not to look like the awkward teenager she used to be.

For the next forty-five minutes, May tried to concentrate, but she couldn't keep her eyes off him. She studied his facial expressions as he thought about his responses before answering the interview questions. May noticed the way one dimple formed in his smile, where the right side lifted slightly higher than the left, and observed the way his eyebrows lifted as he thought and that he gripped the chair on a few occasions. She noted Thomas's blinks and the way his glasses seemed to suit him, as if they were made only for him.

Thomas was successful at the interview and began working at Lawson's. May picked up as many shifts as possible in the month before returning to university. Thomas was a wonderful addition to the office, and May was the moth around his light. It only took days for the rest of the office to notice she had a crush; after all, she had interacted with Thomas more in three days than she had in over three years with the rest of the team. They mocked her playfully, enjoying a softer side to May they had never seen. It wasn't that May didn't like her team, she just found things uncomfortable and overwhelming at times and was never one to talk for the sake of it. Her response to Thomas was as alien to May as it was to her team.

May leant her elbow on her desk and rested her chin on her palm in the quietness of her office. She observed Thomas as much as her eyeline allowed, moving from desk to desk like the most colourful liquid, conducting his tasks with a comfort she wasn't sure she had ever experienced. May felt her face relax as she tilted her head slightly and let her cheek rest on her hand. His presence mesmerised her but also gave her an annoying twinge of envy. She wanted to be like Thomas: assertive, charismatic and with the appeal of fresh, warm dough-nuts. Trish appeared in the doorway with two cups of tea. 'You like him, don't you?' she said quietly, looking over her shoulder to where Thomas was, then back to May.

May bit her lip and shrugged slightly as Trish placed a cup of tea on her desk.

'If I were twenty years younger... well, maybe twen-ty-five.' Trish winked at May. 'I think you would make a sweet couple.' She tapped May's forearm gently before turning around with her cup of tea and returning to re-ception, leaving May to daydream about love.

Trish had welcomed May into the team from day one despite May not wanting or needing new friends. She was there purely to do a job. Over the years, Trish had patiently broken through many of May's barriers to reach the friendship stage, the point where May had really softened to her being last Christmas. The whole concept of Secret Santa made May nauseous. She didn't like the unknown, and that included surprises. She always en-sured her parents and Scarlett knew what she wanted for Christmas or her birthday. When her grandparents were alive, she'd ensured the same. Surprises were not always nice and therefore not encouraged.

Until last Christmas, May had declined to participate in Secret Santa at Lawson's. She had gotten away with it the first year, being new and rarely at work due to her part-time status. The next year, she used not having much money as an excuse.

Then last Christmas, Trish had strode into May's office with determined purpose and stopped in front of her desk, placed both hands on it and leaned forward. 'How would you feel about participating in Secret Santa this year?'

May grimaced.

Seeing May almost squirming like an uncomfortable child, she gently said, 'Maybe you could regift a present you receive if it isn't to your liking.'

May pursed her lips. She didn't want to be a party pooper, but the whole concept of Secret Santa made her teeth itch. She let out a sigh.

Trish raised her eyebrows. 'That bad?' She chuckled, tilting her head back.

May considered the idea of regifting, but she always made sure any gift she purchased was something of need or want. It would be met with a rolling of the eyes when she asked her parents or Scarlett what they would like for their birthday or Christmas. They would laugh and say, 'Surprise me,' then after observing the look on May's face, they would promptly suggest toiletries or a new CD or DVD, a book or something practical, like stationery or socks. She found it much easier for the way her mind worked having a plan and knowing her gift would be appreciated.

Walking over to the photocopier at the back of the office, she thought about the pitch from Trish and how she could avoid feeling more awkward than someone letting out a massive fart in a room full of people.

May frowned as she heard footsteps behind her.

'It's only one gift, love. You could make someone smile, and you never know, you might receive a present you really like.'

May turned to Trish, who had her hands in the air in what looked like surrender but was far from.

It didn't sound like a big deal—to most, it wasn't—but May wasn't most people. She pondered on Trish's suggestion, thinking she could keep her unwanted gift in a drawer until someone said they would like such an item. This might never happen though, and she could be stuck with something of no use for ages, knowing it was there, lying in her drawer like the old pair of jeans she would never fit back into. She could give it a period of time, like ten months, and if no one wanted the unwanted Secret Santa gift by then, she could donate it to charity. Perhaps.

May returned to her office as Trish spun around in her office chair, her inner child enjoying the talk of Christmas.

'It's only a bit of fun, my lovely. And only a tenner,' Trish said gently, picking up on May's still-stiffened body language. She tapped May's forearm and smiled warmly. May quite liked the comforting reassurance of Trish's touch, having gotten used to her tactile nature over the years.

Taking a deep breath, May nodded and exhaled. 'Okay, yes. Yes, I'll take part.'

Trish scribbled her name down on the list at super speed before May could rescind her involvement.

A few weeks before, Trish had commented on May's knitted hat and how much she suited the blood-red colour of it. Lifting her chin at the compliment, May commented that she felt the cold. This was something she had already mentioned each winter as her only contribution of small talk. Trish noticed the way May would grab the neck of her coat, trying to prevent the cold, expectant outside air from getting into the warm sanctuary of her layers. She also noticed May had a hole in one of the fingers on her left-hand glove and that the pair looked a little bobbly and not quite long enough to cover her wrists. She chose May as her person to buy a gift for.

On the day of the Secret Santa exchange, May's bottom lip was tender from her chewing on the inside of it all morning. Not only would she receive a gift from a stranger and somehow have to hide her disappointed face, but she also had some nerves around the gift she was giving. Her person was Jack, the best she could have asked for, even better than Trish. She knew Jack and the way he worked, having completed many of his admin tasks for the few years she had worked there. May had chosen a brown leather A5 page-per-day diary for him that had an accompanying pen. She was as confident as she could be that he would like it, but there was still that possibility he wouldn't.

The team sat around the staff kitchen table. It was 5:30 p.m., the shop was closed and they were drinking steaming hot chocolate, munching on chocolates and swapping gifts. May felt chirpy after managing to obtain four of the orange octagons from the Quality Street tin—her favourites—scattered amongst the soft-centred choices that she would never entertain.

Trish kept bursting into song, singing the wrong words to the background Christmas music playing. Shoulders swaying gently from side to side, Jack tapped the table as if to play the drums. May glanced around as she unwrapped one of the chocolates, observing the childlike energy of her colleagues as they clapped their hands, chuckled as they elbowed one another, and sang as if they were auditioning for a talent contest.

Trish let out a massive 'It's Christmaaassss' as she placed the presents on the table, then spun around with her hands in the air. May couldn't help but smile as she watched her friend and her magnetic enthusiasm. Christmas seemed a release, as if letting the fizz escape from a bottle of pop. There was something about it that brought a bounce, a motivation, an extra layer of happiness along with the extra layer of clothing people wore.

'Get stuck in, then,' Trish said, gesturing to where the gifts sat, proud in their sparkly paper and shiny gift bags.

Following instruction, everyone leaned in, pawing the gifts to find the one with their name tag. Excitement decorated the air. May waited, pulling at her sleeves as she watched Jack find his present. A smile formed on his face as he gently tore the paper off. She observed his every move, almost invisible to the crowd of children that her colleagues had transformed into.

Jack flicked through the diary, as if the days would perhaps hold a different story than expected. He clicked the pen on and off and nodded to himself. 'Hey, thanks, Santa. This is probably the nicest-looking diary I've ever received. You have good taste.' He held it up, a few colleagues voicing their agreement.

May relaxed her shoulders, letting out a breath that could match the winter wind. She was satisfied he was happy. She picked her gift off the table—the last one there. It was squidgy, decorated in pretty holly-patterned paper and with a red bow and string. Thought had been put into its presentation, and it felt a shame to rip it open.

She bit her inner lip and glanced up, aware that everyone else had already opened their gift and the attention could be on her. No one was looking apart from Trish, who lifted her eyebrows slightly before bursting into song again. May began to open the gift, handling it like a newborn chick as her stomach gurgled with trepidation. Peeling back the paper, she saw red wool and felt a little spark of excitement. Ripping the rest of the paper, her Secret Santa gift was exposed—a blood-red scarf and matching gloves that surely must have been made to go with her hat. May stared at them mesmerised, as if they were diamonds. She rubbed them in her hands and put her gift to her nose, smelling the newness, feeling the softness on her skin. She thought she might cry as the reality of kindness went up her nostrils with the slight lanolin-wool scent.

She couldn't remember the last time someone had bought her a surprise present. In her hands, on that day in the office, May held one of the best presents she had ever received.

Chapter 3

Thomas settled into the team quickly. May was in awe of his adaptability and presence, travelling the room like a cool summer breeze, leaving a tingle around her. He wasn't loud, but he wasn't awkwardly quiet like May could be at times. Thomas seemed to be the perfect balance of calm, confident and respectfully charming, like an old-fashioned film star. May liked to think it was self-assurance. It was attractive, and thoughts of Thomas Graham began to sprinkle into May's mind day and night, like delicious dustings of icing sugar on the most perfectly baked Victoria sponge.

Crushing on Thomas was a distraction for May and something she had never encountered at work or university. There had been two crushes, and did Chris O'Dowd in *The IT Crowd* count when she was younger? May had had affection for her first university professor, Dr Adam Armstrong. Was it sexual? She couldn't one hundred per cent say, but she had been drawn to him, like iron filings to a magnet. He was so intelligent and confident and he had a handsome face. May used to find herself blushing in his lectures as her eyes fixated on him, happy to admire from afar, as if being at a concert of her favourite band. Next was Oscar Sullivan. A twelve-hour crush and a necessary evil. May met Oscar after a night out when she was twenty years old, on the fifteenth of July, in the summer of her second year at university. She had gone to visit Scarlett, who was studying drama at the University of Essex.

That was the night she lost her virginity. May had kissed a few boys before that night, but that had been as far as her sexual encounters had stretched. One kiss had been with a boy who used to live in her street when she was eleven. It had been a sloppy, clumsy affair that had left May with a bad taste in her mouth, literally. Another kiss had been with a boy whilst May holidayed with her parents at age fourteen. Her adult kissing encounters had only consisted of kissing two men on separate nights out with Scarlett when she had come home during university break. May had felt neutral about the two experiences but enjoyed the little firework of self-esteem that she desired.

The night May lost her virginity, however, was unexpected. On reflection, May felt like it was almost an out-of-body experience, as if an alien had landed and taken over her being. She wasn't sure if she regretted it, but it definitely wasn't what she had thought it would be and it certainly wasn't like the movies depicted. Sex had never happened until then for May for various reasons, mainly lack of opportunity and lack of desire on May's part. Like a Zumba class, May knew people did it and enjoyed it, but she had no major inclination to try it. She had never really had strong desires for any man except Dr Adam Armstrong. On the whole, she struggled with people, so relationships with guys, who felt like a different species most of the time, were even more challenging. Maybe May just hadn't met the right person, but as soon as it happened, May knew that her right person was certainly not Oscar Sullivan.

Oscar requested May on Facebook after and she still hadn't decided whether to accept him. She didn't go on Facebook much, as she liked privacy, but it was useful for some university stuff and to keep in touch with Scarlett. Life for May as a non-virgin returned to normal. She didn't think about Oscar much, as he'd served his purpose and the earth not moving indicated to May that it was not to be repeated. At least not with Oscar. After all, you don't rewatch a film that left little imprint on your mind, do you? But something good had come of that night because although May had lost her virginity to Oscar and decided that would be her first and last experience with him, Scarlett had got together with his friend, Ethan, and their path continued to much more than a one-night stand.

That was the only time May had experienced sex, and the male species hadn't made a massive impact on her since until, two years after the Oscar Sullivan incident, she met Thomas Graham. It was the summer May left the comforting cloak of her family home and became independent, securing her own flat. The bonus of working at an estate agency meant May was able to rent an upstairs flat not far from university, close to some amenities, without a massive financial outlay. The one-bedroomed flat was in a quiet, pleasant area and only a ten-minute drive from her parents'. A small enough leap to not feel as if she would have to cross an ocean in a dinghy to reach the comforting shores of her family home.

'Will you be okay, darling?' Fran had asked her, furrowing her brow.

'Of course, Mam, and I know where you both are if I need you.' May hugged her mam, needing the warmth and reassurance but knowing she had to fly the nest, so to speak. Even though she found affection hard in general, it was never and had never been difficult to show affection to her parents.

May hadn't been blessed with romantic love in her twenty-two years, but she knew it existed, as her parents were the ultimate production of a Broadway love story. From forehead kisses to perfect cups of tea, the way they looked at each other and laughed at memories. Their love was so much more than words. Victor would always warm Fran's towel on the radiator before her bath and thank her for his dinner, saying it was the best thing he had ever tasted even if it was something as simple as his favourite kind of eggs on toast. Their love was simple, sensitive and sacred. It was pure, natural and effortless. Their love was everything that love should be. What May always wanted her experiences of love to be. Even if intimate love didn't strike her with its arrow, she knew love existed.

May's university studies were going well, with the promise of job options at the end of the final year of her course. Moving into her flat had been a massive step forward that she had managed. She had opened up a little at Lawson's and continued to enjoy her job, especially with Thomas around. She was attracted to him, and although she felt he would likely never reciprocate the attraction, it was nice to feel a fluttering in her stomach.

Then a month later, at the start of August, May's world changed forever.

Chapter 4

'May, my lovely, your father is on the phone,' Trish said gently as she approached May's office. She leaned forward, holding the phone out. 'He's been trying to call you on your mobile.'

May stood up and leaned across her desk for the phone. Her dad always knew her mobile was on silent when she was at work. Panic began to rise. Why was he ringing? She took the phone as Trish stood close by. 'Hello, Dad,' she said, eyeing Trish anxiously as she stood with her arms folded in her lap. She always left the office after handing the phone over to allow for privacy, so why was she still there?

'May, d-darling, it's your ma-mam,' he stammered, voice thick with emotion. 'She's in hospital. Sh-she's had a heart attack, pet. You need to get here.' He breathed out heavily.

May suddenly felt as if she were on a fairground waltzer, desperate to get off. Placing her free hand on the desk, she swallowed. 'I don't understand,' she said quickly. 'Dad, what happened?' She took a step back and practically fell onto her office chair.

'We were just at home, darling, and... I don't know.' He sobbed. 'She collapsed and couldn't breathe. May, please get here, come now.' The last words were said at a high pitch, panic audible in his voice.

It felt as if May's brain were underwater as a wave of helplessness flooded her. 'I'm on my way,' she managed to say before putting the phone down on her desk with shaky hands.

She turned to Trish, who was now by her side. 'It's my mam. She's had a heart attack.' May tried to swallow the weight of worry lingering in her throat as tears began to build in her eyes.

Trish pulled May into her soft, warm body and silently held her for a few seconds. 'I will drive you.'

May nodded, unable to muster any words.

Trish took May's hand and hurried her outside, popping her head around Jack's office doorway on the way. 'I'm taking May to the hospital. Family emergency.'

Trish ushered May to her car, which was parked on the opposite side of the high street. May felt like a lost child in a department store feeling as if they would never find their parents. She could almost taste the bile rising in her throat as they headed to the hospital.

They arrived fifteen minutes later and rushed wordlessly into A&E, straight to the reception desk at the left of the department entrance. May's heart was pounding in her ears as she stood in front of the two receptionists, who were sitting behind a glass screen—a barrier between them and everyone else.

'Can I help you?' one of the receptionists asked, looking at May, then Trish, fingers hovering over a keyboard.

The strip lighting made May feel as if she was going to be sick. She opened her mouth to ask where her mam was, but no sound came out. She turned to Trish, feeling her face crumbling. Trish took control of finding Fran and held May's hand as she navigated the way to the ward entrance.

'I'll wait here, honey,' Trish said, patting May's arm.

May nodded, her fingers over her mouth, eyes wide. She pushed the door open and rushed into the ward, with its white walls and black plastic chairs. Her heels clinked on the polished flooring, adding 'exposed' to her list of current feelings. She found her dad sitting with his head in his hands outside one of the rooms.

'Dad?' she croaked, panic in her voice.

'May, darling, I'm so sorry.' He sobbed, his greying hair dishevelled as he forced himself to look up at her. She stared back into his brown bloodshot eyes. 'She's gone. Your mam's gone, love.' It was as if saying the words killed part of her dad whilst he sat there looking frail and lost, the colour drained from his face. Victor tilted his head back and sobbed to the ceiling.

'No. She can't be.' May shook her head and put her hands over her ears. 'No, Dad, where is she?' she screamed as tears cascaded down her face. 'It's a mistake, it has to be. Where is my mam?' May looked around, frantically searching for someone, anyone to take her to her mam. Her legs felt weak as she spotted the ward reception desk, wiping her face with the sleeve of her cardigan.

'She's gone.' He tried to grab May's hand, but she had already begun moving. 'There was nothing they could do, love.' He rubbed his eyes and walked after his daughter, his baby, covering his mouth to stifle the screams of distress ready to pour out.

'Excuse me, miss, sir.' A doctor with heavy eyes walked towards May and Victor before they reached the ward desk, and gently ushered them into a side room.

'I'm so sorry for your loss,' he said, a small nod of his head as his eyes met Victor's and then May's.

Victor took a seat, almost collapsing into one of the three armchairs in the room, as May remained standing, staring at the doctor, hoping he would transform into a presenter and disclose that this whole scene was a twisted prank. The doctor stood in his blue theatre scrubs, clipboard down by his side. Victor patted the seat next to him, glancing at May through flooded eyes. May wanted to run from the room, to scream all the way down the corridor and into the car park, where her tears could mix with the rain. She wanted to be away—away from this doctor of death, her dad, her mother's dead body and Trish. It felt as if needles were jabbing into every part of her skin as she wrung her hands together and moved to the seat next to her father.

They sat there for the next few minutes, which felt like hours to May, as the doctor calmly explained what had happened to their precious Fran. She had experienced a massive heart attack, but the doctor told them in monotone that she hadn't been able to breathe and had died quickly with minimal suffering. It felt like no consolation to May as a light in her world went off forever. Victor dropped his head into his hands and May remained fixed on the doctor, whose face began to almost melt into a swirl of colour as the noise coming from his mouth became nothing more than a low buzz. As her ears rang and her thoughts suffocated her, he went on explaining that although Fran had no history of heart disease, it was just one of those things, very likely to have been unpreventable.

The doctor, albeit with some empathy in his voice, was talking as if he were reeling off instructions to build a flatpack wardrobe. May couldn't absorb it, her knees bouncing. She rose to her feet and paced the room. Grabbing her scalp with both hands, she tried to breathe deeply. *Is there any air in this room?*

'Where is she? Where's my mam? I want to see her,' May choked as tears seeped out of her puffy eyes.

The doctor nodded calmly, opened the door and quietly led May and her dad to the room Victor had left only a few minutes before May arrived. May froze at the door as her eyes landed on a body that didn't quite look like her mam lying in the clinical bed. She looked as if she were sleeping, but there was also that eerie lingering of death, where the person almost looks as if they have deflated. May advanced into the room quickly, wanting to see but also not wanting the cruel truth. It became immediately apparent that it was her mam in the hospital bed, Fran's light brown, thick hair resting on her shoulders. The woman she had loved all her life. The face she had loved all her life. The face that, over time, was becoming her own.

'I'll give you a few minutes,' the doctor said, stepping away.

May glanced at her dad, who remained standing in the doorway, silent tears falling down his face. She had never seen her dad cry. He was Dad. He was strong and brave and her hero. Now, he was broken, shattered like a plastic toy thrown down the stairs. He shook his head and turned his eyes to the floor, sniffing as he did, not ready to look at his wife again, not wanting to have that definitive death visual ingrained in him deeper.

May turned back to her mam in the narrow hospital bed that almost felt like a coffin already. This is just a dream, a really bad dream. She took Fran's hand, which was neither warm nor cold but felt weird, as if it wasn't her mam's. Please, God, let her just be sleeping.

Fran was too young to die, surely? People don't lose their mothers until they are older. May knew that. It was unnatural. Her mam was only fifty-seven years old. None of this made any sense.

May kissed Fran's hand and contemplated moving the blanket away and just lying with her, wrapping her mam's arm around her. She would close her eyes and pretend her mam was holding her tightly. She wanted, no, she needed a hug from her... one of those hugs that always made her feel safe in a world that sometimes felt unsafe. Who would give her those hugs now? Who would make her dad's dinner and kiss his head when they left the room?

May opened her mouth wide, trying to snatch air from the suffocating space as her head throbbed and her eyes stung like the prick of a thousand needles. She stared at her mam, unable to blink and unsure if she was going to collapse. A tsunami of devastating change had roared through her world in the last thirty minutes. A world that would never be the same again.

May took almost three weeks off work after Fran died. She wanted to move back home to be with her dad, but he insisted she kept her flat even though she spent every day at her family home—something they both needed. It was almost impossible to talk those first few days as grief drove its speed train through the house, through their family, through their hearts. Shock led to denial, then a trickle of realisation. May needed to get things in order, as it was what her mam would have wanted. Victor struggled, unable to escape denial, almost convinced his Fran would come in from her part-time job or the shops, full of joy and thoughts on dinner that evening.

May took control of the formalities, the harsh, emotionless processes that people in their darkest hours have to go through. Registering a death, contacting the endless supply of services that person had in their life, explaining that they are no more to a monotone human that may as well be a robot on the end of the phone. May went into autopilot as Victor sat holding a wedding photo of him and his beloved in an aged frame. May would return to her sparse flat at night, sit on her sofa and realise her mam would never sit there again as they chatted about nothing important that ironically always felt essential to May. She was unsure she could ever love if love meant pain like that her dad was experiencing. Each evening, May would sit and sob silent tears until her eyes felt like shattered glass and her heart felt as if it were being submerged in tar.

A few days after Fran's passing, a card arrived in the post for May. It was signed by the team at Lawson's. It made her smile temporarily before melancholy returned and the day became about processing and running through the heavy mud that was death admin.

Trish had been around to her flat with some cake, bread, milk, cheese, some flowers and a fleece blanket. A package of kindness that made May cry, but a package that she wished wasn't needed, desperately yearning for the past to rewind and change.

Scarlett had also come home and spent some time at May's flat as well as with May and Victor. Fran had loved Scarlett, as did Victor; she was like their second daughter.

Then the funeral was over, and it was expected that May and Victor would begin getting some level of new normal, adapting to walking with their permanent limp.

May returned anxiously to work three days after her mam's funeral despite not wanting to. Luckily, the team were lovely, and the dread evaporated, replaced by support. Trish was the comforter, bringing May cups of tea and biscuits that she would often just stare at, lost in a trance of painful thoughts. Jack gave minimal tasks that helped to distract May's mind for a short period of time.

During one such shift, May glanced at the large, grey clock on the wall to the left of her desk and sighed. It was five minutes into her lunchtime. She didn't have the energy to leave her office or go to the staff kitchen, possibly having to make small talk. She'd stay here, tucked away in the corner, and eat the biscuits from earlier.

There was a knock on her open office door, and she leaned back in her seat. 'Thanks, Trish, but you've only just—'

'Sorry to disappoint, but it's me.' Thomas pushed the door open and stepped into her office, holding up two sandwiches. 'Which one? Egg mayo or chicken salad?'

May studied his lopsided smile and slightly goofy face as he looked at the sandwiches and back at her with a shrug. It made her laugh—something she hadn't done a lot of in the last few weeks. 'I'm okay, but thanks,' she said, giving Thomas a weak smile.

He placed the sandwiches on her desk and put his hands together, leaning forward slightly. 'Now listen here, May McClelland, I know you don't have lunch with you today, as you always put it in the same place in the fridge, in the same container. It's not there.' He tilted his head to one side and raised his eyebrows. 'Unless you want to eat the other half of the pack of biscuits Trish has been feeding you for lunch, which actually would be a great lunch, I suggest you pick a sandwich.' Thomas placed one in each hand, animatedly weighing them up as if they were on a set of scales.

May swallowed, feeling emotional that someone cared. That he cared.

'Chicken salad, please.' She opened her hands, and Thomas placed the sandwich on her palms. 'Thanks.' She sighed before glancing at the sandwich, which developed into a stare and zone out.

Thomas pulled the spare chair over from the side of the room, where it had been next to three filing cabinets. The movement snapped May out of her thoughts as a blast of reality whooshed around the room and kicked her in the stomach.

They sat silently for a minute, Thomas glancing at her a few times, waiting quietly and patiently for her to look up and speak as he opened his sandwich.

Eventually, she repeated, 'Thanks.'

Thomas nodded as he took a bite from the egg mayo sandwich. 'It doesn't get easier, May. We just learn to cope better. I lost my mam to the Big C four years ago. She's never out of here'—he tapped his temple—'but she wouldn't have wanted me to suffer with grief, for my spark to go out.' He glanced at the sandwich that May could smell from across the desk as hers sat unopened. 'I want to make her proud, and I have and will continue to. I'm lucky in a lot of ways to have had her, you know?' He rubbed the back of his neck and took a deep breath.

They looked at each other with silent understanding of shared difficulties.

Thomas opened a bottle of pop, the fizz of the bubbles the only sound for a few seconds. Taking a gulp, he leaned in slightly from the other side of May's desk and said, 'Anyway, I'm here if you want to talk, May, anytime. Here's my number.' Thomas lifted off the seat and leaned further over to May and wrote his number on her notepad. Not in a neat fashion as she liked, but a scrawl across a blank page. The most perfect scrawl she had ever seen.

Chapter 5

It was soon September, and May was due back at university. She was an intelligent, focused student, but life had thrown a big, painful curveball the last month, and May didn't know if she could manage the intensity of the final year of her master's. She was in a battle with her own trajectory she had meticulously been planning for the last five years—seven if she included her college years—and the dilemma of not feeling emotionally ready to be her best. May had experienced both good and bad emotions in the last few months that she hadn't experienced in all of her twenty-two years. The destruction of loss, the crippling pain of grief, the void of loneliness. At the other side of the road lay support from Scarlett around Fran's death, closeness with colleagues, with Trish in particular, and the excitement of being around Thomas. She felt different, for positive and negative reasons, but she prided herself on being organised, diligent and not deviating from the expected, the norm and her own plans. Control and routine were keeping her feeling stable in her challenging life.

There was the option of spreading the final year of her master's over two years, making it part-time. It would mean an extra year added to her job plan, but perhaps that would be okay. Studying for her master's full-time would mean dropping shifts at Lawson's to prioritise her dad, which would impact her income. Even though Victor was always trying to give her money, personal budgeting was a task she enjoyed and something she took enormous pride in maintaining.

Sitting on the sofa, laptop on her knee, May called Scarlett.

'Hey there, stranger,' Scarlett boomed, waving. She leaned against the counter and faced her laptop, which she had placed on her kitchen table.

'How's your day been?'

'Oh, you know, the usual.' Scarlett gave a wave of her hand and crossed one leg over the other. 'How are you holding up?'

May really wanted, needed Scarlett's full attention in person for some much-needed advice and reassurance, not a rushed hour because dinner was waiting or the washing machine needed emptying, but this would have to do for now. Closeness was something she didn't dish out easily, but with Scarlett, a big part of May needed to be closer to her than ever. She swallowed a lump of sadness lingering in her throat and gave the best smile she could, hoping the computer screen would mask the pain burning in her chest. 'I'm doing okay.'

Scarlett nodded slowly, unconvinced, then moved forward and propped her elbows on the kitchen table, resting her chin on her palms. 'How are you *really*?'

The dam showed signs of weakening but somehow stayed strong. 'No, really, I'm okay, I... I'm just wanting some advice.'

May updated Scarlett on her ideas, her attempt to try to sustain some normality. At the end of her explanation, she held her palms up to the screen and let out an exasperated sigh.

Scarlett smiled caringly. 'A year is nothing, honey, and it sounds like it would be too much trying to juggle all those balls if you didn't drop it to part-time. You don't want to be in a position where you can't enjoy your studies or balance between being around your dad and work. Plus, you need time for you after what you've been through.'

May nodded. At times, she struggled to express herself, but Scarlett often described and articulated exactly what she thought. It was as if they were connected mentally despite Scarlett being all those miles away in Essex.

'How's Ethan?' May asked.

Scarlett and Ethan had become official not long after *that* night. The pair made a great couple and had now been together for a few years. He was studying to qualify as a teacher and they were living together in Scarlett's rented flat, waiting to move into their own place. May approved of Ethan—he was focused, kind and put Scarlett first.

'Aw, he's great. He's playing football tonight, so I'm cooking lasagne,' Scarlett said, rubbing her hands together.

'Oh boy, I hope you don't give him food poisoning again.' May laughed. Cooking was Ethan's domain, and there was a good reason for that.

'Cheeky cow. I'm getting better. Oscar asked after you the other day.' Scarlett raised her eyebrow.

'Please, not that one again.'

'You were awful, May; you could have let him down gently.'

'I did; I never contacted him. I never had him up to let him down, plus it was two years ago,' May protested, crossing her arms.

'Well, that's not exactly true, is it? You definitely had him up,' Scarlett teased as May rolled her eyes.

'Change the subject.'

'So, how is your dad doing?'

'He's getting there, I think. He doesn't really talk, and, well, I don't know what to say. I don't want to upset him further. I'm just pleased he has work and some routine. I'd be lost without mine.' May rubbed her collarbone and let out a sigh.

'And how's your work? How're things with tantalising Thomas?' Scarlett grinned.

May felt herself smile, noticed immediately by Scarlett.

'Ooh, what's happened?' she said, taking a seat, May catching a glimpse of the preheating oven behind her.

'Well, nothing really. We've been texting each other quite a bit. Just general stuff, like what we've had for tea, what's on TV and that.'

'Does he like Weetabix?' Scarlett snorted, referring to the fact it was May's breakfast item of choice every single morning.

'Actually, yes, he does,' May replied, a smug look on her face. 'He's just so lovely, Scarlett, and he's easy, you know?'

Scarlett's eyes widened.

'Not in a sexual way. He's easy as in easy-going and takes things in his stride. He's everything I'm not.'

'Hun, he sounds great. Keep texting him and be yourself, okay? You're more than enough. You deserve happiness, so don't settle for anything less. Keep me updated, will you? Even on what he's having for tea, especially if it's something I could manage to cook when Ethan is out.'

The pair laughed.

'Anyway, I've gotta go. Love ya.' Scarlett blew a kiss to the screen and ended the call.

May immediately emailed her university tutor to explain that she wanted to extend the last year of her master's to part-time. She put a read receipt on the email—people didn't answer as quickly as her, but at least she would know when it had been read.

The next week, May returned to university with the ability to extend her master's following a return email from her tutor. She would have fewer lectures but still be in class with some of the few friends she had made. The decision meant she could continue to work at Lawson's and keep an eye on Victor, who was keeping his feelings as insular as possible. He was still Dad in the loving, looking-after-May way, but there was very little talk of Mam and sometimes the house smelt of alcohol. She had to let him work through it. The neighbours, Mr and Mrs Taylor, kept an eye on him, and he was back working at the garage.

Life goes on, doesn't it? It has to. May coped through grief with her routines, controlling what she could and speaking out loud to Fran. May didn't believe in the afterlife and knew she wouldn't hear back. Many would class her as a loner, and she didn't mind that label, but somehow, knowing there was one less person in her world made loneliness real and painfully raw. She wished Scarlett still lived in Newcastle. May had few friends and didn't speak to anyone some days. She would say the odd hello to her neighbours, but that was as far as it went. The woman in the flat below, who May liked, was looking to move to Manchester. The other flats in her block of four had a young man living in who never seemed to be there and a couple who kept themselves to themselves. Her neighbours were pleasant, but she valued her privacy and anonymity too highly to make friends with them.

One medicine for May's grief was Thomas, and on the days of the week she worked, she had a distinct spring in her step. He was her distraction, like a meme of a dog that made you giggle and then smile all day. They had also been texting quite a bit, but May had no clue what their 'relationship' was.

'Get him asked out on a date, May,' Scarlett screeched that night, clapping her hands as they chatted.

If Scarlett weren't purely on a screen, May would have considered playfully throwing a cushion at her, but there was no way she was risking knocking her laptop off the arm of her sofa. 'If you know anything about me in over the decade we've been friends, you would know that I would never do that.'

'Hun, I adore you, but sometimes you need to learn to be kind to yourself. Just ask him. What's the worst that could happen?'

'Let me think,' May said sarcastically, tapping her chin. 'He says no and then I have to work with someone who has rejected me. I've only just begun to feel like I'm not an alien at Lawson's this last year... I don't want to go back to walking around looking at the floor and feeling like the Joker in a deck of playing cards.'

'I quite like the Joker.'

'But he's useless, Scarlett.' May shook her head as Scarlett giggled.

May wouldn't be taking advice from her best friend for a change; instead, she would keep doing what she had been, which included trying her very best to act as normal as possible around Thomas, to not say anything stupid or anything that would make her sound weird and not giggle and blush like a silly schoolgirl in his presence. There was a work night out planned for November for Trish's fiftieth birthday. May would normally avoid such outings, except for once or twice a year; however, it was for Trish, who was a friend, plus Thomas would be going, which was a big six-foot-two bonus.

But there was one major issue: what birthday present to get Trish. May spent so much time with Trish at work, but outside of the office, they had limited interactions apart from text messages that were mainly from Trish checking how May was and offers to catch up after work that May always declined. Scrolling through her phone, she realised just how many times Trish had messaged her to ask about her well-being. She bit her lip as guilt rumbled through her. May didn't want to be one of those needy people, where the relationship was never equal. She didn't want pity. She put her phone down and closed her eyes, taking a moment to try to shut the front door on the spiralling thoughts in her mind that were threatening to run riot.

It felt more important than ever to make an effort for Trish's birthday present. May knew Trish liked ornaments and trinkets, as she had a collection of what May would probably call 'tat' on her desk at work. It made most people smile, but Jack would roll his eyes each time another made an appearance on her desk or even in the staff kitchen, where the tat had begun to encroach. Trish would claim it brightened the place up, but most of it wasn't to May's taste. Trish loved dolphins, and she even had one tattooed on her leg. May had failed to disguise her horrified face after seeing the inked mammal. Perhaps she could get her an ornament, but that felt too hard to decide on given size and the array of different ones she had seen Trish bring in and replace.

May puffed out air and put her fingers to her mouth. Trish also liked jewellery and decorated herself like a Christmas tree with colourful earrings, bracelets and necklaces. Perhaps a bracelet or even a brooch would be a good idea. *Or are brooches old-fashioned?* May put her hand to her forehead, growling to herself.

'What would you like for your birthday, Trish?' May asked intently the next morning at work as Trish delivered a cup of tea to May's office.

'Nothing, my lovely; you keep your money.' Trish smiled at May, placing the cup onto May's leather coaster. The morning cup of tea had become a gesture that May found more comforting than she could express.

She frowned. 'But I want to buy you something, Trish. What do you want?'

'Surprise me.'

May's face went blank, and Trish quickly realised that wasn't the reaction she wanted.

'I do love chocolates and anything candle-related but, lovely, I would rather have your presence than any present.' Trish rubbed May's shoulder, and May's eyes immediately welled up. She couldn't work out if she was emotional because of the kind words or longing for a similar touch from her mam. It didn't take much to set her off nowadays. She wiped her eyes with her fingers.

Shutting May's office door slightly, Trish leaned over and stroked May's hair. 'It's the little pressure that sometimes bursts the dam. Let it out, honey.'

May glanced up at Trish. 'I just feel pathetic so much of the time.'

'Now stop that.' Trish looked over her glasses. 'You're brilliant, May. You're strong and beautiful, and if I had been lucky enough to have a daughter, I would have wanted her to be just like you.'

May pressed her lips together, nodded and remained silent.

'I'll leave you be, love. I'll pop in with a fresh cuppa in an hour or two.' Trish stroked May's hand before placing the packet of biscuits on her desk and leaving her office.

Chapter 6

'Try the leather trousers,' Scarlett almost screamed into the laptop. 'Try them, May, with a sexy sheer blouse.'

May grimaced—she didn't do sexy; in fact, she perceived herself as about as sexy as sciatica. But with her night out tomorrow and a limited wardrobe, she needed Scarlett's help. She'd hoped Scarlett would pick out her floral Bardot dress or navy-blue lace dress, but nope, of course she'd noticed the leather trousers with label still on she'd insisted May buy despite her squeaking like a bag full of mice in them.

'May McClelland, you have a figure most women would kill for. Get those long legs in those bloody leather trousers and tuck in a sexy blouse, with a cami top underneath. Then pick some jewellery and a belt and killer heels.'

'I don't have half the things you just listed.'

'Open your wardrobe and let me see again,' Scarlett insisted.

May carried her laptop around her room, juggling holding it as she opened her wardrobe.

'Ooh, those boots. They look almost knee-high and with a heel. Very dominatrix.' Scarlett laughed.

'*Scarlett*. They are not dominatrix or knee-high... well, maybe they would be on you. They do have a little heel though, so could be okay, I guess.'

'Perfect. Now let me see your blouses.'

May scanned her wardrobe, showing Scarlett on the laptop.

'*Stop,*' Scarlett blared from her end. 'There, that black lace thing. What's that?'

'It's a long-sleeved top.'

'That. Try that on.' Scarlett clapped her hands together. 'And do you have that black biker jacket I gave you last year that you twisted your face at?'

'I did not twist my face, but yes, I still have it.' May placed her hand on her forehead, as if worried she was twisting her face again.

'You did twist your face, May, but I'm sure you didn't mean it. Go and get it and try them on all together. Find a necklace—gold or even pearls spell out classy but gagging for it. Show me once you are ready; I'm bursting for a pee.'

And with that, Scarlett was gone, leaving May to get ready for a fashion show. Pulling on her leather trousers, they didn't feel as bad as she remembered, even maybe only as squeaky as one mouse. She put some fluffy socks on and slipped her feet into the boots. They had a heel but not to the point of discomfort. May put one of her everyday black strappy vests on and pulled the lace top over her head. She looked at her outfit in the mirror, turning to the side and shaking her hair free from the scrunchy holding a loose bun together.

'Not too bad,' she said aloud before having a quick look for some jewellery. She already knew she didn't have anything suitable; May didn't like jewellery except for the small silver hoop earrings that she wore each day and her watch. She wasn't a fan of chunky, bulky bracelets and necklaces that turned her skin green or made her look as if she wanted to be a rapper. Less was more in her eyes. She stopped looking in her tiny jewellery box for something she would never find and instead sent Scarlett a picture.

'*What have you done with May? Where is she? Who is this sexy siren?*' Scarlett texted. Then another came through, '*You just need a necklace, a belt and a little handbag. Then you're good to go! My beautiful bestie!*'

Less than twenty-four hours later, May was standing in front of her bedroom mirror, ready to go out for Trish's birthday with the Lawson's team. She had heard the team chatting about what to wear, arranging lifts and sharing present ideas all week. Some of the younger members of staff, who were still older than May, were talking about a club they would head to even if Trish went home. May was the youngest at Lawson's, although she often felt a decade older than her colleagues. They focused on silly things, such as getting their eyebrows coloured and shaped, leg day at the gym or if a man texted them back. May had most definitely started to adopt the latter, with reference to Thomas.

Tilting her head at her reflection, she smoothed down her hair, reapplied a little lip gloss and looked at herself again, moving around to see different angles. For the first time in as long as she could remember, she felt a sprinkling of self-acceptance.

May's taxi arrived, and she travelled into town to meet her colleagues, firstly just Trish. May had asked her if they could meet half an hour earlier so she could give Trish her birthday presents. Of course, this was because she felt nervous about the present and a possible audience.

May arrived at the bar where they had arranged to meet. She waited outside, looking around, moving on the spot for a few minutes before she saw Trish approaching, a smile as wide as the road plastered on her face.

She hollered a 'Helloooo' in the style of Mrs Doubtfire as she waved frantically until she was right in front of May.

May couldn't help but laugh whilst admiring how naturally confident Trish was. Trish embraced May tightly before she pulled away and waved her arm towards the entrance of the bar.

'C'mon, then.'

The pair got a drink, May sticking to lemonade for now as Trish ordered gin. Taking a seat, May reluctantly handed over the gift bag to Trish, as if stepping into a cold swimming pool. She clenched her teeth as Trish clapped her hands before taking the bag, eyes wide. Her gaze met May's.

'Crikey, love, don't look so frightened.' She chuckled, leaning over and rubbing May's forearm.

Trish delved into the bag, moving her shoulders slightly to the music. She pulled out the gifts and began ripping off the tissue paper.

'*Oh my word*,' Trish screeched as she eventually got through the layers of wrapping. 'These are incredible. Oh, May, you're so thoughtful. I love them.' She leaned across to May and embraced her tightly as May felt sure to burst from the heat of her stressful anticipation. She remained silent, watching Trish as she studied the gifts. *Does she really like them?*

May hadn't bought Trish chocolates, she hadn't even bought her anything candle-related. For once, she had gone into a shop and allowed potential gifts to catch her eye, pushed aside what she knew the giftee would one hundred per cent want and made her purchases with an undertone of uncertainty.

Trish picked up the cup, which had an image of dolphins gliding through waves, their trademark smiles visible. Under the cup sat a book about dolphins, filled with facts and photos. 'Thank you, love, these are perfect.'

May let out a breath and nodded. 'You're welcome.'

The pair finished their drinks before meeting the rest of the Lawson's crew at a nearby bar. Everyone was already there, and as soon as Trish and May walked in, May noticed Thomas. He was standing in black jeans and a bottle-green sweater, almost centre of the group, conducting his audience with his charismatic presence. She was mesmerised for a second before Trish grabbed her hand and pulled her towards the bar.

'No more lemonade for you unless it's with gin.' Trish raised her eyebrow at May before turning to the bar staff and ordering two gins.

There was a chorus of birthday wishes and hugs for Trish as they joined the group. May stood back a foot or so, watching the frolicking before Thomas moved round the group to her side.

'You look pretty, May,' he said, keeping eye contact.

May let out a 'mmm' and glanced into her glass, feeling her cheeks flush.

'Do you come here often?' He laughed at the joke.

May didn't laugh back. 'Not really, although it's nice.'

Thomas grinned. 'Well, I'm pleased you came.'

May bit her lip and was about to say something back before Trish's voice exploded into the air as she began showing everyone the presents May had gifted her. May's shoulders tensed, but everyone seemed to think they were great, so she soon relaxed a little.

The group travelled on to the next bar, followed by the next, and May began to feel less like a duckling amongst a bevy of swans. They finally hit the last bar at 11 p.m. It was busier here and darker too, eighties music blasting at a level too loud for May, but she was pleased to see everyone—as no one had wandered off or gone home yet—especially Trish, enjoying themselves. She closed her eyes and smiled, swaying to the music as she realised she was also enjoying herself. Enjoyment was a feeling she hadn't felt in a while.

The strong smell of mint and beer caused May to open her eyes, and her breath caught slightly at the sight of Thomas right in front of her, his eyes glinting in the low lighting of the bar.

'So, May McClelland, are you going to let me take you out, just us? As much as I love this energetic lot'—he turned to the group next to them, who were dancing in sync—'I would prefer something more intimate with you.'

May laughed, unsure if he was joking and unsure of what to say. She took a sip of her drink and looked at Thomas, her legs slightly shaking.

Thomas held his palm up towards her and tilted his head. 'Well, what do you think? No pub crawl, just maybe a cuppa somewhere or some food, a trip to a museum?'

There was that grin that made May feel as if a kaleido-scope of butterflies were taking flight in her torso. Her mouth was open, but she couldn't make a sound—too shocked, too scared of replying with the wrong words. Instead, she simply nodded and smiled at Thomas, to which he responded by pulling her into his embrace and laughing. When he released her, May was almost certain she would topple over with nervous excitement.

Thomas Graham wanted to take her on a date!

The night out was turning out to be one of the best of May's life. She'd discovered a deeper niceness in her colleagues she perhaps hadn't allowed them the opportunity to show until now and she finally felt included in a way she wasn't sure she had ever experienced before. It was as if she were part of a football team, as important and necessary as the next player.

Thomas touched her hand gently, and a wave of tingles spread through her. 'I find you beautifully intriguing, May, in a way I've never found anyone before.'

She turned a deep shade of red, but the dark bar dulled the new colour in her cheeks.

After losing her mam, May hadn't been sure she could ever be happy again, but maybe her luck was changing.

Chapter 7

It was soon December and the first Christmas without Fran. May was dreading it and tried to be as organised as possible, keeping herself and Victor busy. Being organised was always a form of nutrition or medicine in times of struggle for May, and as Christmas approached, she needed a monumental prescription of it. She was unsure how her dad felt about her taking control but hoped it was a relief to him given it had always been Mam keeping Christmas—and every other important time in the year—on track. Now, it was May's responsibility, and it felt essential and excruciating.

Scarlett was home for the month, and they had been to the Christmas market with her mam, Diane; stepdad, Trevor; and Cumberland, their Dachshund. It was their yearly tradition where, for a few hours, May was able to enjoy time with people who had always felt like family.

In the days leading up to May's date with Thomas, she had the same feelings she used to have when going on family holidays—the excitement and allure of the trip but the nerves that something out of her control might go wrong. She repeatedly ruminated over scenarios in her head. What if she said the wrong thing? What if Thomas thought she wasn't interesting, pretty or 'normal' enough in a one-to-one setting?

Two days before their date, Thomas didn't say much to her on shift at Lawson's, resulting in her thoughts spiralling even further and bouncing all over, like a tennis ball down a hill.

Being her usual intuitive self, Trish picked up on May's nerves over a mid-morning cuppa. 'He likes you, May. He wouldn't ask you on a date if he didn't.' She tilted her head, eyes welcoming as they turned up slightly, gentle wrinkles of the many smiles her face had displayed over the years peeping out of her glasses. 'Men aren't like us; they don't ask people on dates to be kind.'

Reaching over May's desk, she continued, 'Just enjoy it, love, stop spoiling it for yourself before it's even begun.'

May stared into her almost empty cup, watching the remaining golden-beige liquid move slightly as her thoughts began to cannonball despite Trish's reassurance and optimism. By the end of the shift, May had a sore mouth from biting her bottom, inner lip and was convinced Thomas had changed his mind after hardly seeing him all day.

Not long after she got in from work, he texted her apologising for not being able to chat much during her morning shift and explaining that he had been finishing a report for Jack. Relief flooded into her as she texted back, but the feeling was only temporary. She tried to push the worry to one side that night, drowning it in a relaxing bubble bath.

May had planned her date outfit earlier that week, confirming it the night before. Although she was tall with angular shoulders, she was rather in proportion, so she suited most clothes. Suiting clothes didn't mean she had style, well, not one that set her apart—which would never have been something she desired anyway. Looking in the mirror again, she tilted her head back and forth, flicked her hair to one side, put a hand on her hip and smiled. She felt 'enough'.

Thomas and May had arranged to meet at a local Greek restaurant. May was particular about what she ate, struggling with new foods; however, she loved Greek food, mainly due to her family holidays. So, when Thomas suggested the restaurant, she knew he had listened.

May arrived early and waited outside. It wasn't long before she noticed Thomas walking towards her from the edge of the car park. She smoothed down her hair and pressed her lips together, hoping to transfer some of the pink lip gloss where needed.

Thomas reached her and embraced her gently. 'May, you look lovely.'

She let him hold her and lightly held him back, closing her eyes and subtly inhaling his unique Thomas-Graham scent. He let go, and she cleared her throat.

'After you.' He gestured through the door, and May walked into the restaurant first.

The smell of vegetables and meats cooking in their sauces behind the scenes hit her immediately—sharp lemon, minty oregano, rich tomato and warming garlic. They were immediately swarmed by enthusiastic waiters and taken to a table. The restaurant smelt of holiday, and as Thomas grabbed a menu and began scanning the choices, May swallowed the lump of nostalgia in her throat that was threatening to poison the mood.

She looked at the menu despite knowing what she was going to order. She glanced up and down the choices without really reading them, peering over at Thomas now and again to see if he was ready. Once he placed his menu down, she placed hers down too and met his eyes. Thomas smiled, and May rubbed her hands, quickly glancing away and then back to him.

One of the enthusiastic waiters appeared at their table. 'Ready to order?'

May ordered moussaka and a side salad, and Thomas ordered mixed meat skewers. The food soon arrived, and as they ate, the pair talked about work, May's studies and the latest series on Netflix. She was on a boat of emotions, in a sea that flitted from turbulent to calm. She tried to ride the waves, enjoy her night and appreciate the moment. Putting forkfuls of her meal into her mouth, she savoured the taste. Eating moussaka and feta cheese always made her think of good times, family times and now times she wished upon all the stars in the sky that she could experience again. Perhaps she could make new memories with Thomas. Perhaps.

Conversation wasn't awkward like May had feared; instead, they talked about almost everything, from politics to animals, food to film, work and homelife. It was nice... more than nice.

It felt as if they'd not shared enough time together when it reached the point of splitting the bill—upon May's insistence—and leaving the restaurant. As they stood outside the glass doors, Thomas smiled gently.

'I'll walk you to your car.'

As they strolled, May shivered with the cold evening breeze, and Thomas gently took her hand. She jumped slightly but kept her fingers interlocked in his as they continued to walk the short distance to her car. The worry that her palm might be sweaty encased in his despite the temperature stopped her from enjoying the moment as much as she would have liked to.

Once they reached her car, he let go of her hand. He glanced at the ground and moved a small stone with his foot before his eyes rose to meet hers.

'I've had a great night, May.'

He tilted his head to the side and stepped forward, leaning in for a kiss. She automatically leaned away, her body moving closer to her car. Despite having thought about kissing Thomas on several occasions, now that he wanted to kiss her, she felt unprepared, inexperienced and worried she would disappoint him.

He laughed. 'I'm not going to bite your jugular.'

She blushed, but her cheeks were already rosy from the winter air. She opened her mouth to apologise, but Thomas tenderly held her hands and pulled her back towards him before she could. Her heart rate increased as the warmth from Thomas's hands travelled up her arms. He leaned in again, and this time, she didn't pull away. He tasted slightly of the honey and sweet pastry from the baklava they had shared for dessert. His lips moved slowly in sync with hers, and May let herself be desired. She reminded herself she was enough, even just for that night if there was never a date number two.

Pulling away, Thomas raised her left hand to his mouth and kissed it. 'Thanks for a great date, May McClelland. Hopefully we can do it again.'

May stood, looking at the man in front of her, thinking he was more beautiful than a sunset over the Golden Gate Bridge, and she nodded, unable to speak. Date one had been a success. She could have floated home in happiness, surrounded by a bubble of confidence and acceptance from a man she had most definitely developed feelings for. And it appeared he liked her back.

She got into her car, Thomas shutting the door for her before turning to walk to his own. After putting her on, fiddling to hear the click of it securing into place with her still slightly shaking hands, she started the engine and began to drive out of the car park. Waving to Thomas as she passed, she let out a breath she unwittingly had been holding. A smile spread across her face momentarily. Then the bubble popped and reality hit hard as she realised she could never tell her mam.

May kept experiencing pockets of pleasure, of normality. A few hours snatched here and there where she could forget, where she could still be the young adult she should be. Then boom, the trapdoor would open and she would fall into her reality again. As someone who had also lost his mam, albeit years previous to May losing Fran, Thomas knew it would be a hard Christmas for May and Victor. He kept in touch with May in and out of work, and they had a few dates, going to a café, for a walk in the local country park and to see a Christmas display. May used his support and kindness to top up the nutrition and medication her organisational skills weren't quite delivering.

As the days leading up to Christmas approached, Thomas and May spent more time together, Thomas often joining May in the staff kitchen for lunch. Cuppa breaks in her office were still reserved for Trish though.

The microwave in the staff kitchen pinged, and Thomas opened it and emptied his microwave meal onto a plate. He smiled at May as he walked over to join her, his chair scraping against the tiled floor and making a slight squeaking sound as he pulled it back to sit down. The kitchen table could seat many people, and although they were the only two on break, May had still placed herself at one of the end seats.

Thomas took his first mouthful of the chicken pasta, the thin white sauce hardly coating it. 'Mmmm so good.'

The smell of the microwave meal immediately wafted to May, and she smiled unconvincingly and nodded as she wished her sandwich contained a stronger-smelling filling than ham salad. Maybe something like tuna. Something strong enough to cover the smell of vomit it seemed to give off.

She hurried eating her sandwich, struggling to stomach it, grateful when he finally finished his meal and pushed his plate to one side. Thomas wiped his mouth on a tissue before leaning over to his rucksack on the ground, pulling a rectangle-shaped gift out covered in reindeer-decorated red wrapping paper. He placed it on the table to the right of May's plate.

'For you.'

May panicked, feeling hotter as she stared at the gift without saying a word.

Thomas, faced with an initial reaction he hadn't expected or hoped for, tapped May's hand. 'It's nothing dodgy.' He laughed as her eyes rose to his.

She nodded slowly. They hadn't talked about getting gifts despite her having bought him one. But she *knew* he'd be pleased with his gift, so it was different.

'Open it,' Thomas's eyes widened as they moved from May to the gift and back to May.

Pushing her plate to the left and bringing the gift closer, she swallowed. Thomas didn't know about her feelings on surprises, as it wasn't something that would come up in general conversation, like asking someone if they prefer dogs or cats, tea or coffee. She hoped that she could feign enthusiasm.

Thomas leaned in, almost climbing over the table with anticipation as she eventually began slowly peeling back the paper.

'Really, you shouldn't have bothered. Honest, I don't need anything.'

'Ah, most of us never need a gift, but where's the fun in that?' He chuckled.

Far from soothing her doubts, the comment made her feel even worse, and she took a sip of water to delay the reveal. It was bound to be a useless gift after that comment.

'C'mon, it'll be time to go home before you get this open.' Thomas slapped his thighs, amused by May's delicacy.

She squeezed her eyes shut for a second, then opened them and removed the last of the wrapping paper in one go. She couldn't help but smile as relief washed over her.

'Hey, at last.' He threw his head back, laughing.

The gift from Thomas was a useful stationery set with space for lists and tasks. May turned the notepads and pens over in her hands. The notepads were grey and dark blue with stars on each in the other colour. A matching grey pen and a matching blue pen went alongside them. She bit her lip, glanced at Thomas and then the gifts before placing them on the table and reaching for his hand. She didn't need to worry about the message her face might tell.

'Thank you, I really like it.' May gently squeezed his hand, and he nodded enthusiastically.

Perhaps surprises can be okay... sometimes anyway.

She pushed her seat back and got up. 'I'll just be a minute,' she said as she turned and walked out of the staff kitchen area.

May returned with a gift for Thomas that she had been storing in her desk drawer. He brought his hands to his mouth, excited, as if clinging to a lottery ticket, waiting for the numbers to be announced. She felt the pressure, her hands a little clammy as she sat back in her seat.

May knew Thomas needed some new driving gloves, after overhearing a conversation he'd had with Jack. She had promptly purchased him a pair, then wrapped them in candy cane striped paper. She held the present out, grimacing slightly, then attempted to disguise the grimace with a little giggle. Giving the gift felt awkward for many reasons, but mainly because it was their first experience of sharing gifts with one another. The anxiety wasn't helped by the fact it was a surprise gift, albeit one she knew he needed. *What if he's already asked someone else to buy him a pair for Christmas?* There it was again—the anxious voice that always liked to run rampant in her mind. She pushed it away with the reminder that she had the receipt at home just in case.

Thomas didn't indicate he noticed her discomfort as he happily took the present and moved his shoulders side to side as he tore the paper open. May began to relax a little, her impersonation of an ironing board lessening with his widening smile as he discovered what lay within the wrapping paper.

He put them straight on his hands, then held them up in a ta-dah-style movement. 'They're great... perfect. Exactly what I needed. Thanks, May.' He leant over the table and kissed her, then paused. 'How did you know I needed some?'

'I, uh, overheard you say to Jack.' She bit her lip, waiting for a response to her admittance, but he just shrugged and lifted his hands in front of his face to admire his new driving gloves.

May spent the rest of her shift daydreaming about Thomas, daydreaming being uncharacteristic for her usually, but she was up to date with her tasks at Lawson's, so she decided it should be okay to indulge in the nice feelings bouncing on clouds around her mind.

Chapter 8

May was smitten with Thomas but still found accommodating someone in her daily schedule hard. She was going to sleep later each night, often texting Thomas until the early hours about her usually very uneventful day. She liked that someone was interested, it was just weird for her and she had to remember to show interest in things she wouldn't normally, like the rugby score and circuit training at the gym. She had to remind herself that Thomas was getting to know her, just as she was getting to know him. He was becoming familiar with her personality and hadn't made her feel that she had to change anything about herself. May would put 'learn to be less self-critical' on her New Year's goal list. But it all helped to distract her from the loss of her mam and the partial loss of her dad now that his life partner and soulmate was gone.

Victor put on a brave face, and May was thankful he had some level of routine through work at the garage and seeing his friends. His brother, Terence, also visited each fortnight, and on the alternate fortnight, Victor would travel to Terence's, an hour or so away. Victor had never been a big speaker, Fran always holding the metaphoric microphone in their relationship. May was also not the best conversationalist, often preferring silence. Neither had asked those questions that you don't ask because really you don't want to hear the answer. It would just make them feel even more helpless. Much of their time together was silent reflection, Victor often trying to make

May smile with a silly anecdote from work, his lips curling at the end as May watched sadness drawing its curtains behind his eyes. He wasn't the same. How could he be? All those years with his best friend, decades of being in love. And love doesn't end when a life does. Instead, Victor yearned for someone who he couldn't wake up with, spend the day with or go to sleep next to. Fran was now only a photograph in a frame and locked in the memories in his mind.

Christmas was agonisingly hard. May noticed things missing she'd taken for granted. The void left by her mam that would simply never be filled, never heal and the repeated realisation that three had become two and joy had become pain. The homemade sweet mince pies that May used to smell as soon as she opened her bedroom door—warm, golden aroma drifting through the house as she felt her stomach almost smile with what was to come. The Christmas tree coming down from the loft on the right day, twelve days before Christmas, despite Victor complaining in jest each year that it was too soon. The missing reality of May and her mam decorating the almost twenty-year-old tree as Dad ate nuts. Unbeknown to May and her mam, he would sneak the odd glance at the precious women in his life and smile. He would shout the odd order—'That one needs to go higher. Nah, not there, higher up, so you can see it'—referring to the decorations that May had made at school all those years ago that were falling to bits like the slippers he had been wearing all year. He would let his girls get on with it, well almost, as he watched a Christmas movie or *Only Fools and Horses*, which he had seen hundreds of times but still made him laugh. They were underwater, and she knew this would be the time she and Dad would sink or swim.

'I'm not getting the tree out this year, May, I can't be bothered,' Victor said defeatedly as he placed his hand on his cheek. He seemed to sink further into the sofa cushions, as if hiding from the time of year.

'I know it's hard, Dad, I feel it too, but Mam would want the tree out; she loved Christmas. We are already

late putting it up.' She mustered a half-smile. 'We can do
it together. It might not look as nice as when Mam and
me did it, but we can try?'

Victor stared at where the tree normally stood, proud
in the centre of the bay window. There was a strong sadness in his eyes. Was it really that he couldn't be bothered
or that he couldn't bear it that it wouldn't be his Fran
decorating the tree? They were both in pain, but May had
limited tools to deal with her grief, never mind her dad's
as well. She loved him, but it was exhausting trying to
keep things going at times, to keep treading water. She
was still the child; she needed him to be Dad, to be strong
for them both.

Victor glanced at the floor and then held his head in his
hands. A sigh left his open mouth, barely audible, yet May
heard it so loud it could have moved the birds from the
trees. Pain echoed, bouncing off all corners of the room.
She leant over, closing the gap between them on the sofa,
and hugged her dad as they sat in silence in the family
lounge. Her dad almost melted into her arms.

'I'm going up to get the tree from the loft now, Dad. It's
already two days late. Will you catch it?' She stared at her
dad, tired eyes wide, urging him to cooperate. He nodded
weakly, and they got up to bring the tree down from the
loft.

The Christmas tree had so many memories. Covered
with chocolates that would all be gone by Christmas Eve
and decorations that had been passed down from grandparents, handmade by May, purchased on family holidays
and bought by May at the Christmas market with Scarlett
each year. So many memories that only came out once a
year but were sewn into the tapestry of the McClelland
family's history, every stitch created with unbreakable
love.

Each decoration picked out of the box seemed to feel
like another layer of their hearts being cruelly peeled
off. The pair smiled, sobbed and sighed as they decorated the tree that had witnessed so many wonderful tak-

en-for-granted Christmases. But they had to have Christ-mas, for Fran.

Christmas Eve, Christmas Day and Boxing Day were overwhelming despite cousins, uncles and aunts trying to help and bring cheer. May was relieved when it was over and she could return to her more useful focuses. She and Thomas had gone ice skating on the outdoor rink in town and had been to a Christmas carol performance with a local charity. It had helped May to smother the creeping shadow of grief that clung to her neck and shoulders like a restrictive scarf most days. Distractions felt as essential as breathing in those painful weeks of festivities.

During their ice-skating date, Thomas had talked about how difficult his first Christmas was after his mam passed.

'It gets more manageable. Easier is probably the wrong word, as it will never be easy, but we adapt because we have to,' he'd said tenderly, holding May's hand as they drank hot chocolate to warm up in a café afterwards.

May bit her lip and lowered her head. He got off his stool and embraced her. At that moment, May McClelland was convinced Thomas Graham was her destiny.

By the time the university term commenced, she had a year and a half left of her master's degree and began to get back into focusing on the future. Now she was dating someone and the first Christmas without Mam was over, the iceberg of grief was slowly melting somewhat, allowing her to function again.

Chapter 9

As spring arrived, Victor seemed to turn a corner and began doing more in the house and after work. Like water flowing into cracks in the pavement, he began fitting into the gaps grief left that had once been vast and fearsome voids. Just as May had to, Victor adapted and coped to a degree. It meant she could focus more on her studies and Thomas. By this point, the couple were official and she was wrapped in the cosy blanket of love. It was a sensation she had never felt, and it was both amazing and frightening. Love opened a new world to May, where she felt another level of normal. It was a feeling, an emotion, a partnership that made her feel less alien. At the same time, it made her vulnerable and exposed to heartbreak. Victor thought Thomas seemed a decent, hardworking lad and was happy she had met someone.

As spring bloomed into summer, May turned twenty-three on the thirty-first of May. It was the first birthday without her mam, and she tried desperately to remember snippets from her previous birthday. She noted some things down despite having a short video on her phone—her present, the meal they had eaten as a family, what her mam had worn. She watched the video distraught that someday she would forget even though she'd remembered everything perfectly this time. That she would no longer recall her mother's voice, the touch of her skin, her scent. The way Fran would stroke May's hair and kiss her forehead when she sat, as May was too tall for her mam to kiss it standing up. The way May always felt protected, adored. How she always felt at home with her parents, not just in the home. How Fran would clasp her hands together when she laughed and tuck her hair behind her ears when she wanted to be taken seriously. All the ingredients that made Fran, the ingredients that made her mam. There was an axe wound in May's heart that she knew would never completely heal no matter how the days passed by, quickly as the years on the calendar moved. May's birthday without Fran was one of many she would have to swallow, and she would swallow them, but she'd swallow them as easily as she'd swallow a ball covered in razor blades.

By her birthday, Thomas and May had been official for almost six months. Thomas had suggested he plan a night away in a posh hotel for them, but after seeing her reaction of horror, as if a seagull had snatched an ice cream from a child, he suggested theatre and a meal. May was happy with this—she couldn't have someone else planning a trip away, especially as a surprise. Her need for attention to detail, organising and feeling in control was almost on par with her need to eat. May realised she probably wasn't the easiest person on the planet to have a relationship of any sort with, and this became starker in her relationship with Thomas. It may have been the reason she didn't have a massive social circle and why she found conversation difficult at times. May liked silences, but most people referred to them as awkward. She didn't talk for the sake of talking and only asked questions if she wanted an answer. With Thomas, she tried to be more considerate and aware of her reactions.

Thomas was patient with her, and it made her love him even more. Their relationship had been sexually slow to start due to her lack of confidence. Her one and only experience with Oscar Sullivan had been anything but earth-moving and memorable. If she were the problem, it would surely end her relationship and be another thing that broke her heart, another person leaving. After a few months, May felt ready to progress with intimacy. The first time they had made love, it didn't feel as if the world had stopped, with only May and Thomas in their passionate bubble—well, not for May—but she didn't feel like an unattractive, unsexual failure. She still felt close to Thomas and in love with him, and she knew, like anything, the sex would improve with practice.

Thomas seemed happy in the relationship. He was kind and respectful and both appreciated the need for their own space and time, although May, despite always advocating her own company, wanted to spend more time with him and was always thinking of him. She day-dreamed about their future, like a movie of their up-coming lives playing in her head. They had things in common, and although he would snigger sometimes at her ways, it felt more in jest than in malice. It hadn't always been obvious to May when she was younger that she was different to the masses, but living alone, with Thomas staying now and then, showed her that she was different in more ways than had been obvious. But she was okay with being different, as we are all different—it's what makes life interesting.

May felt that so few people in life truly understand other people, so few individuals are in sync organically, like they are cogs of a machine that work and fit together. May didn't have many fellow cogs, but she treasured the ones she had.

Chapter 10

The months passed, and August soon arrived, bringing the first anniversary of Fran's death with it. May went to her dad's and cooked his tea—pasta made over steams of deep breaths and shards of pain. After their meal, which they tried to enjoy despite the taste of the void of their missing matriarch, they sat on the sofa and looked through photos. Eyes glassy with the threat of their emotional dams bursting, they allowed one another to share memories. There were laughs and smiles, glimmers of light in the cloudy tears as the box of tissues was passed between them alongside the photos. May studied the photos, her beautiful mother looking like the world's most stunning portrait. *Did I tell Mam she's beautiful? Did I explain how much I love her?* May had never found paying compliments easy, but she hoped Fran knew May had always seen her as the most beautiful of humans, physically and internally.

Victor and May stopped looking through photos after the second box, both exhausted in grief. They went into the back garden, Victor carrying a spade and May a plant. They walked in silence across the grass that held the vibrant shade of healthy summer in each of its blades—life growing out of the sun-penetrated ground that May and her dad prepared to add more new growth to, as a tribute to the woman they missed so dearly. They were going to plant a yellow rose bush towards the edge of the grass, near the decking where Fran had loved to sit, cup of coffee in hand and often a book in the other.

May stared at the rattan furniture, where she could almost see Fran sitting. She closed her stinging eyes, and hot tears escaped down her cheeks. Once she opened them again, the image was gone and the rattan furniture sat unoccupied, unloved, like a bike with two punctures.

Victor watched his daughter, his hand over his mouth as he stifled the sobs that he had been fighting relentlessly to suppress for the last year. Removing his hand from his mouth, he touched May's arm gently. She glanced at her dad before her eyes shifted to the plot where the rose bush—which would be beautiful and radiant like her mam had always been—would go. Father and daughter, voicelessly in sync, began to plant the yellow rose bush. The yellow rose bush they prayed, despite neither being religious, would keep part of their beloved Fran alive.

Chapter 11

That summer, May picked up a few extra shifts at Lawson's. She was returning to university in September, to her final year of her master's. Next summer, after seven years at university, she would graduate as a research scientist and be able to start her dream career.

The new work week arrived, and with it, the weekly team meeting. May rushed from her office to the staff kitchen with her chair, then set about making Trish a surprise cup of coffee for the meeting. After a stream of cups of tea and endless biscuits from Trish, she'd decided it was time to return the kindness and had already made her two coffees the day before. As she stirred the milk into the coffee, she smiled.

Colleagues gathered in the staff kitchen, leaving one staff member out in the office for potential customers. She pushed through them to put the spoon in the sink, which she'd remember to wash up after the meeting. Noticing Trish walking into the room with Jack, May made her way over to her and handed her the coffee, lifting her chin slightly.

Jack frowned playfully. 'Where's mi—'

'Oh, thanks, lovely, but you didn't have to.' Trish nodded slowly at May and peered at the steaming liquid.

'I want to, you've made my drinks for long enough.' May clasped her hands together.

'C'mon, everyone, get your seats, this is going to be a long one today,' Jack shouted way too loudly for May's liking, waving his hands in a way to move people along.

Trish grabbed her chair from the office and placed it next to May's. As the meeting began, she took a sip of her coffee and coughed loudly after swallowing it, slightly choking.

'Go down the wrong way, did it, Trish?' Jack asked.

Red-faced, Trish nodded. 'Something like that.'

The usual update on tenants, viewings and sales occurred and a discussion on annual leave was had.

'Let's have a five-minute break, as we've got a few more agenda items to go over,' Jack said after the first hour of the meeting.

Everyone obliged, grateful for a leg stretch and cuppa.

'Want another coffee?' May asked Trish, leaning over to grab her cup. Everyone else had moved away from the table, sneaking out for a quick cigarette or toilet break as the kettle boiled.

Trish glanced around to make sure no one was too close. 'May, my lovely, you don't drink coffee and I can tell. Your coffee is like tar; please stop making me it and just let me look after you with hot drinks.' She smiled and got up from her seat, squeezing May's shoulder.

May was a little taken aback. 'Erm okay.'

'Right, I will make your tea.'

May shrugged, glad she'd at least tried.

The meeting continued with a discussion on expenses before Jack announced the big news that they were merging with a company in York, Wray's Estates. It meant that they would be able to expand as a partnership and hopefully establish more branches in the next few years. It was great for Jack, but May just wanted to stay doing what she did for as long as needed before going into scientific research.

Clapping his hands, Jack continued, 'So, that means some of you will get a chance to work in Wray's York office before our merger and rebrand in October. You can all visit, but we need some feet on the ground, so to speak.' He chuckled, but May didn't see the funny side as she stared at her boss and weighed up his next move.

'Trish will go down two days a week for a month and Thomas will be based in York for a few months. The rest of you can each spend a week at Wray's if you wish to before the merge is complete.'

May couldn't take her eyes off Jack, feeling as if a punchbag had been swung into her. *Why Thomas? Why does he have to be sent to York? Because he doesn't have kids? But he has me. I need him.* She began to feel dizzy as her thoughts escalated, and it reminded her of getting lost in Fenwick department store when she was younger. She had to get some air and space away from the muttering.

She left her seat and the chatter, heading for the back door of the office. Opening the door, she gulped in the air to try to calm the negative thoughts and panic encroaching her body. She heard hurried footsteps behind her and felt someone reach for her arm.

'I'm sorry, May. It had been in talks for a few weeks, but Jack only confirmed it with me half an hour ago. I didn't get a chance to tell you.'

May pulled her body away and turned, looking at Thomas as if he had just ripped up her favourite book.

'It's only for a few months. I'll be home at weekends.'

May pressed her lips together and faced the ground. She didn't have the words to express what she felt without sounding as intense as she knew she could be. She nodded and kept her eyes downward, focusing on a stray cigarette butt that had been left by one of the team. She felt as discarded as it.

'The time will fly by and the conveyancing experience of another branch and locality will be great for my CV,' Thomas said, looking at May with wide eyes, eager for agreement as she eventually moved her eyes to him.

She bit her lip, trying to think of what to say. She didn't want Thomas to be away from her for up to three months, even with a not unreasonably long hour-and-a-half commute time and the wonder of Skype, but it wasn't her choice. She knew she couldn't expect him to do what she wanted. She felt impending doom, unable to fixate on the positives Thomas was seeing.

He took her hand, rubbing it tenderly. His hands felt warm, safe, as if they were made to encase hers. May took a deep breath and enjoyed the moment. Their eyes locked, and his charming smile melted her a little. It wasn't as if they were living together, they had only been together for ten months, and although she loved him and he said he loved her back, they still very much had their own lives.

Sensing her need for reassurance, Thomas touched her face. 'It will be fine. We can see each other on weekends and Skype. Think of the bonus I will get for going to York—we could go on holiday next summer with it. Perhaps to Greece.'

May pursed her lips as she ran a hand through her hair. Thomas was so thoughtful and perhaps he was right—it was only for a few months and they would be in touch all the time. She tried to push the feeling of dread away as she plastered on a semi-fake smile for Thomas. Always thinking the worst wasn't one of her better personal qualities.

They chatted some more before going back inside. She felt slightly reassured, leaving embarrassment to hit her that some of her colleagues may have noticed her quick departure from the meeting.

She got on with her tasks for the day, just as she usually did; however, she simply couldn't swallow the self-doubt despite numerous cups of tea from Trish. The thought of Thomas being in York, even for three months, felt like forever. She couldn't help but feel a tight, twisting knot in her stomach that lasted long after her shift.

The day for Thomas to leave for York soon arrived, and his car was packed for his temporary life there. He would come home each weekend but wanted to take as much as he could fit in the vehicle, not that it was a lot given he lived at home with his dad, stepmam and youngest sister.

His first stop was May's. She'd been looking out the blinds of her lounge window for ten whole minutes by the time she saw his car approaching. She smiled as she rushed down the stairs to see him. She'd applied some natural make-up this morning, wanting him to think she looked pretty for the last time he would see her for a week... five days, if she was being technical.

Thomas got out of his car as she opened the front door, and he met her as she walked down the garden path. He embraced her tightly, sinking his face into her hair. 'Mmm, you smell like an ice cream shop. I want to bottle this smell.' He inhaled deeply, then held her at arm's length. 'And you look hot.'

May giggled and kissed him before flicking her hair over her shoulder, glad her new shampoo had done what she'd wanted—given Thomas something else to remember her by while he was away. 'I'll miss you,' she said, feeling sadness dancing around the front lawn.

'I'll miss you too, but we've got weekends and Skype and our phones.'

May nodded and moved back in for a cuddle. 'Text me when you get there so I know you're okay.'

'Yes, Mam.' Thomas put his hand to his head in a saluting motion. 'I love you, May.'

'I love you too,' she replied as Thomas returned to his car. She watched him drive off, waved and continued to watch the back of his car until she could no longer see him.

Chapter 12

Thomas came home each weekend for the first three weeks during his work at Wray's. The couple Skyped most nights, Thomas asking about Lawson's and telling May how much better the systems and technology were at Wray's. May didn't like this, as she wasn't a fan of change and had implemented some of the systems at Lawson's. They may not have been the most up to date and technologically groundbreaking, but they worked and kept order. Those systems were the spine of the business, keeping the skeleton together.

Thomas and May would text in the morning, then after work and throughout the evening. She missed him and would re-read his messages and look through photos of them. On the third weekend home, Thomas visited May on the Saturday afternoon. Despite a cuddle on his arrival and chats about their week over tea and cookies that Thomas had brought, he was less talkative than usual.

'Is everything okay?' May asked, taking his hand as they sat side by side on her brown sofa. 'You seem quieter.'

Thomas rubbed his mouth with his free hand and nodded. 'Yeah, fine. It's just been a heavy week, so my brain's a bit frazzled.' He tapped his forehead before leaning over to get another cookie from the coffee table.

May followed him with her gaze, wanting more from the conversation.

'Ummm, I forgot to tell you, but I actually can't stay over.' Thomas didn't meet her gaze as he bit off half the cookie, a couple of crumbs landing in his lap. 'I'm actually playing rugby with some friends tomorrow morning.'

'But that's tomorrow?'

'I know, but I need an early night.'

May bit back her disappointment and tried to enjoy the next few hours with him before he returned to his family home after a small kiss on the doorstep and a wave as he got into his car. She wrapped herself tightly in her fleece dressing gown after changing into her nightwear. Even though it was a warm night, she felt very cold.

The next week, Thomas cancelled two arranged phone calls, saying he would text instead, as he was working late and going for dinner with his new team. Dread crept into May's body, weighing her down, as if she were carrying heavy bags of sand. She could feel a leak somewhere in their relationship but couldn't find the source. No matter how hard her rational self argued that she was overanalysing, she could still hear an uncomfortable, destructive dripping.

She didn't want to sound like a possessive girlfriend, so she avoided showing any paranoia. She also didn't want Thomas to be lonely in York—him spending time with colleagues and making friends was important. When she sought advice from Scarlett, she said he was probably just trying to fit in with the team and adjust. She was likely right to some extent, but the niggle wouldn't stop; in fact, the warning siren in May's head only got louder.

Thomas didn't come home that fourth weekend, saying he was poorly. She offered to go and look after him, but he declined, saying he was bad company when unwell. It wasn't until Thursday, after nearly a week of no Skype calls, that her laptop sounded the call notification. She jumped, not realising he had been going to call. He was due to come home tomorrow evening, and as far as she was aware, they were only texting until then.

She bit her lip, wondering whether to let the call ring off. Before, she would have answered within less than a second, but after weeks of letdowns and anxiety, her first thought was this couldn't be good.

After countless rings and it being clear Thomas was happy to wait, she plumped up the cushions behind her on the sofa, leaned back and answered. After years of studying people and their expressions, she knew what Thomas's expression was, although it wasn't one she'd seen on him before: sheepish. He sat there silently, as if trying to form what he needed to say properly in his head prior to speaking. It wasn't something May often did, instead rehearsing important conversations before they happened if she had opportunity. She was ready for another letdown to add to the countless ones she'd received since he'd been working away.

'Is this about the theatre tomorrow? If you can't go, that's fine, but—'

'May, listen,' Thomas blurted, cutting her off. 'I've had a lot of time to think.' He took off his glasses and rubbed his eyes. 'You're amazing and clever and beautiful and quirky.'

May leant forward, almost physically feeling the kettle-bell of rejection that had swung into her stomach. She'd seen similar speeches a million times in movies. They usually continued with 'it's not you, it's me'.

'But I just don't know if we are suited. We're so different and... I just dunno. I'm not sure if we have a future, and it feels wrong to keep things plodding along if not.' He looked down momentarily before returning his gaze to the screen and running his hand through his hair.

May licked her lips, which had become as dry as arid soil. 'Plodding along? I'm not plodding, Thomas. I love you.' She felt nauseous as her heart raced to the beat of speedy dance music. 'I'm happy. I see a future. Where has this come from?' She couldn't control the crackling in her voice as distress formed as tears in her eyes.

'I love you too. I really do care about you, May, but I just don't think we are suited long-term.'

'So, I'm just okay for the short-term?' Her words came out louder than she'd anticipated.

'I always want you in my life as my friend. But I just...
I don't think we can be anything more.' He looked away
again, guilt pouring out of his face.

'Is there someone else?' May sobbed. 'Why am I not
enough?'

'You are enough, May, for the right person. You are
perfect for the right person.' He let out a sigh that could
have filled a flat tyre. 'Your right person just isn't me. And
no, there's no one else,' he finished quietly.

And with that, May's fairy tale was over. Dumped
over Skype with no real explanation. Rejection, another
loss and a worry that she would never be enough for
someone. She spent the weekend in denial, certain that
Thomas would change his mind and the storm would
settle to bring calm, more appreciated weather. Surely he
wouldn't throw away the last ten months? After numerous
conversations with Scarlett, where Thomas was referred
to by Scarlett as the biggest shithead on two legs, May felt
confused and out of control.

She went running excessively that weekend. Running
was often the only time she could feel free and switch
off from life, but it didn't seem to be working when it
came to Thomas. He was living rent-free in her head,
and she didn't want to serve him an eviction order. By
Sunday, May was full of dread at the thought of her shift
at Lawson's the next afternoon. Scarlett had delivered
another pep talk, which made May feel marginally better
for the twenty minutes they chatted, only for any balloons
of positivity to be popped as soon as the call ended. May
had cancelled seeing her dad that weekend, saying she
was poorly. She found lying very hard, but she didn't want
to upset her dad with her troubles, still feeling perhaps
there was hope Thomas would change his mind. That he
needed her like a roast dinner needs gravy. Victor had
only met Thomas three times, but it was clear to May that
her dad was happy she had met someone. Another loss.
Another person gone. It was all she could think about.
She decided to send Thomas a last text. She had nothing
to lose; her ship was already sinking.

'I spent my entire life trying to fit in, like a square person in a round world. I fitted with you, then you changed shape. Xxx'

He replied an hour later with just one word: *'Sorry.'*

May re-read the solitary word over and over, as if she could change the narrative if she concentrated enough. She spent her night sobbing into the early hours.

After four hours of sleep, no breakfast and wearing no make-up, May walked into work quite sure she looked as if she were auditioning for *The Walking Dead.* She tried keeping her head down as she slipped past her colleagues' desks, hoping no one could get a close enough look to notice.

'May, my lovely, are you okay?'

May momentarily froze, eyes slightly widening before looking up at Trish. Clearly Trish noticed. She should have expected that. *And I should have at least put some concealer under my eyes and maybe a bit of bronzer on my cheeks for colour. Wait, do I even own bronzer?*

As if confirming her thoughts, Trish leaned for May's arm. 'You're very pale.'

May mustered a pathetic smile and nodded, rushing to her office as Trish quickly followed.

'You're not a great liar, love,' she whispered. 'Now, what's happened?'

May dropped her head into her hands and tried to focus on her breathing, hoping she would be able to speak without the thunder in her heart coming out. As she glanced at her friend, Trish's brow furrowed.

'Turns out I wasn't enough after all,' May mumbled.

'Thomas?' Trish asked, pressing her lips together and taking a deep breath in through her nose.

As May nodded, two tears plopped from her eyes onto the paperwork neatly placed on her desk and spread across the porous white paper. 'He said that he loves me but we aren't suited long-term. Can't love me that much, can he?' She threw her hands up, then grabbed her head with them.

Trish felt the kick in the stomach of seeing your child in pain, quickly followed by the anger that it had been caused by someone else. She moved round to May's seat and pulled her in for an embrace, rubbing her hair gently. 'The bastard. He doesn't deserve you, May,' she soothed through gritted teeth. 'You're special, May, and if he can't see that, it's his loss. He will regret it. Stupid arse of a young man.'

May let out a deflated breath and half-smile at Trish's choice of insult.

Placing a hand on May's shoulder, Trish looked at her, kind hazel eyes almost radiating motherly love. 'I'll put the kettle on. You know where I am if you ever need me for anything, in and outside of work.'

Hours turned into days, days to weeks and weeks to months. The feeling of rejection and heartbreak plateaued. May absorbed the fact that Thomas wouldn't phone and desperately ask to get back with her as they did in the romance movies she couldn't bear to watch. He ended up staying in York whilst the merger of Lawson-Wray's went through. On social media a few weeks later, there were photos of him with a woman. A woman who looked very different to May. She blocked him. It was asking for pain to spy on his life, and she couldn't keep looking in like an outcasted tourist.

Chapter 13

That first Christmas without Fran had been one of the most difficult times of May and Victor's lives. At times, they had both needed to cry on each other's shoulder, instinctively knowing when each other needed a hug or when they needed silence. May had always had a good relationship with her dad, but losing the leader of their pack, the front door to their home, had left them only having one another. It created a stronger bond. Victor began processing his grief after that first Christmas, moving to the next stage in the cycle of understanding the loss they had experienced. For all it felt that she was suffocating with grief at times, May also saw the shards of light as the curtains began to slowly open behind her dad's eyes. This Christmas, she hoped it would be easier.

During the second part of the year, she had agreed to dinner a few times at Trish's house where May didn't know the menu beforehand. Small steps to some, but for her, it was a big deal. Victor had managed better and better as the year had progressed too. He had been more like the dad she remembered before they lost Mam, not fully how he had been, but more like a favourite mug that had smashed and been lovingly glued back together, now used as a pen pot. In many ways, May had altered as a person. Changed felt too strong of a word—perhaps she had adjusted, in some ways not by choice. She reflected on what had worked last year to help the pair get through the festive period and vowed to ensure the same plans for this Christmas. They would honour the routines they'd loved with Fran but avoid sad films and attempting to make sweet mince pies.

'Got it?' Victor asked as he slid the box containing the tree down the loft ladder.

'Yup.' May leant it against the wall before Victor passed the large box of decorations down. She could see the colours and patterns through the transparent plastic container they sat in. Placing the box on the carpet, she sighed and closed her eyes. *Will memories ever stop being painful?*

Victor broke her thoughts as he came plodding down the loft stairs, huffing and puffing as if he had completed a one-hundred-metre sprint. The pair carried the items downstairs, placing them in the middle of the lounge. They both stood in silence, looking at the bay window where the tree would sit, currently occupied by a large footstool. Father and daughter remained still, as if planted in their own pot, trying to keep the roots of their life intact.

May took a gasp of air, not realising she had been holding her breath. She closed her eyes, willing them to open to something else, something in the past that didn't feel like the cutting reality. She felt her father's arm around her shoulder—the tenderness of a man who didn't always show affection but always made her feel loved. She moved her hands to her eyes, trying to stop the moisture escaping.

'There, there, darlin'. It's okay. We're okay.' Victor pulled his daughter in, his little girl, and bit back his emotions, pressing his lips together to stop the sobs of loss. 'Let's make this look like it could be in Harrods' window, eh? For Mam.'

May let out a hmmph. 'You mean I'll do it as you sit and supervise, Dad?' She nudged him, and they both laughed a little.

'Aye, pet, something like that.'

She decorated the tree as he watched from the sofa, the TV off unlike in previous years. As he observed her placing the baubles on the branches, he could almost see

Fran by her side, the two of them racing to get a particular bauble first as they laughed.

'You're putting that bauble there?' He chuckled.

She turned to him momentarily, eyes narrowed. 'I'm the Christmas tree boss. Mam passed the job on to me.'

A half-sad smile travelled across his face. 'Well, to be fair, you're doing a grand job.'

May remained looking at the tree, holding a bauble with Fran's face in that they'd had made the week before. After hanging the Fran bauble lovingly at the front of the tree, she held her upper arms and swallowed, trying to stop the sad whimper that was battling to escape her mouth. Victor quickly rose from the sofa and put his arm around her shoulder. She closed her eyes, trying to remember a time when she hadn't had to deal with adult issues. The child in her just wanted to run to her bedroom and read science books as Mam brought her some juice and homemade rock buns.

'Come on, pet, let's have a cuppa and one of those sweet mince pies I got from the shop, eh?'

May turned to her dad, gave a weak smile and nodded as she got up from the floor, watching him walk out of the lounge with his head hanging down.

The day people either love or loathe soon arrived, and May and Victor succeeded in ploughing through the snowstorm of grief, even managing to have conversations about Fran without May feeling consumed by the sensation that her body would crumble. Dad watched *Only Fools and Horses*, and for the first time, May actually watched too. It had always been a Dad thing, whilst May and her mam decorated the tree. Watching them with Dad felt like the start of an alternative tradition, and her heart felt a little healed as she watched him laugh. She smiled at him, unknowingly to Victor, just as he had all those years, watching his favourite programme but really watching his girls decorate the Christmas tree. *Perhaps things will be okay after all.*

May started the last two semesters of her master's in January and began focusing on late summer or early autumn, when she would hopefully have secured a job in scientific research, having completed her studies. She tried to think positively, focusing on the new year and new opportunities. The problem was that she sometimes found thinking about the future overwhelming.

She missed Thomas still, and it impacted her each day, like a scab that never healed. May knew that grief subsided, it had slightly from her mam's passing, but reminding herself of this proved difficult. It had only been a few months since Thomas dumped her, and she felt certain she would never love again because it was too painful. Instead, she focused on what she could—university, working part-time at Lawson-Wray's, keeping order in her flat and spending time with her dad.

Chapter 14

It was a bitterly cold March, colder than any early March May could recall. She'd been sure many students would have come up with excuses to not come in today, instead staying in the warmth, but the cramped car park she'd encountered earlier said otherwise. She hugged the blood-red scarf Trish had bought her for Christmas a few years back close to her skin as she rushed across the campus as quickly as she could on the slippery, sparkling frost that decorated the ground. She got straight into her car, out of the harsh sleet and wind. May breathed into her cold hands before checking her phone. Three missed calls in the space of fifteen minutes from an unknown number. No voicemails. *Probably salespeople*, she thought, shaking her head.

She decided to send Scarlett a quick text prior to setting off, hoping the engine would warm up the air around her ready to begin her journey home, but before she could, there was a tapping on the car window. May frowned and looked to her right, wondering who it could be and what they could possibly want. Her eyes widened the second she realised it was a police officer, and she quickly shoved her phone into her pocket. She apprehensively opened the car door but stayed inside.

'Sorry, I know, I-I wasn't going to set off with my phone in my hand.' She shook her head quickly. 'I, erm, I was just war-warming up.' It wasn't until now that she noticed another police officer with Sheila, the university's secretary, by her side.

'May McClelland?' the officer enquired.

'Yes, erm, that's me.' Anxiety was pounding in her chest.

'I'm Officer Sue Clegg and this is my colleague, Officer Caroline Myers.'

May nodded, not really sure what she should say in this situation. She glanced in the direction of the other police officer and Sheila, who gave her a smile despite the fact she was standing in the freezing sleet with only a long cardigan on.

Officer Clegg crouched to May's height. 'We tried to reach you at your home address, so apologies for coming here, Miss McClelland,' she said softly, keeping eye contact. 'Is there any chance you can come back into the university with us, please?'

May stared at the police officer. 'Why? What's going on?' she asked, feeling her heartbeat accelerating.

'We can talk in my office,' Sheila interjected, palms out.

'I don't want to go to your office. What's happening? Tell me here,' May uncharacteristically snapped, panic audible in her voice.

'I really think it would be best—'

'*No*, I'm not going there.' Her eardrums pounded and the fear and anxiety whizzing around her insides were threatening to consume her. She wanted to leave. The thought of even getting out of the possible safety of her car, never mind walking past people and into a corporate office, made her feel certain she would have a panic attack.

The police officers looked at one another, then Officer Clegg turned back to May.

'Okay, Miss McClelland.' She bent down slightly, focused on May. 'I'm so sorry to inform you of this, but I'm afraid we strongly believe that your father, Victor, was killed in a road traffic accident earlier today.'

Officer Clegg was leaning into May's car, looking at her with eyes full of sympathy, but May stared back and almost laughed at the ridiculousness of the situation.

'Is this a weird joke?' she asked loudly, shaking her head at the three people standing outside of her car.

'I'm afraid not, Miss McClelland. There was a collision involving your father's car on Bolan Lane, just off Hadrian Roundabout, around ninety minutes ago,' the officer said gently. 'The person, who we believe to be your father, sadly died on the way to hospital despite the best efforts of the paramedics. I'm so sorry.' Officer Clegg tilted her head, soft eyes focused on May as May sat in silence.

'May, this is a massive shock. We should go in the office and have a cup of tea,' Sheila said, coming closer into May's eyeline.

May slumped in her seat and looked straight ahead, mouth open, unable to look at the police officer who had just demolished her world with one fell swoop. She could hear Sheila talking to the other officer, but it was just background noise.

Officer Clegg gently touched May's right shoulder, and realising she wasn't breathing, May took a massive gasp of air.

'I'm so sorry,' she repeated.

'*Noooo*,' May suddenly screamed as her head fell forward, her neck unable to hold up what had become the weight of an iron girder. Her forehead hit the steering wheel with a thump, bouncing slightly before she pulled it back and her head slammed against the driver's seat headrest.

Officer Clegg tapped May's forearm in a gentle attempt to comfort her.

May whipped her arm away before looking at the police officer, shaking her head in desperation. '*Please, God, no.*'

Officer Clegg remained crouched by May's side, watching her patiently through kind eyes that had seen herself deliver this news so many times and witnessed that it never got easier.

There was silence for what felt like forever before May turned to Officer Clegg, pleading, 'How do you know it's my dad? It could be anyone. He wouldn't have been leaving work early. It must be a mistake.'

'We found your dad's ID on him. You will have to formally identify the deceased, and we'll support you with that. I'm so sorry, Miss McClelland.'

SHUT UP, SHUT UP, SHUT UP. May dug her fingernails into her scalp, wanting, needing to block all of their words out, erase them and make them untrue.

Officer Clegg glanced over at Sheila, who moved towards May and bent down close.

'May, darling, are you sure you don't want to come back to my office for a cup of tea?'

May's head flopped forward into her hands, her shoulders shaking. Feeling breathless and realising she was in no state to drive, she nodded.

Sheila leaned in to help May out of her car. Playing the words from Officer Clegg over in her mind as she accepted Sheila's help, it felt as if they were trickling down the windscreen of her car, like the outside sleet. Words not making any sense, just sounds cascading, echoing in her mind.

She stood up straight, then immediately put her hand out to gesture to Sheila to move as nausea literally punched her in the gut. She bent over and vomited onto the tarmac. How can this be happening again? It was as if history was regurgitating itself onto May in a cruel attempt to destroy her. *Surely life can't be this merciless?*

May gasped for air as people rushed past, trying to get out of the cold, unknown to them that someone close by had just had their world stamped on, squashed and crushed.

'Can you please just tell me off for using my phone with the engine on?' she sobbed as Sheila grabbed her hand. '*Please,*' she screamed, looking at the officers as tears ran down her face.

'Let's go inside, and you can call someone for support, Miss McClelland,' Officer Myers suggested, gently ushering May towards the uni.

May looked at Sheila, who nodded, eyes filled with watery pity.

May walked to the office, Sheila on one side of her watching her every step with an outstretched arm, ready to steady her if needed. Officer Myers and Officer Clegg walked closely behind. She felt a cloud around her masking her lucidity, dulling her vision, almost muting the voices and noises around her. It only took a few minutes to reach Sheila's office, but the walk had still exhausted her. She made her way to the closest chair she could see and slowly seated herself.

Officer Myers moved her seat so she was facing May. 'Miss McClelland, we can accompany you to the hospital if you wish. You'll be able to speak to the doctors there.' She had a friendly look about her, no harshness to her pretty, round features. *The type of face to bring you good news, not bad news*, thought May as her gaze became a stare at the officer's face.

'You will have to formally identify the body, to confirm it is your father. Which we understand is an extremely distressing ask. Again, we can support you. Or perhaps you want to ring a friend or family member to take you.'

I don't have family because they are fucking dead, she wanted to scream. Instead, she swallowed the sick that was lingering in her throat and rang Trish, bouncing her legs until she answered.

'May? Is everything okay?'

'Trish, it's happened again. It's Dad... he's dead,' she wailed down the phone, grasping her chest with certainty her heart would stop.

There was an audible gasp before Trish replied. 'Oh, May, my love. I'm so sorry. Where are you?'

'I'm at the university, with the police. Please come, please, Trish. I can't do this again,' May howled, her breath snatched from her by the cruel reality of another loss.

'I'm on my way. Stay there.'

May dropped her phone, her head spinning, her world going dark.

Trish arrived at the university to see May's broken heart etched across her face. May sobbed as Trish pulled her into an embrace, her body almost convulsing with distress. Trish took control of the next-steps discussion with the police before they walked to the car park, May steadied by Trish. She got into Trish's car like a wobbly newborn calf.

They drove to the hospital in silence, Trish sporadically grabbing May's hand with her left hand. May paid no attention to the journey there, her eyes open but unable to see as she sat in a trance of shock, disbelief and pain. As they drove, she could only think about the story her parents had told all those years about her, when she was baking like the most desired cake in Fran's delicate body. The story they would tell anyone who would listen. The account that Dad was unable to tell once Mam died, as if the binding of the book of their lives had come undone and lay on a table, used only as a coaster, never to be read and told again. The story had always embarrassed May and made her roll her eyes, but now she would give anything to hear it again.

'We couldn't agree on a name when I was pregnant. We argued for months, didn't we, love?' Mam would say, her voice filled with nostalgia as Dad nodded.

'She's right. Fran was the boss, but, well, I wouldn't back down on this one.'

At this point in the story, one of them would grab the other's hand.

'Finally, we agreed. Our bundle of joy would be named after the month she entered the world in. Victor wanted it to be June, I wanted it to be May. So, although we still didn't agree on our favourite, destiny would choose.'

Dad would always finish the tale: 'Our little blessing was born on the thirty-first of May, at 11:45 p.m. She looks like a May mind, our May McClelland. I don't think she would have suited June.'

All eyes would then turn to May as she sat, an awkward look on her face, cheeks slightly flushed at the attention, and they'd coo as if she were still a baby.

May sobbed in the passenger seat as she let her head fall into her hands. '*Who will tell the fucking story now?*

she shouted, banging her hands against the sides of her head.

'Hey, oh, May, honey.' Trish's eyes darted for somewhere to pull over. She quickly found somewhere as May continued hitting her head and screaming.

Trish grabbed May's hands and held them firmly in hers. 'May, breathe, my lovely. Look at me. Breathe.'

May stared at Trish, desperate for her to tell her all of this wasn't real.

'May, copy my breathing. Come on, breathe in like this'—Trish breathed in—'and then out like this.' She breathed out. She nodded at May to copy, still holding her hands and staring intently at her.

May duplicated the breathing and could feel her heart, body and mind calming marginally.

'Now, keep breathing like that, honey, we are about five minutes from the hospital. I'm here with you and I'll stay with you, okay?'

May weakly nodded, and Trish left the roadside, heading towards the hospital, where May knew the truth would be there to see, as it had been in August of the year her mam died. Only, this time, Dad wouldn't be there to comfort her.

Part Two

Present year, the month of May

Chapter 15

1st May

In the eight weeks since that horrific conversation in the university car park, it had felt as if May's lungs were slowly filling with liquid pain, preventing the air from getting in. It was only within the last two weeks that she had managed to get out of bed more days in the week than not and just the last week that she had begun eating more than one meal a day after Trish's threat:

'May, if you don't start eating properly, I'm going to have to call social services, like we had to for my dad. I mean it, love. You *have to eat.*' She had leant over May, who lay on the sofa, and put her hand on her shoulder.

May had almost sneered at the woman who had become like a surrogate mother to her, the woman who she genuinely loved. But caring for people was meaningless in the harsh, cruel reality that she now existed in—she would only lose more people she loved.

Trish had been round to her flat from day one despite being ignored for the first three days, yet it was Trish who May had called on the second of March and Trish who had driven her to the hospital less than two years before when her mam died. May eventually opened her front door to Trish on day four. She sat with May in silence for hours as May stared into space, hoping that time would take her back to the innocence of childhood and those holidays in Greece and Spain.

It was Trish who held May up at the funeral whilst Scarlett held her other side, Trish who made her endless meals she couldn't stomach, trying all sorts, including

Weetabix. But May's hunger had completely disappeared until, eventually, her hip bones protruded, her cheek-bones were harsh and her colouring grey. But she didn't care; she had nothing to live for anymore.

She deteriorated further into her hole of grief, the shouting, threats and lectures from Trish and Scarlett practically pointless background noise. It wasn't until one visit from Trish that May finally listened. It was a Friday and the third visit from Trish that week. Part of May wanted to hurt her friend's feelings enough that she would leave her alone, but another part of her felt Trish was her umbilical cord to life despite being in constant conflict in her mind as to what her life even offered now.

'I've brought some homemade soup—tomato and basil—and some crusty bread,' Trish said as she walked straight through to the kitchen, glancing at May, who was wrapped in a blanket on the sofa. May didn't utter a word even after the kettle had boiled and Trish had placed two cups on the coffee table.

Trish sat on the brown armchair, near the sofa where May was cocooned. 'Drink,' she instructed, pointing to the cup.

May rolled her eyes, like a teenager getting told they can't go out until they tidy their bedroom.

Trish lifted her chin and took a deep breath. 'May, I'm going to tell you something that not many people know.' She rubbed her reddening neck and swallowed. 'When I was around your age, I struggled with my mental health. It felt like storm clouds followed me. Then, one day...' She stopped momentarily, closed her eyes and breathed out before staring back at May. 'I attempted suicide. I wanted to die, May... well, maybe not wanted to die. I just wanted the pain to stop.'

May's mouth opened as she listened to her friend, not quite believing that someone like Trish could feel like that. Then she realised how real the pain could be, as she felt broken herself.

Trish looked to the ceiling and pressed her lips together. Placing the orange cushion that was behind her back onto her lap, she continued, 'I know I come over as happy, always positive, and I am. But I wasn't always like this; you wouldn't have recognised me. Jeez, I didn't recognise myself.

'Twenty-two years ago, I had my third miscarriage. I felt a failure as a wife, as a woman. I mean, that's what we are expected to be, isn't it, baby machines?' She let out a sad laugh and wiped under her glasses. 'Even today, young women like you are expected to be able to make new life and bring it into the world, still judged or pitied if you won't or can't. It was worse when I was younger, and I felt like I had a visible stamp on my body telling the world I just wasn't woman enough to grow a healthy baby inside me. I was broken.' A plump tear plopped onto her palm—one of thousands she had shed over the years for her babies.

'My first husband, well, he had lost sympathy by the third time. He didn't understand that I grieved for babies who were never born. My angel babies. It felt real... it was real, and I was a mother each time. I just couldn't keep my babies alive.'

May reached over and took her friend's hand, trying desperately to push her own grief out of the room for just a minute. Trish held on tightly, as if May were going to pull her from a cliffside.

'My husband would shout at me, telling me I was selfish, and when he was drunk, that I wasn't a real woman. He left me two months later, and I wanted to leave the world. It had been too cruel to me, and I thought it was my fault. Those babies, May, I thought it was my fault they couldn't live.'

May could see that the pain was still there in Trish's always rosy-cheeked face, with her eyes that sparkled like the summer sun beaming onto a lake. As she listened to her friend talk in a way she had never witnessed—showing vulnerability—she realised that sometimes we expect people to always be okay, especially our elders, and sometimes we wrongly believe they don't feel as sad or messed up as younger people. Perhaps we just always see them as the adults, the carers, even when we are adults ourselves. She felt like a broken ornament, and the world felt crueller, for not only taking her mam and dad, but for taking the babies that would have been so loved by Trish.

Trish wiped her nose and sniffed. 'I took some tablets one night, but then I rang for an ambulance and stayed in hospital for a week. It wasn't one of my proudest moments, but I just couldn't cope. I had carried the pain for so long, a suitcase of grief in each hand and a backpack to match. I got help from professionals and other women who had miscarried. I began to feel understood.

'I felt less alone and I started to feel like a woman again. I don't tell people that, May, it was a long time ago and I'm now grateful for life and the love of my Brian and stepson, Mark, but there isn't a day that goes by where I don't think of my angel babies.

'Things get better, May. The only way to go when your arse is on the bottom is up.' Trish got up from the armchair and leaned over the coffee table to the sofa where May sat. She kissed May on the head, whose hair was greasy and smelt of illness. 'Get in the shower, wash your smelly hair and then you can have some of my famous soup, else you will be in trouble.'

May gave a blank look back and slowly peeled herself off the sofa, following orders. Walking to the bathroom, she felt drained from the trauma Trish had shared and equally as sad and angry that her friend had given her more loss to think about. After going into the bathroom, she took off the clothes she had been wearing for more days than she recalled. Her washed-out complexion appeared as she turned to the mirror, resembling a prisoner starved of vitamin D. She pulled the bobble free from her grease-ladened hair, then stood for five minutes, not quite seeing the reflection in front of her as she drifted into a hazy thought bubble. Then there it was—an epiphany. May glanced back at the mirror, returning to the room. Despite the repulsion that reflected back, she felt a trickle of relief. Trish had given her an idea, a way out.

After having a shower and managing a child's portion of soup and bread, Trish made May a cup of tea and left her for the evening, telling her she would text in the morning and perhaps they could go for a walk on her lunch break. May nodded, knowing she wouldn't go for a walk with Trish but unable to face another lecture. She felt the tiniest kick of guilt for lying to her friend. It was something she was going to have to get used to; she would be lying to everyone in the short-term.

For the next few hours, she sat on her sofa in silence. She inhaled and almost felt relief travel up her nostrils. The answer to preventing her from having to carry on living like this, experiencing more loss and being a burden to the few people left in her sad life had unknowingly arrived to her from Trish. On the day May would turn twenty-five, in thirty days, the thirty-first of May, she'd commit suicide. May, being May, would have the time to get her affairs in order, leaving no detail unattended to. She would leave the world in a planned way—one thing she prided herself on.

She looked at the photo of her parents on the fireplace, happy memories captured in time. Getting up to go to bed, she put it facedown, not wanting to see the reminder of loss every day. She got into bed with a calm reassurance.

Chapter 16

2nd May

The unbroken sleep May's body desperately needed had made her feel slightly more human. After washing her hair using half a bottle of shampoo to rid her scalp and long locks of the lard-like grease that had become part of her being, she felt less disgusted in herself. But, then again, maybe it was to do with the click in her brain.

She felt a nudge of guilt that she'd taken her idea from Trish's painful disclosure, then shook her head. No one needed extra stress in their lives and May wasn't anyone's problem. Currently, she was the albatross around their necks. Life was painful, lonely and unsatisfying. She had Uncle Terence, but she didn't see him much and he had his own family as well as the loss of his brother to process. Then there was Scarlett, but Scarlett was happy with Ethan, settled and in love. She didn't need May and her pity party on a daily basis. May brought no fun, no support, no laughter to their relationship. And as for Trish, having to mother May wasn't a friendship. May was a boulder encumbering Trish, and if May filled the need for nurturing in Trish, she could find another lost soul to mother.

Sitting on her sofa, hugging a cushion, she reached for her laptop that lay on the coffee table. She typed an email to her tutor. She only had a semester and a half left on her master's degree, but it was the end of it for May. She couldn't even get out of bed, never mind study for finals.

Professor Musgrove,

I'm unable to continue with my studies. Given the recent death of my father, I cannot commit to any more of my master's and therefore wish to withdraw from the course. I appreciate all your support to date. Thank you,
    May McClelland

She clicked send with a satisfied sigh. After what she had been through, losing her beloved science, like everyone around her, was inevitable. *At least this way I'm taking control.*

A few hours later, she received a reply from Professor Musgrove offering to meet her or call to discuss. May replied, declining and insisting her decision had been made. Her tutor sent a final supportive and accommodating email, telling May she would have eighteen months to complete the degree. May shrugged, closing her laptop. Eighteen months was irrelevant.

Leaning back against the sofa cushion, she felt another kick of grief for the career she had always wanted. Something that her parents had supported, her childhood dream, and something she was good at. It was literally part of her DNA.

She had become so numb to the distress she battled each day that she didn't realise she was crying until her vision became cloudy with the tears gathering in her eyes. She clenched her fists.

'Just stop,' she screamed, grabbing her hair and kicking the coffee table in front of her, which only resulted in the immediate throbbing of her foot. Everything was ruined, gone, spoilt like three-month-old milk. Nothing would or could ever be the same again, and that's why she knew that she had to take control of her destiny.

May didn't see her plan as dramatic, harsh or stupid. She didn't see herself as mentally ill or in need of help. No amount of help could make her feel better unless it was to bring her parents back from the dead. No, she wasn't silly, overreacting or insane; in fact, this could be the sanest decision she had ever made.

An alien sensation came over her: acceptance. With acceptance came relief and understanding that her pain would be over within a few weeks. Until then, she would put things in order, tie up loose ends, perhaps even live a little. She would make sure she saw the people she cared about, the ones who cared about her. It would be hard, that last goodbye, she knew that, but ultimately, she wasn't going to get better.

Chapter 17

3rd May

Opening the front door, May pulled the collar of her sweatshirt, tightening it around her neck with her free hand, shivering despite the mild spring. Standing in her doorway, the outside world looked, smelt and felt different than she remembered after not leaving the house for over a month. The blanket, orange squash, notebook and pen filled her bag to an almost heavy level for the weakness in her arms. Today's task was to go for a walk at her local park, but the only movement in her body was her heartbeat as she stared at the tree across the path, not wanting to leave the sanctuary of her flat. She'd known the outside world would be different, of course it was—everything is after your world becomes dark. And now the darkness was spreading, encroaching like a predator, as if the world knew that she had no intention of remaining in it for much longer.

She had lived in her flat for a few years but had never bothered to venture to the local park, partly because she always seemed to be busy with university or work or her dad. The main reason was that she never really felt comfortable around groups of strangers unless she knew what they were there for, like the theatre, where everyone was there to watch a show. There was too much that could be happening in a park—walking, sports, kids playing and often screaming, ice cream vans, cafes, dogs, cycling, picnics and possibly more. Although May loved nature, the less busy and chaotic nature, like a steep hike, was more her thing.

With equal determination and distress, she took a step outside and quickly shut her front door. Hands trembling, she looked at the paving that made up her short path, focusing on the colour and her breathing as she began walking away from her front door. She reached the end of the path and glanced into the street, her head moving left and right as she gasped in the fresh air she hadn't inhaled for what felt like an eternity. Her lips trembled, like a child's whose teddy had been snatched away. She closed her eyes, then took three deep breaths. With her vision switched off, she noticed the spring sun on her face, absorbing into her pale skin. She began to cry silently, the light warmth like a kiss from heaven.

'You alright there?'

The voice broke May's moment, and she turned to her left, greeted with the sight of a jolly-faced elderly man. She nodded unenthusiastically, a fake smile on her face, not wishing to engage in conversation with a stranger.

'It's a lovely day, mild for May. Walking back from the bus stop, it felt like it was beginning to warm up at last,' he said, palms in the air as if to try to catch the mild May sun. 'It's been such a long winter, and a little bit of warmth helps keep my old pins oiled.' The man chuckled as he tapped his knees.

She stared blankly at the talkative stranger, wishing he would walk on to wherever he was going and leave her be.

'I'm Mr Parsley... Peter, to you.' He took a few steps towards her and advanced his hand despite hers being in her hoody pocket.

She reluctantly withdrew a cosy hand from her jumper, aware Peter's hand was pointing towards her with no sign of retracting, like a parking barrier waiting for a payment slip before letting the driver through.

'I moved into the flat below three weeks ago,' he said, nodding towards the flat directly below hers. 'I did knock to introduce myself, but you must have been away, and I didn't want to disturb you further.'

May licked her dry lips, unsure how to answer her new, overly bouncy neighbour. Part of her wanted to tell him to mind his own bloody business and bugger off, as she wasn't in the market for friends or even pleasantries at this point. But then she looked at Peter Parsley rather than staring through him with annoyance. She noticed his eyes curling up, surrounded by a blanket of wrinkles, his thin lips and sagging cheeks that age and gravity had begun to weaken but that still lifted as he smiled. He reminded her a little of her grandfather, Cecil, who had passed when she was ten.

'Erm, yeah, I've not been available.' Strictly speaking, it wasn't a lie.

'Well, it's lovely to meet you, pet, and I hope you have a nice day.' Peter smiled. 'I'll let you get on your way. Thanks for the chat.' He nodded and walked off towards his front door.

May shook her head, unable to fathom how she had missed the fact someone had moved into the flat below her over the past few weeks. The flat had been to let following her neighbour moving away for work, so it was inevitable, but she had heard no removal vans, no furniture being transported or people coming and going. Then again, it was only the last week that she had actually begun to have some level of everyday functioning.

Taking a deep breath, she pushed her shoulders back and began to walk away from her flat, heading in the direction of the park. She arrived at the entrance seven minutes later and couldn't help but smile a little. Flowers were in bloom on either side of the archway, welcoming people in to explore the carpet of grass and strategically placed, bright and beautiful collections of floras. She pulled on the sleeves of her hoody and strolled tentatively into the park, grabbing her bag tighter, as if to comfort and steady herself.

The park wasn't as busy and was much bigger than she had imagined, meaning she didn't feel the suffocation of panic. Inhaling the earthy freshness, it felt like fuel to May's lungs. It was a school day, which limited children and possibly working adults; however, there were a few groups of people and lone runners. That was an idea, running through the park. May had always, until the last few months, run the route of her old school running club out of habit despite having to drive eight minutes to start the run. She hadn't run for over two months, and she missed it. She missed moving through nature like an animal in the wild, the control of her breathing alongside the pounding of her feet and the gentle but strong gliding of her arms. Running had been her saviour over the years. It felt almost like an entity, a counsellor, a friend. The sun on her face, the wind whipping around her ears, the rain dampening her hair and cooling her sweating body. In all weathers, in good and bad times, running had been her ally. The park seemed to be a lovely running route. Maybe it was a route she could try once or twice before hanging her running shoes up for good. She smiled a bittersweet smile before continuing on.

She observed a group of people stretching on the nearby grass, yoga mats of all colours, like an artist's palette, were spread around. Someone ran past with their dog happily running alongside, tongue out and a goofy grin. A woman was sitting on a bench, a buggy with a sleeping baby by her side. She held a cup of coffee in one hand and had a magazine perched on her lap, glancing at it in between checking on her infant, a loving smile decorating her face. With quiet all around, May imagined it was much-needed tranquillity in the mother's day. She kept observing as she walked, absorbing the atmosphere and enjoying being in the moment. She thought about how everyone was so accustomed to the rat race, life being one hundred miles per hour, always thinking about what they had to do next. *When did life become such a pressure cooker of demands?*

Finding a spot to sit down on the luscious green grass, she placed her blanket down. She sat, stretching her arms back to hold herself up. Peter Parsley was right—it was mild for the time of year. She closed her eyes and thought of happy times. Family times, holidays, birthdays, Sunday lunches. Times when the family would sit and watch the latest series of *Dancing on Ice*, where Fran would say May should have been a dancer with her long legs and Victor would say, 'It's never too late', looking at May with a wink and a smile. From the big things to the tiniest of things, her mind was her own scrapbook of family and of love. She sat up and placed her arms across her chest, hands touching her opposite shoulders as she exhaled, exasperated with pain. The memories were all she had now, and it made her feel like the loneliest person on Earth.

She opened her bag and took out her notebook and pen. It was one of those spiral-bound notebooks, the only ones she liked for day-to-day lists, documenting tasks and note-taking purposes. Once she had completed her note writing, she liked to rip the page out. Was there anything more unattractive than a notebook filled with scribbles and lines through words? The first page had a to-do list, with a date above:

28th February
To do in March:
- Search for and try new cake recipes for Dad's birthday cake.

- Confirm Dad's birthday presents — *Just Jonathan* and *Deadly Vendetta* books by Donna Scuvotti, new slippers from M&S and dark chocolate.

- Plan library time for the month.

- Financial summary for end of the financial year.

- Financial forecast for first quarter of the financial year.

- Check and request more shifts at Lawson-Wray's for Easter break.

- Complete three essays and plan work for final semester.

- Schedule an appointment at university with careers advisor.

- Diary in time with Scarlett over Easter break.

- Buy Dad an Easter egg.

None of the tasks had been crossed off and the list was abandoned a few days later when Victor died suddenly. May held the book to her chest and began to sob. He had died five weeks before his birthday, and she had spent the day with her phone off, drinking vodka and crying.

She wiped her tears and lay back on the blanket, sadness pushing her body into the ground. Lying still, the pain in her head throbbed. She felt lonely but hated the thought of spilling her sadness onto anyone and soaking them with her self-pity. Propping herself up on her elbows, she looked around the park. Seeing people in the distance, she wondered if they too were in pain or had been before. Maybe they had got over it, healed and moved on, or perhaps they walked with a permanent scar of misery. She tore the page out of the book and shoved it into her bag before digging her fingernails into her palms and putting her head down, trying to mute the sadness.

After a minute, she took a few deep breaths, a drink of her squash and picked up her pen again.

3rd May
To do (before 31st May):
- Spend time with Scarlett.

- Spend time with Trish that isn't her looking after me.

- Go and see Uncle Terence.

- Visit the cemetery.

- Visit Lawson-Wray's (possibly).

- Take library books back to university and pay fines.

- Run in the park.

- Sort throughout the house; take things to charity and leave notes on things I want to give to others.

- Arrange finances.

- Write letters to Scarlett and Trish—make them as positive as possible and remember to tell them that I love them and why I love them.

- Buy paracetamols.

Chapter 18

5th May

The doorbell rang, and May let out a long, low sigh. She knew Trish wouldn't go away after insisting earlier by text message that she would visit. Dragging herself off the sofa, her legs felt full of lead. She paused at the top of the stairs, closed her eyes and clenched her jaw to the harsh squeak of the letterbox opening.

'It's me, love,' Trish's bouncy voice travelled into her flat.

May walked down the stairs and opened the door to her flat with sloth-like energy. Trish stood there with a bag of God-knows-what, unfazed by May's presentation and distinct lack of enthusiasm. With a smile matching the brightness of a streetlamp, Trish gave a gentle shove past May to travel up the flat stairs.

'Poo, a bit stinky in here, love. Let's light a candle, eh?' she said in her usual jolly tone. Off she went, rummaging around for matches in the kitchen as May stood in the doorway, eyes following Trish's movements. The flat was stuffy from having no air circulating for a few days and May cocooned on the sofa, neglecting a hygiene routine. It was too much of an effort to even change her clothes.

'Get showered. I will heat this pasta bake up and make us a cuppa,' Trish ordered as she placed a lit candle on the coffee table. Her eyes focused on May, and May felt as if she were a dog whose owner was waiting for her to perform a trick. Trish gently clapped her hands in a chop-chop motion. May puffed air out sulky-teenager style and turned from the doorway without a word.

May returned to the lounge ten minutes later, her hair damp after only being towel-dried. Trish sat in the armchair, a plate resting on her lap. A second plate rested on the coffee table. Trish pointed firmly at it.

'Eat.'

May said nothing, reaching for the plate before sitting on the sofa opposite Trish. She swirled the pasta with her fork, watching the red sauce cling to each shell as they slid around. Glancing up at Trish, she was met with serious eyes. After watching May take a mouthful, Trish leaned back slightly in her chair, lifting the plate higher to rest it on her chest.

'Tell me what you've been up to, love,' she said in between mouthfuls.

As she slowly ate, May told Trish about her park visit and how she was thinking of going running there soon.

Trish's head perked up like a meerkat. 'That's great, my lovely, onwards and upwards.'

May felt the usual feeling of being a pathetic burden rather than the encouragement and support Trish wanted to transfer.

Trish soon finished her pasta and watched May eat until half the plate was consumed.

'I've had enough, but that was nice. Thanks.' May put the plate back on the coffee table.

Trish rose from her seat, stroked May on the head and collected the plates, taking them into the kitchen, then returned with cups of tea and slices of cake. May found the cake harder to digest than the pasta, the soft sponge she'd usually find delicious seemingly overly firm and compact when it came to actually having to swallow it. She mostly ate the buttercream, which slid down her throat like silk. She was thankful when Trish's phone beeped.

'That's the stepson. He's finished playing snooker and needs a lift.' She rolled her eyes, but May knew Trish didn't mind being taxi.

Gathering her bag and coat, Trish walked down the stairs to May's front door, with May following. She put her shoes on and opened the door. 'It was lovely to see you, honey. You're doing amazing. I'll see you soon.'

They hugged, and as Trish's arms encased her, May felt she would crumble, like a bulldozed building.

With a cheery wave and a loud, 'See you soon,' on the doorstep, Trish turned to leave.

At the other end of May's garden, a cat strutted past. It stopped and looked at them, and as Trish walked towards her car, they bounced straight over, a loud meow coming out of its mouth.

'Hello, cutie.' Trish stroked the sandy-coloured cat, who wrapped its tail around her leg in approval. 'Who's this, May?'

May shook her head. 'I don't know; I've never seen it before.' She shrugged, hoping Trish would hurry up and get in her car so she could go to bed, exhausted from the effort of having company.

'He's a beautiful little thing, aren't you, baby?' Trish said as the cat flopped onto the concrete and began rolling around on the path. 'I have to go now, fusspot,' she added in one of those silly voices people reserve for animals and babies. The cat watched her get into her car, not ready for the fussing to be over.

May waved her off and shut her front door as the cat looked up the garden path, expectant eyes and another loud meow. She climbed sluggishly back up the stairs and plonked herself on her sofa. Thinking about Trish, she felt a pang of guilt, quickly replaced by the obvious—May was a burden to Trish, and tonight had been an example of that. Having to practically spoon-feed her, as if she were an incapable infant. Sorting her dinner, telling her to wash. It was shameful and unfair. May was the heavy suitcase that you can't wait to drop off at the airport, and Trish would soon, if she didn't already, feel that way.

There was a knock at the front door, and May slid off the sofa with a huff. She looked around the room, trying to see what Trish could have possibly forgotten. There was no handbag on the coffee table, no mobile phone between the sofa cushions that she could feel. Could she want the glass bowl back now that she'd brought the pasta bake over in? No, May was certain she'd said to keep it and wash it up for when they next saw each other, not that she could be certain it would be washed up by then, not in amongst... May felt her whole body heat up as she realised Trish had done all the washing up. Her irritation dropped away. How had she allowed herself to be so irritated by the possibility of her friend knocking at her door after everything Trish had done for her? She sheepishly hurried down the stairs to Trish, but as she opened her front door, the person standing there was very clearly not Trish.

'Hello, pet, it's Peter, your new neighbour.' A proud smile spread across his face, as if he were a toddler who had just discovered how to say his name.

'I know who you are,' May replied in a sharp tone that she often had, albeit not always intentionally.

Peter nodded, his smile fading slightly. 'Of course. Sorry to bother you, pet. Erm, it's just I can't open my kitchen window and wondered if you have a key that might fit my window also? I'm not sure if these four flats might have been two houses not that long ago, and maybe, well, perhaps the windows were put in at the same time.' He cleared his throat, continuing, 'Worth a try, perhaps?'

'I doubt it. It would be a security issue making window locks with the same key,' May said quickly, arms folded.

'I never thought about that, you're right. Sorry to disturb you.' Peter walked away, his head stooped.

May shut her front door and threw her head back, groaning as she went back up to her lounge. *Why are people so damn people-ish at times?*

Chapter 19

6th May

May woke at 7:10 a.m., as she had for most of her adult life. She'd had a restless night and woke in a bad mood. Rubbing her eyes, she got out of bed and stomped through her lounge, into the open-plan kitchen, huffing and puffing. She opened the drawer at the top left-hand side of her cupboards and pulled out the kitchen window key. Turning it over in her hand, her thumb and forefinger touched the cold metal of the tiny key that had contributed to her disturbed sleep. As she stared at it, she realised her anger was with herself and not really Peter and the damn key. She sighed and slammed her palm and the key down on the kitchen countertop. It wasn't Peter's fault that the world wasn't a nice place for May or that her problems weren't as simple as opening a bloody kitchen window.

She bit back her tears and anger. If only she could rewind time to a place when life was normal. Not always easy, not always comfortable, but manageable, happy, safe and with her parents around. Every hour of every day, she felt as if maggots were crawling in her brain, gnawing away. She wanted it to stop. A major thing keeping her going was that she knew there was an end to this painful marathon, a day when she would pass the finish line and reach peace.

May got on with breakfast, usually the only meal she actually had a desire to eat the last few weeks. She prepared her Weetabix and a cup of tea. It was just before 8 a.m. as she put her dishes in the sink. Picking up the kitchen window key again, she wondered if it was too early to knock. Shaking her head, she shut the key in her palm. *It's tough if it's too early.*

She pulled on her running leggings and a hoody and took the stairs down. As she opened her front door, she saw Peter coming out of his. He glanced in her direction, then turned back, locking his door. She couldn't work out if he was in a hurry or avoiding her due to her coldness. She held back her guilt, refusing to dwell on it.

'Peter?' she called out, stepping out of her door as he began walking up his path, away from the flat.

He turned to her, hands in his pockets.

'Here, I found the key. I thought you could at least try it?' She shrugged, dangling the key in the air.

Peter's eyebrows raised. He travelled up his path, along the public path and then down hers instead of cutting across their shared front lawn. May bit inside her lip and smiled a little. Her dad used to always tell her off for crossing the lawn as a child.

'Stop squashing the grass and its resident buggerlugs,' he would half-jokingly say to her.

She would roll her eyes and reply, 'Yes, Dad.' But she'd done it time and time again until she reached an age where she appreciated nature more.

Walking to meet Peter, a smile began to form on his chubby, ruddy cheeks.

'Thanks, pet, thanks so much,' he said, taking the key from her and closing it in his hand as if it were a precious jewel.

'You're welcome, and by the way, my name is May.'

'Thank you, May.' Peter tapped his temple as if to retain her name.

May nodded, turned and walked back into her flat. Peter didn't see it, but she had a smile on her face too. A smile because she had been useful.

The melancholy running through May's veins returned with vengeance within a few hours.

It had been six days since she'd decided she wanted to die, six days since she'd realised how she could take control of and cut off the pain of her unhappy existence permanently. She thought back to a boy at school, Dale, whose father had committed suicide. The boy must have only been around thirteen years old and had a younger sister. Posters had been placed around noticeboards for students, telling them that the school mentor was always available to help, listen and support. She'd found the posters bad taste.

'It's not going to bring Dale's dad back, is it?'

'That's not the point, May. It's to encourage us all to talk about how we feel. The world isn't always black and white like the old-fashioned TV of your mind,' Scarlett had said in a way that was both a dig at her and to try to make her realise that sometimes there was a bigger picture.

May always wondered if Dale had talked to the school mentor, and right now—as she sat on her sofa, cushion on her lap, staring into a cup of cold tea—she wondered the reasons behind his father ending his life and the impact on those left behind. Her heart felt as cold as her tea for a moment, realising that when you're young, you don't really see other's problems. You don't understand, often don't care, too absorbed in your own world. Or you don't know how to care, the right words to say, the questions to ask. Are there even right words to say?

May put her cup on the coffee table and sank back into the softness of the sofa, which sometimes felt like a slight cuddle as her shoulders descended into the padding. Tilting her head back, she looked at the ceiling, her thoughts merging with the white paint. She wanted to speak to Dale's dad, ask him what had been going through his mind in the hours, days, months leading up to him taking his own life. *Did he mean to do it, or was it a cry for help that went too far? Did he think the world would be better off without him? Did he think no one would miss him? Or was his world so dark, so blindly black, that he simply couldn't think about the consequences for anyone?*

May felt the weight in her chest that had started the day Fran died and become heavier since. She realised, unlike

Dale's dad, she didn't have people she thought her death would have a profound effect on. Yes, she'd have people who'd miss her, but they were all people who would be able to get over her loss after a short period of grieving and move on as if she'd never even existed.

Leaning over to the coffee table, May picked up a notepad and pen. She intended to write letters to her few loved ones who might wonder why she'd decided on her course of action, who would miss her temporarily. She wanted the letters to be a celebration of the relationship she'd had with the recipient, something to remember and treasure. She did, however, feel the need to explain why she'd decided to end her life. Perhaps it would be useful to prevent someone from getting to the hopeless stage she had reached. It would also help her process her thoughts, alongside the list of things she needed to do by the thirtieth of May, before her death on the thirty-first.

'My methodical May,' she said, a whimper like a wounded animal escaping her mouth at the end of the words.

Dropping her head, she looked at her lap where her notebook lay. She took a deep breath, opened the notebook and, with a slightly shaky hand, started writing.

'Dear Trish...'

Chapter 20

8th May

May remembered her father telling her that once she had her own house, it would end up being filled with crap regardless of how organised and methodical she was. Standing in her kitchen, drawers and cupboard doors open as she started to sort through her belongings, she realised that although she didn't have a large amount of 'crap', what she did have still seemed worthless and sad. The minimal crockery and equipment screamed loneliness, and looking at it made her feel more of a failure. She wanted to smash it up, scream at it that it had won, that she was alone. But instead, she gritted her teeth and clung to the thought that her pathetic, lonely life could perhaps bring something to someone else via a charity shop—affordable kitchenware for a single mam on benefits or for a couple just moving into their starter home. Someone down on their luck or even just someone who liked to reuse and recycle.

Rummaging through her cutlery drawer, she wondered why she had six forks when she rarely cooked for anyone and (usually) washed the dishes daily. *Probably because they are bloody bought like that, for families, not for sad, lonely women.* Frustration and sadness swirled around her as she placed two on the countertop that would be taken to the charity shop, leaving herself with four. She copied the same process with knives and spoons. Then she spotted her bottle opener, and she snatched it up, clenching her fist around it. She felt the edges of the oblong shape press into her palm for a few seconds as she closed her eyes and tried to recall the moment it was bought in Greece, on one of the family holidays to Mykonos.

She and Fran were strolling and mooching in the many tat shops, as Victor called them, whilst he remained by the pool, in the shade, book in hand, snacking happily on Pringles. Mother and daughter approached a small gift shop, undistinguishable from the three they had already been in, except for the jolly woman greeting them as they entered and slid their sunglasses from in front of their eyes onto their heads.

May, being a shopping-for-a-purpose customer, glanced around without great intent behind Fran, who loved to browse, as she studied the shelves, battery-operated fan blowing in her face as she wafted the neckline of her striped sundress with the other. Not one to buy for the sake of it usually, May's eyes flitted to a metal bottle opener with the most beautiful tile print along the top of it. The design felt almost out of place for something that helped free the seal for a thirsty beer drinker.

'Mam, look at this, isn't the design pretty?' She handed the bottle opener to Fran, who nodded in agreement. Looking at her daughter and enjoying seeing the slightly more carefree May that was always visible on holiday, she said,

'Tell you what, let's get two. We can use one at home... well, your dad can. We can keep the other one for you for when you're older with your own place. Then you'll always have a bit of our holiday with you.'

May felt the dampness of tears on her cheeks. She wanted to stay in that moment, in that small, stuffy shop in Mykonos with her mam, when they'd had a future. May put the bottle opener back in the drawer and, after wiping her face with the sleeves of her top, continued with her sorting.

She wanted things in order, although that didn't require much, as her flat already exceeded the general population's level in that department. However, she still had items to dispose of and it was important that she had everything tied up. This included taking items to the charity shop. Things she didn't need for the remainder of her time on Earth and things she didn't want someone else to have to deal with when she was gone. Sorting houses of passed people was traumatic and tedious, and she knew it would likely be Uncle Terence, Trish or Scarlett sorting hers. Maybe all three.

She stopped for a moment and stared out of her kitchen window, the memory of sifting through her mam's belongings with her dad whirling in her head. They had put it off, not wanting to face the reality that Fran wouldn't come in and grab her favourite handbag, that she would no longer put the light-blue cardigan on that was years old and bobbly. But it was as if each bobble had a memory in it that rendered it essential to keep forever. They had only made a small start sorting through Fran's belongings, her life, before giving up.

And now, sorting through her own belongings was proving to be exhausting, as most things these days were. But this had to be done, as she didn't want this burden to fall to someone else and she really wanted to ensure that the few items of sentimental value went to the right people. She didn't have much, but she had memories in knick-knacks and photographs.

She turned away from the window and returned to the task in hand.

After an hour, she stepped back and blew her hair out of her face. Most people would have found tons to donate, but she had only found a small number of items in her kitchen, which were now in a row on a countertop. There was the small pile of cutlery; a sandwich-toasting machine that always seemed to pull the sandwich apart and spill the contents, which was a nightmare to clean despite claiming to be non-stick; a soup maker, which made a good few portions in less than thirty minutes; and two thermos flasks. Being minimalistic, she wasn't surprised this was all she had found.

Picking up one of the flasks, she turned it around in her hands. It was grey and had been her dad's flask.

She grabbed her mouth as nostalgia sharply winded her. Memories of helping her mam get packed lunches ready for the next day. May had never had school dinners, as she liked to know what she was eating and school meals never had a great reputation. Although the dinner staff seemed lovely and May knew they would be trained and hold a food hygiene certificate, the supposed edible produce always seemed to be an undesirable shade of brown and looked as if it would bounce upon hitting the floor. Pieces of fruit and baked goods lay where children would riffle through. Instead of this anxiety-provoking lunch experience, she would take a packed lunch every day, dropping the worry of snot-flicking and urine-sprinkled hands rooting through what she had to eat.

Each evening, she would help Fran prepare for the next day, with military precision. This included Dad's packed lunch, who would eat almost anything. One of May's roles was to get his thermos flask out, and the next morning, she would fill it full of coffee—something he always claimed got him through the day. She took this crucial requirement seriously. Carefully, as if a surgeon at the operating table, she would place the specified number of spoonfuls of coffee into the dark grey flask, watching in case any brown granules spilt from the spoon and landed on the kitchen countertop below. Next, it would be time to add the boiling water. She would grasp the full kettle, holding it tight as a trophy, determination etched on her face as Fran watched on. She would take her time; perfection couldn't be rushed. Then, she poured the kettle with her steady hand as coffee-fragrant steam tickled her face until around fifteen per cent volume of space remained in the flask. To finish her dad's daily essential, she would pour the milk, watching it dance with the brown liquid until they created the perfect colour for Dad's beverage. It took practice and patience to perfect her offering, but since the day she'd begun making her dad's daily flask, he'd always say it had the 'May magic'. She didn't like coffee and was rubbish at making it for anyone else, but for Dad, she'd been the best.

Walking into her lounge, nostalgia drew her eyes to the mantelpiece where the photo of her parents still lay facedown. Sighing, she pushed her shoulders back and looked at the grey flask still in her hand. She had seen Peter going out each morning at 8 a.m., returning at lunchtime. She was curious, like a magpie in a new garden. It was unlikely he worked, as he looked to be in his early seventies. Although, of course, she couldn't be sure he wasn't working, given the cost of living these days. Maybe she would ask Peter if he wanted one to keep him warm. She always felt drinking out of a flask on a cold day was like a hug to the soul.

May continued to potter around her flat, cleaning inside drawers, creating a pile for rubbish and another for charity. She felt almost content but knew the fleeting feeling was because she was taking control of her life and her death. Sorting her flat, running, Trish and Scarlett. All of those things she enjoyed were time-bound and were not enough for her to feel any quality of life. It had felt hard for too long, as if she were knocking down a castle with a toffee hammer. Impossibly hard, with no feeling it would become easier. And to her, it was inevitable that she would lose Scarlett and Trish, as she had lost her parents and Thomas. Loss followed her, teased her and haunted her. Maybe she was the problem. A bad omen. *Well, not for much longer.*

The cup of tea was hot against May's chest as she clasped it to herself and stared out of her lounge window. She had been contemplating a walk to the park, but she wasn't sure if she had the mental or physical energy. She spotted the sandy-coloured cat waltzing past as if he owned the street and couldn't help but smile as the cat jumped on a leaf that the mild wind lifted at just the right time, before stopping, plonking on the pavement and beginning to clean itself, one of its white legs stretched out as if it were in a yoga class. Taking a sip of tea, May glanced at her watch—it was almost 12:30 p.m. As predicted, when she looked back out at the cat, it was Peter now in her view walking quickly towards the flats.

May placed her cup on the coffee table, grabbed the flasks from the kitchen bench and rushed down her stairs to the front door. Putting the flasks on the bottom step, she flung the door open. 'Peter,' she called as he walked past her path, beckoning him over with her arm.

He turned her way, and although she wasn't always the best at reading new people despite studying body language over the years, Peter's downturned mouth and the tissue scrunched in his hand were an obvious giveaway of his upset even to her.

He cleared his throat and attempted a smile. 'Hello, May, how are you?'

'Erm, I'm alright, thank you, Peter. Are you okay?' She stared at his red eyes and bit her lip, wondering if she should have waited to speak to him another time, but it was too late to go back inside now.

Peter swallowed and rubbed his hands together. 'Oh yes, pet. Don't worry about me.'

May nodded, unsure but not wanting to probe. She turned around and picked up the flasks from the stairs. 'I wanted to know if you want a thermos flask? I was going to take them to the charity shop, but, well, I noticed you go out each morning and thought you may want one to take a drink with you?' She held the flasks out towards Peter.

He put his head in his hands, turning silent, his body shaking slightly.

'Peter?' May squirmed, not sure what to do.

Taking his hands away, Peter pulled a handkerchief from his pocket before dabbing his eyes. 'Sorry, May. I've had a rough morning. Your kindness just sent me over the edge a little. I'm feeling a bit silly now.' He dropped his eyes to the ground, then back to May, who stood in silence.

May was never very good when people were upset, but she often thought sometimes the best thing to do was be quiet—it's what she preferred anyway.

'It can be cold sitting at the bus stop each morning, especially when the bus is late, so a flask would be very welcome. Thank you, May.' Peter's voice cracked on the last few words.

May smiled, still holding the flasks out. She gently shook them, indicating for Peter to make his choice.

He reached for the flask on the left, the grey one that used to be her dad's, his other hand on his heart. 'This will do me perfectly. Thank you, May, you've made my day.'

'You're welcome,' she replied before quickly turning around and heading back inside.

Once back in the sanctuary of her flat, she leaned her back against the door and exhaled, feeling a mixture of happiness and sadness. Peter was very grateful, but why was he crying, and where was he going each morning? She shook her head and turned the key in the lock before walking away. It was none of her business, and quite frankly, given her plans, she simply did not want to know.

She decided she would get ready for a run to clear her mind, plus she was ready to re-explore the park she wished she'd discovered sooner. She took her mobile phone from her pocket and saw she had a missed call from Jack. Rubbing her face with one hand, she held her phone to her ear with the other and listened to the voicemail.

'May, it's Jack, from work, Lawson-Wray's.'

'I know where I work,' she said sarcastically to the phone, missing the next few words of Jack's message.

'And we hope you can come back to work soon. You're a miss, to us all. Anyway, keep in touch. Bye.'

No doubt Trish had fed back that she no longer looked like a zombie who soaked their hair in chip fat, and having supposedly perked up slightly, Jack had taken this as she would be returning to work. She deleted the message and tipped her head back, still holding her phone. Were people genuinely concerned about her, or were they just saying it out of obligation? Was it just to get her back into work? It was exhausting having her thoughts conflicting constantly like a screaming baby who couldn't be placated.

Chapter 21

9th May

May tried to clear her head of the rush-hour traffic that seemed to constantly be at a standstill in her mind, tooting and revving with nowhere to go, as she stared out of her lounge window. It was something she had only started to do with intent the last week or so, as if she were trying to imprint her observations into her mind, appreciate them while she could. She would watch birds land on the branches of the tree across the road. Away they would chirp to one another, some surprisingly loud for their little bodies. May wasn't certain, but she thought there was a regular blackbird that visited the tree, and as she stood in silence, sipping her cup of tea that morning, she waited for it.

It was another five minutes before the bird arrived. Her eyes widened as she leaned forward slightly. He was almost staring at her from the branch. For a split second, she wondered if the small blackbird with the vibrant yellow beak could be her dad coming to say hello. Then she pressed her lips together and looked into her now empty cup.

'Don't be so stupid, May,' she scolded herself.

When she glanced back up, she spotted Peter going out as usual at 8 a.m. Walking past her garden, he gripped the handle of her dad's old flask in one hand, his other hand resting in his coat pocket. She rubbed her lips. Despite the pang of nostalgia, she was pleased. She would leave her soup maker on his doorstep later that morning, with a note and a hope that he would also give the item a new home.

At 5:30 p.m. that evening, May had a Skype call with Scarlett.

'You look perkier,' Scarlett said within seconds of the call starting.

May shrugged and changed the subject. 'What have you got your mam for her birthday?'

Scarlett raised her eyebrows. 'May, I haven't bought her present yet; it's not for two weeks. There's plenty of time,' she said, head tilted, sounding as if she were trying to convince a child that the tooth fairy was real. 'But, on the plus, I already know what I'm buying you for your birthday.' She moved her shoulders, doing a little dance in her seat.

May laughed but then felt the axe of guilt carve into her. 'You shouldn't bother.' She looked down, feeling that if she looked directly at Scarlett, even through the screen, Scarlett would sense that there was a deep problem.

'Shut up, you daft mare. Of course I should bother; you're my bestie.' Scarlett blew a kiss as May's eyes returned to the screen. 'And if you don't like it, well, you can shove it.'

May chuckled. 'Charming.'

'So, I'm thinking in the summer we could perhaps have a break away somewhere. Even for a few nights?'

A bowling ball dropped into the pit of May's stomach as she struggled for a response. Would she love to? Yes. Could it happen? No. Was it better to agree with this knowledge or to decline the offer?

'Earth to May.' Scarlett tapped on the screen. 'A holiday? Us. You and me.' She made a heart with her fingers and thumbs to the screen. 'It'll be fun. You bring the Weetabix, I'll bring the music.'

May allowed a warm feeling of hope and care inside before a gust of despair and reality blew it away. 'We can talk about it when you come up.'

May wanted to ensure the friends had a nice time when Scarlett visited. She would try as hard as she could to celebrate for others. She didn't want to be the Eeyore, so she would wear a mask for the short time she planned on being around, even if the mask felt as if it were burning her face.

They chatted a while longer before saying their good-byes, Scarlett blowing kisses, then waving with both hands. May hung up and shut her laptop. She slumped back on the sofa, letting her back and shoulders sink into the cushion. Putting her hands to her head, she dragged them slowly down her face and thought about her oldest, most treasured friend.

Their calls had become less frequent over the last year or so, and May sometimes felt she was in Scarlett's way. Alongside some acting work in Essex, Scarlett was now teaching drama and she and Ethan had busy lifestyles. Sometimes, May felt as if the Skype calls snatched time from Scarlett that she didn't have, remembering that other people had more going on in their lives than she had and that as people got older, inevitably, their priorities changed. Scarlett had always been one of May's priorities, but like Trish, May felt she had taken and not given a lot to the friendship in the last few months or even years.

Life was good for Scarlett, and May, of course, was pleased, but it felt strange not being 'Scarlett and May' as life pulled them both in different positions and further apart in ways. At one point, May had felt envious of what Scarlett had. She wanted one of the most important people in her life to be happy and to have all of her dreams come true, but she couldn't help but long for those things also, like a prisoner yearns for freedom. She desired those normal things that felt so abnormal to her—another flashing light that she just didn't fit in with 'the norm'. Always walking on the outside, always in the dark with happiness as fleeting as a bird flying across the sky.

May grabbed the fleece blanket, gifted by Trish, from the side of the sofa and wrapped it over her, needing the comfort of something against her as she sat, feeling lost. She wanted to go back to childhood, when the friendships felt unbreakable, when the risk of bullying and not fitting in felt like a jump over a puddle compared to the mountain she'd had to try to climb over the last few years. She groaned, pulling the blanket up to right under her chin as she tucked her feet up on the sofa.

The stark reality was that she and Scarlett were edging apart as the years continued, like a worn sweater with a hole emerging, the gap only likely to become bigger. She picked up her glass of water from the coffee table and took a gulp, her head pounding from overthinking.

A text alert came through. May picked up her phone and saw it was from Scarlett.

'Great to speak, lovely. Can't wait to see you in person soon! Yay! Love ya xxx'

May stared at the screen and wondered if she was overreacting. Then the feeling began to crawl all over her, creeping up her body until she felt like a burden once again. She acknowledged their friendship would never be exactly as it used to be when childhood innocence was a protective armour they both wore, when the worst things they worried about were what they would do at the weekend and getting homework in on time. But the point was that the pair, although sometimes polar opposites, had never been troubled by adulthood issues. She'd had her May worries, but they hadn't had to think about houses and work meetings, relationships and parents dying.

Now as adults, they couldn't hide from things. There was no tree to giggle behind, no games and nothing fun about life anymore for May. She had to face the big stresses and the minuscule issues alone—her food shopping delivery giving a green pepper as an alternative to a red pepper, unexpected roadworks meaning a detour from a route she was comfortable with. It sounded trivial, insignificant, but it wasn't for her. She didn't have the energy for all life's challenges anymore.

May closed her eyes, wishing she could go to sleep and wake up as someone else.

Three quick knocks on her door thumped her thoughts away. Startled, she jumped before pushing the blanket off herself and checking her watch. It was just after 7 p.m. She walked down the stairs with her arms folded for warmth and opened the door hesitantly.

A jolly Peter presented her with a plastic container as if he were presenting a trophy to the winning team on match day. 'Here, my kind neighbour, this is for you.'

May looked down at the plastic container. Her face must have indicated an unimpressed curiosity, as Peter quickly added, 'It's vegetable broth. I made it this afternoon in the soup maker you so kindly donated. I hope it's okay.' He moved the container a little closer to May, nodding at her as her eyes raised to meet his. 'I had to follow a recipe I found online. I'm getting better at this cooking malarky.'

May bit her lip. Peter wasn't to know that she was opposed to eating food made by others unless in a professional, monitored kitchen. Trish had already pushed her to the limit, but she used to work in the kitchen of a local community centre, meaning she must have some food hygiene certificates, even if they had expired.

Remaining standing, Peter held the rectangular box of soup as May studied it and him, brow furrowing.

'I've tried it myself. It's not bad for a newbie. You see, my Anne used to do all the cooking, I just did all the eating. But now, well, she can hardly eat, never mind cook.' He glanced at his feet and took a deep breath before lifting his head back up to May, who hadn't moved a muscle.

'Anyway, there you go, pet. I hope you enjoy.' He thrust it into May's hands and nodded. 'Oh, and that key worked, thanks. I will get a copy and bring yours back. Erm, have a good evening, May.' He walked away with his shoulders slumped.

She looked at the soup and then Peter's back as he walked down her path. 'Thank you,' she called out.

As she closed the door of her flat, she kept wondering what Peter's story was. Why had he moved there? Where from? Where was Anne? And the question that was starting to really intrigue her despite trying to expel it from her brain: where did Peter go every morning at 8 a.m.? She tutted, knowing it wasn't her problem and she had no right knowing his personal circumstances, but something about him made her want to know more, and it irritated her that she felt this way, given her focus for the end of the month. Peter Parsley was becoming the loose thread that kept forming on a shirt despite cutting it off several times.

Chapter 22

10th May

The traffic was pretty light on the roads, which May was thankful for, as she wanted today's task to be over with as quickly as possible. She didn't particularly want to visit the place where she'd received the news of her dad dying, where the trauma would no doubt bubble over like a pan full of vegetables, but she had library books that needed returning. A heavy bag of them that was currently on her passenger seat. Most were late and there would be a fine she'd have to pay, but she was okay with that, as she wouldn't be needing money for much longer and didn't want to chance anyone else having to clear her debt once she was gone.

She'd watched Peter leaving his flat at 8 a.m., and the thread had dangled again, urging her to desire more information on her neighbour, but even that hadn't been enough for her mind to completely wander from the library books.

Visiting university would be another goodbye in a place she had never really been visible and that was another stark example of failure. She had come so near yet so far from achieving her goal. Whilst Scarlett had dreamed of Broadway and other children her age focused on being a singer, a professional sportsperson or a nurse, she'd always wanted to be a scientist. Now all her studies had been for nothing. She would never finish her master's, never get the job of her dreams, and if she wasn't so damn diligent, she wouldn't bother returning the books.

Nevertheless, she parked a five-minute walk away, not daring to even attempt to park in *that* car park. The one where her world had been destroyed again.

As May walked across campus, towards the library, she could see the car park peeking out in the distance. She looked the other way, feeling nausea run over her. She took a deep breath and focused on carrying the bag of heavy books and returning them to their rightful place.

She entered the library and looked around the building that always made her feel comfortable—the peace and quiet, endless rows of books that all had their own place. She closed her eyes and inhaled the slight mustiness, leather and polish. Although university now felt a place of trauma, the library still evoked sanctuary.

May made her way up the stairs to the third floor, to her favourite part of the library—the science section. A few people were sat at tables, some on computers and the odd student was looking at the rows of books. She walked down an aisle, running her fingers along the spines as she strolled. She felt the patterns on the covers and the odd gap where one had been removed. She stood back and stared at the shelves, thoughts of how her future could have turned out playing like a slideshow in her mind.

'Excuse me.'

May coughed back into the here and now as she stepped closer to the books to allow a librarian past, then guiltily followed them to the desk, returned all the books and paid the seventeen pound ninety-five pence fine for the books being two months overdue in their return. She was relieved it was done and that she could cross that task off her list. She began walking to the exit, wanting to be back in the comfort of her flat.

'*May.*'

She grimaced and turned around at the mention of her name to see one of her tutors, Elizabeth Irving, standing by the library noticeboard.

'May, oh, hang on a second, please?' Elizabeth shouted, waving her hand in the air.

May felt panic and the overwhelming desire to run. She waved and pretended she couldn't hear Elizabeth as she scurried out of the exit, then dashed across campus, out of sight. Panic turned to an exasperated giggle as she walked back to her car. She wasn't unfamiliar with ignoring people, perhaps not always so obviously, but running away like that felt so childlike and a bit naughty.

May hadn't eaten the soup from Peter the evening before. Granted, he could have been a former Michelin star chef, but it was unlikely. However, on returning from university, after sorting through her paperwork and shredding out-of-date documents, she felt a pang of hunger and an intrigue about the soup. She opened the fridge and took out the plastic container. After opening the lid, she studied the beige liquid that appeared to have chunks of vegetables and some pulses in it. Taking a spoon from the cutlery drawer, she dipped it in the liquid, stirring it tentatively to see more of the meal, studying it as she would a scientific paper. Orange—that would be carrots, a few slithers of pale white onion, potato chunks and some faded green stringy leeks. Leaning closer to the tub, there were definitely some pulses in there—barley, by the looks of it. Peter had made an effort; this was a soup that had taken a lot of prep time. She couldn't help but feel impressed. She gathered a spoonful, raising it to her nose. It smelt nice, similar to the broth her mam used to make. A stab of grief assaulted her, and she had to hold her weight up on the kitchen bench whilst she took a deep breath.

Pouring some of the soup into a pan and letting it warm slowly, she stirred it as she began to daydream. Thoughts turned to the song her mam used to play when she was little. She recalled giggling in delight at her dad trying to slow dance with her mam around the kitchen to it. The words came straight to her head, and she began singing Billy Joel's *Make You Feel My Love*. Her mam used to say it was about them and their love—Fran and Victor's and then May's. Each time they played it, Fran would say, 'It may have been Bob Dylan's, but Billy Joel made it.' May asked Alexa to play the song on repeat as she sat and ate the soup. Spoon in the soup along with the odd fallen tear, she tasted memories and love.

Chapter 23

12th May

A knitted blanket of brightly coloured squares that created a rainbow woollen comforter used to lie on the back
of the sofa at Grandma McClelland's house before she
passed some years back, and when May visited, Grandma
would put it over her knee and give her a big mug of
tea and some homemade fruit cake. May looked at the
vibrant blanket now as she sat on her bedroom floor,
the drawers of her double divan open whilst she sorted
through excess bedding. May didn't have a massive number of belongings—she wasn't frugal as such but wasn't
wasteful, more a considerate consumer. The blanket was
important to her, cherished memories woven into it, and
she didn't want it discarded; however, it wasn't to everyone's taste. Scarlett would hate anything like that in her
home, as she was very much about modern décor; May
already had a few items of importance in mind for Trish;
and Uncle Terence already had a very similar blanket,
also knitted by his mother.

May thought about Peter. It was almost 1 p.m., so he
could be in. *Maybe he would like the blanket.*

Standing up, she folded the blanket and brought it to
her face. She buried her head in it, her eyes closed, and
smelt her history one last time. Swallowing back tears,
she slid her ballet pump shoes on to take the blanket
next door. She would prefer someone she knew had the
blanket than take it to charity. If Peter didn't want it,
perhaps Trish would.

She tucked the blanket under her arm and walked down the stairs and out of her front door. Instead of crossing the shared lawn, she walked up the path, reached the top and then rushed down Peter's path. As she neared his front door, she frowned, realising it was ajar. She approached slowly and knocked gently, waiting for a short while, then slowly pushed the door open.

'Peter? Are you here?' she said quietly, peering into the hallway.

After receiving no answer, she put her hand to her mouth and reluctantly stepped into the flat. She first noticed the doormat that displayed the word 'WELCOME' with a rainbow above the word. It made her smile as she considered how appropriate of a doormat it was for Peter, with his welcoming nature. He was so much more of a people person than she was, and his happy disposition was growing on her, even if she didn't want to admit it to herself.

Moving off the mat and into the hallway, she looked at the magnolia walls, decorated only with a coat rack and a mirror that felt far too small. Catching a glimpse of herself in the unproportionate mirror, she looked away, anxious that being in Peter's house uninvited wasn't right. She shuddered at the thought of someone coming into her space uninvited. But she just couldn't ignore the niggle that something could be wrong.

She walked tentatively along the short hallway to a room on the left with the door open. Blue carpet almost dazzled (not in a good way) through the open door. She wrinkled her nose in distaste at the awful, garish bright blue, and although she wasn't the most fashionable and certainly didn't have an interior design eye, the carpet was intense. Despite recoiling, she continued towards the room.

She heard a movement and held her breath as she stopped and considered running away. She bit her lip, then slowly reached in her pocket and retrieved her keys before moving the next few steps that would lead her into Peter's lounge. May tiptoed, her keys in her hand (as her mam had taught her), wondering if there was an intruder. She was prepared for an attack—well, as much as a set of keys and a granny-style knitted blanket can prepare you. Then the sound came again, this time increasing in volume. It only took her a second to realise it was Peter snoring like an English bulldog, and a few steps later, she could see him. She stifled a giggle at the sight of Peter slouched in his recliner armchair, glasses skew-if, mouth open with an almighty noise coming from it that would rival the revving of a motorbike.

There was a battered armchair opposite where he sat, an aged TV in the corner and a small table next to him. The only part of the room that wasn't sparse was a wall, which was decorated with photos. May couldn't help but look at the pictures of babies, weddings, holidays. Most of the photos showed Peter with a woman who must have been Anne. Trying to be quiet, she leaned in to look at her. She was a beautiful petite woman with almost white-blonde hair and a smile that made her eyes curl up. The same type of smile as Fran, a Duchenne smile, where laugh lines occur outside the corners of the eyes—the most genuine of smiles. Peter hadn't changed except for the decades of ageing softening his skin and muscles, but his happiness was evident in the photos, eyes wide, expression animated, and his smile was infectious even in the faded photos. There were pictures of Peter and his wife on their wedding day and pictures of her alone. Photos of children, then young adults. So many memories in assorted frames collected across the years. A pick-and-mix of precious times. May was mesmerised, wondering what had happened to the people in the photographs.

She turned back to Peter, who was still asleep in the chair, lying like a hibernating bear. After one last hug of the knitted blanket, she tiptoed over and placed it on him. There was a notepad and pen on the table by his side with some scrawls on it. She didn't dare read his notes, but she turned to a fresh page and left a note explaining his door had been open, then she put the pen down and stepped back. Peter stirred but didn't open his eyes. As she left the room, May looked back to the memory wall and then to Peter and wondered if he was as lonely as she was.

She went back into her flat thinking about Peter. Sighing, she put the kettle on. Her uneventful life was making her nosy.

As she was just about to sit down, cup of tea on the coffee table, her mobile phone rang. It was Uncle Terence.

'Hi, May, how are you doing?' he asked, his voice chirpy.

'Hi, Uncle Terence. Yeah, I'm okay. How are you?' she asked back, significantly less chirpy as she picked at a loose thread on her cardigan.

'Not too bad, pet. Plodding along, you know?'

She nodded, not that he could see her.

'I had a call from Alison, Mrs Taylor, your dad's neighbour.' Clearing his throat, he continued, 'She was asking after you and wondered if you have any plans for the house?'

May felt immediately discombobulated with the comment but also because she hadn't even remembered to put sorting out her family home on her final list. She felt a stabbing of guilt. The house had come to her following her dad's passing, but she had put it in a box in her mind, the lid firmly shut, unable to deal with it. She had only been there twice, the first time two days after Dad died, accompanied by Trish to retrieve documents that she did nothing with for another few days before Trish stepped in and assisted. The second time was for the wake. Even those times felt like a million years ago. She couldn't face the house afterwards and still couldn't now.

'It's none of her business,' May said sharply, breathing deeply to try to control her escalating emotions.

'She wasn't being nosy, love; Mr and Mrs Taylor thought the world of your parents. They've been checking on the house, running the taps weekly, firing the boiler up and making sure it's secure.' Terence sighed. 'Alison sends her love. She said you're welcome for a cuppa anytime, and Imarah would love to see you and show you her drawings.'

May swallowed, both touched and feeling harassed by the gesture. Her list of people she was a burden to was also getting longer. She wondered if it would eventually be longer than her to-do list.

'She said she's tried ringing you and not heard back. I think she's worried about you,' Terence said gently.

'Well, I'm fine and I will sort it,' May said quickly, starting to sob. 'I'll move in when I'm ready or I'll sell it or rent it. I'm just not there yet.'

'I know, love, I know,' he soothed. 'I'll pop up once a fortnight to alleviate them from doing as much and, May, I'm here for you. I know you like your own space, but we are family and I do care, pet.'

May put her hand to her mouth and swallowed. She wanted to scream, cry, ask her uncle for help to make the world bearable. But he wouldn't have the answers... no one did. She felt completely beyond anyone's help. 'Thanks, Uncle Terence,' was all she could muster.

She hung up the phone and stared into space for a few minutes before getting her notebook from her bedroom. She looked at the list she'd created over a week ago, reviewing what had been crossed off, and then she added something else at the bottom of the list.

3rd May

To do (before 31st May):

- Spend time with Scarlett.

- Spend time with Trish that isn't her looking after me.

- Go and see Uncle Terence.

- Visit the cemetery.

- Visit Lawson-Wray's (possibly).

- ~~Take library books back to university and pay fines.~~

- ~~Run in the park.~~

- ~~Sort throughout the house; take things to charity~~ and leave notes on things I want to give to others.

- Arrange finances.

- Write letters to Scarlett and Trish—make them as positive as possible and remember to tell them that I love them and why I love them.

- Buy paracetamols.

- Write will to include Mam and Dad's house to go to Uncle Terence.

May tried to process the thoughts that were whizzing around her head like a fireworks display as she jogged over the tarmac and towards the pond in the park that afternoon. Passing the ducks, swans and coots living in feathered harmony, she began to feel less angry with herself, the world and everyone in it. She smelt the tang of the freshly cut lawns as she jogged past the grassed areas, which she knew, as a scientist, was actually the smell of organic compounds called green leaf volatiles. She regulated her breathing despite the vigorous run and almost felt strong for a fleeting moment.

Moments like this made her feel almost normal. She wasn't the type of runner to play music as she ran; instead, it was as if she could transport herself to her own world where the birds sang louder in the sky and the wind rustled through the grass with an echoed breeze. There was something therapeutic in running, and for May, it wasn't just the exercise. It was the solitary feeling. Even in the running club at school, she had run alongside folk, not uttering a word. It was almost as if they were part of her team but separate, like gazelles in South Africa. A herd doing their own thing. When she ran, she could almost be anyone she wanted. She could be a film star, a model, a rock star, but more in keeping with May, she could be a top scientist. She felt invincible. She could feel happy. But the rush never lasted, and when she got home after her run, she went in the shower and cried silent tears that mixed with the warm water cascading down her thin frame.

In that moment, she felt sad to be alive and sad to know she was going to die.

Chapter 24

13th May

May had been avoiding the cemetery where her parents were buried, but she felt she had to visit one last time. It was not something she had done much since her mam passed two years ago, especially in the first year, and she hadn't been since her dad's funeral eight weeks ago. She had occasionally been to Fran's grave with Victor, more to support him, who'd gone each week. It all felt exposed and weird, and for that reason, she avoided it when she could. She hadn't felt connected to a headstone when her mam's ashes had been at the family home on the lounge mantlepiece. Both her parents' ashes were now in her flat, in the hallway cupboard, safe on a shelf but not ready to be on display or even thought about if possible. Despite not wanting to go and still not understanding how she could feel any sort of connection, she could almost hear her dad's voice in her head from the conversation they'd had about the cemetery around a year after Fran died.

'I know you think it's creepy or whatever, May, but it's important to your mam for us to visit. It's showing our respect, and actually, it can be quite reflective and spiritual.'

May had raised her eyebrows at her dad, who had never used the words reflective and spiritual in her lifetime.

Victor glanced into the distance. 'It makes me feel like I'm in a corridor between the living and the dead. A place where we can almost touch those on the other side of the door we are all walking to at different speeds. All those gravestones, the collective loss. It's sad, deeply sad, but there's something else, May.' He placed his hand on his chest, still looking away from her. 'A peace, a respect, an understanding that everyone there hurts. And when I'm in that corridor, the cemetery, I hurt in a different way because I know it's not just us that feels it.'

May had said nothing to Victor; she hadn't known what to say. Instead, she'd put her arm around him and vowed to go with him to the cemetery as much as she could. And she had. Now, she had to go to see them both, even just the once before her time ended.

She puffed out air, straightened her shoulders and grabbed a packet of cleaning wipes to put in her bag. Getting her shoes and coat on at the bottom of the stairs, she was ready to go. It was three miles away, but she decided to walk. As she stepped outside and locked her front door, she heard a meow. She turned around and saw the familiar cat jauntily strutting towards her, its tail straight up in the air like one of those ornamental ring holders. It arrived at May's feet and boldly rubbed against her ankles, looked up at her and meowed as if to say, 'Here I am.'

Smiling, she bent down to stroke the cat. The moggy purred and rubbed its head against her hand, eyes closing in satisfaction.

'Aren't you a happy little boy or girl,' May commented as the cat immediately flopped onto the ground and began rolling around. She couldn't help but enjoy the interaction as the playful puss purred in delight. 'And maybe you're the biggest attention seeker on the block,' she added as she fussed over her visitor.

The cat was a lovely sandy colour with tabby markings, white patches and beautiful golden eyes. It moved its head around to get the sweet spot from May's rub, purring with contentment with its mouth ajar.

'What's your name, then, and where do you live?' she asked her new pal, in a high-pitched voice, to a response of an even more vocal purr as it continued to enjoy the affection.

She giggled. 'I've got places to be, little one, I can't stay here fussing over you all day.'

She rose up, much to the cat's disappointment. It rolled on the ground, stretching out a white paw in one last flirt for attention. She remained standing, looking down at the cat's fluffy belly. Shaking her head, she smiled and turned to walk away. A pathetic meow came from her visitor, who was now standing by her feet. She had never much cared for animals and had never had pets as a child. Although not scared of them, she'd had no experience of looking after or having the company of one. Patting its head one last time, she set off on her walk to the cemetery.

Arriving at the cemetery an hour later, she took a deep breath and began the route of the 'corridor', up to where Fran and now Victor were remembered. It was early afternoon and the sun was shining. She stopped at the garden of remembrance, flowers in bloom, with the spring sun nourishing them. There were a few people quietly contemplating in the area. She was mesmerised by the rainbow palette of flowers and inhaled the soft scent as the flowers brought a calmness to her soul.

How come I never noticed how beautiful this is when I came here with Dad? May placed her hands on her stomach and pressed her lips together, staring at the yellow rose bushes. Fran's favourites. She closed her eyes, willing to open them to Fran standing next to the flowers, looking as stunning and radiant as them, but when she opened them again, her wish hadn't come true. Wiping a tear from her eye, she turned and began walking the corridor again.

Her parents' plot was in a short row adjacent to a footpath where wooden benches had been placed, providing seating space to grieve and reflect. She stood a metre or so from the headstone, eyes transfixed. Her thoughts came and went for a minute or so as she blocked out everything else. Then she opened her mouth, wanting to talk, to say something to her parents. But she shut it again, feeling stupid, feeling a failure, not really knowing where to start. Instead, she returned to her thoughts, hoping that perhaps her parents knew what she was thinking, as they had when she was a child.

Taking the wipes out of her bag, she ran a few over the headstone, the sharp lemon fragrance tickling her nostrils as she followed the carving of her parents' names with her encased finger, tracing the dates of their lives—numbers that had changed her life. She had never cleaned the headstone; it had always been Victor's job. But now he couldn't.

She began to cry silent, lonely tears, holding her head down, not bothering to wipe them away. Then she heard a small noise. Head back up, her eyes widened. A blackbird was perched less than a metre away on the top of the gravestone, looking at her. Marble eyes, vibrant yellow beak. Just like the one who regularly visited the tree opposite her house. Tilting its head, it stared at May. Its beak opened slightly, and she leaned gently forward, almost certain it was going to speak. Then it flew off. Her heart was pounding and she felt a tingle in her body. Even though the scientist in her said it was impossible, she hoped with all her might that maybe it was her dad thanking her.

An hour and a half later, she returned home from the cemetery. She felt emotionally spent but pleased she had gone and had a new understanding of her dad's need to visit. May wished she could have felt it sooner, when Victor had perhaps needed her to. It was another punch in the stomach of uselessness, another point in her failure score.

Walking up her path, she looked towards Peter's front window. She hadn't seen him leave this morning, and as much as she had tried to not think about him, she wondered if he was okay. Part of her felt a little disappointed he hadn't knocked about the blanket. She didn't want the attention, the thanks, the disturbance or a new friend, but as much as she had resisted, she was developing a soft spot for Peter that was challenging to smother. Caring about more people made her plan for the end of the month harder and she was already on track to get everything in place for her departure. She didn't want anything getting in her way.

Chapter 25

14th May

May's hallway cupboard was a massive storage space for a small flat, and it felt overwhelming to even an organised May. Her eyes immediately focused on the very top shelf and the urns containing her parents' ashes. She gritted her teeth and lowered her gaze from the top to travel along the other shelves that held boxes, most of which were labelled. A few larger unlabelled boxes sat on the floor of the cupboard, mainly ones she had taken from the house after Dad's wake. Glancing at the shelves that contained much of her memories and her life admin, she thought of her parents' home still full of decades of memories of life and death. Memories of her grandparents and probably her great-grandparents. Now, her parents were where the memories stopped. Ceased and left behind, as May would be. She put her hands together, took a deep breath and shook the thought out of her head. She had a task to try to declutter, and she would do it.

She grabbed a cushion from the sofa and placed it on the laminate floor. She sat down, dragging the nearest box out of the cupboard to begin organising. It was from her parents' house. There were favourite cups in the box, papers she had quickly collected in a time of distress. Then she spotted a familiar item peeking out from under some documents—one of the family photo albums. Instinctively, she smiled, knowing it would be filled with snapshots of a happy childhood. She pulled it out and rested the album on her knee, running her hand across the cover that showed a beach with a hypnotic blue sea

and sun-kissed golden sand. She had never been an ornament person and didn't like prints and pictures cluttering
wall space. There was one shelf on her bedroom wall
that housed her books and there was a clock hanging in
her lounge. Apart from the photo of her parents that still
faced down on her mantlepiece and a mirror above it,
that was about it décor-wise; however, she loved photo
albums and had fond memories of going to the supermarket with Fran after each holiday to excitedly wait for the
photos to be printed off. Once home, they'd placed the
photos in an album as they talked about the meal or the
drink or the architecture or beach pictured.

She opened the photo album and could almost smell
the scents of holiday escaping the pages. The first few
pages showed the family in Greece, big smiles, tanned
skin, the look of rest that adults only seem to have when
away etched across her parents' faces. May and Dad in
the pool, splashing and laughing. The beach and all the
inflatables that always lasted just a few days before developing a puncture. Closing her eyes, she held the album
to her chest and tried to inhale the warm evenings of
Greece. The salty sea breeze mixed with the sumptuous
aroma of herbs and spices, meats and vegetables cooking.
The tang of feta cheese and the freshness of the olives,
which she'd never liked but Dad loved. The scent of the
salt water in her hair and on her skin after the sun had
penetrated it throughout the day. Fran's perfume and the
local beer Victor had loved. May lifted the album from
her chest and inhaled the pages, desperately trying to be
back in any of the moments.

She flicked through the remainder of the album,
touching her parents' faces. As she closed it, she wondered if Victor had looked through the albums after Fran
died, touched Fran's face as she now touched both their
faces.

Picking up the next album, which was older, thicker
and cream in colour, May knew it was of her parents'
wedding. She remembered looking through it as a child
with them, querying the fashion and asking about all the

people in each photo. She'd sniggered, viewing her parents in the 1970s as a young couple and on their wedding day. Now, she smiled at the fashion, shed a couple of tears over the reappearance of her grief before pulling herself together again. Her parents looked so young, even being older than she was now, but they looked so happy, so in love. That Duchenne smile on Fran's face, as beautiful as May always remembered. Her dad, standing tall, proud to have the most stunning woman in the world as his bride. The pair kissing outside of St. John's Church—their new life as man and wife celebrated in the oldest church in town. The world was their menu, inviting them to order and taste its delights. May traced her dad's eyes and her mam's hair, knowing they must have thought they'd have many more years together than they'd had. She would never get married and look at someone the way her mam looked at her dad in those wedding photos. Pure devotion.

Sighing, she scrunched her eyes, annoyed that she'd allowed herself to be taken to a place of hurt. It always felt like this—something nice and happy snatched away and set on fire to leave pain and emptiness. Placing the album on the floor, she reached back into the box.

Ding-dong.

May's hand froze in the box. Trish was due to come over that night, but not for another forty-five minutes. She grumbled as she quickly put the albums back in the box and into the cupboard. She rushed down the stairs in a huff at the earliness, which she'd also have done if Trish had been late. On time was just fine.

May opened the door. 'You're earl—' She paused and frowned, but with confusion rather than disappointment. 'Oh, um, hi, Peter.'

'Hello, May. I've made you this.' He held out a glass container with an oblong cake inside that was golden in colour, varnished in icing and sprinkled with specks of lemon zest. He smiled broadly, proud of his creation.

'Oh, Peter, honestly, you shouldn't have.' And emotionless-faced May absolutely meant it.

'Pet, I wanted to thank you for the blanket. I was meant to come round sooner, but I'm not my best when I wake and, to be honest, I was feeling a bit under the weather. But your kindness and the blanket... well, it was just such a nice thing to do.' He moved from foot to foot where he stood and glanced at the cake, then back to May. 'And I'm a daft old sod leaving the door open. Thanks, May.'

May blushed slightly, uncomfortable at the praise. 'I was going to give the blanket to charity, but it was knitted by my grandma, so I thought it would be nicer to go to a frie... someone I know.'

Peter nodded, then looked at May with a frown. 'Pet, why are you giving so much away? Are you moving? I sure hope not.'

'No, just getting rid of the clutter in my flat,' she quickly replied.

Peter didn't respond for a few seconds, and she was sure he knew she wasn't telling the truth. Why would a blanket knitted by her grandma be classed as clutter? But instead of questioning her, he continued, 'Well, take this cake anyway. It was another recipe off my iPad. I'm getting used to it and I'm quite enjoying cooking. I've made one for the nurses, but theirs is a little burnt.' He giggled.

May nodded, not wanting to pry. 'Thanks, Peter.' She took the cake from him, which she was now certain was lemon drizzle, one of her favourites. 'Why don't you come by tomorrow when you get in and we can have a slice of this and a cuppa?' she blurted. She would have kicked herself if her body had been hidden; instead, she internally winced.

Peter's face lit up like Blackpool Illuminations. 'Well, that would be lovely, May, just lovely indeed. About 1 p.m. work for you?'

'Yes. Great, that's settled. See you tomorrow,' May answered, shutting the door and almost regretting what she had just done. Small talk was hard for her and she had just exceeded her comfort zone exponentially by inviting her neighbour round for cake that he had made and she would have to eat.

'What's happening to you, May McClelland?' she said, throwing her head back.

Trish arrived a little later, ringing May's doorbell, with a takeaway pizza in one arm. May hurried down the stairs, opening it to an ever-chirpy Trish, who hugged May with her free arm as she came into the flat.

'Alright, my lovely? You look well.' She squeezed May's hand before handing her the pizza so she could take her shoes off. Going upstairs, Trish went straight to the kitchen to get plates. May found it both strange and comforting how relaxed Trish was in her home.

'I'll get us a drink,' she said, trying to feel useful as Trish took the pizza, plates and kitchen roll through to the lounge.

As May made her way to the sofa with two glasses of water, Trish began talking, 'So, you must be getting bored here by now, with your active brain. How about popping into the office next week?' She tilted her head, eyes wide like a dog waiting for a treat.

May placed the glasses of water on the coffee table and sighed as she took her seat. She knew Trish had been discussing her with Jack, as the phone call from him had been too much of a coincidence. She couldn't face returning to Lawson-Wray's, and quite frankly, it was pointless unless to say goodbye.

'We all miss you.'

May wanted to scream out the words she really needed to say, but she couldn't. She had loved working at Lawson-Wray's over the years and it had been so much more than just a job, so it felt like another big loss to her. But it had been almost three months now. Although Jack had kept her position open and everyone was asking after her, she still couldn't face people. Her pendulum-swinging emotions made it an impossible goal to see a future at work even if she hadn't been planning on suicide. The solemn stares, the hushed voices, the pity stirred into her tea. She didn't want the attention, the sympathy, the attempts to tell her everything would be okay. It wasn't okay and it hadn't been for a long time.

Trish slid over the pizza box. 'Just think about it, eh?'

May nodded, taking a slice of pizza that she had no appetite for. As they ate, Trish talked about what had been happening with her family and at work. May mainly listened and nodded. Trish asked May questions about her running, Scarlett and university. May knew Trish cared, but she really had very little to say, given the secret situation, although this in itself made her just appear to be almost back to her usual self. She did enjoy Trish's company and listening to the funny way she would talk about her husband or her menopausal symptoms. Trish was the closest thing she had to a mother now and to a nearby friend, and time spent with her always felt bittersweet.

May swallowed a lump of emotion. 'I'm just going to get a drink.' She gave a weak smile and headed to the kitchen. With both hands on the countertop, pushing her weight against it, head lowered, she let out a couple of deep breaths. She heard Trish coming over with the plates and spun around.

'You mean to say all this time I have been cooking for you and you can bake cakes?'

May turned to the lemon drizzle cake on the kitchen bench, which Trish was pointing at, eyes wide with excited hunger. 'No, Peter made it.'

Trish looked over the top of her glasses and smirked. 'Oh yeah, who's Peter? You little flirt.' She puckered her lips and blew a kiss.

May grimaced. 'Urgh, Trish, stop it. He's my neighbour and he must be at least seventy.'

'Oh.' Trish let out an awkward chuckle. 'Well, bless him, making you a cake. How lovely. Christ, I can't even get Brian to make me some bloody jam on toast,' she said, rolling her eyes.

'I wouldn't either if I was Brian; your cooking is delicious, and I'm very fussy.' May laughed.

'Giz a slice, then. It looks divine.'

May took a knife out of the drawer and placed it on the top of the cake. She glanced at Trish, who beckoned the knife further along for a larger slice. May chuckled as she sliced the cake and served Trish a piece, cutting herself a smaller piece.

The friends remained in the kitchen, leaning against the countertop as they ate their cake.

'Wow, this would give *Bake Off* a run for its money, I reckon,' Trish commented.

May licked her lips, in full agreement with Trish.

In between mouthfuls, Trish continued, 'This Peter chap, what's his story?'

'I don't know. He hasn't said, and, well, I haven't asked. He lives alone though.'

'Do you think he's lonely? Maybe could do with a friend?'

May shrugged as Trish kept talking.

'Sometimes it's nice to make new friends, and sometimes the closest of friends can be very different people who just click.'

May nodded. She didn't know much about Peter, but he did bring a smile to her day. Perhaps it was his age—not massively older than her dad when he passed—or perhaps it was that similarity to her late grandfather. Of course, she wasn't looking for another dad, he was irreplaceable, but it did feel a little strange that Peter arrived at a time when she had lost the second of the two most important people in her world. There was a kindness evident in him that her dad had always had, even if she didn't want to be the recipient. You see, making friends would only make her plan harder, and she wanted an easy few weeks before her exit from this world.

After wrapping up a slice in foil to take home for herself and 'definitely not for Brian', Trish left. May's flat was empty and quiet once again, like a school during half term. She turned all the plugs off except the timer light, the fridge and the oven, as she did every night, then went to bed.

She was more afraid of living with hurt, anxiety and monotony than dying. She had a high pain threshold but didn't want to end her life in a painful or gruesome way; instead, she had opted for taking a cocktail of tablets and vodka. She had bought several packets of painkillers and would continue to buy them through the month, stock-piling them. She wouldn't google anything—processes, consequences or details of death—as it would only complicate the matter and the internet could be a place of untrust and exaggeration. She knew she wanted to escape, that she had to escape. The last fortnight had been okay at times, like a bright spring coming out of a dark winter, but she didn't trust her future or even her present. Happiness was fleeting. She had let her guard down to the world before and been knocked to the ground by the wrecking ball of destruction. No, she couldn't trust the world and knew her current reality was only real and only tolerable because she knew it was coming to an end.

She sat up in bed, with her bedside lamp on. She reached into the top drawer of her bedside cabinet and took out her spiral-bound notebook and a pen. Taking in a deep breath, she stared at the page for a moment where she had previously written 'Dear Trish' and began to write.

Chapter 26

16th May

May watched from her lounge as Peter left his flat at 8 a.m., the hand-me-down flask in his hands. She banged on the window, then laughed as he jumped a little. She quickly covered her mouth in shame for laughing at giving an old man a fright just before he spun around and waved, his jolly smile decorating his chubby face. Pointing to the flask, he held it up like the World Cup trophy. May smiled before Peter trundled off to wherever he went each day, the location that she was still not clear of but had the desire to establish.

Peter was coming over around 1 p.m. to have some of the cake he'd made the day before. It was extremely unlike her, but she had already tucked into a good half of the cake. She had to admit, it was very tasty and she could see herself finishing it off by the evening. *And why not?* In two weeks, she wouldn't have to worry about how much sugar she ate.

May went into her kitchen and stood for a moment, as if arriving in an unfamiliar country. She turned around, glancing at the small dining table for four with the chairs neatly tucked under it that was almost hidden in the corner of the room. Furniture she had never used for eating, instead just sitting at the table a few times to study. It should have been for her family when they visited. Putting her hand to her forehead, she wondered what life could have been like had she been saved from loss—both her parents and Thomas. The meals they could have shared sat around the small table, Fran helping May cook as Victor and Thomas talked about politics or sports. She tilted her head back and let out a low wail, her mind and body wounded and tired. And then she turned silent again as her eyes moved to the kitchen bench where Peter's cake sat. She shook her head and took a bowl from a cupboard, milk from the fridge, then grabbed the Weetabix box from another cupboard. Her lips parted as she held the box in front of herself, the thought of Weetabix feeling somehow unusually unappealing. After staring some more and debating back and forth in her mind, she put the box back and grabbed a knife from a drawer. She cut a big chunk of cake and ate it there and then, standing at her kitchen bench. She couldn't recall the last time she hadn't had Weetabix for breakfast. It felt naughty and strange but delicious.

She savoured each mouthful, smelling the tart lemon as her fork cut through the golden, bouncy sponge cake. Once she had digested her out-of-character breakfast, she decided to go for a run in the park. Leaving the house an hour later, she stood on her doorstep and inhaled the fresh spring air as a gentle breeze tickled her arms. She heard a meowing. It was her visitor from a few days before. This time, the cat came running over.

'Whoa, you have some speed on your little legs,' she said gently as she crouched to pet her new friend. The cat immediately flopped, showing May its belly and looking at her with pleading desperation for a stroke. She rubbed the cat's head and sides, its warm little body vibrating as she stroked it. It was clear to see it was on the skinny side, and she frowned at the very obvious feel of its ribs. She wondered if it was old, but it didn't particularly look it. Not that she could one hundred per cent be sure.

'Do you have a home? Is anyone feeding you?'

The cat carried on with its soothing purrs. Maybe it had a medical issue? She wasn't sure which option to hope for, as none were positive.

'I need to go, little one,' she said in a high-pitched voice as the cat looked at her. 'You sure are friendly.' She put her hand to her forehead, realising she was doing that annoying baby voice people do. But the cat was rather cute.

She went to step past but found she couldn't. Everything was drawing her back to the cat. She looked away but ended up glancing at it again. The hunger worry lingered in her mind. 'Do you like chicken?' she finally asked, as if the cat could answer.

Going back into her flat, she took a little bit of fresh chicken from her fridge. She didn't want to encourage the cat and she still fretted that it could be on medication, but it was very skinny. And she wouldn't be able to continue her day without constant panicking if she did nothing.

The cat had its front paws on the doorstep in anticipation of her return, but it didn't enter her flat, as if there was an invisible barrier. She handed it the chicken, which it devoured with delight. Patting the cat's head, it almost gurgled a massive purr in gratitude.

'You're a sweet little thing, aren't you? And definitely hungry,' she said as its tail swished around her ankles. 'I think I will call you Alexander, after one of my favourite scientists.'

May found herself looking for Alexander when she returned home an hour later, then shook her head, as if to shake the nonsense out. Why would she want to get attached to a cat when she planned to end her life in two weeks? She was thinking about death in such a nonchalant way that it was almost starting to surprise her. But there was relief in acceptance that her last few weeks on Earth could be enjoyed, as she wouldn't have to deal with the everyday crap after that.

After a quick shower and change, it was almost time for Peter to come over. May sat down on her sofa and checked her mobile phone. There was a message from Scarlett saying she was shopping and had seen the biggest box of Weetabix ever and it reminded her of May. Putting her phone down, May felt a slap of sadness for her old life, the closeness she'd had with Scarlett dissolving. Or was it her pushing Scarlett away, knowing the inevitable?

The doorbell rang, and she rushed down the stairs and opened the door. Peter stood there with a sandy tail peeking out from behind him.

'Hi, May, is this cutie yours?' Peter pointed to Alexander, who was rubbing around his ankles.

May smiled, bending down to stroke the cat as he boldly stepped forward, almost into her flat. 'Hi, Peter, come in. And no, he isn't mine. I think he has just become a regular visitor. Now, go home, you,' she said to Alexander, weakly shooing with her arms as she shut the door behind Peter.

'Should I take my shoes off?' he asked.

'Don't worry about that,' she said, ushering him up the stairs and into the lounge. Previously, she hadn't let anyone in her flat with shoes on; now, well, she didn't really care.

'Lovely place you have here, pet. Very neat and tidy,' he said, glancing around at the clean white walls and the orange curtains at the lounge window. He nodded with approval. 'Minimalistic they say these days, don't they?'

'Thanks, Peter. Take a seat, and I'll put the kettle on.'

Peter sat on May's brown armchair, moving the orange cushion that leaned against the back of the chair to the side, as if in fear of squashing it. He stroked the cream fleece blanket that lay folded on a footstool to the side of the armchair whilst noticing a photo frame above the fireplace, facedown.

Once the kettle was boiled and the water poured into a teapot, she carried the teapot into the lounge on a tray with a milk jug and small bowl of sugar, as she didn't know how Peter liked his tea. Two stacked cups and two plates with a slice of cake on each were also balanced on the tray. She put it on the coffee table, making her tea how she liked it and leaving Peter to make his. After Trish's distaste for her coffee, she thought it best to stick to making her own hot drinks.

She took one of the plates and sat on the sofa, taking a big bite of the cake. 'Peter, I thought you couldn't bake. This is delicious, and my friend Trish thought so as well.'

Peter beamed and picked up the other plate. 'Thank you, May. Well, I never used to cook or bake. You see, my Anne looked after us all so well.' A light giggle left his mouth. 'But that was before she became poorly.'

May bit her lip, unsure as to whether she should ask the question in her mind. There was silence for a few seconds, nothing but the ticking of the clock in her lounge. 'Will she, erm... will Anne get better?' she finally said.

'No, pet, she won't.' He glanced out the window and then to his hands, as if searching for words to say. He didn't look up as he continued, 'I miss her. I miss her, and she is still alive and I see her every day. Where is the fairness in that, eh?'

May saw tears in his eyes as he lifted his cup from the coffee table and took a sip of his tea.

'That's where I go every day. To see my Anne. She's in a care home in town.' Peter looked into his cup and swallowed before returning his eyes to May. 'Every morning, I go and see her, sometimes helping the carers with breakfast, feeding Anne. But... she's more and more like a shell of my wife. As if daily, someone else crawls further and further into her body. Taking her, snatching her, poisoning her. My Anne.

'She doesn't know who I am, pet. Forty-two years together and she doesn't recognise me. The face she looked at all those years, as familiar as her own. Now she asks who I am.' Peter's lip trembled as he stared out the window. 'As time goes on, I think I recognise her less and less too. It's like a little part of her dies each day, and a little part of me dies with her.'

May felt a tear fall down her face and quickly wiped it away, not wanting Peter to see. He began sobbing and put his cup down, as if worried he'd spill his tea because of his quivering hands.

'May, I'm so sorry for putting that onto you. It's torturous at times, keeping it all in here.' He tapped his heart. 'I can't talk to the kids about her. It just feels so lonely. And you're good to talk to.'

She sat frozen for a few seconds, watching the old man sobbing and sharing his pain in her lounge as she overthought the best way to comfort him in a situation she couldn't make better. She was also astounded that he felt she was good to talk to—no one had ever said that to her before. Peter's gaze remained down and she saw his shoulders shaking slightly. Eventually, she went to him and gently placed her hand on his forearm, which felt a bit uneasy but appropriate given the situation. He turned and clung to her, holding her arms as if they were a lifebuoy to stop him from drowning. She stiffened with awkwardness, only to feel herself soften as she slowly put an arm around him.

The pair were silent for a minute or two before Peter took a deep breath in and spoke, 'May, I'm so sorry. I didn't mean to pour that onto you, pet.'

May tapped his shoulder gently and returned to her seat. 'It's okay. I'm sorry you have to go through that.' She looked down at her lap. 'How long has Anne been poorly? You don't have to tell me if you don't want to.' She wasn't sure why she was asking or if she actually wanted to know, but she sensed Peter needed to talk and she knew he may not have many people who listened. In all honesty, she could see that she and Peter didn't seem that different.

'It began almost six years ago, but I hid it for a few years. Denial probably. I still feel guilty for that. Like, maybe I could have helped her by actually accepting there was a problem and searching for help back then.' He wrung his hands together.

'The kids, Sam and Gina, they were adults themselves and worked away. Sam is in Birmingham and Gina is in Australia with her own family now, so they didn't come home much, didn't notice their mam's deterioration at first. We think these things won't happen, that it's just forgetfulness and that. But Sam began to notice, him being home more. Gina only comes over once a year, but we used to go there before Anne got worse.' Peter's voice crackled, and May gave him an encouraging smile.

'Anne got some medication from the doctor, and we just thought she would be fine. I buried my head, like us old men do. At Christmas, Sam managed to get some time off work and was going through a messy divorce, so he came home and spent some actual time with us. And he noticed. He was really concerned, and so was I. But I'd hoped it would sort itself out and I was scared. I feel bad about that every day. I could have done more.

'After Christmas, Sam called social services, saying we needed help as a couple. They put Anne in respite, where poorly people screamed in their rooms all night. It was awful, and she used to just cry when I visited. I couldn't leave her there.' Peter shook his head as he recalled the memory. 'I worked in homes when I was younger, you see, a bit different to care homes for elderly people, but I know what can go on.

'I wanted the best for Anne, the best care and support money could buy. That's why I'm here, pet, renting this flat. I sold our house, gave some money to Sam and Gina, telling the solicitors we owed them, else the robbing bast— else it would get taken off them. But it left me enough to get Anne into the best care home in the North East. We lost our home, but if it means keeping Anne around a bit longer, in the best place with top care, I'd do anything.'

May sat in quiet disbelief that he could still be the jolly, kind man he always presented as. 'That's so sad,' she finally said, clearing her throat as she felt the lump of emotion.

'Thanks, May, and for being a nice neighbour. More than that actually, pet. I class you as a friend, and I don't have many of those in the world.'

May watched Peter. Peter her neighbour whose story she now knew, who was crying in her lounge. Peter her neighbour who she couldn't help but also see as a friend and who seemed to feel as alone in the world as she did.

Chapter 27

18th May

It was soon Saturday morning, and May decided to go for a run in the park. It had become a four-times-a-week event for her during the last few weeks, and she enjoyed the surprising peace and quiet there. Maybe people didn't realise it was on their doorstep, a hidden oasis, just as she once hadn't realised. Either way, she was happy running around the lovely green space and inhaling the clean air, the earthy smell of the trees and the delicate, powdery scent of the flowers.

She walked to the park as her warm-up, stretching her arms in circles as she travelled and contemplated her weekend plans. Scarlett was coming home for Diane's birthday. Ethan would be joining Scarlett, but there would be time for them to catch up alone, which was something critical for May that she had repeatedly asked for reassurance about from Scarlett that week.

'Ask me that one more time and I will block you,' Scarlett had joked as May faked a smile. But things were getting real for May and the countdown was on for the day she'd end her life. Like a box of eggs in a fridge, she was reaching her expiry date.

There was a party planned for Diane in the afternoon on Sunday, and she was invited. Although social situations more often than not evoked a cold sweat and racking of her brain for excuses, it was different with Diane and Trevor. May had always liked Scarlett's parents, including her birth dad, and had fond memories of time spent with them. When the friends were fifteen years old,

Scarlett's parents divorced, leaving Scarlett devastated and cracks in May. Scarlett's parents had always felt so solid, so happy, untouchable from the stresses and pressures of life, love and relationships. Then it was over, their love melting away like ice cream in the sun.

For a good eighteen months after Scarlett's parents split up and her dad moved to a flat above a shop in town, May panicked, thinking her parents would be next; after all, Scarlett's parents had always seemed so in love. She became obsessed with asking her parents daily if they still loved each other. Victor and Fran understood and tried to reassure her, but it wasn't enough and it became a massive distraction in the year of her GCSE school exams as she tried to make sense as an outsider of the rotting wood that Scarlett's parents' relationship had become. She internalised the divorce in an unhealthy way, demonstrating another example of how she struggled with the unpredictable, with emotions and things out of her control. She would go so far as to say it had impacted her more than Scarlett, who although upset, quickly adapted. Eventually, Diane met Trevor, and Scarlett gained another caring man in her life.

May crossed the road and ran her hands through her hair. There were so many of Scarlett's traits she wished she had.

Despite the flip side of the coin, May was looking forward to Diane's birthday, especially since she knew it was afternoon tea being delivered by a local patisserie that had a five-star hygiene rating. Her stomach rumbled slightly as she thought about the offering. She'd purchased Diane a navy-blue umbrella for her birthday that was small enough to fit in her handbag, and it was wrapped and ready to be gifted along with a pretty card. Of course, it was something Diane had mentioned she wanted to Scarlett and Scarlett had then relayed to May. She had her usual social anxiety still despite one less stress of not having to attempt a surprise gift, but she wanted to see Diane, Trevor and Cumberland the dog for the last time.

May reached the entrance to the park. Walking in, she looked around, tilted her head back and inhaled. She almost felt in a bubble, content in a place that had become an escape. As she jogged her usual route past the lake, she watched a train of baby ducks noisily following their mother. She observed the regular coots and swans gliding in the water as she took in the slight musky smell of the vegetation in the lake that had become somewhat of a comfort in her routine despite not being exactly pleasant. The morning sun reflected off the water, making it gleam with inviting splendour.

A squirrel bounced across her path and up a tree, zigzagging with ease as she watched and smiled. There was a beauty in nature that she had never fully realised. The smells, sights, sounds and animals. It felt as if she were on their stage, watching and partaking in their stunning performance.

Why had she never appreciated the simple things around her? We walk around with our eyes and mind closed, wrapped up in the pressures of life. It wasn't until she didn't have that heavy load to carry that she could see. Yet it wasn't enough because her life as it was wouldn't be sustainable. She would have to return to the rat race, be hurt by someone else, lose people over and over. She would return to being that square person trying to fit into a round world. She often blended into the background, unseen and invisible. Yet she had always been seen by her parents and by Scarlett. Then by Trish and Thomas. Now by Peter. She finally thought she was possibly being accepted, not just by people who *had* to accept her due to an obligation—family and childhood friends. But the pain was too deep, the fear of loss too strong as it blared in her mind like an ambulance siren. She couldn't face any more rejection, distress and invisibility.

She stopped running, suddenly having to hold her side and bend over in fear of vomiting. She slowly made her way to a nearby bench, hunched over, noticing the wooden seat had a plaque screwed onto the backrest as she sat down. After taking a moment for the sick feeling to pass, she turned her body slightly to see the plaque.

To Keith, eternity wouldn't have been long enough to spend with you. Love always, Brenda.

May pressed her lips together as a tiny welp escaped her mouth. She sat for a minute, regulating her breathing before she rose from the seat, took one last look at the plaque and began to walk home. On her journey back, she thought about Peter. He had been so upset at her flat the other night that she had decided to give him a little space. She wasn't sure if this was the best thing to do, but it was the decision she'd made.

She was sad for Peter, who, as much as she didn't like to admit it, had made an impression on her. He had referred to her as his 'friend'—a responsibility she wanted like a dose of the flu. She wasn't meant to be making new friends.

She kicked an empty pop can in frustration as she walked, then, feeling bad, she picked it up and carried it to recycle at home despite her mind going into overdrive about where it could have been. Sometimes, she felt she was in a bubble that no one could ever understand, just floating slightly away from people.

As she reached her front door, she noticed the car that had been outside of Peter's house quite a bit since Friday night. She hoped it was one of his children that he had mentioned, but she hadn't seen anyone around. She panicked in case there was a problem but worried about intruding, so she pushed it to the back of her mind, instead thinking about the nice weekend she would have with Scarlett. Going into her flat, she put the empty pop can in the recycling and then washed her hands. After a quick shower, she sat on the sofa and opened her note-book. Looking at her list, she began crossing off what she had achieved since the last time. She put a line through 'Spend time with Scarlett', as she would be seeing her later. May had also discussed meeting Trish somewhere outside of the flat over the next few days and would finalise a plan. The letter writing had begun, but she was finding it too emotional to write them in one go.

3rd May

To do (before 31st May):

- ~~Spend time with Scarlett.~~

- ~~Spend time with Trish that isn't her looking after me.~~

- Go and see Uncle Terence.

- ~~Visit the cemetery.~~

- Visit Lawson-Wray's (possibly).

- ~~Take library books back to university and pay fines.~~

- ~~Run in the park.~~

- ~~Sort throughout the house; take things to charity~~ and leave notes on things I want to give to others.

- Arrange finances.

- Write letters to Scarlett and Trish—make them as positive as possible and remember to tell them that I love them and why I love them.

- ~~Buy paracetamols.~~

- Write will to include Mam and Dad's house to go to Uncle Terence.

- Sort through some things at Mam and Dad's house.

May heard the music blasting from Scarlett's car and saw headlights lighting up the road for a few seconds before Scarlett pulled up outside May's flat, ready for a takeaway and a catch up. There had been previous talk of a night out, but May had shared her disinterest, feeling it would be a waste of their time together to be around other people and knowing that alcohol, her mood and plans wouldn't be a good mix. She rushed down the stairs and opened the door. The immediate area was temporarily illuminated, practically putting a spotlight on Alexander, who was lying half under a hedge, his head poking out, eyes fixated on May. As Scarlett turned her headlights and engine off, May walked a few steps out of her door to the approaching Alexander.

'Hello, you,' she cooed, about to crouch to stroke his head.

'And hello, you,' Scarlett said, grabbing hold of May tightly, Alexander going completely unnoticed. 'Oh, hang on.' Scarlett pulled away and bounced on the spot. 'I forgot something in the boot.'

May followed her, asking about her journey as Scarlett grabbed a rucksack and the two headed into May's flat. Knowing the usual routine, Scarlett took her shoes off at the bottom of the stairs and May handed her a clean pair of fluffy socks that had become Scarlett's when she visited. The pair went straight upstairs and into the kitchen. May made a pot of tea and grabbed some shop-bought cake slices, which weren't a patch on Peter's baking. They moved to the lounge, talking as they walked. Scarlett headed towards the sofa first, abruptly stopping.

'Erm, May, have you bought a cat?'

'What?' May stepped past and looked to the armchair. She burst out laughing at the sight of Alexander the opportunist curled up tightly. He even had his eyes covered with a white paw. 'No, I haven't. But this little dude, who I've named Alexander, clearly wants somewhere to snooze. He must've snuck in when we went to your car.' Standing hand on hip, she looked at Alexander, who was paying no attention. She was secretly pleased that he saw her home as welcoming and her company as acceptable.

Scarlett put the tray of tea on the coffee table and leaned over to the armchair. She gently stroked Alexander, who didn't even bother to open his eyes, instead showing his appreciation with a low, soothing purring. 'Aw, he's lovely. Where does he live?'

'I don't know. I'm not sure if he's homeless. He's been hanging around the last week and, well, he's pretty small.' May stared intently at him.

'He clearly wants to live here, and you can't say you don't want him to. You've even named him, no doubt after one of your favourite scientists?' Scarlett looked at May knowingly.

'It suits him though, doesn't it?'

Scarlett nodded, still stroking the new house guest as he remained cosy on May's chair, as if it had been made especially for him. They both took a seat on May's sofa.

'How's Ethan?' May asked.

'Oh, he's good, thanks. Sends his love and looks forward to seeing you tomorrow. He's settled into the new school and thinks it's great. It also means he can do DIY on the house when it's the school holidays. All part of my plan.' Scarlett faked an evil laugh and rubbed her hands together.

'Hey, look at this.' She leaned over to her rucksack, made a drum roll sound and pulled out a photo album. May recognised it straight away, and a smile crept across her face. 'I found it when I was looking for some photos for Mam's birthday. Oh my gosh, May, we were such geeks. And our fashion sense back then is hilarious. Look at that bubble dress.' She placed the photo album between them both.

They began to flick through, laughing, gasping and cringing.

'Our matching rhinestone jeans.' May threw her head back and clutched her stomach. 'Scarlett, we loved them.'

They grabbed hands, giggling. The photos were no older than fifteen years, but May loved that even in the age of mobile phones and photos taken in the blink of an eye, Scarlett had taken the trouble to get the photos printed off. It was something May had always done. Even if her walls were parched of memories hanging from them, she had the photos in her albums as well as in her head.

'And those coloured leggings. I mean, I've never been one for fashion, but they are vile. Emerald-green leggings,' May added, holding her head.

They flicked through the album, commenting on every page. It was a wonderful trip down memory lane for May and her lifelong friend. May had been through so much and Scarlett had always been there no matter the miles.

'Remember that holiday?' Scarlett pointed to a double page of photos from the time she'd gone with May and her parents to Greece. 'Oh wow, it was brill. Remember that sleazy waiter who was trying it on with me? He was ancient, and your dad went mental at him, screaming and shouting at the creep even though he didn't have a clue what he was saying in his broad Geordie accent.'

'Yeah, hadaway an' shite yer knacker doesn't really mean much to a Greek person.' May howled with laughter.

'Oh, May, it was a precious time. I have such lovely memories of your family and being part of it.' She grabbed her friend's hand and looked at her, the mood turning serious instantaneously.

May felt her bottom lip quivering, then the tears began to fall, knowing those times were gone and soon all that Scarlett would have would be memories of her.

'I'm sorry, hun, I didn't want to upset you. I thought it would be nice to take a ballet-pump walk down memory lane and see photos of us and some of your parents. I should've asked.'

'No, I'm pleased you brought them. They're lovely. It's just so hard, Scarlett. It's like a niggle that never goes away. A dull ache that just rushes back into your day, your night, your mind.' She swallowed. 'I don't feel in control of it, and the people who always made me feel better—well, alongside you—they aren't here anymore. I can't ask them the simplest of things, they can't help me or comfort me. I'm lonely and feel I won't ever not be, and I miss them so much that I can't breathe at times.' Her shoulders drooped as she let the tears fall, wanting Scarlett to offer the answers, a solution to keep her alive.

Scarlett took May's hands and placed them both in between hers. 'May, I can't even pretend I know how you feel. You've had the shittiest of times these last few years, and I wish with all my heart that I could take your pain away. I'm sorry I'm not here much physically, but always reach out to me. You know I'll always try and help.'

Scarlett gave May a soothing hug, and they had a minute of silence. When May pulled away, she looked at her closest friend and down at the opened photo album that showed the innocence and happiness of youth.

'We have loads more memories to make. Your parents will always be in your heart, May, but I'm still here. Love you.'

May nodded, bit her lip and flipped the page. There were photos of Scarlett and May pretending to be at a wedding. The pair laughed and looked at each other as May's tears started to stop and dry on her face.

'You can get dressed up like that again, May; you'll be maid of honour for me in a few years, I just need to coerce Ethan into proposing first,' she said, rolling her eyes. 'And I better be your chief bridesmaid when you find your lucky future husband,' she added, giving May a playful nudge.

May sighed quietly. 'You've always been the bestest friend anyone could ask for, you know that, don't you?'

Scarlett tilted her head and fluttered her eyelashes in joke of the comment.

'I'm serious. You made my school life and beyond bearable. The times I felt like a complete freak, I was always accepted by you.'

'You were never a freak, May, I wish you wouldn't use that word.'

'You've always had my back. I know I'm not the easiest person at times, but you never gave up on me or thought I was dragging you down. Even though at times, I definitely dragged you down.'

Scarlett shook her head. 'Hey, what's this all about? Stop being silly, May. You've always been there for me as well. We are stuck with each other, and remember what we used to say?'

May looked at her, unable to not smile. She did remember. They'd been saying it since they were eleven, back when they used to play Scarlett's bingo game.

They spoke in unison, 'When we are eighty-eight and two fat ladies, we'll move into a retirement home together and get fatter.'

'I love you, Scarlett, and I'm sorry if I did ever upset you or you felt you had to look after me.' May looked to the floor as guilt crept in. Not giving Scarlett time to answer, she took a deep breath and said, 'Right, let's get those pizzas ordered; I'm famished. And I will have to find something for that one to eat.' She pointed to a cosy Alexander on the armchair, who had remained in his blissful ignorance throughout the photo album flicking.

A few hours later, May waved goodbye to Scarlett as she drove away, her music blasting again. She rubbed the sandy fur off her sleeves from carrying Alexander outside, who had now disappeared back under the hedge. The same car was still parked outside of Peter's, and worry twisted in her torso. *Is he okay?* She ran her hands over her head and then visualised putting the thought in a balloon and watching it float away—something her mam had always told her to do. It was a shame she couldn't make her sadness, loneliness and grief float away as easily as Mam had always made everything sound.

After locking her front door, she sighed, guilty and exhausted from lying to her friend. She'd had a lovely night with Scarlett—distance and time always felt redundant when they met up—but she did miss having her friend at home. However, May knew what the future held for her, and being with Scarlett felt bittersweet.

After washing her face and brushing her teeth, she climbed into bed. Her bedroom window, as always, was open, as she couldn't stand sleeping in stagnant air. The street she lived on was quiet, and being a cul-de-sac, it had limited traffic through. She reached over to her bedside cabinet, picking up her notebook to finish off

Trish's goodbye letter, ignoring the tiny fleeting feeling that maybe there could be another way. The tip of her pen touched the paper and stopped there as she heard a noise. Taking her pen away from the page, she held her breath to listen intently. She heard it again.

She put her notebook and pen on the bedside table, then climbed out of bed and pushed the window further open. Leaning out to look for the disturbance, she discovered it looking up from outside at her. The disturbance's tail was in the air.

'You have a big mouth for such a little thing, Alexander.'

He talked back at her, looking up with golden pleading eyes. She peered up and down the street, wondering if he lived in any of those houses, but she couldn't help but still feel that strong suspicion that he didn't have a home at all. She imagined him lying back under that hedge all night or wandering the streets, dodging speeding cars if he ventured too far. The cat who craved affection out there on his lonesome.

Stepping away from the window to the tune of Alexander's meows, she headed downstairs. Alexander was already waiting on her doorstep when she opened her front door, and he bounded inside and straight up the stairs, like the king of the castle.

'Oh, come on in, then, Alexander. Make yourself at home, I guess.' She rolled her eyes playfully and locked the front door again.

She headed to the lounge, ready to give him a stroke goodnight before going back to bed, but he wasn't on the armchair. She figured that he was probably hiding, not wanting her to put him back outside.

Returning to her bedroom, she paused in the doorway, smiling. 'Hey, cheeky.'

Alexander vibrated and padded on her fleece blanket as she headed over to him. He pushed his little head into her hand, purring with delight. She looked at his small body and thought how brave, or maybe just desperate, he was, demanding to be in her house and trusting her. She looked at him and swore he looked back at her with a type of love she had never felt before. She felt it too—a warmness and calmness in her chest as she stroked him on her bed. She could have stroked his beautiful sandy coat all night, and she was sure he would let her.

Eventually, she managed to slide into bed, Alexander lying almost in the centre. She curled around him, listening to him purr as she fell asleep.

Chapter 28

20th May

—

May woke early as usual. She moved her legs slowly across the bed as her body began to wake until she felt a lump next to her. Leaning up, she was met with Alexander's gaze and a good-morning meow. She couldn't help but smile as she stretched over and patted his warm head. He closed his eyes in contentment, beginning his addictive purr before getting up from where he had slept all night and moving towards her. When he reached her, he stretched up and rubbed his head on her face before yawning.

'Urgh, Alexander, your breath stinks.' May laughed, giving him a quick stroke before moving to get up. Her guest jumped off the bed and sauntered off into the lounge. Putting her slippers on, she thought about how trusting animals were and how much humans could learn from them.

'Have you not got a home to go to, mister?' she said, walking into the lounge.

Alexander sat cleaning himself. There was a chance she was allowing an owned cat into her house, and that made her feel guilty, but the thought of that not being the case and him having no one made her feel worse.

She thought about Alex, her university friend, who loved cats. He always said that he'd never bought a cat in his life. Instead, his family had adopted about ten moggies over the years, all of them finding him and his family, homing themselves there. It was as if they knew there was a vacancy at a cat-loving house. May didn't feel she gave off the cat-hotel vibes, having never owned a pet in her almost twenty-five years on Earth. She had also heard cats were a bit psychic, but she struggled to absorb and give any remote validation to something that could be questioned around proof. Whatever it was with this cat and however much she didn't want to admit it, the skinny, little sandy boy made her happy. Maybe she could keep him for a week and try to rehome him, perhaps with Peter. She wasn't even sure if the persistent cat was homeless. Maybe she would put some posters through people's doors or leave them on lampposts—found rather than lost posters. There were a lot of maybes.

Alexander got up and slowly made his way out of the room. As if he'd navigated her flat countless times, he sauntered into the kitchen and sat beside the fridge. He looked at her, then the fridge and meowed.

'Oh my word, really?'

After feeding the expectant cat some chicken, Alexander strolled down the stairs. She followed, opening the door. He stepped out, then turned back to May as if saying thank you and goodbye, like a guest checking out of a B&B. She patted him on the head, and he meowed before going off on his travels.

She noticed the car had gone from outside of Peter's house. She decided she would have her Weetabix and then give Peter a knock, just to check all was okay. Rushing her breakfast, she pulled on a sweater and practically jogged to Peter's door. Knocking, she leaned from foot to foot. He soon answered, his jolly smile appearing upon seeing her.

'Oh hello, May, how are you diddling?'

'Hi, Peter, erm, I really just wanted to check you're okay, as I haven't seen you for a few days and, well, there was a car and I was a bit worried in case you weren't well or something,' she spewed and then blushed. She realised she was probably sounding silly, nosy or overreacting. Maybe all three.

'Ah, pet, I'm really touched that you were worried. Well, no, that sounds like I'm pleased you were worried, but I'm absolutely not pleased.' He frowned at himself. 'I mean, it's nice you care. You're a lovely lass, May.'

May half-grimaced at Peter, feeling awkward at the compliment. 'Well, as long as you're okay,' she said, starting to back away from his door. She felt as if she'd shown herself up and now wanted nothing more than to get away.

'Are you okay though?' Peter asked, tilting his head.

May stopped, eyes slightly widening. She could lie, but she'd never been the best liar; something in her almost prevented her from telling fibs, just like she couldn't keep secrets. The past few weeks, she had felt like an Olympic-winning liar despite technically only holding back what she planned to do on her birthday with regards to living or dying. It was more she hadn't offered her thoughts. But it was hard, and her shoulders felt heavy.

There was something in Peter's voice, the way he'd asked if she was okay. A tone, an expression, an emphasis perhaps that she had not heard from him before. Turning back to face him, his eyes stared into hers, and in those seconds, she felt she would cry. Biting her lip, she put her hands together and desperately wanted to be honest, even just for a moment.

'Sometimes I am and sometimes I'm not. Most of the time, no, I'm not okay.'

The colour had drained from Peter's usually flush face, and he nodded slowly. 'Oh, May, we can't have that. Can I help you in any way? Sometimes big thoughts and problems can feel better shared.' He looked at her, his eyes kind and his palms facing up.

Could he help me? She wasn't sure he could. No one could bring her parents back and she didn't want to be talked out of her plan to end her life. She certainly didn't want him to help her find a reason for living, because even if she could feel almost complete again, it would only be temporary.

'No, Peter, but thank you.' She felt wrong for burdening him, so she feigned a smile and changed the subject. 'But I'm going to my best friend's mam's birthday party this afternoon, so that will be nice.'

Peter mirrored her smile, but concern lingered in the frown on his forehead. 'That's great, pet. Bring me a slice of cake back, will you?' He rubbed his hands together but looked at May seriously, as if awaiting a doctor's diagnosis. 'Oh, and the car is Sam's, my son. He's coming home,' he added in an instantly more upbeat tone.

May nodded before walking away, pleased for Peter but feeling a compelling need to get quickly into her flat, her sanctuary.

Once inside, she put her hand to her forehead. People, emotions, life... it was all just too much for her at times. *Why am I so incapable of being normal? Why can't I just be better at pretending?* She sniggered, realising that actually, she had become pretty damn marvellous at pretending, considering in ten days' time she planned on ending her life and no one had the foggiest. She laughed, then it immediately hit her that there was nothing in the slightest that was funny about her situation, and sadness ran into her, assaulting her like a punch from a heavy-weight boxer. She dropped to the floor, against the back of her door, where she sat and sobbed for her mam and dad. She sat there, at the bottom of her stairs, until her bum went to sleep and her tears dried to her face and neck. She wanted to stay there all day and avoid the world, but it was the day of Diane's birthday afternoon tea and she could hear a text message alert on her mobile phone upstairs.

Running her hands through her hair, as if to comb out the defeat she felt, she pushed herself up and walked up the stairs. After checking her phone and replying to a text message from Scarlett and ignoring one from Trish, she had a long, hot shower. The water helped soothe her fragile mind and, once out and wrapped in her dressing gown, she decided to paint her fingernails and toenails. Pampering wasn't a priority on her life list and she was nowhere near high maintenance, whatever that was these days.

She thought about a girl at Lawson-Wray's, Chloe, who spent almost all of her wages on self-care—filling her face with syringes full of what could be anything and constantly searching for a perfection that didn't exist—and was only May's age. She claimed to spend hundreds on hair extensions, face rejuvenating concoctions and teeth treatments that made her mouth look so bright that it could be used to search caves. Her eyebrows had been arches, then slugs, then something that represented a cartoon expression. One time, she'd come in and mentioned she was injecting herself with chemicals that tanned her skin from the inside out. May was beyond perplexed and asked Chloe why she couldn't just be happy with who she was. She answered, as she looked May up and down, 'Cos no one is these days, May. We're all looking for perfection, including you in some way.'

May never forgot what Chloe had said because she was right. We are all searching for something, the seed of satisfaction that keeps growing and stops us from envying others too much. All of us hunting for perfection, the unobtainable. We spend life wishing we had this and that, wanting what we haven't got and not appreciating what we have. May was just like Chloe: searching for something. The only difference was May had given up on her search, tired of looking, defeated. She didn't have Chloe's staying power, and at that moment, she realised how wrong she had been about her.

There were only a few cars on and around Diane and Trevor's drive when May arrived, helping to ease her social anxiety. She pushed open the side gate to the back garden, and Cumberland came darting over. She bent down to stroke him as his tongue hung out and his little body almost shook with the joy of a familiar face who would provide extra attention. Glancing up, she saw Trevor standing by the recycling bin to the left of the gate. He lifted the lid and emptied some cardboard out of a plastic tub. Turning, he spotted her and smiled.

'Oh, May, hello.' He wiped his hands on his trousers and walked over. 'It's so lovely to see you,' he said warmly, embracing her.

'Thanks, Trevor, how are you?' she replied, bending over to stroke Cumberland again, who was jumping on his tiny legs with excitement.

'I'm good ta, and you? Is it getting any easier?' He looked at her, frowning.

'Sometimes, and then other times I feel I'm going backwards and I won't ever move forward.' She shrugged and, trying to be dismissive, added, 'It's life, isn't it? It is what it is.'

Trevor tilted his head and nodded slowly. 'Our Scarlett's always said you're mentally tough and braver than you realise, and I saw it at the funerals. You're strong, May, and I for one admire you. But remember, we are all here if you ever need us, okay?'

May's face dropped as she temporarily went inside her mind. *Do people really mean it, or do they just say things because they feel they have to?* She knew Trevor cared, just like Diane did, but it was all time-bound. People had their own stuff to deal with, good and bad. They couldn't be the protective quilt that she could wrap herself in forever. The intensity of asking, texting, calling, offers of support, kind words and compassion had a shelf life for grief and low moods. Even the most patient of people break off, dropping like petals as the seasons change.

Trevor tapped May's arm and gave her a reassuring smile, bringing her back to the here and now. 'Right, come on in, let's get you some of the most delicious brownies I've ever tasted before Ethan inhales the lot.'

She was greeted by more hellos and hugs from Scarlett, Diane and Ethan. The afternoon tea, spread across tables under a gazebo, looked delicious. On seeing the display of baked goods arranged as edible artwork, her stomach growled louder than Alexander's strong purrs. She moved over to the tables and glanced at the tempting delights. There were cupcakes with thick icing piped on top, finished with a chunk of chocolate in each. Slithers of cheesecake with ganache coverings and sprinkles of biscuit crumbs that made them look almost too pretty to eat. A large red velvet cake that popped with alluring colour and thick frosting. Chocolate brownies that appeared to be the perfect mix of fudgy, gooey, chewy heaven. Then there was a selection of scones. Some had succulent sultanas popping out, others flashes of colour, some chunks of chocolate and all with an inviting golden top. She could smell the sweetness and was almost salivating. Her appetite had really increased the last week, especially for sweet things, and she couldn't wait to tuck in.

After filling her plate, she spent the next few hours enjoying the party. Diane was like royalty for the day and rightly so, with Trevor rushing around, checking on guests and constantly topping people up—mostly Diane—with champagne and tea.

Sitting on the rattan furniture, May put the last forkful of cake in her mouth. Closing her eyes as she ate it and feeling the spring warmth on her face, she leant back against the sofa cushion. 'Scarlett, those raspberry and white chocolate scones are unreal, and so is the red velvet cake,' she exclaimed, turning to the cake table for something she hadn't yet tasted.

'I know. I've consumed at least 8,000 calories this afternoon, and I ain't stopping anytime soon.' She made a snorting noise as she patted her stomach, and the two started laughing. 'It's so nice to see you having a good time, and you look lush, as always.' Scarlett leaned against May's shoulder, and May kissed her head, not quite able to answer.

Scarlett looked over at Ethan, and May noticed the tenderness in her gaze.

'I'm pleased you found someone who makes you feel whole, Scarlett. Some people search a lifetime and never find love. You're very lucky, as is Ethan.' May smiled through a stab of longing.

'Aw, thanks, hun. Yeah, he's a keeper. I know you'll find your happy ever after as well.' Scarlett grabbed May's hand and looked at her the way a patient parent looks at a child who is reluctant to jump in a swimming pool.

'I don't know about that; I feel pretty unlovable, well, except for the love from a stray cat.' May never meant it to be funny, it wasn't, and she wasn't joking, but Scarlett pressed her lips together and then let out a squeak of laughter. May followed, and the friends sat there, holding hands and laughing as if the funniest thing on Earth had just been said.

The rest of the afternoon was wonderful. Diane loved her umbrella and May chatted with Ethan, who thankfully didn't mention Oscar Sullivan.

'I love her so much, May,' he said when she talked about how brilliant Scarlett was. 'I can't imagine a world without her in it.'

May looked at him watching Scarlett with such affection at the other side of the garden. All we ever want for our friends is for them to be happy, safe and loved. She knew Scarlett had that with Ethan, her mother and step-father. Love floated around the air in the back garden, and even May breathed it in that afternoon.

Scarlett mentioned she would try to come back up for a day or two on the weekend of May's birthday; if not, they would celebrate in a month's time. May held Scarlett tighter than she ever had as they said goodbye that afternoon, unsure as to whether she would see her again. She slipped away without saying a proper goodbye to Diane and Trevor or even Cumberland, unable to take any further emotion. For those five hours before her departure, May not only felt normal, but she felt a sensation that had been so fleeting for the last few months—happiness and a desperate yearning to make it last.

'Cake delivery,' May said, holding out a cardboard cake box.

Peter's hands reached for the box, like a toddler's hands stretching out of a buggy. 'Oooh lovely. Thank you, May, that's really kind. Won't you come in for a cuppa?'

May nodded and followed Peter into his flat.

'I'll make them, Peter, I've been getting looked after all day,' she said, moving towards the kitchen as Peter followed.

'That would be lovely.' He clasped his hands together. 'I don't get that many cuppas made for me these days, and doesn't it always taste so much better when someone else makes them?'

May nodded. 'My friend, Trish, makes the best cup of tea. She would make me two or three a day at work and always bring a few biscuits. At times, it felt like the best thing I had ever tasted.' She glanced around Peter's clean and tidy kitchen. The walls were painted a pale lemon and a sky-blue blind hung at the window. The light was pouring in, making the walls even sunnier.

She rubbed her neck, then turned to find the kettle. It stood on the kitchen countertop next to three blue canisters. There was a teapot covered with a knitted dark blue cosy on the other side of where the kettle sat, and she smiled as she filled the kettle with water. She hadn't seen a tea cosy for years, but her mam used to have one that made an appearance when visitors came round.

'Do you not work now, May?' Peter asked as he watched her look for the cups. 'Top left cupboard, and the spoons are in the drawer in front of you there.'

May followed his instruction and replied to his question, trying to sound flippant. 'No, erm, I've had a few months off. I'm not sure if I will ever go back, to be honest.'

'Well, you've your whole life ahead of you, pet, a long, prosperous career I bet. The world's your gift, May.'

May put the made tea onto a tray, which she'd found behind Peter's kettle, and carried it through to the lounge, placing it on the little side table as Peter cradled the box of cakes, some kitchen roll in his other hand.

'Where was it you worked?'

'Lawson-Wray's, the estate agency in town.'

'Ah, I see. I bet you're brilliant at your job.'

'I only work there part-time, but I've been... was there years.'

Peter nodded in silence as he opened the box of cakes, eyes widening as he saw the selection. He picked out a brownie, sliding the box to May, who put her hand up as a decline of the offer of more cake.

Peter looked back at May expectantly as he took his first bite, eyes immediately displaying pleasure at the taste.

'Well, I was at university as well, doing a master's in science.'

Peter's eyebrow raised. 'Crikey, May, you must be very intelligent, pet. Good on you.'

'Not so good. I didn't finish it, and now, well, it's too late.' She picked at the sleeve of her hoody and looked the other way. She couldn't help but feel disappointed in herself. She'd always known what job she wanted, the studies she would do to get there, and now she'd dropped out at one of the last hurdles to reaching her dream.

'Of course it isn't too late; you're only a young lass. Please go back and finish your studies. The world needs more scientists, more people like you. That's how they will help so many, like my Anne.' Peter looked at May hopefully as he leaned his shoulders forward.

'It *is* too late, Peter. I can't.' She bit her lip, unable to express exactly why it was too late.

'Poppycock. You know, I didn't graduate until I was almost thirty-five years old, and I'd do it all again if I could.'

Peter had a degree? She'd expected he had maybe worked in a shop or in a factory or something until he retired. But he was an academic? She had made an assumption, perhaps because of his age and the way he talked, similar to her dad. She had never asked, but now she wanted to know. 'What did you study?'

'Ah, that's a story for another time.' He flicked his wrist, as if he could flick all to do with himself away and put pure focus on May. 'I'm more interested in why you quit, May, and why you won't go back to university or Lawson-Wray's.'

May lightly clenched her fists, holding back the anger at him for not dropping the subject and the upset it was making her feel thinking about all she'd given up. 'You're very nosy, Peter.'

'No, pet, I'm interested, not nosy.' He chuckled.

May shook her head and looked at the floor, unclenching her fists. She hoped he hadn't noticed. Peter had some way of making her talk, and she couldn't decide if she liked or loathed him for it.

'I've had a hard few years. My mam died nearly three years ago and my dad passed away in March.' She swallowed. Her life, or what was left of it, felt like broken glass on the floor, waiting for someone to sweep it up and put it in the bin. Even with people around her, she felt unimportant. 'I just feel as if things will always be hard.'

'I'm sorry,' Peter said quietly.

'It's not your fault; you don't need to be sorry.'

'But I am cos you're a lovely lass and I bet your parents were so very proud of you. I'm sorry you've had so much pain, May, I truly am.'

He spoke with such a compassionate softness that she felt a validation of feeling so broken. That perhaps feeling hopeless was normal given the trauma she had experienced. She let a tear fall down her face before wiping it away with her sleeve. She sat with her head down, and the pair remained silent for a few seconds until Peter spoke again.

'If you ever want to talk, I'm here.'

May looked up at Peter and smiled a half-hearted smile. As someone who at times struggled in social situations, especially with people she didn't really know and following an afternoon of chatting with many people, she was regretting coming to see him. She worried she had said too much, not wanting to burden him or for him to pity her. Caring complicated things, and she equally didn't want to begin to care about Peter. But she had felt compelled to check on him and now she felt compelled to know more of his story.

Fran used to always say to her, 'May, darling, in life, most people will like you if you show interest in them. It can sometimes be hard, and sometimes people are like you and prefer to listen rather than talk. Some people love the sound of their own voice and you will wish you never asked.' At this point, May would always giggle. 'But kindness is something that never goes out of fashion. Ask questions, show interest and be kind.'

May was thinking about her own sadness and loss, but being here with Peter, she knew that maybe he wanted to talk and that she needed to show kindness. She had never been a great talker nor a great listener. She often failed to see the rainbow-coloured spectrum that lay between black and white. But she was certain Peter was trying to help her whether she wanted it or not. And she had to help him back despite her reluctance to get close. So, May asked the question because she knew deep down that she already cared despite the searing pain in her own heart. 'So, tell me, Peter, how has Anne been this week?'

For the next hour, she listened as Peter shared how his week had been with Anne, from the detail of taking his flask from May to helping with breakfast a few times during the week. He described Anne's room at the care home and pointed to the most recent picture of her on the wall before she'd begun her cruel health decline. May stood up and went over to the wall that was filled with photos of precious times. Peter joined her and pointed to a photo of them both.

'Look at us on our wedding day. I was thin back then and had more hair.' He chuckled, and May laughed too. 'And my Anne, she was always a beauty.' He ran his fingers delicately over an aged small photo in a frame. 'My Samuel—he is, was, my brother—he used to say I was punching above my weight courting Anne. He was right. She was a head-turner... she still is. A smile that shines so brightly it could melt an iceberg. It was instant love.' He rubbed his hand over his mouth and cleared his throat. 'Some days, I visit Anne in her home and I can almost see the twenty-six-year-old nurse she was when I first met her. She's in there, hiding behind a wall of confusion and fear as her brain gets weaker. But sometimes, just sometimes, she peeks out and I get to fall in love with her all over again.'

May continued to look at the wall, side by side with Peter. She heard him sniff and, glancing to her right, she saw him wiping his eyes.

'It's the cruellest of illnesses, it really is. This is why you need to finish your science studies and help find cures for these killers.'

May didn't acknowledge what Peter said and instead kept looking at the photo of him and Anne on one of the happiest days of their lives. A blow of sadness hit her; Peter still had Anne, yet she was so far away physically and mentally. She thought about her own parents and how her dad had never got over losing his love. Even with her scientific brain, she hoped that they were together now somewhere, somehow, maybe.

Was there someone for everyone? She didn't know, but she knew Fran was for Victor and Anne was for Peter. She couldn't not believe in love, as she had seen it and she had sampled it with Thomas. But it wasn't Peter and Anne love nor Fran and Victor love. It wasn't Diane and Trevor love, Trish and Brian love nor Scarlett and Ethan love. May wanted that love, and even though she had resigned herself to never getting it and leaving this world without it, as she continued to look at the wedding photo on the lounge wall in Peter Parsley's flat, May McClelland wanted love more than anything.

Chapter 29

21st May

May turned her head and got a face full of Alexander, who was half on her pillow. He stirred, and his tail gently flicked her face.

'Make yourself comfortable, why don't you,' she said, yawning. She moved her body, and he startled, staring at her as if to say, 'How absolutely dare you.' She took her arm out of the quilt and stroked his head, feeling the warm, soft fur. He began purring, and she closed her eyes again, continuing to stroke him, listening to the tune of his happy voice that felt like a spoonful of medicine. She'd let Alexander in on her way to her flat from Peter's, just as she had the night before. This time though, she'd snapped a photo of him by her fridge as he'd waited once again for his evening chicken. She was enjoying the feline's company and having something to look after, but he wasn't hers and it could only ever be temporary. Opening her eyes, she stopped stroking Alexander, who remained content, stretched out. She rubbed her face as she climbed out of bed, sliding her feet into her slippers.

'Come on, then,' she said to Alexander, patting him gently to alert him as she put on her dressing gown before shuffling out of the bedroom. She knew her exhaustion was mental, but it always seemed to massively affect her physically too after spending time with people. Today, it was as if her social battery had completely drained, and she wasn't sure how many hours or days it would take to charge.

Although she was glad she'd checked on Peter, by the time he was talking about his son being there until Friday while he looked for somewhere to rent in order to move back home following his divorce, Big Ben had almost been ringing in her head. Like May, Peter was lonely; unlike her, he liked to talk and talk and talk.

May forked some tuna from a tin onto a plate for Alexander whilst he impatiently meowed and stretched his white front paws up the kitchen cabinets.

'For sir,' she said as she placed the plate down and Alexander's face dived into the fishy feast.

It was then time for her breakfast, and after deciding against leftover cake from Diane's party, she prepared her Weetabix and sat on the sofa. She turned on her laptop, snatching mouthfuls of her cereal before it soaked up all the milk whilst the laptop powered up. Alexander strutted in and sat near the coffee table, looked at her in case there was anything interesting in her bowl, then began licking his paws. After quickly checking her emails, her task was to create a poster to try to locate Alexander's home and therefore dissolve the responsibility she was beginning to feel for her vocal visitor. Firstly, she uploaded the photo of him.

'You didn't think I took a picture of you just because you're cute, did you?'

Alexander looked up at her from where he'd chosen to lie—straight across her feet.

She smiled. 'That's not me saying you're not cute though, because you are.'

Ten minutes later, the poster was complete with a photo of Alexander and May's email address, as she never answered her mobile phone to unknown numbers. Printing them out, Alexander walked over to where she had plugged the printer in at the very time his image was coming out of the machine.

'Oh, come on, you know I have to do this,' she said defensively.

Alexander, unconvinced, walked to the top of the stairs. She followed, and he ran down the stairs, wanting out.

Opening the front door, she said to him huffily, 'Okay, whatever, I know you'll be back.'

'Hi, morning.'

May looked up from Alexander, to the end of the drive, where a man was standing by a car. He waved and gave a closed-mouth smile. His smile was framed with a red beard that matched his hair colour.

The uneasiness and lack of preparation that came with this interaction with a stranger made her want to just shut the door, but as she glanced at the car again, she realised it was the same car that had been parked outside of Peter's a few days ago. The car that belonged to his son, Sam.

'Umm hello,' she replied, feeling her cheeks warming as she bit her lip. He was a bit older than her, but she couldn't tell his exact age. Tall like Peter and with the same stocky build.

'Looks like decent weather,' he said, palms turned up as he began walking up Peter's path.

May noticed his blue eyes, bright against his pale skin. She ran a hand down her hair, gave a nervous laugh, nodded and quickly closed the door to her flat.

After rushing up the stairs, she looked in her lounge mirror, staring at her tatty locks. 'Crap, I look like my hair has lost a fight with a toffee apple.' Then she shook her head. *Why am I even bothered what I look like to a stranger?*

She felt odd. She was noticing things and didn't like it. It wasn't part of the plan and it needed to stop.

May's eyes moved straight to Peter's door as she set off for a run in the park. Sam's car was still there, and she wished he had seen her now rather than in her dressing gown earlier. She tapped her temples as she walked, annoyed with herself again for thinking about it.

When she reached the park entrance and walked through the arch, she inhaled the familiar earthy scent she loved, her senses immediately perking up. She began doing a few leg stretches, tilting her head to the mild sunshine.

'Hi there,' a voice said.

May turned to her left to see a woman standing in leggings and a hoody. Smaller than May, she had a head full of tight brown curls that resembled springs, held back from her face with a headband.

'Sorry to bother you. I've seen you running here a few times and wanted to give you this.' She smiled and passed May a small flyer. 'It's a park run. We do it here every Saturday morning, and you are very welcome to join us. It's no cost, just a bit of support and company while you run, if you want that, of course.'

May's mouth was open as she moved her eyes from the flyer to the woman. She didn't know what to say. She hadn't ever been invited to join a group, especially not like this by someone who had noticed her. She thought of Fran and being kind and showing interest—that was exactly what the woman was doing to her.

The woman began closing the bum bag that was strapped around her waist, where May assumed she had taken the flyer from. 'No pressure though. I know running is meant to be solitary as well, but I much prefer it in a group. My number is on there. I'm Maddie.' She pointed to her number on the flyer. 'Anyway, sorry to disturb you. Have a great run, and maybe we will see you one Saturday morning.' Maddie put her hands in her hoody pockets and began to walk off.

May realised she still hadn't uttered one word. 'Thank you,' she shouted after Maddie, who turned, smiled and waved.

May stared at the small photo of Maddie with her bouncy hair framing her pretty face on the flyer. The park run was called Mad's Park Run, and she read the story snippet on there about how Maddie had suffered from depression and anxiety for many of her adult years, eventually getting into running as part of her therapy. May's eyes widened as she read on, discovering that Maddie needed something to help her to process her thoughts in a positive way and used running as exercise for her body and brain and to complement EMDR therapy.

She wondered what the therapy was and felt in awe of how brave Maddie was to put her story onto a flyer to give out to strangers. Reading the final bit of the paragraph about Maddie, May discovered that once Maddie had felt she was in recovery, she wanted to meet other runners and make new friends as well as create a group for people who had experienced mental ill health, but Mad's Park Run was open to everyone regardless of their experiences. It was to connect the community, keep fit and enjoy the beautiful park.

May read the flyer over and over again, as if it were a love letter. Maddie hadn't seemed poorly or as if she could have ever been someone who had struggled with her mental health, not with her confidence. Then she thought of Peter, who on first impression presented as a jolly, happy man. Always-positive Trish who hadn't had such a positive past. May realised people only showed what they wanted the world to see and that some were just better actors than others.

Folding the flyer in four, she placed it in the back pocket of her running top. She started jogging her usual route, trying to be in and appreciate the moment; however, her mind was dominated by questions and no answers. She ran to the beat of confusion, frustration, fear and the unknown. She thought of the things right now in her life that made her happy—the new people and opportunities that seemed to be coming into it. There seemed to be a surprising number of positive distractions presenting themselves in her path, but she pushed them out with the things that made her sad, the voids that could never be filled, the things that would never improve.

By the time she arrived back at her flat, she was utterly exhausted. Sam's car was gone and there was no sign of Alexander. Once inside, she headed straight for the shower, then pulled on her cosy joggers and made herself some eggs on toast and a mug of tea. She put the radio on, not wanting to hear her thoughts, then checked her phone for the time—11:30 a.m.—and saw she had a text message and a missed call from Trish. She immediately remembered that she hadn't finalised the plan they had discussed to meet up. It was unlike her to be so distracted, but, well, she did have a lot going on.

'Meet for lunch, my lovely? Xxx'

The text message was followed by a voicemail that said she wanted to catch up with May that day if possible.

May sighed. She really couldn't be bothered to put on the mask today. Her head was ringing and it felt as if a game of tug of war was going on in her body. She just wanted to rest. Placing her phone down but taking it off silent, she sat in her armchair and ate her eggs on toast, cooked how Victor had loved and Fran had perfected for him before May took over—poached. Finishing off her food, she stood up and glanced out of the lounge window, immediately noticing a blackbird on the tree opposite.

'Is it you, Dad?' she said quietly. Pressing her lips together, she turned away and went into the kitchen. She'd never believed in an afterlife, so why did she keep getting this wonder? Was it a coping mechanism? Silly hope? Or had her black-and-white mind closed her off to the possibility and now she was slightly bleeding out into grey areas?

As she dropped her plate in the sink and began to tidy the kitchen, Trish's name flashed up on her mobile phone. She decided she couldn't put off the contact any longer.

'Oooh, so you are alive, then,' Trish exclaimed as May answered. May almost laughed at the irony. 'Can you meet today for lunch?'

'I've just eaten, so no, not really.' May's voice was flat, but it didn't deter Trish.

'Dessert, then? I've missed you.'

May bit her thumbnail. Deep beneath that feeling of not wanting to see Trish, she knew she just wasn't ready to say goodbye.

'C'mon. We can meet at 1 p.m. That's an hour to make room for a cake.' Trish's voice was pleading, like a child asking to stay up late.

'Fine, we'll meet at the library.' It had a cosy café and she could mooch around in one of her favourite places, although she wouldn't take any books out, as that would mean having to return them and more hassle.

'Perfect. See you then.' Trish hung up before May could change her mind.

May finished cleaning the kitchen after her call with Trish, then went back in the lounge, took her laptop off charge and glanced out of the window to see if the blackbird was still there. It wasn't, but Sam's car was back. A smile crept across her face.

Changing out of her jogging bottoms into jeans and a khaki jumper, she located her handbag and then put some mascara on, followed by some blusher and a spritz of perfume. Looking at herself in the lounge mirror, she combed her hair and put it in a loose bun. For a moment, she glared at her reflection.

'What are you even doing?' she asked her reflection, looking at her lengthened eyelashes and rosy cheeks. Rolling her eyes at herself, she grabbed her bag and went downstairs. She put on her sandshoes and denim jacket.

Opening the front door, leaving and locking it took longer than usual—without wanting to admit it to herself, she was nosing on her neighbour, in particular wondering what her neighbour's son was doing. After locking her door in slow motion, she walked up her path and strolled away from her flat, towards town. For a few minutes, she didn't think about death.

She'd left her flat early to arrive at the library with plenty of time to mooch. The stairs were in sight as soon as she entered through reception, and she took them to the second floor, then moved to the side and stopped for a moment to inhale deeply, closing her eyes tightly. The smell of books, older and new, was one of her favourites. The underlying mustiness. If it were a scent of anywhere else, it would be unappealing, but here, the smell was a comfort. She walked to the shelves and saw the new publication section. The latest edition of *New Scientist* stood proudly on the shelf. She smiled. Her parents used to get her a subscription to it each Christmas before Fran died and the Christmas presents became less organised, just as life had.

May sat on one of the padded blue chairs and flicked through the magazine. Science had become a lost love recently, but she could have sat there all afternoon indulging in her passion. Once it reached almost 1 p.m., she stood up and travelled down the stairs quickly, feeling the air rush around her and the lightness of her feet clipping each step.

At the bottom, she headed to the café, where Trish was waiting at the entrance.

'Hi, love.' Trish greeted her with a warm smile and an embrace, squeezing her like a grandmother squeezes her young grandchildren. From her view over Trish's shoulder, she saw someone else standing to the side. Jack lifted his hand in a nervous wave.

She internally winced, her arms dropping from around Trish to stay firmly at her sides. It had been hard to come here knowing that this could be the final time she saw Trish. She didn't want bloody Jack here, prattling on about Lawson-Wray's. She looked at Trish dejectedly.

'Just hear him out,' she whispered to May, squeezing her hand and giving her a raised-eyebrow look.

May felt her jaw clench and her cheeks heat up. She wouldn't have agreed to meet Jack and Trish shouldn't have brought him, but he was here now. The anger at being put in an uncomfortable situation was radiating from her, and she was sure Trish was showing signs of unease, but she couldn't work Jack out.

'May, so lovely to see you,' he said, smiling. 'Shall we?' He pointed into the café.

They headed in, and Jack took a seat whilst Trish and May went to look at the cakes on the counter.

'Trish, what are you doing bringing Jack?' May said in the tone of an eight-year-old who has been told they are going home from the fair.

'Honey, they all miss you at work and they're worried about you. Jack, me, the whole team want you back, okay? So you're going to listen to him and go home and think about it afterwards,' Trish said firmly, turning to May before transforming back to her usual bouncy tone. 'I'm going for the rocky road. What are you having?'

May glanced over the cakes, then crossed her arms and huffed. 'Caramel shortcake.'

Trish ignored May's attitude, only listening to her cake choice. 'Jack, what do you want?' she shouted over to the small table where Jack had his head down, phone in hand. His face flushed.

'We are still in a library, you know, not at a concert,' May said, shaking her head at Trish.

'Bugger off, grumpy. Go and sit with your boss. I'll order these and three teas.'

May dragged her feet over to take a seat next to Jack. The little round table had mismatched seats and vintage sugar pots that made it feel old and quirky like the library. As she sat down, Jack smiled at her. It wasn't his fault, none of how she felt was his fault. In fact, he had never been anything but nice to her.

'How are you?'

May swallowed. *How am I? I don't even know where to start.* Her body language often gave her thoughts away before she opened her mouth, making her a terrible liar; however, in the last few weeks, she had somehow managed to dupe most people around her. Rubbing her fingers together, she answered, 'So-so. Some days are easier than others. Some days, I still feel lost.' She faced the table, not wanting to see pity in his eyes. Luckily, Trish arrived with her tray of goodies and a teapot shaped like lined-up books.

'Eeeh, this teapot is amazing. Look at it, May, I bet you love it.' She almost spilt the tea with excitement.

May and Jack both laughed, and May was thankful it changed the subject.

Taking a seat, Trish pushed a chocolate muffin over to Jack, then stirred the tea. 'Got you this.'

'Thank you,' he said, then turned to May and laced his fingers on the table as if he were about to conduct an interview, though he didn't hold the power in this particular conversation. 'May, I won't bother with any more small talk, I know you're not a fan of it,' he said gently, placing two sachets of sugar from the vintage pot by her cup.

May slightly frowned at Jack remembering how she took her tea, caring to recall such detail. She didn't want people to care. She pressed her lips together as Trish got on with pouring the tea.

'The truth is, we miss you at Lawson-Wray's. I miss your organisational skills, and we would love for you to return, even just for a few hours a week at first.'

May emptied the sugars into her now-poured tea, stirred it and took a sip. She raised her eyebrow at what she was certain were rehearsed words, then glanced at Trish, who was nodding her on like a punter at the horse racing.

'I don't think I can, Jack.'

'Oh, May, come on, of course you can. You can't sit in that flat all day.'

May snorted at Trish's tone—Was it irritation? Perhaps impatience? 'Actually, I'm not sitting in my flat all day. I've been running most days and I'm thinking of joining a park run. I've got a neighbour, Peter, who's elderly and, well, we are friends and help each other.' She took a deep breath. 'I've been seeing Scarlett and her family and I have a cat who wants to live with me. So, you see, I am *very* busy.'

She looked sternly at Trish and the massive grin that was starting to spread across her face.

'That's my girl. Sounds like you're doing lots of normal, routine things, May, so to me, you're getting better and doing amazing. Meaning you can come back to work.'

May realised she had been set up by Trish, a trick statement to make her defensive and reel off things that made her seem, well, normal. And the strange thing was they did exactly that. It didn't take away her loss and her sadness, but it showed them that she was getting better and could function. So why couldn't a return to Lawson-Wray's be part of that?

'I'll think about it, okay? Please no more talking about it.'

Jack and Trish looked at each other and then at May. They nodded, and both of them had an annoying grin that made her think they thought they had won. They hadn't and she wouldn't return, but part of her deep inside was glowing from feeling needed.

After a bit more general chit-chat and May avoiding any in-depth answers to their questions, Jack and Trish returned to work.

May stayed at the library, deciding to peruse the shelves. She strolled around the ground floor, glancing at the new releases, touching the books, inhaling the smell of them and the café. Then she had an idea and rushed back upstairs to the non-fiction. The space was almost empty except for a few people on the computers in the corner. She took a deep breath and closed her eyes, absorbing the feeling. Once she opened them, she felt irritated with herself for having never appreciated the library as fully as she did at that moment.

She found the medical science section and touched the spines of the books as she walked ever so slowly, as if deciding on the most sumptuous piece of fudge in a Parisian chocolatier. Eventually, she pulled out the treats she wanted: a book on medical research around age-related illnesses, followed by a few further on the same topic. Ever since Peter had opened up about Anne's dementia, she'd wanted to know more. Degenerative diseases had been a topic of study during her degree and master's, but she had focused her assignments on heart conditions following Fran's passing and also Parkinson's, which her grandfather had had.

She wanted to know more than her existing knowledge base, out of respect for Peter but also to try to help if he talked more about Anne in the future. Then she remembered she didn't plan to be around for much longer. She felt a melancholic sinking feeling in her stomach, as if she were watching jewels running down a drain, unable to stop the flow. She held the books as if they contained the answers to all her problems as she stood as still as the King's Guard, staring through the shelves at rows and rows of knowledge and information aligned alphabetically.

She had been in denial of pleasant experiences the last week or so, smothering them with a heavy hand, but she was experiencing more of these moments that made her feel torn about what to do. A few weeks ago, it had felt so clear, so definitive that she couldn't live, as life was just too painful and she would always feel let down, ill-fitting and on the periphery, watching other people's happiness. But some days, most days now, it felt as if the anchor of grief, unhappiness and defeat was retreating a little, allowing her to navigate to the port of possibility. She didn't want to feel like this. It confused her, frightened her and she simply didn't trust that things would be okay for long. She had felt that before. Then Mam died, Thomas left her and Dad died. Trust was a dangerous thing. Belief was a dangerous thing. Hope was a dangerous thing.

So why couldn't she put those books back on the shelf?

An hour later, after sitting in the peaceful library and looking over the books she had removed from the shelves, she wanted to know more. It was as if the researcher in her had been revived and she required knowledge like the oxygen she breathed. After selecting a few more books, she recalled some of what she had studied briefly at university through the pages and learnt a little more. She felt empowered with knowledge to converse with Peter about the subject and perhaps offer more support than a silent look and a tissue.

She went back to browsing, coming across the mental health section, where she glanced at the shelves, ignoring the books on the topic of suicide. She thought about the flyer Maddie had passed her way that morning for Mad's Park Run.

What was the therapy that Maddie mentioned? May tapped the books as she slowly looked across the rows of information. She was sure it was a four-letter therapy. Collecting a few books on mental health therapies, she sat down, beginning to look in the contents pages. Scanning book after book, her confusion increased with the many options. Was it CBT? DBT? No, they were three letters. She picked up the next book, which had a colourful cover, and looked at the contents page.

'That's it,' she said a little too loudly for a library, jabbing the page hard with her finger. EMDR. Most of the book seemed to explore and explain it. Eye Movement Desensitization and Reprocessing therapy uses eye movements and other rhythm stimulation, like tapping, to work through traumatic experiences. 'Recommended as a treatment for post-traumatic stress disorder.'

During her studies, they had covered mental health conditions and researched medical advancements, especially medication and trials, but she hadn't heard of this treatment. Perhaps it could have helped her. She let out a sigh. Asking for help was so hard, and when her parents died, no one suggested she get help for her mental health. She wasn't sure why. Perhaps people thought she was young and clever and strong, so didn't need help. Maybe because she was quiet, people saw minimal difference in her presentation.

She regretted not asking for help, but she wasn't convinced her voice had been or was loud enough. Maddie had found support and she'd seemed so together in those few minutes they had conversed. May held on to the book, not ready to put it back on the shelf, not ready to stop learning, and at that moment, she questioned if she was ready to die.

Chapter 30

As May left the flat with 'found' posters in a document wallet and some sticky tape and zip ties in her jacket pocket, her thoughts kept flitting between wanting to find Alexander's owner and to hoping no one came forward. As much as she didn't want to acknowledge it, he had left a little impression of his paw print on her heart already. Nevertheless, she began her mission, starting with the lamppost closest to her flat. Taping the poster was harder than she'd thought, the sticky tape not doing what it claimed, meaning she had to tighten a zip tie around the lamppost. Shaking her head, she continued on, walking down the street and repeating the action several times.

As she walked and looked for places to display her posters, she heard knocking on glass. Slightly startled, she touched her throat and looked around. A young child was waving frantically from a downstairs window, face beaming. May chuckled and waved back, to a response of a two-handed wave by the delighted child.

She passed a telecoms cable cabinet she had never noticed before. She had probably been blind to a lot of things as she wore the dark sunglasses of grief, boring broadband units and all. Strategically placing a poster on the cabinet, she added an extra strip of tape, then set off towards the nearest bus stop at the bottom of the street, intermittently tilting her face towards the sun that was warming the air.

Arriving a minute or so later, she identified a place to display the poster in the bus stop, just under the timetable. As she began to wedge the poster into the edge of the large plastic frame displaying travel information, trying to not cover any important information about the local transport, she heard a beep. Turning around, she saw Peter and Sam waving from Sam's car. Her cheeks heated up as Sam's car pulled over on the opposite side of the road.

Peter wound the passenger window down. 'May, pet, do you need a lift? I've got my own chauffeur here,' he said, pointing eagerly towards Sam.

'Hi, erm, no, thank you. I'm not going anywhere. I mean, I'm not just hanging around the bus stop.' She laughed a silly, awkward laugh. 'I'm just putting these up.' She grabbed the document wallet and sticky tape off the bus stop bench, checked no cars were coming and then stepped towards the car to show Peter and Sam the posters.

'Ah, what a lovely cat,' said Sam, leaning over his dad and taking one of the posters from May. 'He was the one coming out of your flat this morning, wasn't he? Is he just a temporary guest?' He chuckled, his ocean-blue eyes looking right into May's.

May's heart beat faster, and she looked away from him temporarily, embarrassed about possibly unblinkingly staring or just being generally awkward. 'I'm not sure if he is homeless. I just don't want someone worried about him and, well, I haven't got time for pets.' She shrugged. She wasn't technically lying, she just meant time left in her life rather than within her life.

'Aw, May, he's a little champ, I think he wants to live with you,' Peter said, winking.

A car tooted. Peter put his hand out the window in a go-around-the-vehicle movement. The car passed, the driver shaking his head.

'Think we are getting in the way,' May commented.

'I tell you what, pet, let us just get home to put our shopping away and then we can come and give you a hand putting those flyers up.'

'Oh no, honest, don't worry about that, Peter. Thank you though.'

'Well, how about coming over for a cuppa and some cake when you are done, May? I've tried a carrot cake recipe. It's got real carrots in, so it must be healthy. Isn't that right, Son?'

Sam nodded at May. 'He's right, and it's pretty delicious for a dad who used to burn water.'

'Cheeky bugger.' Peter looked at his son fondly.

May laughed. 'I would love to. Thank you.'

She watched Sam and Peter drive away, already looking forward to seeing Sam again. She shook the thought out of her head, feeling silly and realising it would lead to rejection. Plus, it was completely redundant anyway.

May ran her fingers through her hair in front of the mirror in the lounge, staring at her reflection. She had never felt attractive or alluring. She remembered seeing magazines full of fashion, music and pretty girls when she was younger, knowing she would never compare to them. She could never achieve that level of beauty, confidence and self-acceptance.

Despite this, people saw her. Trish, Jack, Scarlett and even Thomas had, albeit for only a short time. Then Peter, Sam, even Alexander and Maddie.

She picked up the photo of her parents that lay facedown on her mantlepiece in its frame and looked down at it in her hand. 'I miss you both so much,' she wailed, pulling the frame into her body. 'It's not getting easier.' She stepped back and sat on her sofa, with the frame on her knees.

'Help me, Mam, Dad. Help me to be brave and strong and to want to live.' Tears dripped onto the glass, distorting the image underneath. Silence echoed around her, and after a minute, she wiped away her tears, put the photo on the mantlepiece upright and went into the bathroom.

She placed both hands on the sink and took some deep breaths before applying some mascara, some tinted lip balm and perfume, then walked down the stairs.

Knocking on Peter's front door, she felt ridiculously nervous, her stomach fizzing like citric acid and sodium bicarbonate in water.

Sam quickly answered with a smile and a 'Come on in,' standing to the side and moving his arm to gesture her in.

May walked past him, self-conscious at being so near to him. Up close, Sam was just a smidgen taller than her and his red beard had a touch of golden amongst it. He had the same smile as Peter, with round cheeks.

'You look pretty, May,' he said, pointing her in the direction of the lounge.

She didn't bother telling him she already knew where it was and that the flats were identical in layout except for May's having stairs. Instead, she thanked him. She couldn't remember the last time a man had told her she looked pretty, and she hoped Sam meant it. Then, she immediately panicked that perhaps she should have complimented him back.

'Oh, here she is, my neighbour and friend.' Peter tapped the armchair opposite his recliner for May to sit down. There was an old wooden chair that looked as if it might collapse at any time that she assumed Sam had brought in from somewhere.

'Sam's ordered me a brand-new sofa, May, I can hardly wait. I think it will end up being my bed as well,' Peter exclaimed, clapping his hands.

Sam leaned forward and rolled his eyes. 'He does have a bed, by the way, he's just been a little scared to spend money in case Mam needs more for her care. But we've chatted, haven't we, Dad? You have to be comfortable also.' Sam looked at Peter seriously as Peter turned to May, slapping his own wrist and chuckling.

'He's right, pet. I've bought myself some bits of furniture and our Sam has bought me the sofa. It's one of those L-shaped ones, May. Spot on it is, in a lovely grey colour.'

'It sounds really nice, Peter.'

Sam got up from his rickety chair. 'Cuppa, May?'

'Yes, please. Would you like a hand?'

'That would be grand, thank you.'

She followed Sam into the kitchen and got three cups out as he topped up the kettle.

'You know where things are in here?' Sam tilted his head.

'Oh... yeah. I've been in for a cuppa with Peter before. Your dad is a lovely man. He's been kind to me.' *I knew I should have said something when he invited me in.*

'He's mentioned you a few times. My dad is very fond of you and is pleased to have a nice neighbour. It's been hard for us all, but Dad didn't just leave a home he had all his married life, he left lots of memories there that my mam no longer retains.' He leaned against the kitchen bench and ran his hand through his hair. 'At one time, well, I wasn't sure if he would cope. So, thank you for looking out for him. Anyway, I'm coming home now, so at least I can help. And it's been lovely to see Mam. Bittersweet, but still.'

May wasn't sure whether to say anything or not, so she nodded, then simply said, 'I'm pleased you are coming home. For your dad.' She felt a flutter in her stomach.

The kettle clicked, and May's shoulders relaxed as the pressure of the deep conversation left her.

'Would you mind getting some plates for the cake, please?' Sam asked as he started pouring water into the cups. 'And do you take milk and sugar?'

After sorting everyone's tea preference, they carried the cups and cake back into the lounge area. Placing the plates on the side table, May watched Sam hand a cup of tea to his father, who looked at his son with a love she recognised. It caught her breath. It could have been her there with Victor, handing him his poached-to-perfection eggs as his face lit up with gratitude. She wanted to sob with overwhelm, but she was also happy that Peter had Sam and Sam had Peter and that they had a love that seemed as precious as hers had been with Victor.

'There's yours, May.' Sam handed her a cup of tea as she perched on the armchair, breaking her thought trance.

Mouth open and not quite ready to speak, she nodded.

'Serve that cake, Son.' Peter pointed to the carrot cake.

'Alright, greedy guts. You're worse than a kid.' Sam laughed, and his dad joined in, tapping his stomach.

'Ladies first.' Sam passed May her cake, and she thanked him, having swallowed her emotions in a gulp of tea.

The three sat, eating the carrot cake in silence for a moment except for an 'mmmm' noise from Sam.

'Peter, this is so tasty. Are you sure it isn't a shop-bought one and you are pretending?' May asked, half-serious. The icing was like a buttery whip and the grated carrot only just noticeable in the soft golden sponge.

'Well, he's done that before, haven't you, Dad?'

Peter burst out laughing.

'He used to pretend he had made cakes all the time when we were kids, even at school fairs. He was such a billy bullsh—'

Peter glared at Sam.

'Oh sorry, May, I didn't mean to almost swear.'

May laughed. 'It's quite okay, Sam, I don't mind.'

'Well, I do. Not in front of ladies, Sam, you aren't too old to get a telling-off from your old man.' Peter waggled his finger and smirked.

Sam rolled his eyes. 'Thirty-four years old and still the baby of the family, aren't I, Dad?'

'Always, my lad. And a brilliant big baby you are as well.'

Sam shared that he had been living in Birmingham for the last six years, after meeting his wife at a former work function in the city. He had worked as an accountant in Birmingham, but following a divorce and his mother's deteriorating health, he was moving back to the North East.

'I've secured a job with Bilton and Co's as an accountant, so now I just need to find somewhere to live and I'll be moving up in the next month. New start, and I'm looking forward to being back around Dad and Mam.'

'Your mam needs you, Son, we don't know how long she has.' Peter looked at May with watery eyes. 'But having my boy around will help me no end. I've said he can move in here, on my new sofa. Or you can have the bed, Sam; the sofa will do me.'

'Dad tells me you are a scientist, May?'

May's brain took a moment to process the jump in conversation. She wondered if the prospect of sleeping on his dad's sofa was a massive downfall from married life, and she couldn't blame him for not agreeing there and then to his dad taking the sofa. Maybe he just didn't want to discuss private matters in front of someone outside of the family.

'Well, not really. I studied science at university and began a master's, where I was specialising in research. That's what I want... wanted to do. But it didn't work out, so I guess that's that.' She glanced at the floor and bit the inside of her cheek.

'You've got all the time in the world, May, and I hope you return to your dream when the time is right.'

'She will,' Peter said confidently. 'She's a clever lass and it would be a waste to not. Just waiting for the right time, aren't you, pet?'

May let the side of her mouth turn up a little. She was grateful Peter had belief in her, but it was wasted in the reality of things.

'And she works at the local estate agency, Lawson-Wray's. She's very organised, and I bet she helps keep them right,' Peter added, his shoulders back, looking between May and his son.

May wasn't enjoying the focus being on her, especially in front of Sam with whom she had a strange sensation of wanting to impress, but quite frankly, her current existence was anything but impressive.

'Another cuppa?' Sam asked, studying May intensely. He didn't wait for an answer; instead, getting straight up and taking the cups and plates to the kitchen. She got the impression he'd picked up on her awkwardness, and it made her feel giddy he'd noticed, yet she couldn't help but overthink how easily he could read her and wonder if it was just in that moment.

'It's nice to see you laugh and smile. I'm sorry if I embarrassed you a bit there, but I think you're great and I want our Sam to know it.' He leaned forward and whispered, 'Not that he can't tell himself.'

May looked back at Peter and grinned, unsure as to how to take the comment. Regardless, even with a tiny bit of questioning and pushing her out of the comfort zone she had wedged herself in the last few weeks, she was pleased to be there. Peter and Sam were great company, and it was nice to adapt to someone new without her usual social anxiety. Although she didn't want to admit it, in that moment, she felt an emotion she didn't often feel anymore: happiness.

Chapter 31

23rd May

May frowned and opened her eyes slightly, shielding them from the morning sun.

'Alexander?' She sat up and looked around the room, then remembered he wasn't there.

Meow.

May jumped out of bed, her tiredness completely forgotten, and ran to her bedroom window. 'Alexander.' She'd assumed he'd finally gone back home and had wanted relief to drag her mind away so she could focus back on her to-do list before the end, but she'd be lying if she said she hadn't missed him. She'd even placed some scraps of meat and a ramekin of water by the front door each morning and night. The meat had gone on the occasions she had left it, but there were many animals who would take advantage of an easy meal.

She rushed down the stairs, his meows getting louder the closer she got. His two white front paws were already on the doorstep as she flung the door open and crouched down to greet him.

'Where have you been, you little cutie?'

He looked at her, letting out little meows between purring like a tank. May didn't care if it was just food he was after; she felt wanted, needed and loved. She stood up, and Alexander darted into the flat and up the stairs. A little meow escaped his mouth as he jumped straight onto the sofa and flopped down. She watched his confident performance. He looked at her, made another meow and closed his eyes.

'Well I never,' she said as she walked to the kitchen to make her usual breakfast of Weetabix and a cup of tea. As the kettle boiled, she leant against the countertop and wished she could be as carefree and bold as Alexander. Once her tea was brewed, she poured milk onto her cereal and returned to the lounge, squeezing into the little space Alexander had left between his stretched-out body and the arm of the sofa. She placed her cup on the coffee table, then stroked the cat's head. His eyes remained closed, but his paw opened and closed in contentment.

Trish had rung yesterday asking May to come into work again just to see everyone. It was the fourth time she had asked, and May had decided she would go in. It was on her list as a possibility and it could be the last time. Breakfast finished, she got up from the sofa and looked straight over at her parents' photo. She smiled at their happy faces etched in the joy of love, then put her hand to her forehead and sighed. She felt sad, happy and confused all at once.

An hour later, Alexander was still stretched out on the sofa.

'Come on, I need to go for a run and you need to leave.' She tried to shoo him off the sofa, but he looked at her blankly and then shut his eyes again. She reluctantly picked him up, her heart fluttering with love as he settled in her arms and nuzzled her neck. She had spent a lot of time wanting love in the form of a relationship, always watching everyone else, wondering if she would ever find it, and while it would be nice to, his love felt enough.

She placed Alexander outside and turned away as she closed the door, knowing he was watching her and wanting to come back in. She didn't know cat behaviours regarding needing the toilet and how often they ate, so he needed to be outside until she could research. She bit her lip. Who was she kidding? He wasn't hers and she wasn't going to be around much longer. Yet when she passed the bus stop where her poster was still displayed half an hour later, she had the overwhelming urge to pull it down.

The ticking of her wall clock was all that could be heard as May stared into space as she stood in front of the toaster, elbows on the counter, a plate of crumbs in front of her. She'd already eaten two slices of toast and wanted more. *Stress eating? What am I stressed about?* Her life was no worse than yesterday or even last week; in fact, the grief that felt almost certain to crush her with its brutal weight, in all honesty, felt lighter most days. At the park earlier, she'd said hello to almost everyone she crossed, which was a huge achievement, and yesterday, she'd even made a list of her possessions and where she'd like them to go. Her biggest item was her car, and she'd decided to leave it to Peter. He could drive but had sold his car when he found a care placement for Anne. Although he had his bus pass, the weather would soon turn cold again and she didn't like the thought of him freezing at the bus stop. The list was in an envelope with 'Uncle Terence' on it, sat in one of her bedroom drawers.

Speaking of Uncle Terence, she was going to visit him on Sunday—a call she'd actually made, unlike the Skype call she'd cancelled with Scarlett after a day of reflecting on things she regretted, chances not taken and people she wished she would have seen more of or spoken out against. But the reality was that the percentage of her that wanted to die was decreasing as the days went by.

The toast pinged at the same time her phone beeped. She took her phone from her pocket and opened the message.

Trish: *'Are you coming over? Pop in to see the team, then I will take you for lunch. xxx'*

May: *'Be there soon. xxx'*

She placed her phone back in her pocket and rested her elbows on the counter again, staring at the toast. She craved her old normality and routine, her safe, boring, trouble-free life. The newness felt overwhelming and very un-May and, dare she say, a tiny bit exciting. Leaving the toast to grow cold, she grabbed her car keys and left her flat. She'd bin the toast and wash the plate later—another very un-May thing.

Driving into town, she went around a roundabout twice, then sat in a car park a few minutes from Lawson-Wray's while edging on whether to return home. She had spent ninety-nine per cent of her life seeing black or white, yes or no, go or stop. There wasn't a grey, a maybe or an amber; therefore, she had never been indecisive. But that had all changed, and she didn't like the alien feel.

She wanted to see most of her colleagues, but she was worried people would pity her or even think badly of her for not being in touch and not returning to work. Perhaps they would just be pleased to see her, but she wasn't sure she wanted that last visit, and there was something about not doing it that made it easier than reigniting the flame only to extinguish it forever an hour later.

Rubbing her hands together, she looked at the charm dangling from her handbag on the passenger seat. It was more of a keyring, but she didn't like a big bunch of keys with more knick-knacks hanging off them than a drag queen's jewellery box, so this bag charm, or keyring, was on her favourite bag, the keyring itself one of her favourite things. It had been a Christmas present from her dad last Christmas. He'd presented it in a tiny cardboard jewellery box. She had automatically hoped it wasn't a bracelet or necklace, as her dad knew she wasn't one to wear jewellery. A watch, however, was always welcome if it had the required features.

She closed her eyes and smiled as she watched her dad's excited face in her mind as he handed her the box saying, 'There you go,' followed by an impatient, 'well open it, then' and a clapping of his hands.

May held her face, replaying the scene in her head. Dad with his ill-fitting party hat on and May holding the little box, hating the thought of a surprise that she would likely not enjoy.

With Dad eagerly looking on like a dog waiting for scraps of meat to fall to the floor, she'd opened the little cardboard box. Her face must have lit up brighter than the Christmas tree lights, as he'd had tears in his eyes. It was a little Lego woman with long dark hair like she had, wearing a white scientist coat. It was a silly, simple, inexpensive gift, but she thought it was magnificent.

Opening her eyes, she looked at the Lego scientist, touching it and letting a tear fall down her face. Then she lifted her bag up, got out of the car and went to the parking ticket machine, knowing that it would be exactly what her dad would have told her to do.

Lawson-Wray's was about a two-minute walk from the car park she had parked in, and she needed all the time she could get to compose herself. It only felt like a few steps before she could see the front of the shop. She stood opposite, looking over as nerves played paintball in her stomach. She could see the odd figure milling about in the office, but she couldn't work out who was who from where she stood. She looked up at the sign above the shop, remembering the old Lawson's signage that felt like another home and a time before the world shat on her life like pigeons on a statue.

With no vehicles coming either way, she forced herself to put one foot in front of the other and cross the road, going straight into the building. As she walked in, some staff were busy with customers but most eyes turned to her, and she was greeted with smiles, waves and hellos. Her cheeks flushed under the awkward spotlight that seemed to be shining on her. She stood near reception, moving from foot to foot and looking at the noticeboard for a minute before Jack and Trish approached from the back of the office.

Trish gave May an enveloping cuddle. 'Lovely to see my favourite month here,' she said as she cupped May's face. May felt like a puppy getting ready for a Crufts competition, all the attention on her. If it were anyone else, she would have run away, but Trish did have a soothing effect on her, even if it pushed her out of her rigid comfort zone at times.

'May.' Jack gave her a light hug that made them both feel a little awkward. 'It's so nice to see you.'

'I only saw you a few days ago,' she replied, glancing around the office.

'Erm yes, I know, but I mean it's nice to see you here, in a work environment. We've missed you.' He gestured around the room, then continued quietly, 'My diary, my filing, my accounts. Christ, May, they have been abysmal these last months. You've been a huge miss and not just to my organisational abilities.' Jack chuckled.

'I'm only here to shut you both up from asking me to come in.'

'I know. But you won't regret it.' Trish winked.

May glanced around again. 'There's something different in here.' She tapped her lip as Trish's brow furrowed.

'Nah, nothing different, love.'

May looked down and then back at Jack. 'You've cleaned the carpets.' She pointed to the burgundy carpets that looked brighter than the last time she'd walked on them.

Jack clapped his hands together. 'You're right, and that's why we love your attention to detail, May.' He walked off, waving his hands in a beckoning motion for May and no doubt Trish to follow him to May's office.

'Hi, May,' one of her colleagues said, walking past. 'Want a cuppa?'

She nodded. 'Thanks.'

She felt almost nauseous with each step on the cleaned carpet as they walked through the main office to get to her office. It was a mixture of nerves, fear, sadness and finality with a chunk of wanting to rewind time. Rewind to a time she was happy at Lawson-Wray's, back when it was Lawson's, and her parents were alive. When she was studying and felt she had a future. When she would Skype with Scarlett almost daily and Fran would make her sandwiches for work just the way she liked them. When she would still make Victor's flask with the 'May magic'. When she would hear her dad singing in the morning and her mam's beautiful laughter.

Her feet seemed impossible to lift for those last few steps. Then she was there, in the doorway, staring at her chair and desk. Almost seeing her former self that she was proud of enjoying her job and knowing she was good at it—a massive deal for her in her world where she often felt not good enough in so many ways. The beech wood effect desk looked pristine, her pen pot and document rack neatly on the top. Untouched, but she always left it neat and tidy, adhering to the clean desk policy.

'It won't bite,' Trish said, placing a hand on May's shoulder. Jack stood in silence a few metres back.

May wanted to scream and run away, to cry and smash her desk up and tip the filing cabinets over. How come it was still here when the people she loved weren't? Time stood still as she remembered all those chats, cuppas, biscuits with Trish. The glances she would snatch of Thomas as he ventured to the photocopier. The lopsided smile on his face as he winked behind his glasses. When every moment at work was enjoyable.

Squeezing her hands together, she moved towards her office chair and pulled it out. The leather headrest was cold against her hand. Trish and Jack stood in silence as she sat in the chair. Tears fell down her face like plump raindrops on a winter's day and landed like ink spots on her grey trousers.

'Hey, hey, hey. Come on, my lovely.'

A colleague appeared at the door with a cuppa for her and a packet of biscuits in her other hand. Jack took them, placed them on May's desk, then left the office to give May and Trish some space. Trish rushed round the desk, pulling May's head into her chest and stroking her hair. May sobbed and sobbed, unsure as to whether she would ever stop. The pain was breathtaking. Trish silently remained next to her, allowing her the time she needed to calm down. It was only once she'd stopped crying completely and had drunk half of her drink that Trish spoke.

'May, I hate to see you upset and I hate to think of you like this alone. I wish you would reach out more.'

'I've been okay-ish the last few days, I suppose. And I've got to not rely on everyone else to be my crutch, Trish.' May looked at her, chin trembling and the threat of the floodgates opening again.

Trish placed a hand on her hip. 'Listen, my lovely, we all need help in life, we all need support and a little arm around us to keep us up at times. *All of us*, including you. There have been times I would have crumbled without my friends. And you know what? I asked for help and they came running. That's what friends do, May.'

'You've already helped more than I could ever repay,' May said quietly, staring into her cup.

'I don't want you to bloody repay me, May; you're my bloody friend. More than that, you're like my daughter and I love you,' she said, clasping May's forearms. The love from Trish's grasp darted through her like a current of compassion and care.

'May McClelland, what will we do with you?' Trish beckoned her to stand up, then hugged her. 'Now, come on, I'm starving and want some lunch. Have a minute, then go and say goodbye to Jack and that lot out there so we can go for some food.'

May said a quick goodbye to Jack, feeling as if she wanted, needed to say more, hug him. Something to show her thanks for all the years she had worked there. But she couldn't, and he didn't initiate anything other than gratitude for her coming in and a see-you-soon farewell.

In the café, Trish sat opposite May. 'Was that as bad as you thought, then?'

May shrugged, feeling gusts of guilt as she looked at Trish. She held a menu in front of herself and looked at it, then realised how obvious her awkwardness was, considering they'd already ordered. She put the menu down, her eyes glancing to the counter, where she could see the barista making drinks. 'I don't know, I'm struggling to explain how I feel about a lot at the minute, Trish. Some days, I want to run away and stop the noise and thoughts in my head; other days, I feel happy some of the time.'

They stopped talking as a waiter placed a blueberry tea and caramel latte down on the table alongside a panini each.

'Oooh, if I was twenty years younger,' Trish said, staring at the waiter as he walked away.

May giggled. '*Trish.*'

'Well, you would, wouldn't you?' she said, wide-eyed.

May rolled her eyes and picked up her panini.

'Come back to work, my lovely. We miss you. You're doing really well, but I promise that extra routine and using your skills will help.'

May paused with the panini near her mouth and looked at Trish. *If only you knew my plan.*

'Just a few shifts, May? And it's such easy work for you, but Jack needs help. You know he's useless at times; in fact, he's trying to palm his shitty work onto me, so you'll also be saving my bacon coming back because otherwise I will end up telling him exactly what I want him to do with his stupid receipts.'

May coughed, choking on her mouthful. 'I would actually like to see that.'

'You wouldn't, my lovely, it wouldn't be pretty.'

The two giggled and continued talking for a bit. May told Trish about Alexander and Trish commented that the cat was 'going nowhere' and May had to keep him.

It was soon time for Trish to return to work, and she told May she would come over on Monday with her birthday presents and to meet Alexander properly.

'Have a think as well if you want to go for dinner for your birthday or perhaps the theatre?' Trish said as she hugged May goodbye.

Sadness engulfed May as she watched her friend cross the road back to work, knowing the next time she saw her would be the last.

But she was beginning to question what was braver—to live or to die.

Meow. Alexander's sandy face popped out of the bushes, then out came the rest of him, full of chatter as May grabbed her handbag and got out of her car. He fussed around her ankles and stretched up for attention. The guilt and stress weren't gone by any means, but he seemed to have a soothing effect on her.

'Come on, then.' She held the front door open so he could go into the flat first, then noticed an envelope with her name handwritten on the front on her doormat. She frowned and picked it up, opening it as she walked upstairs, an impatient and vocal Alexander waiting at the top.

'Oh, you are a diva, aren't you?' she said as he pushed his head on her hand. She walked to the fridge and stared inside, glancing at two yoghurts, a container of leftover pasta, melon chunks in a bowl and a variety of condiments. 'I'm not sure there is anything here you would like, little man.'

Alexander looked up, meowing frantically.

Moving to her tin cupboard, Alexander quickly followed and pushed through her legs to also have a nosy as she opened it. She giggled and stroked his back as he pushed his head into the cupboard. A second later, he removed it with an unimpressed meow.

'Don't think you will like soup or baked beans.' She pulled a few tins out of the way. 'Oh, here, tuna. You love tuna.' She tapped the top of the tin with her fingernails, which immediately alerted Alexander, and he began rubbing his body against her leg. She opened the tuna to the loud tune of meows as he impatiently waited for his food. The plate barely touched the floor before he was munching away.

Now Alexander's only interest was in the fishy treat he was devouring, she picked up the envelope again and slid out the piece of paper that was inside. The note was handwritten in black ink, the paper lined and ripped carefully from a notebook.

Dear May,

Sam and I would be delighted if you would join us at my flat for dinner tomorrow night.

Don't get too excited, it will only be lasagne and garlic bread. However, pet, I am making it all myself from scratch.

Master Chef next year, eh?

Hope to see you at 7 p.m.,

Peter and Sam

May re-read the note and then read it again. She put it down while she filled a glass with water and then she read it again before holding it to her chest. Perhaps she wasn't such a burden to people after all, and maybe, just maybe, it wasn't always pity that they felt towards her.

She left Alexander to his food and went to the lounge to Skype Scarlett. Curling her legs under herself on the sofa, she placed her fleece over herself and waited for an answer, laptop perched on the sofa arm.

'You're late,' Scarlett immediately commented. She was lying on her stomach on her bed, her head propped up on a pile of pillows. Before May could reply, she smirked. 'What's tickled you?'

May hadn't been aware she was smiling, but now she could feel the big grin on her face.

'You look like you're buzzing. You're *soooo* pretty when you smile.'

'Shut up,' May said jokingly, shaking her head. 'How are you?'

'Erm, no, May, you aren't doing that. You aren't coming on a call looking like you've just won the lottery and then not telling me why. Come on, spill the beans.' Scarlett cupped her ears and leaned closer to the screen.

Alexander interrupted with a big meow followed by walking in front of the laptop screen.

'Oooh, Alexander baby, look at me, your auntie Scarlett. Here, baby,' she said in a silly voice, patting the bed next to her, as if he could possibly walk into May's laptop and out the other side at Scarlett's.

Alexander turned to May, showing Scarlett his bum and rubbing against May's head.

'Oh my God, I've just seen a cat's shitter *in full HD*,' Scarlett screamed, clasping her hands to her mouth.

May burst out laughing and tapped her knee. Alexander hadn't sat on her lap before and she hadn't tried coaxing him to, but after Scarlett tapping her bed, she was curious. He climbed straight on and sat down. 'Alexander says sorry for flashing.'

'Gross. Tell him I will be having words with him when I come up.'

May's eyes flitted from Alexander to Scarlett with potential excitement. 'Are you coming up?'

'Yeah, for your birthday. A few days beforehand. I've got no auditions and I have diary days clear.'

'You don't have to come up just for me, you know. I'll be fine.'

'It's not just for you, I want to come up and see my mam and Trevor.'

May nodded, unconvinced.

'Anyway, you did a proper sly move there, you and arse flasher Alexander. Why are you so buzzy? What's made my May a happy gal?' Scarlett laughed. 'Come on, man, spit it out.'

'Nothing big, I just got invited to dinner at Peter's,' May said quietly. 'Nothing big' felt like an understatement when she really thought about it.

'Oh, hun, you haven't started to fancy your old man neighbour, have you?' Scarlett asked, eyes wide.

'Jeez, Scarlett, you're weirder than me at times. No, I do not find Peter attractive.' She grimaced and then softened at the thought of Sam. 'But, well, his son is visiting, and he's just lovely.'

'Get in. Oh my gosh, this is brilliant. Tell me *every detail*,' Scarlett screamed, pounding the sides of her fists against her pillows with excitement.

'*Ow*,' May said as Alexander jumped from her knee. She rubbed at it, knowing for a fact there were now claw pin pricks in her leg. 'This is why you are an actress.' She laughed. 'You are beyond dramatic.'

'Tell me, May McClelland, *immediately*.'

'There isn't much to tell. I've only met him three times, two of which were very brief.'

Scarlett rolled her hand, waiting for May to continue.

'Well, I went round for cake the other night and the three of us chatted. He seems really nice, a little older than us and he's been living in Birmingham but is divorced and coming back up here.' May took a breath. 'So, yeah, that's Sam.'

'Is he super hot?'

May smiled. 'Well, you wouldn't fancy him, but I think he's quite handsome, and he has a wonderful personality.'

'Have you looked him up on social media? What's his surname?' Scarlett asked, grabbing her mobile and looking with anticipation at May.

'I haven't even thought to look, to be honest. It's Parsley, Sam Parsley.'

'Great name.' Scarlett snorted. 'Right, give me a second.' She typed away on her mobile as May took a drink of water. 'Is that him?' She pushed her mobile phone to the front of the screen. It showed a man with another man on a beach.

'No, he has red hair.'

Scarlett continued searching. 'Here we go, this has to be him?' She held the phone to the screen again. The image was of a man sitting at a table in what looked like a pub, smiling and holding a pint glass.

May grinned. 'Yeah, that's him.'

She turned her phone back round and took another look, smiling. 'Oh, he's sweet, May. I can see why you think he's a cutie.' She tapped the screen, then proudly stated, 'I've friend requested him.'

'*Scarlett*. He won't know who you are.' May bit her lip, her heart beginning to race.

'No, but he soon will.' She winked. 'Relax, May. On a serious note though, it's lovely to see you excited about a man and even better that it's Peter's son. Despite me joking around about him, Peter seems a lovely guy. He clearly thinks the world of you. Maybe I can meet him when I come up?'

May nodded. 'What day you coming?'

'Monday, I reckon. Can I see you Tuesday night?'

'Erm, yeah, that sounds good.'

'Ok, hun, will look forward to seeing you. I'm knackered, so having an early night. Lots of love.' Scarlett blew May a kiss.

'Night, lovely, love you.'

May hung up the call and turned to see Alexander on the armchair, curled up on her hoody. She smiled as she watched his body gently moving up and down.

Chapter 32

24th May

May opened her eyes to an almost smiling Alexander looking at her. 'Hello, boy,' she said as he headed up the bed to reach her face. She stroked under his chin, and he stretched his neck. *I wish I was a cat; what a life.*

May thought about her dinner with Peter and Sam that evening. She felt a flutter of excitement through her body, like dandelion seeds floating around in the breeze. She couldn't ignore that over the last few days, she'd felt more interested in life than she had for a long time.

Added to this, for the first time in ages, she had slept in.

Alexander stretched before jumping off the bed. He pranced into the lounge and straight through to the kitchen, over to the fridge. His meows gave away exactly what he wanted.

'I'm coming, I'm coming.' May opened the fridge and put some of the tuna onto a plate. Alexander tucked straight in when she placed it on the floor, and now that he was sorted, she put the kettle on and prepared her breakfast.

Alexander's insistent meows interrupted her.

'What's the matter now?' She looked down at his empty plate, which he'd clearly licked clean. He meowed again and licked his lips, a flake of tuna hanging from one of his whiskers.

'You still hungry, or do you want to go out?' She went to the top of the stairs, and sure enough, her four-legged house guest followed and began descending the stairs.

She unlocked the door and opened it for Alexander, who ran straight outside and into the warm morning air and the sound of laughter. She followed the noise with her eyes and saw Sam walking from his car, arms linked with a pretty woman. Reality smacked May in the face with a harsh, cold hand as she pulled back, trying to hide behind the door, but as Alexander darted between the happy pair, Sam's gaze turned her way, knowing exactly where he'd come from. Her heart sank like a brick in a bath, and she wanted to slam the door shut, but it was too late.

'Morning, May,' he shouted over, waving. The woman with him turned her gaze from Sam, towards May, and smiled.

She winced and wished it was purely for the fact she was in her dressing gown, then lifted her hand, which felt like a ten-kilogram medicine ball, and waved back. 'Morning.' She quickly slammed the door and ran back upstairs, both hands on her face, as if she were stopping it crumbling. Because it sure had crumbled.

She felt stupid for having feelings for a man she didn't even know, because yes, this sure as hell felt slightly past the crush stage. It was unlike her, as were many of the things she'd done and felt the last few weeks. She'd always controlled many things, including who she let into her life, and even then, she'd been left broken-hearted.

She dug her nails into her scalp, scolding herself for getting wrapped up in the stupid, childish feelings she'd actively avoided as a teenager. Of course Sam wouldn't be interested in her; what did she possibly have to offer? *It doesn't matter anyway because I'm not going to be around for much longer.*

She put her pyjamas on and finished the letters to Trish and Scarlett. She realised now, once again, that her future was categorically one that would be full of let-downs. Sam owed her nothing, of course he didn't, she hardly knew him and he hadn't shown her any inkling he felt any sort of way for her. However, she was embarrassed that she'd mentioned him to Scarlett and had thought there could be any possibility. She was exhausted from the emotional tennis that she had unwillingly been recruited into, and she needed to take control again.

She got another two photo albums out of her cupboard, and they sat on the armchair for over an hour as she sat on the sofa, wanting but not wanting to go through them. Eventually, she picked them up, plonked them on her knee and opened the first one. Memories stared back at her. There were photos of times when her parents would tell the Story of May and she would cringe. Christmas photos with the wider family where she would insist on wearing her choice of outfit and would never wear anything with that itchy glittery material despite it being in fashion and her mam trying to convince her. Nor would she ever wear a Christmas jumper, thinking the cartoon-like illustrations woven into the fabric should be on the TV or on a Christmas card only. She'd always done her own thing, and although her parents had tried to convince her otherwise sometimes, they'd both been secretly pleased she had her own mind.

She flicked through the heavy album, looking at her young and carefree parents smiling at the camera. She kissed her fingers and placed them on her parents' faces, sure that without their love in her early years, life would have been even more challenging for her. On bad days at school, they had been there. When she doubted herself, they had been there. She pushed the scientist out of her mind and hoped her parents were together. Then she hoped she would be with them soon.

Tears led to sleepiness, and she had a nap on her sofa, waking up mid-afternoon. She watched her favourite movie, *Titanic*, a film that both she and her mam loved, with a cup of hot chocolate and the biscuit tin. It didn't exactly help her mood.

She looked at the clock in her lounge and bit her thumbnail. It was 7 p.m., the time she was due at Peter's. She had decided immediately when she saw Sam with the woman this morning that she wouldn't be going.

She wanted to switch off the constant dripping tap of her thoughts. She straightened the coasters on the coffee table for the fourth time, glancing back at the clock, the hands only moving to the next minute. Sam telling her she looked pretty at Peter's played over in her mind. Throwing her head back, she let out a groan. She couldn't decipher what his intentions had been, but she was hurt and didn't want to see him despite the fact it most likely would have been an innocent comment she'd taken hope from. She walked over to the kitchen area and filled the kettle. The clock would soon move and she would just distract herself with the news on TV. Unfortunately, not seeing Sam also meant she wouldn't see Peter until Sam had left and it would probably be a bit awkward, but she didn't care. She wouldn't be around much longer to worry.

After pouring boiled water over the teabag in her cup and giving it a couple of minutes to brew, she carried it into the lounge. She grabbed the fleece and plonked herself on the sofa, refusing to look at the clock. Switching on the TV, she glassed over staring at the screen, unable to smother the Rolodex of thoughts flicking around in her mind.

At 7:15 p.m., her doorbell rang. She knew who it would be and sighed. She stood up and began slowly pacing the room, ignoring the doorbell. A knock followed. Then a few seconds later, 'Hello, hello, May. It's Sam. Are you in?' came through the letterbox.

She covered her ears with her hands and scrunched her eyes closed as she remained standing up. She wanted Sam to go away. Luckily, he soon did, and there were no more knocks on the door.

She remained standing for a further five minutes, a ball of emotions being kicked around her body. Going into her bedroom, she retrieved her notebook from her bedside drawer. She returned to the sofa, cocooned herself in the fleece blanket and looked at her to-do list and crossed off a few more items.

3rd May

To do (before 31st May):

- ~~Spend time with Scarlett.~~

- ~~Spend time with Trish that isn't her looking after me.~~

- Go and see Uncle Terence.

- ~~Visit the cemetery.~~

- ~~Visit Lawson-Wray's (possibly).~~

- ~~Take library books back to university and pay fines.~~

- ~~Run in the park.~~

- ~~Sort throughout the house; take things to charity and leave notes on things I want to give to others.~~

- ~~Arrange finances.~~

- ~~Write letters to Scarlett and Trish – make them as positive as possible and remember to tell them that I love them and why I love them.~~

- ~~Buy paracetamols.~~

- Write will to include Mam and Dad's house to go to Uncle Terence.

- Sort through some things at Mam and Dad's house.

With just three items left to complete, she felt a sense of achievement. She would be seeing Uncle Terence that weekend and had an appointment booked to make her will on Monday. Then she just had to muster the strength to spend a little time at the family home.

If someone had asked her if a person could grieve for things they had never had a few years ago, she would have said it was impossible. But as she sat in her lounge, she did just that. She grieved for not finishing her master's in science, she grieved for never going to countries like America, for never being brave enough to go skinny dipping, for never having been in a helicopter. She grieved for not reading all the books on her list, for never staying up all night watching movies and for not doing karaoke. Then she grieved for the big things, the life blocks that she would never build. Engagement, marriage, children, buying her first house with someone she wanted to spend the rest of her days with. So much that would never be.

Chapter 33

25th May

May woke up with the type of banging headache you get from drinking red wine, but no alcohol had passed her lips. Rubbing her eyes, she sat up and slid her legs out of bed, locating her slippers off the floor with her feet. Cracking her neck as she walked into the bathroom, she opened one side of the mirrored bathroom cabinet and grabbed some painkillers from the shelf. She laughed an ironic laugh when she saw all the packs, stacked up as if part of a game of Jenga, in preparation. She stared at them as she popped two tablets out of a packet into her hand and then into her mouth. Her gaze moved to the closed, mirrored half of the cabinet, then back to the piled-up boxes of tablets. In that second, she wanted to smash the glass of her bathroom cabinet so she didn't have to see what stared back at her. The ugly face of depression, loneliness and failure. Anger bubbled inside of her, and she didn't know whether to cry or scream.

Going back into her bedroom, she returned to bed, falling asleep for a few hours and waking after lunchtime with a rumbling tummy. She heard a car outside and peeked out from behind the bedroom curtains. Sam was in his car, and Peter dashed down the path with a packed lunch that he passed to him through the open window.

'See you Monday, Son,' he shouted, walking away and waving.

May's heart sank. Feeling foolish and sad, she decided she would get up, have a shower and change out of the clothes she had been wearing for well over twenty-four hours, then she would have some food.

After washing and getting her loungewear on, she straightened her bed and then stood with her hands on her hips, wondering what she was going to do with the rest of her day. She'd already wasted half of it in bed. Then again, it wasn't as if she had any commitments today.

Another sound floated in from her slightly open bedroom window—a distinctive call.

'Alexander.' She ran downstairs and opened the door. Alexander was standing there. Unfortunately, so was Peter.

'I guess this cat is your new doorbell?' He laughed as Alexander shot up the stairs.

May shrugged.

'What happened last night, pet?'

May hated lying despite having become a champion deceiver in the last few weeks. Peter had what her mam would have termed an honest face—open, transparent. It was always in the eyes, Fran had told her. His eyes looked sad and concerned.

'I-I was-wasn't well,' she stuttered, rubbing her nose.

'Well, I've brought you this.' Peter held out a container. 'It won't be as nice warmed up, perhaps a bit dry, but hopefully it'll still be edible.'

May took it and looked at the ground. 'Thank you, Peter.' Seeing the portion of lasagne made her feel even worse. Not only had he cooked for her, he wasn't angry that she hadn't turned up and had still made sure she got the food even if it was the next day.

'I'll come in for a cuppa if you want?'

'Well, I'm a bit busy, to be honest.' She bit the inside of her lip, sure he could sense her unease.

'Okay, but don't be a stranger, May. I've missed our chats even though Sam has been here.' Peter dropped his head and started back up the path.

'Wait.' She didn't like how she felt watching him walking away disheartened. She'd let him down, she was in the wrong with that and she had some making up to do. 'Maybe just a quick cuppa?' She stepped to the side, and Peter turned back around with a small smile and a nod as he entered her flat and followed her upstairs.

'One second,' she said to him as she popped her head around her bedroom door. She stopped and smiled as she saw Alexander curled up on her bed.

'Tea or coffee?' She made her way to the kitchen, thinking Peter would answer and sit down, but he followed her.

'Tea, please, pet.' He leaned against the kitchen bench. 'So, you were poorly last night?'

May had her back to Peter as she got cups and spoons. She was pleased he couldn't see her face and pick up on the lie she was about to tell. 'Yeah, I just wasn't feeling well. Sorry.'

'I was worried. Sam knocked on your door.'

'Did he?' She turned around and gave an apologetic smile. 'I was flat out. Exhausted.'

'I think we should swap mobile numbers, pet, just in case, you know, in the future. One of us may be ill and, well, sometimes it's nice to check in.'

May swallowed and nodded. 'Right, here you go.' She picked up both cups and passed Peter his. 'Let's go and sit down. I'll get the biscuit tin. Sorry I haven't got any cakes.'

They moved into the lounge, and Peter sat down on the armchair.

'Sorry, there might be cat hair on there.'

He shrugged, unphased by any evidence left over from Alexander.

'It's been wonderful having Sam's company this week and it's been lovely to see him with his mam despite Anne not recognising him when he visited.' Peter paused for a moment and raised a clenched fist to his mouth. 'It's taken a bit of the burden off, you know what I mean? A problem shared is a problem halved as they say.'

May bit the inside of her lip and didn't respond. Her mobile phone rang, breaking the silence. She picked it up from the coffee table and looked at it. It was a withheld number, which she never answered; however, she was waiting for a call back from the bank and had already spent over sixty minutes trying to get through to them. *Surely they'll ring back?* She could always ring them tomorrow.

'Answer it if you need to.' Peter took a biscuit from the tin.

'Erm, no, it's okay.' She turned her phone facedown on the sofa next to her and put a hand to her forehead. When returning her gaze to Peter, he saw her watery eyes.

'May, pet, what's wrong?' He leaned over from the armchair and gently placed his hand on her forearm.

'Please, Peter, it's okay. Please don't be nice to me.' A tear slid down her cheek, and she turned away.

'May, I'm going to say a few things that I've wanted to for a while.' He sat forward, moving his body to mirror her sitting position opposite. May glanced down at her lap. She was almost on the edge of the sofa, and she grabbed the cushion from beside her, hugging it to her stomach.

'I'm going to tell you a little bit about myself, May. I know you're aware of my life now, with my Anne being poorly and of course Sam. But I wasn't always an old codger.' He looked at her, a twinkle in his eye as he smiled, and she let a weak laugh escape from her sad face.

'When I was younger, I worked in a job I loved supporting people who had poor mental health, and I did it for over twenty years. I didn't get into it until my late thirties by the time I did all of my training. A bit like with you and your science studies, there was a lot to learn.'

May stared silently, partially intrigued and partially confused as to where he was going with this conversation.

'Before I worked with people who had mental health issues, I was a landscape gardener. I loved that as well, but it wasn't so nice in the winter, pet, and I blame my dodgy knees on years of bending and resting them on concrete. Never mind, I'm going off track.' He scratched his head before continuing. 'Anyway, something tragic happened that led me to decide I wanted to help people who were struggling. You see, my older brother Samuel took his life.'

It was as if May's strength left her, and the cup fell from her hand. It bounced across the carpet, spilling the entirety of her tea. 'Oh gosh, I'm so sorry.' She fumbled to pick up the cup and ran with it to the kitchen, dropping it in the sink almost in the same way as she'd dropped it on the floor. She watched her shaking hands holding the sink and tried focusing on her quickening breathing. First, Trish had confided in her about how suicide had nearly ended her life, and now Peter was telling her about how it had ended his brother's. And what was she supposed to do with that information?

She quickly composed herself, knowing Peter would soon join her in the kitchen if she didn't go back, grabbed a cloth and used it to absorb the majority of the spilt liquid. She put it on the table as she sat down—something she wouldn't usually do.

'I'm really sorry, I just wasn't expecting it. Please, go on.'

'Don't worry, pet, I'm sorry if I gave you a shock.'

'No, it's not your fault,' was all she could muster as she felt a heavy beat pounding in her chest. She nodded, indicating Peter to go on.

'It was a horrendous time, May. My parents under-standably never fully recovered, and for me, well, after Samuel passed, it was like my world had been replaced with someone else's. He was my hero, my big brother who'd showed me how to play footie and would give me the answers to my homework. He was my idol and apparently a top-class actor. No one knew he was strug-gling. He was over the river, working in Durham, and had his own flat. He was only twenty-eight years old and had achieved so much. Young and with a lifetime to look forward to.' Peter looked intently at May, and at that moment, she felt as if he could see all her secrets. She realised he was sharing his story not with her but for her.

'Samuel didn't tell us—me and my folks—but he had lost his job managing a building firm, and a fortnight before that, his girlfriend had left him for another man. He would come over each weekend, usually for Sunday dinner, but he was a busy man, so it wasn't unusual to get no answer on his landline if we called. On the Saturday, Samuel's best friend rang us saying he couldn't get through to him by telephone and he hadn't come to footie practice. That Sunday, my father found Samuel dead in his house.' Peter wiped his nose, tilted his head back and took a deep breath.

'You could have given me a list of people and I would have put Samuel at the bottom of that list when it came to mental illness and suicide. The problem was, he'd had no one to check up on him except for the odd snippets through the week. We don't know how long he was struggling before his world imploded. They say sometimes you can't stop people doing what they will do, but, pet, I never even got a chance to try.' Tears welled in Peter's eyes.

The emotion in his voice and the words spoke of such pain and loss. May felt as if a herd of bulls had stampeded through her. She wanted to comfort Peter, but she just couldn't. How could she when she knew exactly what she was planning?

'He thought we would be better off without him. That's what he had written in a diary that was found in his house afterwards. Dark words of despair. It was hideous to read... it just wasn't our Samuel. Well, not the one I knew.' Peter's chin trembled and he sniffed. 'He felt so low that he didn't want to ask for help and didn't want to drag us down. He had no history of mental illness that I knew of, although in those days, almost fifty years ago, no one asked, especially when it came to men. I couldn't accept it for months, then I couldn't forgive him. I was so angry. How could he leave us? It didn't make any sense. I was in my early twenties and I needed my big brother.

'It took me so long to even try to understand, and I didn't think I ever could or would. It was a few years after Samuel died that I decided I didn't want anyone to feel how myself and my parents had and still did. If I could help one person to stay alive, it would be magical and our Samuel's death wouldn't be in vain.'

Their eyes locked across the coffee table as May wrung her hands together, knowing Peter was almost reading her mind.

Eventually, he spoke again, 'I studied and trained to be a mental health worker for almost five years, and it's where I met my Anne. Then I spent over two decades working with people with a range of emotional needs. It helped me, and I hope I helped them.'

May swallowed. 'I had no idea.' Peter was such a kind soul, so it made sense that he would have used his trauma to help others. She wished she could be like that rather than just wanting to escape and seeing her pain as ir-reparable.

'I know. You know the biggest thing I learnt while working with people in mental pain, May? I learnt that the best medicine of all is kindness. It's taking the time to say hello, ask how someone is, show an interest, talking and listening. It costs absolutely nothing. And you know what else? Things can *always* get better. Sometimes we just need a helping hand to get us back on our feet and learning to walk again. And there is *always* a hand ready to help.'

May's breath caught in her throat as he held his hand out across the small table separating them. She stared at it, considering whether she wanted to or was ready to take it, but Peter's face remained understanding and his hand determinedly outstretched, like a life raft in a sea where she was drowning. Eventually, she leaned forward and took his hand. He held on tightly, determined to keep her head above water as waves crashed around her. She began to sob.

'I don't know exactly what's going on in your head, but I know something sad is. I've worked with enough people over the years to know, and more than that, May, you're my friend, and I think I know you well enough to see something is wrong.'

May felt many things she didn't want to feel—caught out, embarrassed—but she didn't feel invisible anymore. Someone had noticed. Peter had noticed. And she felt relieved.

She looked up from her lap and sniffed. 'I'm sorry.'

'Stop apologising. You're human. I could and can see in your eyes that you're struggling, and I might be older, but my hearing is like a fox's. I've heard you sobbing and I've heard the nightmares, pet, yet you still listened to me go on about Anne and still managed to help me so much. May, you haven't given up, you just don't necessarily feel the strength I can see in you right now.' He squeezed her hand and nodded. 'I know you aren't happy, but pain passes, I promise. We never forget, but we do heal. Do you believe in serendipity?'

'No, not really, I'm a scientist. Or I was,' she replied flatly as she wiped her eyes.

'Well, I do. I believe that we accidentally find good things and people, often at times we really need them. May, I think we are each other's serendipity, and the fact that my Sam has asked about "pretty May next door" most of the week makes me think it even more.'

This caught her by surprise, and she didn't have time to let her hair fall forward to cover her face before she felt her cheeks heat up.

'Then there's that cat who is on your bed. Alexander, right? He's part of it, put in your path. He needs you. Just like your friends, including me. So, whatever's going on, let me help.'

Chapter 34

26th May

Yesterday, May had told Peter she wasn't ready to talk, which was true. Her brain would swim in the most beautiful water only to be caught in a poisonous sea in the next stroke, and the conflict was confusing. Peter was kind and patient, asking her if she would come over for cake tomorrow (today). Alexander slept on her bed again last night, his purrs soothing her to sleep.

She was going to see Uncle Terence tomorrow and needed to visit her family home today, knowing Uncle Terence would ask about the house. It was something she had been putting off, the sore that wasn't healing. But before that, she wanted to try Mad's Park Run to challenge herself, commit, not just drop out as she usually did when it came to plans that weren't firmly arranged. She would avoid them and people, often chastising herself for it afterwards. It was simply too hard sometimes. She had been curious about Maddie and her recovery since she had been handed the flyer, and she'd spent a lot of time researching EMDR. Perhaps it was somewhere between a distraction and an attempt to rescue herself.

Alexander fussed around her ankles as she got her trainers on and opened the front door.

'And what are we going to do with you, boy?' She patted his head, and he left alongside her, heading on his own little run around the estate.

She arrived at the park fifteen minutes before the park run was due to start. Walking through the entrance arch, she inhaled, the fresh scent fuelling her as usual. She strolled towards the mobile coffee hut, where the flyer stated the run started. Getting closer, she could smell sharp coffee and saw customers chatting with the woman serving them. Stopping near enough but not to get in thirsty folks' way, she began to stretch, snatching glances of people as they passed in case they may be potential runners. Her watch indicated it was now ten minutes before Mad's Park Run. Nerves started to do gymnastics in her stomach, and she contemplated taking off solo and doing her own thing. Yes, that's what she'd do. She took the first step of her jog.

'Hi.'

Turning, she saw Maddie behind her wearing leopard print leggings and a brown top. Her bouncy curls were held back with a bandana.

'Oh, hello,' she answered, suddenly feeling a slight calm in her stomach.

'Lovely to see you again. Are you here for the park run?' Maddie touched May's arm gently, and she had to force herself to not pull away from Maddie's touch.

'Erm yeah, I am,' she said as she moved from side to side.

'I'm so pleased. It's a great little group.'

May nodded. 'It was interesting, your flyer.'

'Oh, thanks. Well, I had a really bad time and running massively helped me.' Maddie glanced around and waved at two people who were approaching, 'Lots of the people who come to the group have had mental health issues, and others know someone who has. It's so common, and it's nice to meet and have a shared understanding, you know?' She smiled and turned her hips side to side, beginning to stretch.

The couple reached them, and Maddie beamed before making introductions. Several minutes later, there was a group of around ten people, all stretched and ready to begin the park run. They seemed a friendly bunch, smiling at or greeting May, and although most appeared to know one another, some turned up solo. She would have normally been anxious for days before something like the park run—actually, she knew she simply wouldn't have participated unless it had been compulsory. It was stretching her comfort zone to the point of an elastic band snapping. Weirdly, she hadn't felt so consumed by doubt and the unknown of a new situation. Her nails were intact, she had slept the two nights before and she felt uncharacteristically herself despite a few nerves. Perhaps she had stopped caring, given her plan. She wasn't sure. But for this morning, she would enjoy this more carefree version of herself.

The run soon commenced, with Maddie reiterating the route and a few health and safety points. It was a slightly different course to the ones May had been on the last few weeks. Instead of feeling strange about it, she embraced it. They ran deep into the wooded area, along a short track surrounded by silver birch and oak trees. Squirrels scurried up the trees, some stretching their neck once in a place of safety to observe the army of feet coming their way. The air was damp and refreshing, and May tilted her head back, looked up at the sky through the trees and almost laughed. She felt free. And despite the unfamiliarity of the route, this one was in fact better, with fewer people—not taking into account the ones she was running with—and a more intimate look at nature.

After forty minutes, the group was back at the meeting point, everyone stretching off, full of endorphins. Some grabbed a cuppa from the coffee hut. The run hadn't been about chatting, yet she'd felt connected to the other runners. It had been a whole new experience for her and very different to the running club from school. With each pound of the ground, she'd felt an energy, a bond with nature. In a way, she felt as if the park had a silent understanding of her turmoil.

'Nice to meet you.' One woman raised her hand in a wave at May as they began to walk away.

'You too.'

Maddie stepped towards May. 'It was great to see you again, May. I'm so pleased you came along, and hopefully you'll come back again?'

'Yeah, erm, definitely. Thanks so much,' she said, rubbing the sweat from her brow.

'Magic. If you need to get in touch before next week, any questions and that, here's my card.' Maddie handed over a business card, and the pair said goodbye.

May strolled home turning Maddie's business card over in her hands and feeling a sense of achievement.

Although the run had mentally energised May, it had left her feeling sweaty and hungry. With her hair left wet to naturally dry after a quick shower, she placed two slices of bread in the toaster and put some baked beans in a pan on the hob. She was dreading the visit to her family home, replaying the ghosts of memories. As she waited for the toast to pop, she stirred the beans with one hand and unlocked her mobile phone with the other before opening Facebook. No notifications, but there was a friend request. She raised her eyebrow and clicked it.

'Oh gosh.' She took her hand from the wooden spoon and put the tips of her fingers to her lips. It was Sam. She quickly put her phone down on the bench as if it were hot out of the oven. *I have to accept him,* she thought, *otherwise it will be weird.* She reflected back to a few days ago when she'd seen Sam arm in arm with a woman. *Why would he request me if he has a girlfriend?* Then she shook her head, berating herself and realising that in most social circles, men and women were friends. She picked up her phone quickly and pressed accept before placing it facedown and serving her lunch.

She ate her food, cleared up and drove to her parents' home. As she entered the street where her parents had lived all her life, she saw their house in the distance, the welcoming royal blue door that she'd helped choose. *Oh God, oh God, oh God.* She pulled over as the first feeling of nausea hit her like an axe in her torso. Opening her car window, she gulped in the air. Her legs were shaking, and she placed her hands on them, trying to control the movement. She hadn't been there for two months, and somewhere in her mind, she had locked the door of the house and thrown the key far away. Maybe she should have asked Trish to come with her. No, no, she shouldn't have; she needed to stop being everyone's pity case.

With her legs still too wobbly to drive, she turned off the engine at the top of the street and stepped out of the car, the small breeze hardly enough to even begin to take the edge off the hot sweats accompanying her light-headedness. She closed her eyes and tried to ground herself—listened to a car door slam nearby, chatter floating to the street from one of the gardens, where she assumed the smell of sausages and burgers was coming from—before opening her eyes again and forcing herself to walk. The street was like a treasure map of childhood memories, and she could almost see herself as a teenager walking home from school next to herself now on the pavement, a younger her running around, playing with the few other children her age who didn't think she was too weird. She wanted to sit on the curb and rewind time to fifteen years ago, when playing with swing ball in the front garden was the ultimate answer to happiness, when the sound of the ice cream van was the highlight of the week and the only decision she had to make was ice cream cone or ice cream sandwich.

She stopped, stood and stared as her teenage self passed her, crossed the road and walked down the drive to her parents' house. She clutched her stomach as sickness crawled around her insides. After taking a deep breath, she walked closer on unsteady feet, balancing on the tightrope of collapse. Then she was there, on the other side of the road, facing the top of the drive, staring at her past. With shaky hands, she fumbled with the zip on her bag, successful in getting it open but failing once it came to finding the keys. She sat with a huff on the curb opposite her family home, which she used to dance on, balance on and throw balls off.

Then she heard a door open and looked up and saw Mrs Taylor from next door.

'Oh, May, darling,' she said, rushing over. 'Are you okay?'

'Hi, Mrs Taylor. Erm, yes, thank you,' May lied, glancing at the ground.

Surprisingly, Mrs Taylor sat next to her, letting out a little groan as her legs bent and her bottom touched the pavement.

'May, darling, I've known you almost all your life. Please call me Alison.'

May smiled, and Alison patted her hand. They sat side by side, looking at the McClelland house.

'Scary, isn't it? Coming back to the past.'

May nodded but didn't speak, her voice too thick with sadness to make a sound. It began to rain lightly, but neither of them acknowledged the drizzle.

'I was very fond of your parents, May. They were incredible people and the best neighbours anyone could ask for. I remember when I was pregnant with Imarah all those years ago and I felt unwell and frightened. Johnny was at work and I couldn't get in touch with him. Your parents were in, and I knocked. I was so scared.'

Alison squeezed May's hand, and May turned to her, noticing her eyes filled with tears. 'They looked after me, your mam and dad, and I won't ever forget that. They were very special, and they loved you dearly.'

May dropped Alison's hand and let out a little yelp.

'Come on, darling, let it out.' Alison gently pulled May's head onto her shoulder as May sobbed. For someone who always shielded away from human contact, she had been hugged, embraced and patted a lot over the last few weeks.

Straightening her head, May wiped her eyes with the sleeve of her jumper. Her face felt blotchy and puffy from crying and her head was pounding. She wanted to sit there all day, in the rain, too frightened to go into the house. She pulled her legs into her chest, hugging them gently before getting up from the ground. Once up, she turned to Alison and held her hand out, helping her neighbour up from the cold, damp pavement.

'Thanks so much, Mrs... Alison,' she said quietly, rubbing her face.

'No worries, darling, we don't mind popping in as much as you need us to. And if you decide to rent the property out, we're happy to help any prospective tenants look around. I know you probably aren't ready to put it up for sale, but if and when.'

May nodded.

'I can come in with you now if you want?' Alison said softly, glancing at the house.

'It's okay, but thank you.' May sighed, then pushed her shoulders back.

'Well, you know where I am if you need me, May.' Alison smiled and began to walk away, leaving May staring at the front door as she tentatively took steps across the narrow road and down the path of her past.

Her hand wobbling, she put the key in the lock and turned it. The door opened, and she stepped over the few bits of mail on the doormat as she entered the house. She inhaled, taking in the familiar, comforting smell. She found it funny how you would never know the smell of your own home, but you could always smell someone else's house, as each seemed to have its own unique fragrance. Walking through to the lounge, the furniture was still all there, but most of the memories from the wall had come down—some after Fran had died, and some when Victor died, May frantically taking them and storing them in her flat. She hadn't been able to face beginning to tear the place apart and sort the house out despite her renowned organisational skills and had only grabbed a few things the two times she had visited since Victor died.

May sat in her dad's chair, rubbing the armrests and wishing he would come in from the kitchen and tell her to 'bloody move', in the jokey way he used to. She moved around the house, smiling at the things that had seemed so important—the special cups bought on holidays or for birthdays in the cupboard, the Monet print in the dining room. As she walked around downstairs, she saw memories everywhere. Conversations on the sofas, the space where the Christmas tree always went, the candles that her mam loved but that Victor said smelt like a pot of all the Duty Free perfumes mixed together.

She wanted to turn around, run out of the house and never go back, but she knew she had to do something, at least make a start, for Fran and Victor. Placing her hands to her mouth, she was overwhelmed as to where to begin.

'I'll start at the top,' she said aloud, as if trying to convince herself. The loft. She would go in the loft, just for an hour. There may be important things there that Uncle Terence might deem unimportant due to being in the loft.

She walked up the stairs and pulled the loft hatch open. The loft stairs slid down, and she locked them in place, took a massive breath and climbed up them, switching on the light at the top. The Christmas tree was in its box to the left. She placed a hand on her heart, stared at it for a moment and then looked away. There were boxes neatly stacked at the far end of the loft, behind the suitcases that the family had seemed to collect over the years, the bashed ones becoming storage; therefore, none ever getting thrown away.

May reached the boxes and lifted the lid off one. It had some of her childhood toys in—teddy bears, dolls, Lego and books. Another box had similar items. Then she opened a third, which was full of hardback books. She picked one out and realised they were diaries. She scratched her head, not recalling ever seeing them. 1987 was on the front of the first one she retrieved. She pulled out a few more—1991, 1998, 1981. The box was filled with decades of documented thoughts.

She flicked them open, and they displayed the day and date, just like a normal diary; however, each day was filled with a few lines, a paragraph, sometimes more squashed into the space allocated for the day. She gasped and ran her fingers over what she knew to be Fran's handwriting, the words blurring beneath the tears welling in her eyes. She wanted to wipe the tears away to read the words, but another part worried that her mam wouldn't have wanted anyone to enter her private world. After a time of going back and forth in her mind, she started pulling the diaries out carefully but hurriedly, determined to keep Fran alive and to gain the hope these pages could bring her.

May put the diaries into year order, and for the next two and a half hours, she sat on the boarded floor and read some of them. She laughed, she sobbed, she gasped with new knowledge. She felt closer to her mam than she had in all the time she had been dead. Going in chronological order, she came to the diary of the year she was born. The sickness, the body changes and emotional changes that came with pregnancy. Fran had documented how much she loved May before she was born, preparing for the new arrival, how it was all she and Victor had ever wanted. Tears streamed down May's face. She had been so loved and so lucky. She had been cherished, protected, adored. She then came to the entry for the day after her birth and read it between the blurring of her tears.

'We have her, our beautiful May. I feel like I've waited all my life to hold her, all 7lbs 6oz of joy. She's perfect. I know all parents say that, but she is. Our perfect May. People talk about love, they talk about being parents, but you never know. You can't know the love until it's yours, and after what's felt like forever, it's mine now, ours. And I promise, my beautiful baby May, that I will love you forever. Your dad and me, we will love you forever. Because you are the most precious gift, and for as long as I live (and beyond) I will always cherish you and look after you. That's my promise, our promise.'

Dropping the diary, May grabbed her mouth. She thought back to the story told countless times about her birth, the one everybody almost knew the script of. She crumpled into a ball on the loft floor, holding her legs to her chest. She wailed like a wounded animal. For the first time in her life, she saw the true meaning behind the words, the true love that they'd always had for their daughter and they always would, even in death.

That afternoon, as she turned off the switch lighting up the loft, a light that had been broken, leaving her soul in darkness for so long turned back on in her, although dim. Could it be that her parents, as her mam had stated, were still looking after her and loving her from beyond? She was still struggling with that concept, but after seeing the blackbird countless times and reading her mam's promise, she wasn't as closed off to the idea as she'd previously been.

Perhaps it isn't my time to die after all.

Leaving her family home and walking back up the street to her car, she checked her phone and found a message from Sam. *'Hi May, just wanted to check after the other night that you are okay and of course to say hello! x'*

May bit the inside of her lip. She was pleased Sam had texted her, but the message also just reminded her of the woman he had been with and that her response would be more lying. She shook her head, wanting to disperse the thoughts, but she typed a quick reply.

'Hi, Sam, thanks, yes I'm fine. I was feeling poorly. I didn't have your dad's number to tell him, but we've swapped numbers now. Hope I didn't cause too much inconvenience.'

May thought about what Peter had said the night before about serendipity. She was usually a factual person, but he had a point. Some things that had happened in the last few weeks seemed odd. They could have been a coincidence, of course, which would be what the scientist in her would conclude, but at the time in her life when she needed them more than ever? They almost felt like a sign. Something to keep her eyes open when she wanted them to permanently close.

'May, pet, come on in,' Peter said, his usual pleasant greeting, after she'd knocked on the door. She'd been researching EMDR ever since coming home from her parents' and had slightly lost track of time; however, she was only five minutes late, so Peter didn't seem to notice.

After cups of tea were made and slices of coconut cake cut, the pair sat down.

Peter leaned back on his armchair with a sigh, his already flat cushions flattening further behind his back. 'My new sofa will be here on Tuesday. I can't wait,' he said, eyes lighting up as he shoved a forkful of cake into his mouth.

'Sounds like it will be lovely, Peter.' May tucked into the tasty cake herself, relishing the butter icing, mouth almost tingling from the sweet coconut.

'Well, Sam will be sleeping on it for a few nights next week, staying between here and Rachael's. He's coming up Tuesday, as he has some house viewings. He's going to rent for six months or so, to make sure the new job is secure and all that.' Peter's cheeks lifted in a satisfied smile.

Nodding uncomfortably, May dug her fork into the soft golden sponge, certain Rachael was the woman she'd seen Sam with.

'He was asking after you, pet. I think he might like you as more than a friend.' Peter's eyes remained on her, inviting her to comment.

May coughed, almost choking on a bit of cake she had swiftly put in her mouth. She uncomfortably swallowed. 'What about Rachael?'

Peter tipped his head back and started laughing as if they were watching a comedy sketch on TV. She frowned, her shoulders stiffening.

'Rachael's gay. She and our Sam are old college friends.'

May closed her eyes, wanting to disappear.

'I'm so pleased Sam is coming home. Both Anne and me need him. I would never have asked, as he's an adult and needs his own life, but I can't pretend I'm not over the moon. Anyway, enough about me, I hope you feel more positive about the future after our chat yesterday?'

'For the last few months, I've felt so alone, with no point or purpose. Like I'm a burden to the few people in my life that always have to pick me up. And I miss my parents so much.' May took a breath and rubbed her fingers. 'The grief was and kind of still is suffocating me.'

Peter leaned forward, towards her. 'May, you've had the hardest of times and you did one of the bravest things—you opened up. I'm honoured you could open up to me, and I'm proud of you, pet. I promise, May, the days will become kinder to you, easier. You're a strong lass.'

May put her hands to her face and breathed out. She wanted to cry, the whirlwind of emotions threatening to blast through her composure. She had struggled her whole life to open up to people, fearing and experiencing rejection and mocking. Peter cared so much about his family, and for some reason, he seemed to care about her.

'That's what my dad used to always say, that he was proud of me. You almost sounded just like him there.' She bit back the tears, pressing her lips together.

Chapter 35

27th May

May didn't have grief as her first thought waking up on Sunday. She wasn't immediately reminded of what she didn't have; in fact, her first thought was Alexander, who she instinctively turned to stroke upon waking. His rumbling purring commenced immediately, and she lay, listening to his calming audio, wondering what was going on in his head. Her thoughts drifted to Sam and the reality of him being around more and what that could mean. It was hard for her not to escalate in her thoughts, but instead of thinking the worst and that she would be hurt, abandoned and experience more loss, she flipped the coin and thought about possible friendship if not dates and romance.

She took her hand away from Alexander, tucked her arms back under the quilt and stretched her legs out. She looked at the ceiling and focused on her breathing—in and out, in and out—letting the quietness surround her as the sun snuck into her room through the ajar curtains. She felt a calmness, as if floating in the sea on one of the many lilos purchased over the years during family holidays. She remained in her own bubble until a paw gently tapped her face and she heard a meow, indicating Alexander wanted breakfast.

By the time grief reached her, she was up and making a cup of tea. As her tea brewed, she thought about the diaries. Instead of the punch of loss right-hooking her stomach, she pondered reading more of them. The dread of going back to the family home was smothered slightly by the thought of the diary entry from the day after her birth. It had been so upsetting to read, but there was a comfort in the words that stuck with her and that she could almost recite. She had left the box of diaries, not sure how she felt about moving them from their space. But she was sure that she was ready to read more.

After feeding Alexander some chunks of chicken, he started licking a white paw before giving himself a full bath on her lounge rug as she ate her breakfast. Leg in the air, he stopped mid-clean and glanced at her. She giggled at his yoga pose. She decided she'd buy him some cat food today, as it wasn't practical or affordable to keep feeding him tuna or chicken or ham despite her inclination to believe he would be more than okay with that. He was staying most nights now, and although she had been out for periods of time over the last few days, he hadn't seemed to roam too far from her flat. She had become fond of her furry companion and he seemed to quite like her. No one had responded to the posters, but she still didn't know if he was indeed homeless. After researching, she'd discovered cats usually have a few homes they visit. *Must be their flirty and persistent nature.* As if knowing he was occupying her mind, Alexander moved from the rug, towards her, meowing and rubbing against her ankles.

'C'mon, then, I bet you want out.'

She got up from the sofa and headed towards the stairs, Alexander trotting a few steps ahead. She unlocked the front door and let him out, glancing at the tree opposite her flat, where a few birds were chattering away, including a blackbird. Smiling, she shut the door and went back up to her lounge.

She had a quick shower, pulled on some jeans and a jumper, then headed off on the almost ninety-minute journey to see her uncle. As she drove, she thought about how Uncle Terence might have felt these last few months, losing his only brother. *The thing with grief,* May thought, *is that you can't see beyond your own. Everyone else's is too much to consider when you're suffocating.* It was only now, as she drove along the motorway, that she considered her uncle. She had been unintentionally self-ish, her desire to not live having taken her to a place of inability to think of others, consumed by her own desperation, depression and worthlessness. She wanted to make amends, and it started with recognising her uncle had feelings, just as she did.

Motivated by her internal pep talk, she continued on her journey determined to make the visit positive for him. When she reached her destination, she spotted Uncle Terence sitting next to and looking out of the large lounge window. On spotting her car, he rose and went to the door.

'May, it's so good to see you.' He greeted her with open arms and then they went inside.

The last time she had been to Uncle Terence's, Victor had been with her, and as she and Uncle Terrence en-tered the lounge, she glanced at the green armchair her dad had sat in.

'Cuppa, May?' Uncle Terrence headed into the kitchen without her response, and she followed.

Returning to the lounge with their cups of tea five minutes later, the pair sat in silence for a minute.

Gripping her cup, May looked into it and spoke, 'I miss him, Uncle Terrence. And I know he isn't coming back, but I can't help but wish so hard for it.' She sniffed and raised her eyes to her uncle sat opposite.

'You'll always miss him. It never goes away. I still miss your grandad and your nanna. And now your da's added to the list.' One side of his mouth curled up into a sad smile, the same one Victor had. 'But you know what, May. The dead don't want us to be sad for long. Your da would want you to mourn, to miss him, but only for a short time. He was so damn proud of his May, loved the bones of you. He would be gutted if you were upset all the time. You won't forget him, nor your ma, but don't forget to live.'

May couldn't speak. She felt as if she had been waiting all this time for someone to say those words to her and to be able to listen, not just hear them. Uncle Terence knew

Victor like no one else, as only a sibling can. He was right, and she just had to remember what he said.

The pair kept talking anecdotes and memories. They brought comfort and made May smile rather than her usual breakdown into a pool of salty tears. Sharing stories with her uncle felt a stark contrast to the days when her parents used to repeat the Story of May and she'd wanted to shrivel up in the corner of the room. Terence mentioned the story, and they both laughed.

'It's tragic they're gone, it really is. I wish with all my might I could bring them back for you, for everyone. But it's magical you had them and how much they loved you. Never forget that. I hope in time you go back to your studies. Your folks would want that.' Uncle Terence had the same kind eyes as her dad, and although physically they looked different, for a second, May saw Victor in him and felt comforted.

She nodded, that seed of hope growing inside her again. 'I'm going to sort the house out over the next few months, then maybe rent it for now. I'm not sure I'll ever be ready to let it go, but I'm not ready to live there. Does that make sense?'

'Perfect sense. Just take your time, May, there's no rush. And remember, I'm here if you need me.'

May left her uncle's feeling as if her mind were cracking through a thick layer of ice and she was able to see the sunlight. She headed back home, stopping off at the supermarket on the way, where she purchased a range of cat food for Alexander alongside a few items for herself. As if he knew, Alexander was sitting in her garden when she pulled up, front paws stretched out on the grass. As she gathered the bags from her boot, she could hear him approaching, vocalising his hello.

'Alright, alright.' She laughed, struggling with her shopping as she tried to open the door for an impatient Alexander. 'You just go on in, then, don't bother helping me.' She smiled, looking up the stairs as his tail disappeared around the corner.

She unpacked her shopping and fed the incessant Alexander, then sliced some cheese and placed it on top of two pieces of bread that she then slid under her grill. The pale cheese bubbled under the heat, turning stretchy as the salty smell and the nuttiness of the bread scented the air. When the cheese was speckled with burnt crispiness, she removed it from the heat, plated it and carried it over to the sofa, where Alexander was curled up on the armchair opposite. As she ate her lunch, she thought about the last few days and weeks—things that had happened, little and big. Conversations, meetings, discoveries that felt like signs. She shook her head. Her mind worked on fact, not speculation, yet still the thoughts crept back in.

She retrieved her notebook from her bedside cabinet and returned to the sofa. Rubbing her fingers down the spiral-bound side, she took a pen from the coffee table and opened her notebook. Just like a few days ago, there were only two points on her to-do list to complete. She studied the list and turned it on its head, realising how much she had achieved despite feeling so hopeless.

3rd May
To do (before 31st May):

- Spend time with Scarlett.

- Spend time with Trish that isn't her looking after me.

- Go and see Uncle Terence.

- Visit the cemetery.

- Visit Lawson-Wray's (possibly).

- Take library books back to university and pay fines.

- Run in the park.

- Sort throughout the house; take things to charity and leave notes on things I want to give to others.

- ~~Arrange finances.~~

- ~~Write letters to Scarlett and Trish—make them as positive as possible and remember to tell them that I love them and why I love them.~~

- ~~Buy paracetamols.~~

- Write will to include Mam and Dad's house to go to Uncle Terence.

- Sort through some things at Mam and Dad's house.

May's pen hovered above the list. She had made a start on sorting through her parents' things, but there were decades of items to organise. Slamming her pen down on the coffee table, she glared at the list, then ripped it out of her notebook. She tore it into pieces, got off the sofa and put the paper in her kitchen bin, then kept her foot on the bin pedal, looking at the pieces of paper scattered across the top of the rubbish. She gasped and began to cry tears of release, sadness and relief. She would send an email cancelling the appointment to make her will. She would make one, but perhaps in June.

Chapter 36

28th May

Meowing and purring woke May.

'Shhhh,' she pleaded, trying to pull the quilt up and over her face, but Alexander's entire weight was on it. His whiskers tickled her cheek before she got a faceful of fish breath as he yawned. Her eyes immediately opened as she twisted her face away and held in a gag. 'Urgh, Alexander, your breath is the worst.'

He just looked at her, wondering why she wasn't marching to his demanding beat. Her feline alarm clock headbutted her face and walked all over her chest until she was forced to get out of bed.

They both went through to the kitchen, where she put some cat food down for him and made a mental note to research something for his death breath as she made and ate her breakfast. If she was going to keep him, and it was looking probable, she would have to take him to the vet and make it all official, purchase toys, a litter tray and a bed of his own. It was a lot to consider, but perhaps the decision had already been made for her, as it seemed he was becoming a tenant of his own choice.

Even though she felt increasingly positive about her near future, it was still a big commitment, and she teetered on the edge of focusing on that he too would die at some point, most likely a long time before her. Her dad would have loved Alexander, but her mother had been severely allergic to animals.

On cue, Alexander started chatting.

'C'mon, then, boss.' She moved from leaning against the kitchen bench and gestured for Alexander to go first. She followed him down the stairs and opened her front door. He dashed out as Peter was dashing up his path, ready for his morning visit to see Anne.

Peter held his flask up to wave as he rushed past May's flat. 'Morning, pet, I'm late for the bus, but are you okay?'

'Yes, thanks. Have a nice morning.'

As she closed the door, she thought about how committed Peter was to his wife. He visited her every single day even though, by the sounds of it, she wouldn't know if he missed a day. *That's what love is about*, she thought, *never giving up*. She admired his devotion.

She thought about all the strangers walking around and their untold stories. We see the face, but we don't know what's going on or what has gone on for them. She would try harder to be emotionally available to people, to give support and show interest. She would try to help people how people had helped her these last few weeks and the many weeks in her almost twenty-five years. Yes, she would try harder.

Trish was due to come over after work that evening and Scarlett was also travelling up. She held back a pang of guilt that she had seen these meetings as a final goodbye, while her friends would have perceived them as the start of her birthday celebrations. They'd be distraught knowing how she had felt the last few months. How she still felt in some ways.

She went into her bedroom, reached into her bedside cabinet and picked out her notebook. She perched on her bed and held it in her hands, not wanting to read the words she had penned from such a dark and desperate place. She thought about her mam's diaries and some of the simple yet special things she had documented, the life-changing events, the distress and the celebration, loss and love. Then she thought about what she had written in her letters and how reading those would have caused so much distress. She had been blind to it at the time, her vision only being the end.

A tear dropped onto the cover of the notebook. Taking a deep breath, she slowly opened it. The words tried to jump into her eyes, willing her to read; instead, she closed her eyes and ripped the pages out, scrunching them into balls. She took them to the kitchen and threw the ball-shaped pages into the bin. It felt liberating, even with the guilt hanging over her. Then she went back to thinking about her birthday. In three days, she would be a quarter of a century old. It would also be her first birthday without her dad. She felt that kick in the stomach again as the pulsating pain of sadness began throbbing in her mind.

Over the last few weeks, some nice things had happened and she almost felt happy in some ways. Added to this, she felt a pleasant taste in her mouth every now and then of what her new normal could be. Some things had occurred over the last few weeks—messages and obstacles—that felt as if they had been brought to her to stop her on the assault course of destruction. Perhaps thinking she was going to die had made her appreciate things more. She wasn't sure. Either way, Peter had a point about serendipity.

Routine and control had always felt essential to her, but recently, she had let those aspects of her life soften a little, and the irony of it was that no one had died (despite her plan) and nothing terrible had happened. Thinking her life would end had allowed her to stop worrying about things out of her control, push herself a little and live with less fear. Perhaps with being less May, she was beginning to live.

May opened the front door and smiled down at the sandy fluff ball on the doorstep next to Trish. Trish raised an eyebrow, then hugged May as if she hadn't seen her for a year.

'Ah, lovely to see you,' she said as she let go of May and entered the flat, which allowed a patiently waiting Alexander to also come in and dart up the stairs.

May laughed. 'Have you missed me?'

'Yes, actually. Plus, you've been a little quiet these past few days.'

'Come up. I'll tell you why.'

Trish removed her shoes and followed as they made their way to the lounge. She turned to May's armchair where Alexander was getting comfy and let out a chuckle.

'Oh yeah, I think Alexander might be my new, non-rent-paying flatmate.'

After making hot drinks and buttering some scones, they sat on the sofa, without so much as an eye-open from Alexander, who had claimed a regular spot on the armchair. May updated Trish on events of the past few days, including meeting Sam and Mad's Park Run, leaving out what her intention had been for the end of the month.

'Wow, you've had a busy time, and, my lovely, I can tell by your face that you like this Sam. The last time I saw you like this was with Thomas. But, May, please look after yourself. I know how much Thomas hurt you. I would hate to see you hurt again. But saying that, I have to be honest, I already know who he is.' Trish giggled.

May's eyes widened. 'How?'

'He's been in Lawson-Wray's. It must be him unless there are two Sam Parsleys and two Peter Parsleys and, in fact, two May McClellands.' Trish laughed loudly.

'He mentioned me?'

'Yup and then obviously I commented. He's got a few viewings booked. He seems lovely, to be honest, but I still want you to be careful.'

'Of course I will be. His dad, Peter, has been really useful to talk to. I've been struggling, Trish, I think I've always struggled, but these past few months have been intolerable at times. Without you and Scarlett and Peter, I wouldn't have coped.' May's voice cracked, and she raised her hand to her mouth.

Trish instinctively leant forward and patted May's leg. 'May, my lovely, I love you, you know that. You've had a hard time, but look, you've worked through it, you're still working through it and we all care about you. It sounds like Peter and Sam care also.'

'You're the closest thing to a mam to me, Trish. I'm sorry if I don't always show and tell you how grateful I am.' She glanced down at her hand, then back to Trish. 'Sometimes I find it hard to do that, but I'm working on it.'

Trish shook her head. 'I always know you're grateful, May, you don't have to change who you are. I, we love you just the way you are. Jack was so happy to see you at Lawson-Wray's last week. We all were. The door will always be open.'

May gave a close-lipped smile. If she were being honest with herself, she missed the place, the routine and feeling useful.

'Can't you even think about just coming back one day a week?' Trish stuck out her bottom lip, like a child asking for more sweets. Then she added, placing her hands together, 'For my sake, even?'

'Trish, you can't do that and make me feel guilty.'

'But it's worked, hasn't it?' She giggled. 'Oh come on, May, please bloody come back. Just try a shift. If it's no good, don't do it again.'

'I will, I'm just not ready yet, Trish. There's been so much going on. I want to feel right and ready. I feel like I've just gone on autopilot and if I don't deal with the things that cause me pain, they'll just resurface.' She licked her lips and glanced at the TV, as if trying to look busy and absorbed in something else, but it wasn't turned on.

'I know, I'm being selfish. I just want you back to the May I know. But don't be harsh on yourself; you've come such a long way.'

May pulled at her cardigan guiltily. 'I think I might look into some therapy. I've done a little research, and I think it's worth a try.'

Trish smiled and nodded frantically. 'Absolutely. I think that would be a great idea. After my breakdown, I got CBT through the doctor. It really helped, but there are so many options around now.' She lifted her cup. 'A toast, May, to the future.'

May chuckled and lifted her cup to meet Trish's. 'To the future.'

She was concerned that life would throw her another curve ball and she would go back to the thoughts she'd had a few weeks ago. She knew dark feelings could come knocking on her door and let themselves in as uninvited guests for a room in her mind. Encroaching sadness, loneliness, desperation and depression are hard to evict. Although she had almost stopped thinking that the only way to prevent her head and heart from continuously hurting was to end her life, she was still grieving.

Did she feel happy more times than not? Yes, probably.

Did she trust that she would always feel more happy than sad? No.

Did she worry that she could never manage her grief? Yes.

She wanted to recover as much as she could, knowing that living meant she would be hurt, lose more people and feel unhappiness at times—no one was immune to that—but she needed a way to manage her emotions and digest her past as much as she could.

Chapter 37

29th May

'Give me a second.' May giggled as she picked her keys up off the coffee table. Alexander's fur rubbed against her calf as he hurried past her and down the stairs for his morning toilet. As she opened the door, he dashed out across the path and past Peter, who was looking up the street as he leaned against the wall.

'Morning, Peter. How are you?'

He turned quickly. 'Oh, morning, May. Yes, I'm good thanks. Well, I would be if this blooming taxi would turn up.'

May frowned as she noticed his lack of flask. It was the first time she'd seen him leave in the morning without it since giving it to him. 'Where are you going? Are you not off to see Anne?'

'I am, but, well, I had a little bit of a fall last night. Tripped on my new rug, and I've got an ankle like a pudding this morning.' He let out a little laugh as he pointed to his ankle. 'I don't want to walk on it, pet, and it's about a three-minute walk at the other end of the bus journey, so I ordered a taxi.' He shook his head, looking at his watch. 'Well, I thought I did, but it looks like they might have got a better offer. I've tried ringing the taxi firm and got no answer. No customer service these days.'

Normally, May wasn't a fan of driving with company, as they usually wanted to talk and she liked to drive in silence, but she knew this was one of those times she needed to push herself out of her comfort zone a little. Peter's time with Anne was precious and he'd looked out for her a lot. 'Give me a minute. I'll just quickly get changed and take you there, Peter.'

'Ah, pet, I don't want to put you out.'

'It's no bother. Give me a minute, I'll just put some jeans and a sweater on.'

She turned and ran up the stairs, promptly changed and ran her hands through her hair before putting it back in her bobble. Brushing her teeth in record time, she then put on her trainers and joined Peter outside. It was times like this she was pleased she didn't need to have a full face of make-up, immaculately straightened hair or a co-ordinated outfit and bag ensemble when she left the house.

'Okay. Let's get going.' She locked her door and walked up her path.

'Thanks, May. I've been a bit worried about Anne the last few days. They said she's off her food, so I want to be there for breakfast, you know.'

'No bother, Peter, it's the least I can do.'

Peter hobbled to the passenger side of her car and plonked his bum in the seat, then swung his legs in. She noticed his knees were touching the dashboard, not that he moaned or mentioned.

'The lever is under your seat. Just lift it and push your-self back,' she instructed.

Peter followed instruction and rapidly jerked back. 'Bloody hell.' He laughed, making May smile.

They began the ten-minute car journey to the care home Anne lived in, with Peter giving directions and chatting non-stop. May interjected a few times to con-firm directions and predicted a headache would engulf her once she got him to his destination.

'So, the singer will be in later. He comes once a week to the home, not a bad voice on him either. Sings the oldies, you know. Songs you've probably never—'

'Is it left or right at the next junction, Peter?'

Peter looked around, checking where they were. 'Ah yes, pet, it's left. Next left, then it's about three buildings down on the left.'

They pulled up to the entrance of the home, which was set back behind some green space with what looked like plenty of wooden benches. The building was an old Victorian structure that had a grand yet welcoming exterior. *More like a hotel.*

'Looks like a nice place,' said May.

'Oh, it's lovely. Only the best for my Anne.'

May drove Peter as close to the entrance as possible.

'There you go.' She smiled despite her head ringing from concentrating on a route she didn't know and Peter chuntering on in the car.

It took Peter a while to get out of the vehicle, trying to put the least amount of weight possible onto his ankle. 'Thanks so much, pet, you're a gem.' He closed the door behind him and waved.

'Do you want a lift back?' she called through the open passenger side window, then immediately wondered if her head could stand it.

'Oh no, you've done enough. I'll hopefully get a taxi and it'll be less of a rush on the way back. Or maybe our Sam will be here by then.'

May watched Peter hobble into the building before manoeuvring her car. As she pulled onto the main road, she heard a text message alert ping. Her phone was on silent. She groaned and looked for a safe place to turn her car around.

She returned to the care home car park and reversed into a space, then looked around for Peter's phone. She found it on the floor of the passenger seat, tucked into the side of the footwell. With Peter's phone in hand, she walked into the building the way Peter had entered, hoping it was reception, then pressed a buzzer at the side of some sliding doors.

'Cookson House, can I help?'

May moved closer to the intercom. 'I have something to drop off for a visitor, his phone.'

A beeping noise followed, then the doors opened and she went inside. There was an enormous mat at the entrance with the word 'Welcome' across it. She glanced around the large reception area that displayed comfy seats, small tables and a bookcase. Bright paintings decorated the crisp, white walls and the place smelt of fresh lemon. There were a few elderly people sitting and some people milling around. One lady passed holding a doll like a baby and gave the happiest smile. May smiled back, then looked past the lady, spotting a man in uniform approaching.

'Hi, are you alright?' he asked.

'Hi, erm, can you tell me where Anne Parsley is, please? Her husband, Peter, I have his phone,' May said as she held the mobile phone up.

'Of course. He'll be in the hall with Anne. It's down the corridor all the way along to the end, then the hall is on your left.' He nodded, then approached a woman who was sitting down. 'Okay, Pat, let's get you down for breakfast.'

May thanked the worker and followed his instructions. As she walked down the wide corridor, she saw a painted bus stop with a comfy bench next to it and a painted postbox. There were A1-size pictures on the other side of the corridor of the 1920s up to the 2010s. She slowed briefly to view them. At the end of the corridor, the hall entrance was to the left and another corridor to the right, where she snuck a glance and saw a seating area and a bookshelf.

She could hear music and smell breakfast—toast, pancakes, eggs and oranges—coming out of the hall right before she entered. It was warm, bright and felt like a giant family kitchen. People were sitting at wooden tables or on sofas, and some were sat in wheelchairs. Some residents had staff sitting by their sides, whilst other staff were walking around in uniforms. A counter displayed fruit, cereal, pastries, and there was what looked to be a kitchen area behind it.

Peter was right, only the best.

She rubbed the back of her neck, trying to spot Peter amongst the sea of people. Despite the lovely setting, she felt an overwhelming sadness for the residents in their battle of deterioration.

'We are all living too long, May,' her dad had once said. 'The world can't manage the number of people in their late eighties and nineties. It was practically unheard of when I was younger to live so long. Medicine, lifestyle—it's only a good thing if we have social care to match the needs of people.'

She smiled to herself. She would have looked after Dad even if he'd reached 110. Her parents would never get to the age of many of the people here, but she was grateful their minds and bodies hadn't been ravaged by cruel dementia or other age-related illnesses. Her mam's parents had both died before May was ten years old and her dad's mam when she was thirteen, followed by his dad, Cecil, the year after. It meant she'd had limited interactions with older folk. She had studied dementia and Alzheimer's, the most common cause of dementia, briefly at university, and recently, she had revised and learnt more to try to support Peter. After standing for a minute or so and probably looking completely lost, a woman in a tabard came over.

'You okay there?'

'Sorry, yeah. I'm looking for Peter, Anne Parsley's husband.'

'Erm, he's just over there, sitting at the table with the yellow tablecloth. Do you see him?' She pointed across the room.

Peter had his back to May, but she could see the side profile of who must have been Anne sitting at the table with him.

'Thank you,' she said, smiling at the carer.

She walked over to where Peter sat. He was holding a piece of toast to Anne's lips.

Anne looked at her. 'Lydia?' she said as Peter turned around.

'Oh, May, is everything alright?' Peter asked, eyes wide.

'Yes, erm, you left your mobile in the car.' She handed him the phone.

He sighed and put it on the table in front of him. 'Thanks, I'm all to pot this morning.'

'Lydia?' Anne said again, her hand reaching out towards May.

'No, darling, this is May.' Peter leaned over Anne and pulled a seat out at the table for May, to the left of Anne.

Not wanting to seem rude, she sat down. 'Hello, Anne.'

Anne's mouth curled, and May recognised the smile from the photos on Peter's lounge wall. Anne leaned towards her, took her right hand from the tabletop and held it. The sudden touch made her flinch slightly, but the look in Anne's eyes showed her that Anne needed to hold her hand way more than she wanted to take it away.

Peter looked at their hands interlocked and swallowed. He glanced at May and gave her a smile before returning his gaze to Anne.

The three sat almost in silence as Peter encouraged Anne to eat a little toast, and Anne remained holding May's hand, calling her Lydia every now and then. Neither May nor Peter corrected her again. May watched the way Peter supported his wife with eating. He was so tender, patient and kept a smile on his face despite the fact he was very likely crumbling inside. It was one of the most selfless things she had ever witnessed and one of the most beautiful gestures of love. Anne was still Peter's everything even though she was fading in front of him.

'Lydia, will you brush my hair?' Anne asked, looking at her with such brightness in her eyes.

May bit her lip and turned to Peter for the answer.

'You don't have to, pet, don't worry.'

The thought of brushing hair felt intimate, but it also felt important for Anne, important for Peter and perhaps even important for herself. 'Erm, no, I will,' she replied, nodding and realising that Anne's gaze had never left her. 'I used to brush my grandma's hair when I was younger and put her rollers in, although I don't think I would remember how to do that.'

Peter put a hand to his chest. 'Thank you, thank you, May. Her room is number twenty-four, along the corri-

dor, on the left. There is a Christmas cactus plant outside
the door on a shelf.'

May took Anne's arm, gently easing her up. Anne held
on to May as if she were a precious childhood teddy
bear as they walked slowly and silently to her room. May
wasn't sure what to say, but the silence and synchronised
walking with Anne glancing up at her with every other
step felt like a moment she would never forget.

After reaching Anne's room, May opened the door and
assisted her in. Anne had a lovely small dressing table
opposite her single bed. On it was the same wedding
photo Peter had on his wall. To the other side was an
old-fashioned brush and mirror set that was beautifully
adorned with a pearl-like backing. Anne silently took a
seat and smiled up at May, then looked at the brush.
She sat straight, staring at the mirror that was part of the
dressing table structure, awaiting May to pamper her.

May gently took the brush to Anne's hair. It was shoulder length, white-blond with a platinum shine, changing
little from the photos on Peter's lounge wall. Although
Anne was a stranger, May felt she knew her through
Peter's shared memories. Despite this, she felt nervous
as she tentatively brushed Anne's hair. Anne closed her
eyes and gently hummed the familiar tune of *Unchained
Melody* by The Righteous Brothers.

Anne finished humming the song and opened her eyes,
looking straight at the wedding photo on her dressing
table. She then looked at May through the mirror and
reached up to hold her hand. May heard a sniff behind
her and turned to see Peter standing in the doorway,
leaning on the door frame to alleviate his sore ankle,
wiping his eyes.

'That was our wedding song. She forgets who I am most
days and could never tell you the day of the week or what
she had for lunch, but she won't ever forget our song.' He
looked the other way, swallowing pain that he didn't want
his beloved to see.

May placed her hands on Anne's shoulders and softly
kissed her head. 'Goodbye for now, Anne. Hopefully, I

will see you again soon,' she said, deciding it was time to leave and give Peter time with his wife. She squeezed Peter's upper arm gently as she left the room.

'Lydia, come back soon,' Anne said, still looking at May through the mirror.

Chapter 38

There was plenty of time to waste before May was due to see Scarlett at 7 p.m., so she'd decided to make an important stop on her way home. The aisles of Pampered Pets were pretty much empty as she walked up and down them.

'Ah, great.' She leaned into a shelf to pick up a litter tray. Stepping back, she noticed more choices, some smaller, some with hoods that made them look almost futuristic and even one that claimed to be 'self-cleaning'. Her eyes widened at the thought. She placed the litter tray she had selected back on the shelf. It now felt too basic. Scratching her head, she read the product descriptions of the five available litter trays, eventually deciding on the hooded version for privacy and hygiene reasons. She hoped Alexander wouldn't use the litter tray much, her lip curling at the thought of the smell and having to clean it out. So far, he had always told her in his own way that he wanted out to do his business, but she still needed a backup plan.

She continued browsing for the next item: toys. There were three aisles containing toys, but given the low stock and that most were for dogs, this diminished the choice significantly. She picked up one dog toy that was almost the size of Alexander and laughed at another that contained imitation items from a full English breakfast, plate and all. She took her mobile phone from her pocket and snapped a photo of it. Her finger hovered over her chat with Sam, but worrying he might think she was silly, she sent it to Scarlett instead. After a few more minutes, she decided on a cardboard scratcher, some small toy mice, a fish on a string and some woollen balls.

Next was the aisle for beds and blankets. There were a number of choices that varied in size, shape, thickness and furriness as well as colour and pattern. She furrowed her brow as she tried to decipher.

'Everything alright there?' an assistant asked, who had been stocking the shelf behind May.

'I'm wondering, erm, what's the best bed for a cat?' She knew it was likely Alexander would continue to sit on her armchair in the spot that seemed to be his favourite, but he still needed choice and a dedicated bed regardless of his preference.

'Is it for a kitten or an adult cat? How big is it?'

'Well, I'm not sure of his age. He's kind of found me. Or maybe we found each other.' She smiled. 'He's only little in height, but he's not a kitten.'

'Okay, well, these cocoon beds can be good. They flatten down to make a more exposed bed but can be enjoyable for cats to snuggle into and be covered up, warm and a little hidden, which they often like.' The assistant pointed to the bed, and May reached for it. It was a brown velvety material and would look nice in her lounge.

'Great, I'll take it.' She put the bed in her trolley and thanked the assistant before picking up a beige fleece to go with the bed.

Lastly, a cat carrier. There was only one type on the shelf at Pampered Pets, but it seemed to be right for Alexander. Not too large or too small, and as she fiddled with the front, she worked out how to open and close it. Pushing her trolley to the checkout, she noticed some cat treats and picked up a few packets of biscuits, including one that claimed to help dental health, which he really needed for his smelly breath.

As someone who hadn't grown up with pets or been around them much as a child, she had found something special in Alexander. Despite her initial desire to not get attached, his persistence was a quality she admired. Truthfully, she felt a love from him that she had always thought a bit silly when hearing other people talk about how much they adored their pets. She had never been able to grasp the connection until now. Alexander was her companion, and more than that, he was her best friend. And in a way, perhaps he had saved her.

May paid for her purchases, packed the items into her car and drove towards home. She couldn't help but smile the whole way as she thought about Alexander playing with his new toys and sleeping in his new bed. But then, as she drove into her estate, she passed a bus stop and the smile immediately dropped away. She indicated and pulled over outside of the empty bus stop, racing to get her seatbelt off and out of the car. And then she stood staring at one of the posters she'd put up, gazing at Alexander's sandy fur and almost kitten-like eyes. Panic filled her as she imagined him having a family, them spotting this and calling her, their tears at being reunited with him, her tears after saying goodbye. Biting her lip, she ripped down the poster and scrunched it into a ball. *I've had no calls, seen no missing posters or missing online posts.* She unscrunched the poster and considered putting it back up. *No, I've waited long enough for them to come forward. Plus*, she argued with herself, *I'll give him back if they do contact, I just don't need to actively seek them out.*

She got back in the car and drove the long way to her street, jumping out at another bus stop and the lampposts where she had placed the posters, ripping them off with satisfaction. Alexander had accepted her from day one, and now she knew she couldn't possibly part with him. Not through choice.

After parking outside her flat, she gathered all her new purchases from the boot and took them inside, then set about finding a home for each of the items. She laid the new fleece out on the armchair cushion that Alexander had claimed for himself. There was an impatient excitement within her to see how he'd react when he finally decided to show his sandy face.

She sat on the sofa and checked her mobile phone, after having it on silent, and found a message from Sam. *'Hi May, how's things? I've just stopped off at Scotch Corner for a comfort break. Why does service station coffee always taste so vile? I'll be at Dad's soon and wondering if you would like to go out for dinner tomorrow night? X'*

May dropped her phone on her lap and clasped her hands in delight. Was it a date? She couldn't tell, but either way, Sam Parsley had asked her out for dinner, and she felt a surge of excitement whizzing around her. There was something different about Sam, an anomaly you could say. The difference with Sam Parsley was that, weirdly, she already felt she knew him. Perhaps a little through their interactions, but mainly through Peter, and not just him talking about his son. She didn't necessarily see Peter as a father figure, but he had those dad qualities that we all hope for in a real dad. The dad qualities that Victor had. The kindness, the gratitude, the silly humour. The learning to cook, the wanting to know she was okay. The silent thinking that gets articulated at the right time, with thought and sensitivity. If Sam was even half the man his dad was, he was one of the good guys.

She grabbed her phone and immediately responded. *'Hi, Sam. Yeah, all good thank you. Hopefully, your dad will make you a decent cuppa when you get here. Dinner on Wednesday would be lovely, thank you! x'*

Not long after 7 p.m., May's doorbell rang. She rushed down the stairs and opened the door to Scarlett.

'Oooh, so lush to see you,' Scarlett said, entering the flat and giving May a big hug. Holding her at arm's length, Scarlett looked May up and down. 'You've put on weight.'

May coughed and glared at her friend. 'It's only been just over a week since I saw you.'

'In a good way. You needed to; you looked deathly the last time I saw you despite stuffing cakes down your neck quicker than a seagull.'

The pair laughed.

'Well, in all honesty, all I've done these last few weeks is eat cake. It's ridiculous and has to stop.'

'Never stop eating cake, May. Never.'

Scarlett took her shoes off, and May handed her fluffy socks over before they headed upstairs.

As they entered the lounge, Scarlett peered over at Alexander cosy on his new blanket on the armchair. 'Aw, my four-legged mate is here.'

'I think he knows his name,' May said, stroking him as he stretched his front legs out and gave a big yawn. 'I called him earlier and he came running. He's been lying there ever since.'

'So, you are keeping him, then?' Scarlett pointed to the cocoon bed under the window.

'I think we are keeping each other.' May smiled as she stroked Alexander, who stretched a paw to her, rubbed his head against her hand and then closed his eyes.

'Aw, that's cute, May. Now tell me about Sam.'

'Well, he asked me out for dinner tomorrow night. I'm not entirely sure if it's a date though.'

Scarlett's mouth went from an O shape to a big grin. 'Of course it's a date. Peter would be made up if you two got together; you're like his bestie. He's stolen you from me.' She touched May's hand as she laughed.

'Don't be silly; no one could take me away from you.'

'Seriously though, this all sounds amazing. I'm so pleased for you, and I hope it continues going in the right direction.'

'Yeah, me too. It's so nice to see you, I really wasn't expecting you to come up, Scarlett.'

'Obviously I wanted to see you on the first birthday, well, with your dad not being here and all that.' She paused for a second, checking that May was okay. 'But there's something else I want to tell you, and really, it had to be in person.'

May's breath caught in her throat. The problem with her brain was that it always automatically jumped to the worst. Her heart began racing as she went through what felt like a million possibilities, none of which she liked. Was Scarlett poorly? Was she moving country? Had Ethan broken up with her?

'What's happened? Are you alright?'

'Yeah, yeah, I'm fine. Well, sort of. Erm, the thing is, May...' Scarlett momentarily placed her hand over her mouth, a massive grin creeping out the side. 'I'm pregnant.'

May opened her mouth wide and looked across the sofa at her lifelong friend, whose face looked as if her heart was beating with sheer happiness. Scarlett let out a squeal of delight, and May joined in before jumping up and leaning over to hug her tightly. Alexander glanced over, disturbed by the joyous racket, before turning back and burying his head into his body.

May hadn't been expecting such news; it wasn't something they had talked about lately. Then the excitement was immediately squashed by one particular negative thought. *Was this planned, but she couldn't tell me because my crap life has been dominating the friendship recently?* The negative thought threatened to pop the balloon of joy in the room. She scrunched her fist and let go, hoping it would disperse as her fingers opened.

Her best friend's face was a picture of happiness, and she knew that Scarlett's caring nature would make her a wonderful mother. She had to let go of any negativity for Scarlett's sake. She couldn't spoil this moment for her.

Grabbing her friend's hand, she spoke, 'Oh, Scarlett, that's just incredible. The best news ever. I'm so happy for you and Ethan. How? When?' She shook her head. 'I mean, I know how, I don't need details, but how far along are you? Were you trying?'

Scarlett laughed. 'I'm only a few months. It's early days, really. I haven't even had my first scan.' She touched her stomach. 'My body just felt weird... this whole thing is so weird. But it's brilliant despite being super weird. And no, we weren't trying.'

The balloon of happiness grew bigger, suffocating any negativity, and May smiled.

'But it's been the most amazing surprise and we are both made up. We'd talked about babies, in the future, but I wanted the wedding first. I still feel like I'm not an adult yet some days.' She ran a hand through her hair. 'This tiny curveball was thrown in, and really, now I've got my head around it, we're chuffed. Ethan will make a great dad and, of course, you the most amazing auntie.'

A tear fell down May's cheek as the realisation of the situation really hit her and as she hoped she'd make Scarlett proud as an auntie. She'd doubted herself and her abilities the past few months and she'd been working on herself recently now her mindset was changing, but now she *really* had someone to aspire to be better for and something to look forward to. The gravity of her previous decision to end her life smacked her in the face as she contemplated the grief and stress she could have put onto Scarlett through her pregnancy.

Scarlett wiped May's tear away. 'Aw, May.'

'I'm so proud of everything you've done, Scarlett. I know I don't say it enough or show it, but I am. You've always been there, and well, you're going to be the best mam. I hope I can be the best auntie.' May wiped her eyes with the palms of her hands. She didn't have siblings and had never been close to her cousins. The thought of being involved with Scarlett's baby's life felt like a gift.

'You will, you'll be the best, and of course I know, you daft mare.' Scarlett playfully nudged her. 'We're going to try and come back closer to home to live. I really need the support now more than ever.'

May's shoulders lifted and her eyes widened as she listened to Scarlett.

'Even Teesside would be close enough, between here and his parents near Leeds. We can both get work in schools, and even though the acting opportunities might not be as fruitful, family will always come first.'

May leaned in, not certain she had heard right. 'You're coming home?' she said in a high-pitched voice as the floodgates threatened to open again.

'Yeah, well, as near as I can.'

'This is the best birthday present I could ask for. My bestie having a baby and coming home,' she gushed, grabbing Scarlett.

With the good news about Scarlett, a date planned for the next night with Sam, Alexander officially moving in and some ideas floating around in her head, it did indeed feel as if things were starting to look up.

Chapter 39

30th May

Standing at the entrance of the university, May could feel her heart racing and her throat tightening. The last time she'd been here, she'd deliberately parked in a different car park—the same place her car was now. She tried facing away, focusing on the entrance, but she couldn't help but glance at the car park in the distance that held her grief. Even the slight image of it made her feel as if an elephant were trampolining on her chest. How could she ever park there again? She didn't associate it with the university anymore, just with the pain of losing her dad. That pain she'd felt the exact moment she'd found out about his car accident. And there was no way to undo that link now.

She took a step forward before turning on her heels, an overwhelming need to get out taking over her. People were passing by as she stopped at the exit, hardly able to get enough air in her lungs and feeling she was going to collapse. She stood breathing in, her mouth as wide as it would go, her head pounding. *Why didn't I feel this bad when I returned the books?* The answer came to her as soon as she asked the question: she wanted to live, whereas last time, it almost felt like part of the punishment she was continuing to inflict on herself.

She sat on the wall by the side of the path for a minute and held her head in her hands, just as she'd done on the curb outside her parents', but Mrs Taylor wasn't there to comfort her now. She watched her knees bouncing, thinking people would have thought she was drunk or insane. Perhaps they would be right; nothing much about her felt sane right now.

She sat until her breathing became less erratic, then stood slowly, her legs wobbling a little but holding her up. Her appointment with her tutor wasn't until 9:30 a.m., in ten minutes, but she knew no length of time would be enough to prepare her today. She slowly walked back to the car.

Calling her tutor from her car, she lied, saying her car had broken down, and instead, they talked on the phone about her returning to finish her last semester and a half and final exams in her master's in science. Her tutor, Professor Musgrove, was encouraging and said May could return in September for the autumn term. Happy with this, May agreed to some distance learning to catch up and a meeting with her tutor in five weeks. As she drove back home, she had the sense of moving forward and achievement but knew she wasn't quite there yet and still needed to push herself a little further, like learning to ride a bike without stabilisers.

Once she'd had a cup of tea and was sure her nerves were calm, she would go for a run in the park. She was keen to try the group again on the coming Saturday. She wondered if sometimes in life she had settled too much or if her adherence to routine had prevented opportunity. She felt that in the last month, she had lived more than in the last decade, and it made her sad that her parents weren't there to see it. Running helped her think about things—the good and the bad. It gave her some space to reflect, but she needed to work through her thinking and not have it keep her in an unhealthy routine that threatened to destroy any changes in her life.

May was already at the top of the stairs when Sam rang her doorbell. She'd been ready for forty-five minutes and pacing for the last fifteen. Biting the inside of her lip, she reminded herself of what Scarlett always said,

'May, just be yourself. Don't apologise for being who you are, warts and all.'

Scarlett had been keen to help her get ready, but she had declined. She had to be herself and wear what she wanted, not what Scarlett thought she should. As much as she respected her friend and her advice, she was an adult and needed to be able to decide what to wear on a possible date. After all the decisions she had made this last month, surely she could pick out an outfit for a meal.

'Be yourself. Be yourself,' she quietly said as she descended the stairs. She wasn't even sure if it was a date. *Stop putting pressure on yourself,* she thought, her kitten heels clicking on each step. Reaching the bottom, she took a deep breath, straightened down her tight black dress that had moved slightly with each step and opened the door, hoping she looked okay.

'Hi, May, lovely to see you, and I see you look lovely.' Sam laughed awkwardly at his own wordplay and then cleared his throat. 'I got you these. Not sure what you like.' He handed her a box of chocolates as his face flushed a light shade of pink.

'Oh, thank you.' They were a selection from a chocolatier in town. Her eyes travelled to the box, *Summer Selection – an assortment of luxurious chocolates.* Turning over the box, she saw they were soft-centred chocolates in lemon, strawberry, champagne and orange flavours.

'I don't like soft centres, but these look lovely. Thank you.' She smiled at Sam, then turned to place the box of chocolates on the stairs.

'Huh,' Sam muttered, running a hand through his hair. 'Erm, shall w-we get going?'

She nodded and stepped outside, locking the door behind her and putting the key in her handbag. Sam looked as if he wanted to make some sort of move to help her to the car—whether that was taking her arm or holding her hand—but he seemed to think himself out of it and walked beside her instead. He opened the passenger side for her, and she got in before he walked to the driver's side and took his seat.

'Erm, you do look lovely by the way.' He beamed at May as he fastened his seatbelt.

Little fireworks sparked in her stomach. 'Thank you, and you too. You look nice, I mean.' She turned to Sam, who was now facing forward and pulling away from the drive. The buttons on his pale blue shirt slightly stretched over his belly and his smart navy chinos. He did look nice, and he smelt nice as well.

They soon arrived at the Italian restaurant, and Sam parked up. He quickly undid his seatbelt and got out of his seat, dashing round with little grace to the passenger side to open May's door.

'Thank you,' she said as she climbed out.

No man except Dad has ever opened a car door for me. And not just her, he'd always opened it for her mam too. Despite May's insistence she was capable of doing it herself, she'd secretly loved it, and the thought of her dad landed in her heart, making her smile instead of feeling she could cry.

May and Sam walked the twenty or so metres to the entrance of the restaurant, and upon going inside, a symphony of smells greeted them. Tomato richness, strong cilantro, slow-cooked meats in caramelised onions and the comforting smell of baking dough coated the air. Glancing round, they could have been in a little corner of Italy. Instrumental folk music played quietly in the background and the small wooden tables had a backdrop of terracotta walls, wooden shelves displaying bright, intricate crockery and prints. Taking their seats, a red candle stood tall in a wine bottle, nodules of wax decorating the side of it. May thought it was the perfect setting for a date.

The waiter took their drink order and then they opened a menu each. Although May had been making a habit of doing things differently, she had, as she'd always done, viewed the online menu earlier and knew what she was going to order.

'I already know what I'm having; I had a look at the menu online.' There was a proud grin on Sam's face as he shut the menu.

May shook her head and smirked.

'What? I'm just saving time so we have more time to talk.'

'No, it's funny because I did exactly the same.' She closed her menu too and placed it on the table.

Sam chuckled. 'Well, there you go, a great thing to have in common.'

'How are the house viewings going?'

'I saw one today, but it was no good and very small for the price. I thought Birmingham was expensive, but it seems just the same here.' He blew his cheeks out. 'There's another one I'm viewing tomorrow, but they want a minimum of a twelve-month lease and really I want six months so I'll have passed my three-month probationary period at work, got some payslips and can sort out a mortgage. Something will turn up though. Actually, it was through Lawson-Wray's. The receptionist said she was your friend. Tish?'

'Trish. Yeah, she's a really good friend.'

'She kept telling me how great you are. As if I didn't already know,' Sam said, playing with the serviette by the side of his plate.

May let out a nervous laugh and stroked her hair. Her cheeks warmed, and she hoped the subdued, soft lighting would mask any visual signs of her embarrassment.

The waiter brought the drinks over. 'Is madam and sir ready to order?' he asked, shoulders back and pen poised on his notepad.

Sam put his hand out in May's direction, indicating for her to go first.

'I'll have the lasagne, please.'

Sam tilted his head back, and May glanced at him. 'Make that two lasagnes, please. And a garlic bread to share.' He turned his eyes from the waiter to May to check she was happy with the side order. She nodded, handing the menus to the waiter.

'That's another thing we have in common.' Sam chuckled, and May felt the tiny fireworks in her stomach again.

Whilst they waited, Sam talked about Peter and how happy he was to have the new sofa.

'It's great spending time with Dad. I just wish I would have come home sooner, more for Mam. But I guess I had to give my marriage a chance, even when I knew it was doomed. There's something innate in us that doesn't like to give up.' He glanced at the wall behind May and shook his head. 'My ex-wife, well, let's just say we were polar opposites and grew even further apart. Then there was the clearing up from the fallout. I'll be pleased when I'm back up here for good.'

May nodded, not really knowing how to respond. 'It took me ages to get over my relationship and it was only short-term. I guess it's just hard. I've not been on any dates since.'

'I've not had a date in so long, but I just couldn't wait for this evening.' Sam bit his lip awkwardly and pulled at the sleeves of his shirt.

May looked at her lap, trying to hold her big grin back as a small smile. *So, it is a date.*

'You've been a breath of fresh air, May. I think that sometimes things happen to make way for better things, and sometimes things come into our life at the right time.'

'You mean like serendipity?' May said, thinking of the conversation with Peter.

Sam paused and slightly scrunched his face. May wondered if he'd got those words from his dad and was now putting two and two together. 'Exactly like that, May, serendipity.'

The mains arrived, and the pair tucked into their meals. May shared how kind Peter was to her, without going into too much detail. She asked about his ankle and mentioned the care home the day before.

'Who's Lydia? Your mam called me Lydia.' She tilted her head and rested her fork on her plate for a moment.

Sam gave a half-smile coated in sadness, which was a stark contrast to his usual cheek-rounded grin. 'Lydia is my niece. My sister Gina's daughter. They live in Australia.' He put his hand to his beard and sighed. 'God, it's a bastard of an illness.' He paused for a second, and

May took a sip of her drink, not wanting to probe the conversation further. 'Sorry for swearing.'

May gave a slight flick of her wrist, indicating it didn't matter to her.

'Gina was here until about ten years ago, and Mam helped raise Lydia. Gina was a single mother. She had to work, so Lydia and Mam were super close.' Sam's eyes glazed over momentarily, as if recalling memories in his mind. 'Gina still visits, but Mam, well, she struggles, as you've seen. Lydia is twenty-one now.'

May felt a pang of sadness reflecting back on meeting Anne. 'I've thought about your mam a lot since I met her yesterday. It's strange how you can hear about people, yet until you meet them, they aren't quite real in your head. Will you tell me about her, if you feel okay to?'

Sam nodded. He touched May's hand as it sat on the top of the table. It felt so natural that she had no urge or thought to pull away.

'Mam and Dad have always been best friends, always together. They had the perfect marriage and they were and are the most perfect parents.' Sam went on to tell her a little about his childhood, how Anne had always told him happiness was the most important thing in life, whilst Peter had emphasised the kids pursuing a 'decent career'. His eyes were glassy as he rubbed his beard and smiled at the memories.

'Mam always made us feel loved. So did Dad, but in a different way, you know?'

May knew exactly what he meant, as she had felt it with her parents.

'She had endless energy as I grew up and even up to five or so years ago. Always rushing around, socialising, doing errands, volunteering. And then it started.' Sam placed his finger and thumb to his mouth.

'I suppose like most people with Alzheimer's,' he continued, 'it was subtle, an insidious monster creeping around her brain.' He paused for a moment as May watched him in silence. 'We didn't know, we just assumed she had lots going on, like we all do at times. Dad began doing a bit more than usual—shopping lists, things like that. Tasks Mam always did. We even joked about her memory, unconcerned.' He took a gulp of water, and May wondered if it were his way of taking an emotional pause and collecting himself from the obvious guilt he felt. 'Things happen to other people, not us. That's what we all think.'

It was exactly how May had felt before the death of her parents, not realising, not appreciating the fragility of life. She couldn't change it for Sam or Peter, but she hoped she could help, in even the smallest of ways. And she felt certain that Peter was even more amazing than she had first thought.

'It's such a silent killer, May. Listening to Dad and then seeing Mam. It's as if she's forgotten so much these days. Despite prompting, she just can't reach the memory. The dementia has consumed her brain.' Sam pressed his lips together and then rubbed his chin. May wasn't sure, but it looked as if his eyes were filling with tears. She wanted to take his pain away.

'I'm sorry, Sam, and I'm sorry if I've upset you.'

'Thanks, May, and no, it's actually nice to talk about her. I sometimes can't do it with Dad and Gina. It's hard.'

The waiter passed, and Sam took the opportunity to have a break in the conversation, ordering a tea for May and a coffee for himself.

'So, what's your story, then? Do you have family?' he asked.

May's body stiffened. She had assumed Peter would have told Sam, but then she remembered his former career and how he would have been used to confidentiality, and it showed her even more how special he was. Because really, it wasn't his place to tell anyone about her life, and that was the attitude she'd always had about people's business.

The drinks arrived, and Sam blew his coffee before taking a sip.

May stirred her pot of tea, eyes fixed on the motion as she spoke. 'My parents are both dead. Mam nearly three years ago, and Dad...' She paused, still not looking up, her bottom lip quivering. 'Dad died just a few months ago. So, there's just me.' She lifted her head up, and two tears plopped onto the table.

'Shit, May, I-I'm so so-sorry.' Sam shook his head. 'I didn't me-mean to pry,' he stammered, leaning in.

'It's okay. It's not your fault, and you weren't prying,' she said quietly, dabbing the serviette under her eyes with her free hand. 'I'll tell you more about it some other time.'

'Well, I'm always here. Me and my dad. If you need us.'

'Thanks, that's kind. Trish, from the estate agency, she's a great support. And my best friend, Scarlett, and your dad. He's really helped me this last month, in ways I'm not sure he'll ever understand.'

Both of them sat in silence for a minute or so absorbing their thoughts and the words spoken as the gentle music played in the background.

Sam fixed his gentle eyes on May. There was something in them that made her feel safe. Something in his smile made her believe she could perhaps be herself—with her imperfections and her flaws—and that he would accept her just as she was.

'I guess I've always felt a little out of place, like there is something wrong with me, perhaps. I've never really felt like I fit in.'

'Normal is overrated, May. And anyway, what even is normal? We are all different, we are all a bit odd, and that should be celebrated.'

The pair left the restaurant, breathing in the evening spring air. Sam drove them home, talking about Alexander on the way. May told him what she had bought and that she really wanted to keep Alexander, hoping that no one got in touch and claimed him.

'I've taken all the posters down, so fingers crossed,' she said, giggling as they pulled up outside the flats.

'He definitely wants to live with you by the sounds of it, May, and he seems lovely company,' Sam replied before getting out of his car to open the passenger door for her.

'I've had such a great night, thank you for spending it with me.'

'Me too. Thanks, Sam.' May stepped out of the car and began to slowly walk up her path.

'May?' Sam called after her.

She turned to look at him as he walked the few steps up her path to meet her.

'Goodnight.' He leaned in and kissed her gently on the cheek. Sam's lips felt so soft against her cheek, the bristles of his beard pressing against her momentarily. He quickly walked back down her drive and up Peter's, waving to her as she stood on the spot, surrounded by a bubble of happiness.

She walked into the flat, holding her cheek. It had been so long since a man had shown her any affection, and Sam wasn't just some man. He was automatically more special because of Peter, but he had such a way about him as an individual. She only had her relationship with Thomas to compare it to. She had loved Thomas, she really had, but she and Sam had talked that evening about such deep topics already. He seemed ordinary in a special way, and he saw her as someone who, despite her circumstances, didn't need pity, just understanding and kindness. He was most definitely special, and she couldn't wait to see him again.

After letting Alexander out for his evening toilet and then back in, she put her pyjamas on, brushed her teeth and got into bed, shaping herself around the ball of Alexander. Her mobile phone beeped with a message from Sam, thanking her again for a lovely night and asking if she would like to have a cuppa at Peter's tomorrow evening. She beamed and instantly replied with a yes, not wanting to mention it was her birthday. They eventually said goodnight, and she put her phone on her bedside cabinet.

She lay looking into the darkness. It was hard to believe she'd devised a suicide plan four weeks ago, that her life had got to such a desperate point, a storm in her mind that had felt too heavy to ever pass. She had a new appreciation of how low and despairing people could get, not knowing where to turn. It felt as if that person four weeks ago was a stranger, someone possessing her through the impact of her trauma.

Because what she had really wanted was to live, she just hadn't known how to enjoy life when she had so much pain. But when she thought about what she had done the last month—new experiences, pushing herself out of her comfort zone, making new friends—it all felt rather magical; in fact, it felt as if she was living, not dying.

The only thing that cut through all the happiness was that she didn't have her parents there to share it with. They would never meet Sam, Peter, Alexander or Scarlett's baby. They would never hear about the great date or how much she had changed. They were gone, and the scar would never heal, she just had to learn how to live with it.

Chapter 40

31st May

Alexander woke May with a birthday head rub. He would never know how much it meant to her, especially on that day.

'Why thank you, stinky mouth,' she said as he purred and then yawned straight in her face.

She patted his head, his fur soft and warm. A shower of tears followed. It was her twenty-fifth birthday. The day she had planned on taking her life and the first birthday without either of her parents.

She remained in bed, curled in a foetal position. Alexander jumped off and headed towards the lounge, no doubt looking for some food. She frantically scrolled through her phone, her heart racing as she searched for photos of the last birthday she'd had with both her parents. It was three years ago, aged twenty-two. There was one of the birthday cake Fran had made, another of May and her mam drinking hot drinks out of the special tea set that only made an appearance on exceptional occasions. Smiling at the screen, May touched her mam's face as tears cascaded down her cheeks. The next photo was of May and her dad in matching grey sweatshirts. She laughed through her tears, recalling the conversation before the photo as she'd opened her gift. Victor had gotten sick of her stealing his grey sweatshirt to replies of, 'But it's comfy.' To prevent it, he had bought her one for her birthday. The exact same plain grey sweatshirt, in the same size. She had been delighted and put it straight on as her dad raced to the bedroom to get his and put it on as well. The three of them had been in stitches as May and Victor posed for the photo.

'How will we know whose is whose though, Dad?' May had asked.

'Oh, I never thought of that.'

They had all roared with laughter, and Fran had said she would do what she did when May was little at school and used to come home distraught that another child had taken her sports T-shirt or plimsolls—she would stitch her name into the grey sweatshirt. Problem solved.

May rubbed her face and pulled herself up in bed. There were a number of text messages that she couldn't bear looking at just yet; instead, she got up, made her bed straight away in an attempt to detract her from getting back into it and then went into the kitchen to find Alexander. He was sitting patiently by the cupboard that he now knew his food was kept in. She couldn't help but snigger and be grateful to him for being a distraction, even if he was demanding with it.

After feeding Alexander, she put the kettle on but was interrupted by a meow informing her that her lodger wanted out. She walked over to the stairs, Alexander darting past her and towards the front door. As she put the keys in the door, he pawed it impatiently.

'Okay, okay, one second, boss.' She laughed as the lock turned. He ran out and headed to the garden. Peter and Sam were getting into the car, likely going to see Anne. They saw Alexander, then looked over to May's flat.

'Morning, pet. Happy birthday,' Peter called out with a wave.

'Yeah, happy birthday, May,' Sam added.

'Thank you.' She pulled a shoulder up to her ear and held her dressing gown to her chest as she half hid behind the door in her nightwear. *How on Earth do they know it's my birthday?* She didn't have it on social media, so Sam couldn't have found out there, and she knew she had never told them.

'See you tonight for your birthday cuppa,' Sam shouted out of his open window, a big grin on his face. 'Enjoy your day.'

May watched the car drive off and remained peeking out of the side of her front door for a moment, thumb to her mouth, still wracking her brain as to how they could have known it was her birthday.

Back upstairs, she finished preparing breakfast and went into the lounge area to sit on the sofa. She may not have her parents to help her celebrate today, but she had a busy day to help distract her from what she didn't have, even though the thought of all the socialising she'd be doing today was intense and far outside of her comfort zone. She was going to Diane and Trevor's house for lunch, where Scarlett was staying until tomorrow. She was grateful she had Scarlett there on such a difficult day and relieved that Diane and Trevor always seemed to make her feel welcome and prioritised.

This evening, she had plans to go to dinner with Trish and then, as arranged last night and confirmed this morning, to Peter and Sam's at 8 p.m. for a cuppa. She was determined to not spend the full day in distress, knowing how heartbroken her parents would be if she wallowed in misery and loneliness on her birthday instead. She leaned her head back on the sofa and hugged her arms around herself. From as young as she could remember, Fran and Victor had talked to her about what they would do for the milestones in her life.

The holiday to Cyprus for her sixteenth birthday, tickets to go and see Brian Cox on her eighteenth birthday, *Phantom of the Opera* at the West End on her twenty-first birthday. Victor had even talked about a holiday together this year, possibly for her birthday. Now it would never and could never happen. She gritted her teeth, trying to bite through the thoughts that were pulling her into a dark cloud. She shook her head and refocused on her plans for the day once more. After the busy day ahead, she hoped Alexander would come back that evening. His company was proving to be an unexpected but now almost essential medicine. She glanced at the armchair where his fleece blanket lay and smiled. It was going to be a strange and hard day.

She had received a few cards in the post. She stood by the lounge window as she opened them, looking for the blackbird on the tree opposite her flat. It wasn't there, but still she remained, hoping. One card from Uncle Terence, one signed by a few friends at university and one from Mr and Mrs Taylor. She was pleased that Trish and Scarlett had asked about gifts that she wanted or needed earlier in the month, reducing the anxiety of surprise on a day that didn't need any added stress.

To waste some time, she decided to do some house-work. Hoovering had increased in frequency since Alexander had become a regular guest, and although he didn't shed a lot of hair, she noticed it, having never had pets. She didn't mind though, as his company far outweighed any increase in chores.

An hour later, the flat was spotless, and she felt the buzz of satisfaction. Clapping her hands together, she surveyed her space. It wasn't much, but it was home. She placed her birthday cards on the windowsill and glanced out. Her eyes widened and she took an intake of breath—the blackbird was on the tree. She held her hands together and brought them to her chest, then stood still, worried sudden movements might scare the bird off as she observed it. It remained motionless for a minute before hopping along the branch, then up to the next branch before flying to another part of the tree. It stopped again, almost looking at her until it took flight.

May pulled up at Scarlett's family home and parked on the road outside of the semi-detached house. She leaned to the passenger seat for the flowers and got out of the car. Scarlett opened the door, singing *Happy Birthday* loud enough for the whole street to hear. With arms out and a few hip wiggles, Scarlett had perfected the per-formance. Walking down the driveway, May put her free hand over her face, but she couldn't deny that Scarlett had a beautiful singing voice, which made the situation slightly less embarrassing. Diane and Trevor appeared behind Scarlett and began joining in with the singing.

May smiled. Feeling a little awkward with the attention being on her, she held the flowers out that she'd picked up from the supermarket on the way and passed them to Diane.

'Thank you, May, but it's your day, you shouldn't be giving gifts.' Diane chuckled, pulling May in for a hug.

Scarlett grabbed May next, squeezing her, then she received a light embrace from Trevor and a barky greeting from Cumberland, who bounced on his small feet, tongue out.

She eventually got into the hallway and was rushed through to the lounge by an excited Scarlett.

'Sit down.' Scarlett plonked onto the sofa and tapped the seat next to her with childlike enthusiasm. May joined her with significantly less enthusiasm.

Trevor and Diane headed into the kitchen.

'How's your morning been?' Scarlett took May's hands and stared at her friend.

May bit the inside of her lip. 'I dunno. Strange. Sad. Grateful. I'm glad I'm here.'

Scarlett looked over May's shoulder. 'We have *cake.*'

Another rendition of *Happy Birthday* started as the cake was carried in by Trevor and hot drinks by Diane. May felt her cheeks redden, but today, she found great comfort in being fussed over despite her natural embarrassment. She could immediately tell the red velvet cake was from the local patisserie Diane had used for her birthday as she blew out the candles.

'I saw how quickly you put this away at Mam's party, so we knew we had to get it for your birthday cake,' Scarlett said as Diane began to cut slices. May could smell the creamy butter icing, and once cut, the sumptuous red sponge made her lick her lips.

'I think I've got cake running through my veins the amount I've eaten this month.' May tapped her stomach.

'Well, love, it's done you the world of good; you look healthier for it.' Diane rubbed May's upper arm as she handed her a slice of cake on a plate.

Trevor raised his cup. 'To May, our second daughter. Happy birthday.'

Diane and Scarlett repeated the sentiment and even Cumberland fussed around her, likely for crumbs of cake. She quickly wiped a tear away from her eye, took a sip of tea and put a forkful of cake in her mouth. The room was silent as they all took their first mouthful, followed by ooohs and mmms of sweet delight.

'Time for presents.' Scarlett put her plate onto the floor and did a little dance in her seat.

May was given three presents—two from Scarlett and one from Diane and Trevor—alongside two cards. As they were placed on the sofa next to her, she rubbed her hand along her thigh and moved slightly in her seat, noticing an extra present than she'd expected. She thanked everyone as she began opening them, now more self-conscious of the eyes on her and the unwavering excitement from Scarlett that was filling the room. Diane and Trevor had got her a box of her favourite orange chocolate and a book token (which she had asked for).

'Thanks so much, both of you, this is perfect.' May smiled, grateful not only for the gift but for knowing which books she would buy after a few months of not even contemplating one of her favourite pastimes.

Scarlett tapped her legs as she watched May reach for the presents from her. She leaned in as May opened the first of two gifts from her best friend. The larger gift was a laptop case (also what she had asked for).

'This is brilliant. Thank you, Scarlett.' May leaned over to hug her.

'Open the other, that one, there.' Scarlett pointed to it even though May was fully aware.

Under Scarlett's watch, May rubbed her thumbs and forefingers together, then picked up the gift. It was a little pale pink box, and she felt a flutter of anxiety wondering what it could be.

Scarlett, reading her best friend, shook her head slightly and said, 'If you don't like it, you can hide it away. It takes up no space. But, well, I just saw it and had to get you it.'

May opened the box tentatively and looked inside. She reached her fingers in and gently pulled the gift out as a smile formed on her face. It was a beautiful silver bracelet with an engraving on.

'Look, I've got the same. It's a friendship bracelet and that's the friendship symbol,' Scarlett said, pulling her sleeve up and pointing to her wrist.

May touched her friend's wrist as she held her gifted bracelet in her other hand. She didn't wear jewellery as a rule, but this was elegant and subtle. And perhaps it was a gift she needed today, a gift to help her with the worries she'd been having over their friendship. Because with the celebration today, Scarlett calling her an auntie and looking at moving back and the thoughtfulness of the gift, May couldn't deny that their closeness felt as strong as ever in that moment.

May hugged Scarlett tightly. 'I love it.'

Scarlett hugged her back momentarily, then pulled away. 'Look at me, I can tell when you're lying because you're shit at it.'

'*Scarlett.*' Diane glared at her daughter.

'It's okay, Mam, she's not lying.' Scarlett began laughing, and May joined in.

'Can you fasten it for me, please?' May asked, holding her wrist out to Scarlett.

Scarlett fastened the delicate bracelet. The metal felt strange against her wrist, but she decided it was a feeling she could get used to.

'There you go, it looks gorgeous and it means we're always connected even if apart. Take a photo, please, Mam?' Scarlett asked Diane, passing her mobile phone. 'And another of our wrists.'

They posed.

'Let's get one of us all,' said Diane.

'Wait a minute, someone else wants to be in it,' Trevor added, looking down at Cumberland, who was sniffing the carpet for crumbs. Picking him up, Trevor held Scarlett's phone out with his free hand, and they all squashed in for a selfie.

Trevor and Diane cleaned the dishes whilst May and Scarlett chatted. They talked about Scarlett's pregnancy and a little about May's parents—just enough for May to share a memory or two with someone who'd known them, but not enough to open the floodgates and spoil the enjoyment she was feeling.

'What are you doing for the rest of the day?'

May explained she was meeting Trish for dinner, then about Peter and Sam. 'I don't know how they knew it was my birthday though. I didn't mention it.' May rubbed her forehead.

Scarlett bit her lip and began giggling.

May's mouth dropped open. '*Scarlett.*' She prodded her friend.

'Facebook can be handy for chatting to people you've never met.' She grinned. 'They would've wanted to know, May. They are your friends, and Sam, well, maybe more.'

'You're pretty nosy, but I love you.'

'May, he sounds right into you. How exciting. Give him a proper snog tonight, will you, and perhaps he will give you the birthday humps.' She burst out laughing.

'You mean birthday bumps.' May rolled her eyes, making Scarlett laugh even louder.

After Diane filled a glass container with slices of birthday cake for May to take home, it was soon time for her to head off. As much as she enjoyed their company, she wanted a little time at home before seeing Trish. A social conveyor belt was no good for her. It was overwhelming and exhausting. She needed to socialise today more than any day, but, well, small steps and all that.

Chapter 41

May practically dropped onto her sofa as soon as she was back in her flat, leaning her head back against the chocolate-brown velvety material. Alexander just looked at her from his blanket, seemed to consider how tired he was and where he'd prefer to lie, then got up, stretched and moved onto her knee, curling into a ball and purring.

Her phone beeped, and she could see Scarlett was sending through the photos of her birthday lunch. She smiled, putting her phone to her chest. She'd look at them later and eventually print them off and put them in a new photo album, just like they used to. In ten years, Scarlett and May and Scarlett's child would sit somewhere, looking through the photos and laughing. Just as May and Scarlett had done only a few weeks ago in May's flat. She looked at her right wrist where her friendship bracelet sat neatly. She touched it and smiled. 'Thank you.' No one but Alexander heard.

Something Sam had said the night before on their date had been niggling at her:

'We are all waiting to die, but you can get on with living until then or you can sit and wait. Some people can't help it, like my mam, but my dad is living and learning to live in a world that's not what he prepared himself for when he married my mam. He's just getting on with life. We all have to do that. We have to do our best.'

He was right, and May had to do her best to live before she died.

She reached for the laptop on the coffee table, gently so as not to disturb her purring knee warmer, then went back to the page she had been looking at online in recent days. She read it again, for the third time, and then, taking a deep breath, she picked up her mobile phone and dialled the number on her laptop screen.

It rang three times before a bouncy voice answered the phone. 'Hello, SCT Therapy, Sandra speaking.'

May swallowed, slight panic seeping in now everything was becoming real. She'd rehearsed what she was going to say over and over again, but her mind hit a blank, as if she were an actress with stage fright. 'Hello, erm, my name is May. I saw your website, and I am wondering if I can possibly come to meet with you, please?'

'Thanks so much for calling, that's the first step, and I would love to see how I could help you,' said the gentle voice. 'Let me tell you a little bit about what we do here and then we can maybe book an initial meeting. Does that sound okay, May?'

May felt immediately relaxed by the warm, calming voice on the phone, and after a further ten minutes of chatting, she made an appointment with Sandra for just over a week's time.

After the call, she sat in silence. She hadn't even had a session yet, but it was as if all the pain she'd pushed into the back of her mind had been dragged up. Maybe her brain was pulling everything to the front ready to sort through. A clutter of pain, grief and sadness ready to be rearranged into an orderly, neat stack on a bookcase or in a cupboard in her mind. It had taken her so long to seek help, which was a surprise in itself considering she'd just discovered how easy it actually was to reach out. She realised now that sometimes it seems easier to let the depths take you when you're already drowning rather than to swim hard against the tide and search for a life raft. She wanted to be happy, she wanted to move on, but part of her was intentionally stuck in grief. What if she forgot her parents? What if the guilt for not constantly being in a state of grief was too much? She had to work through it with a professional. She had to try living.

It was a few hours before she was due to meet Trish. Sitting on the sofa, she rested a small plate with a slice of cake on the arm. A cup of tea cooled on the coffee table, and she reached for her laptop from the table shelf. After quickly checking emails, all of which were rubbish, she clicked onto the site of the bookshop her voucher from Diane and Trevor was for. Fully aware of which books she wanted, she browsed around the site rather than heading straight to the virtual basket. As she spooned cake into her mouth, she enjoyed looking at the new releases and even the sale section before eventually going to her pre-chosen books and paying for them.

Soon, it was time for her to get changed. Pulling off her jumper, she reapplied some deodorant before opening her wardrobe and taking out one of her favourite floral blouses—one her mam had loved. Putting it on and looking in the mirror, she let a long, slow sigh out before leaving the bedroom. It was time to go and meet Trish.

Fifteen minutes later, she had parked her car and was standing outside of a gastropub near work, waiting for Trish. She had passed Lawson-Wray's on her way to their meeting place and smiled at the empty office, shut up for the day. As she stood, she thought about what Scarlett had said about Sam possibly liking her. Things seemed to be going okay at the moment for her, considering, but she was fearful of it all going wrong. She hoped the therapist could help her manage her emotions, some of her responses and behaviours. Her thoughts were dispersed by shouting from across the road.

'Hello, my birthday girl.'

Her eyes travelled to the opposite side of the road where a frantically waving Trish was starting to cross.

'Happy birthday, my lovely,' she said, reaching the pub entrance and hugging May with all of her might.

'Thank you,' May replied as Trish hurried them into the pub.

It was busy inside, pop music just about audible under the murmur of customers and intermittent clattering of crockery.

'Let's find a quietish corner,' Trish suggested, taking May's hand and leading the way.

A waiter passed them with a plate of sizzling grill in each hand. The smell of fried mushrooms, onions and meats wafted under May's nose. She couldn't believe she was hungry after double cake, but her stomach rumbled.

'Oooh, here we go.' Trish found a cosy booth set back slightly from the main bustle of the pub. They both reached for the menus, although May already knew what she was having—the same meal she'd had the last time she was in the pub and likely the same meal she would order the next time: chicken burger in a bun with home-made rainbow slaw and chunky chips.

Trish went to order, choosing the beef burger for herself, and brought back two lemonades to the table.

Placing the drinks down and sliding back into the booth, Trish grabbed May's hands across the table. 'How have you been?' she gently said. 'I've been thinking about you all day.'

'It's been better than I thought it would be, to be honest. I rang a therapist this afternoon and I've booked an appointment. I know I need something.' She stopped, swallowing. 'It's getting easier, but sometimes I feel stuck and I think the worst and, well, it's stopping me from living how I should. How my parents would want me to live.'

'I'm so flipping proud of you, May, you're an amazing lady.' Trish squeezed her hands quickly and then let go. 'Right, my lovely, here's your presents. And here's another card, not from me.'

May raised her eyebrows as she took the card.

'No world cruise ticket or anything. It's from Lawson-Wray's, they all wanted to sign it,' Trish clarified.

'I'll open it later, thank you.' May put the card to the side as Trish pulled up a gift bag onto the table.

She'd heard the word 'presents', although she was sure she'd only mentioned wanting a new notebook when Trish had been pestering her about her birthday. She wrung her hands as she glared at the gift bag.

'Eeeh, what you like. Open the bugger, will you.'

May pulled out the presents and placed them on the table in front of her. She looked at them, then to Trish, who nodded. May began to slowly open the first present, delicately peeling back the wrapping paper. Scarlett had already surprised her once today. *But it was a nice surprise, so perhaps this will be nice as well.* Trish leaned forward, almost crawling onto the table between them. The first present was a floral spiral-bound notebook.

May smiled. 'It's perfect and spiral-bound. Thanks, Trish.'

'I know you like your spiral-bounds. Open the next one,' Trish said impatiently.

May began opening the second present, neatly and slowly pulling the paper off, putting off the surprise for as long as possible. But she didn't have to fake a reaction. It was a photo of her and her parents on the last Christmas they'd had together, taken by Uncle Terence. Beaming smiles from their three faces as they all wore paper party hats, Victor's balancing on his head, as they were always too small for him. Fran was holding a glass of sherry in the hand that wasn't wrapped around May, raising it in a *cheers* motion.

Rubbing a finger over the faces in the photo, May recalled how happy they had been that day. Carefree in a world that often caused worry about so-called 'little things' for May. But that day, that Christmas, she had felt carefree and happy, and she knew her parents had felt it too.

May and Trish had shared Christmas photos that year by text, and Trish had saved it. And now she had printed it out and put it in the most beautiful frame.

May stared at the frame, speechless. Tears fell down her face as she kept her eyes on the photo, unable to take them away. She wanted to look at it forever.

Trish leaned over and kissed May's head, then passed her a serviette to wipe her eyes. 'Your walls are bare, and I want you to start filling them with all your precious memories and new experiences. This is the start.'

May almost felt back in her parents' house, on that Christmas, when her world had been so different. She took a gulp of air and brought her eyes up from the frame. 'Thank you, I love it,' she managed in a croaky voice.

'There's something else in there.' Trish nodded to the gift bag.

May took out the small envelope she'd mistaken for a birthday card and hoped to open later while alone. She hated having to read cards aloud. Gently lifting the flap of the envelope, she slid out two vouchers, one for a garden centre and one for a plaque-making service in town. And there it was—the reason she hated surprises. Having to fake happiness or, in this case, not even understanding the gift in the first place. She glanced at Trish, attempting a smile, but her furrowed brow gave her away.

'It's for you to pick a bench to put in your back garden. I'm sure your neighbour won't mind now you are friends. The other voucher is for you to get a plaque to dedicate your bench to your parents. Then when you sit there, you can just be.'

May burst out crying as their burgers arrived, unable to control the emotions she felt at such kindness from her friend who never faltered in her care. Even when May could seem and be ungrateful, Trish was always there. She felt happy, sad, guilty and overwhelmed all at once.

'Sorry, miss,' the waiter said, quickly putting the food on their table and giving a nervous smile before dashing away, leaving a crying May with Trish holding her hands.

'I can't believe you'd do that.'

'Well, with a present perfectionist like you, I was cacking myself.' Trish grinned.

May laughed, wiping her eyes with a serviette. 'They're amazing. Thank you so much.'

'You're welcome, my lovely. Now, let's tuck in; I'm famished.'

The pair ate their burgers, and May talked about her week, Scarlett's pregnancy, going back to university and her date with Sam.

'Oh yes, he was very keen to know more about you when I mentioned I was your friend,' Trish said, tapping the side of her nose.

'Oh crikey, what did you say?'

'Just that you're gorgeous and brilliant and if he hurt you, I'd break his legs.'

'*Trish.*'

'Okay, well, not the last bit.' Trish chuckled. 'He seemed very nice, May. Very genuine and complimentary about you. He's coming back in tomorrow. The poor bugger can't find anywhere to rent; there's not a lot on the rental market at the moment.' She stopped talking and looked at May, who had begun stacking their dirty plates. 'Would you consider leasing your parents' house when the time is right?'

May turned her gaze from the plates. 'Erm, yeah, actually. I was talking to my uncle about it. I'm not sure if I'll ever be ready to sell it. But I have started sorting a few bits to possibly rent it out in the future. It's just a big deal and renters can be dreadful, as we both know.'

Trish nodded. 'That's brilliant, love. If I can help you with the sorting, let me know. As for renters, too flipping right, we've had some nightmares over the years, haven't we?'

The pair started to laugh.

'But if you did want to rent in the future, how about someone like Sam, when the time's right? Someone you know? At least it means you wouldn't have a stranger living there in the short term.'

'You know, it would be great to have someone I sort of know living there.' May ran a hand over her hair. 'Sam did say he only wanted a six-month or so lease until his job up here is permanent. I'm not sure if I'm ready right now, but someone I know would definitely make it easier.'

Trish nodded. 'Could be a perfect solution, and perhaps he could even help you sort things out, if you felt comfortable with it of course.'

May thought about all the memories in the house, each room with its own stories. The things she couldn't possibly ever change and that a lodger would have to leave the same. *Would a stranger understand the importance of such things?* The whole concept felt overwhelming, like running a marathon when she'd only just learnt how to walk again. But Trish had a point, and as pushing herself out of her comfort zone had become the theme of the last few days, perhaps it could work.

'I don't know. It's probably too big for him and, well, I haven't even begun to sort all the years of belongings and rubbish in there. I'm not sure I could ask him to help or if I would want him to.'

'I understand. You could put some items in the main bedroom and rent it as a two-bedroomed to him.'

'Maybe, I don't know. But I guess it's worth thinking about.'

Alexander was waiting at the front door when May arrived home. He gave a chorus of meows and rubbed his body against her legs. It was later than usual for her to be out, and she felt bad at the thought of him waiting to be let in.

'Perhaps we need to get a cat flap put in the door, my little boy,' she said, patting his head as he pawed the front door, trying to get in quicker. She smiled and repeated, 'My little boy.'

Alexander ran up the stairs, and she followed, slower after taking her shoes off. The meowing went into double figures as she tried to quickly meet his demands. She laughed to herself at how bold he was and that he had already assigned himself the boss of the household in a matter of weeks.

She made her way to the bathroom and took out her make-up bag from the cabinet, then opened it and stared inside at the little make-up she had. She was already wearing a thin coat of mascara but decided to apply a little blusher and some tinted lip balm—minimal, as always. Then she saw some eyeshadow in the make-up bag and fished it out. It was usually one she wore for nights out with Scarlett. Opening it, she rubbed a little of the grey, shimmery shadow on the applicator and applied it to her eyelids. Staring at her reflection, there was still a dull sadness in her eyes, but she saw something else, perhaps a little flicker of self-belief and acceptance. She took a deep breath, smiled at herself in the mirror and took the sixty-second walk to her neighbour's front door.

She had only just taken her finger off the doorbell when the front door burst open to Peter and Sam squashed together, a helium balloon bobbing in between them as they sang *Happy Birthday*. She began laughing at the wonderful sight. They moved their arms, beckoning her in. She smoothed her hair as she walked into the flat and followed the joyful pair into the lounge, where she stopped and gasped. They had put bunting up in the lounge that spelt out 'Happy Birthday'. She put her hand to her mouth, shocked at the kind effort.

'Happy birthday, pet,' Peter said, giving May a hug.

'Happy birthday, May,' Sam said, hugging her before rushing out of the room.

'Sit yourself down, pet, on my new and fancy sofa.' Peter clapped his hands together and then pointed to the L-shaped sofa taking up much of his lounge as if she could have missed it.

'Thanks, Peter. Wow, it's a really nice sofa.' May sat down and rubbed the grey velour cushions before looking at Peter with an approving nod as he sat next to her.

Sam came from the direction of the kitchen with a large box in his arms that was decorated in colourful wrapping paper. 'May, this is for you, and it isn't a cat carrier.'

She laughed. 'Good, as I already have one of those and Alexander doesn't seem keen.'

After Sam placed the box on the floor in front of her, Peter looked at her, at the box and back at her. With the excitement he seemed to have when it came to giving a gift, she felt sure Sam's Christmases must have been magical as a child. Perhaps they still were.

'C'mon, then, get it opened.'

'You both shouldn't have bothered,' she said, feeling under the spotlight and worrying about what might be in the box. She smiled as if she were joking, but there was seriousness behind her words. She'd had more than enough surprises today to last her a lifetime despite them being incredible, and she worried about what they could have possibly decided on buying for her just from the short time they'd known her.

As she moved the box around, looking for where to start opening it, she bit her lip. She tore a large strip of paper, which was decorated with colourful cupcakes, then pulled the remaining wrapping paper off, revealing a cardboard box. She stared at it blankly, as if that could possibly be the gift.

Sam started laughing, observing her face. 'It's inside the box. Go on.' He leaned in towards where she sat.

May opened the cardboard box and carefully lifted out another box from inside. A beautiful wooden box that had been carved into with stunning patterns and pictures, with a clasp at the front. She stared at it, eyes wide, mesmerised, rubbing her hand over it, feeling its intricate, detailed carving. Opening the clasp, she lifted the lid of the box to see inside. It was unlined, with a smooth, neat wood finish.

Turning her eyes back to Peter and Sam, she spoke, 'I don't know what to say. This is absolutely gorgeous. Thank you, both of you.' Her smile displayed her gratitude, and Peter and Sam nodded, pleased their present had been a success.

Today had been a catalogue of surprises and so different to all the previous birthdays she had experienced. But instead of the sheer horror that usually accompanied surprises, today, she'd learnt that they could be good too. The box was something she never would have thought about asking for, but it would be perfect for her to put some of the memories of her life in.

Peter placed his hand on her shoulder. 'This was one of Anne's boxes. She had many in our home, filled with knick-knacks and memories. We've kept some but gifted others to only special people.' He half-smiled. 'This one was one of her favourites, as she said the carvings almost told a story. The memory box of memories.'

May put her hand to her heart as Sam put an arm around his dad.

'I couldn't possibly...'

'Yes, you can,' Peter stated firmly but lovingly. 'I know my Anne, and she would've wanted it to go to someone who needs it.' He pulled his collar to the side, trying to cool the hot flush of grief he was feeling. 'Anne's memories are hardly there now, but Sam and I hold them and try to help her remember. We are Anne's memory box now. We want you to put your memories in it, May, and it's a place for all your new ones.'

'It's beautiful. I'm a bit speechless,' she replied, her eyes focusing back on the stunning creation. She felt herself filling up, but she didn't want to cry. It was such a thoughtful and kind gesture, and she was touched that Peter and Sam wanted her to have something of Anne's.

Peter wiped his eyes before smiling at May. 'Put the kettle on, Son,' he said to Sam.

Sam headed into the kitchen, and Peter turned to May.

'How have you been today, pet? I've been thinking about you.'

May smiled. 'Actually, it's been a lot easier than I thought it was going to be. I'm pleased I didn't—' She stopped, shocked at how she'd almost given her former intention of suicide away. Peter was just so easy to talk to sometimes. She could see why he would have been great in his career in mental health support.

Peter squeezed her hand and stared at her with serious eyes. 'Me too, pet, me too.'

She looked at Peter, not clear on what he meant or what he understood. She went to speak just as Sam popped his head around the corner.

'Dad, I can't find the you-know-what. Can you help?'

Peter shook his head and got up, smiling at May as he followed Sam through to the kitchen.

A few seconds later, the singing duo started again as Sam carried a birthday cake. May's mouth opened—it was a ginormous, family-sized cupcake, piped with thick, swirling icing and with a candle in the top. Peter carried a pot of tea into the lounge, holding it in the air as if it were champagne. At the end of the performance, she applauded them, and Sam crouched, holding the huge cupcake in front of her. Despite usually feeling uncomfortable with the attention, she had relaxed, and she soaked it up as if it were the medicine she had so desperately needed the last few months.

She took a deep breath in, closed her eyes and blew out the candle that almost looked lost amongst the masses of inviting icing. As her breath extinguished the flame, she squeezed her hands and made a wish that she hoped with every fibre of her being would come true.

Part Three

Present Year

Chapter 42

November

May's hand searched blindly for her phone on the top of her bedside table as she struggled to open her eyes and let out a loud yawn. She eventually found it and forced her eyes open to turn the alarm off. Despite being an early riser, *this* was too early. After taking quite a bit of time off university, she was determined to do whatever it took to refresh her mind on what she'd already studied, even if it meant rising extra early to study before planned university lectures continued for a while. She'd already managed it for two months, after doing some distance learning before going back, so what was another few months?

She rose from her bed and wrapped her dressing gown around herself before stroking an undisturbed Alexander as he lay curled on her bed. After pushing her feet into her slippers, she shuffled into the lounge. Too early for breakfast, she boiled the kettle and made a cup of tea, then sat on the sofa and switched on her laptop. She was relishing in her studies and could see her end goal, reachable at last. A small smile crept onto her face as Alexander walked into the room and curled up on what now seemed to be his armchair, wanting to be near her.

After an hour of research and note-taking, she got up from the sofa and closed her study book, then stretched her arms up and straightened her back. She moved to the kitchen to get a glass of water, then brought it back to the lounge and looked out the window as she sipped it. Her eyes immediately widened and she blinked quickly, leaning slightly forward, nearer to the window. There he was, the blackbird. She hadn't seen the bird since the end of May, over five months ago. He had been there at her hardest time, almost watching over her. Then in June, he was gone. And there he was now, on the branch, looking in her direction.

She placed her fingers on the glass. 'Thank you,' she said quietly as a silent tear slid down her cheek. The blackbird seemed to understand, cocking its head, then a minute later, it flew off. Her fingers lingered on the glass as she wondered if she'd ever see it again.

One thing that was constant in her life though was Sam. She thought about him, as she did most of the time they weren't together, then smiled to herself. She couldn't believe they'd been together for five months already. But with her need to leave for uni lectures fast approaching, it was time to get Sam off her mind and focus on what she would pack in her lunch bag instead, making sure to include an extra sandwich for her shift at Cookson House after, the care home where Anne lived and where she now brushed her hair weekly. With her new busy schedule of housework, uni, studying at home, making time for social plans and volunteering at Cookson House, she'd had to make the decision to leave Lawson-Wray's after almost five years. The hardest part had been leaving Trish, but the pair kept in regular contact, and Trish now served May tea and biscuits at home rather than the workplace. But volunteering made her feel useful in a way Lawson-Wray's never had been able to and it allowed her to learn so much about degenerative diseases in a way no textbook could ever teach her.

She took the last mouthful of water from her glass and turned away from the window, having decided on a cheese sandwich and a ham sandwich. A door slammed, and she looked back to the window, leaning forward. Peter was rushing up his path, towards a taxi, his usual cheery face now serious and hard to read. She banged on the window as hard as she could, but he jumped into the taxi and headed off without even a gaze in her direction.

Concern immediately crept up her back. *Maybe he has an appointment before going to see Anne.*

The situation ricocheted around her head, and after making both sandwiches and packing her lunch bag, she texted him.

'Saw you dash into a taxi earlier, hope everything is okay?'

She put her mobile phone on charge before going in the shower, not wanting to call just in case, but sure she was worrying about nothing and that she'd get out of the shower to a text. But after finishing her shower, drying her hair and getting dressed, he still hadn't texted back.

Once May arrived at uni, her morning passed quickly as she became absorbed in lectures. At lunch, before going to the canteen, she visited the library, keen to get a book advised to the class by the professor. Grabbing one of only two copies on the shelf, she let out a gratifying sigh before taking the book to the front desk to check out. Whilst in a short queue, she checked her phone again, but still no text.

Leaving the library, she headed for the canteen, her stomach rumbling as she walked. The canteen was bustling with big queues for hot food and drinks and students catching up. She walked past the noisy queues and took a seat at her regular table, next to one of her course friends, Alex.

'Did you get the book you wanted?' Alex asked before taking a bite of his sandwich.

'Yeah, last one on the shelf.' May patted her tote bag containing the book before pulling her lunch bag out. As the other friends arrived at the table, she checked her mobile phone again. This time, there was a text from Sam.

'Hi May, can you please call me when you get a chance? Thanks. Xxx'

She stuffed her lunch bag back into her tote bag and took her coat from the back of the seat, draping it over her arm.

'I'll just be five minutes.'

Before anyone could respond, she walked away, grasping her phone as if it were a bar of gold. Reaching a quieter spot outside the canteen, her fingers began shaking as she called Sam, the coldness in the air already feeling as if it were sucking all the heat from her coatless body.

'Hi, Sam, are you okay?' An anchor was already down in her stomach as she waited for the bad news. Something was wrong and something had felt wrong all day.

She heard a light cough as Sam cleared his throat. 'It-it's Mam.' He gasped in some air before continuing, stuttering, 'She-she's gone.'

There was a pause as a gush of grief hit May, leaving her unsteady on her feet. She put her hand to the canteen brickwork and used it to guide herself slowly to a nearby bench, where she practically collapsed, hand to her head.

'What happened?' she managed as she tried to keep it together for Sam.

'The carers, th-they found her this mor-morning. She must have die...' A whimpering sound came from him as he struggled to get the word out. 'Died in h-her sleep.' There was a sniff followed by a muffled sob. 'Sorry.'

May shook, partly from the winter chill but partly out of shock and sadness. Anne had been terminally ill, but it didn't mean any of them had been prepared for the end, especially not Peter or Sam. She wished she could transport herself to be with them. Wiping her eyes on a red glove from her coat pocket, she gave a nauseous hiccup.

'No, Sam, I'm sorry.' She knew that didn't help. People saying sorry had never helped her, and what were they actually sorry for? It wasn't their fault. She pressed her lips together and said what she actually wanted to say, not what people had said to her. 'I'm, I'm devastated for you, Sam. Your mam, she's... she was amazing.'

Sam breathed in between sobs. 'Thanks,' he mustered.

'I'll come to you. Where are you? At the home?' she asked, trying to sound calm despite an avalanche of emotions in her mind.

'Yeah. Dad's here. He's not spoken, May. I don't know what to do.'

'Okay, I'm on my way, Sam. I'll be less than half an hour.'

'Thank you,' he replied quietly. 'I love you.'

Trying to control her breathing, May rushed to her car and threw her coat into the boot. As she jumped into the driver seat and turned the engine on, she sat there wondering how she was going to drive with her legs tingling so much.

'C'mon,' she scolded herself, knowing that this was about Peter and Sam, not her. She had to smother the feelings she had worked so hard to control. She took ten deep breaths and focused on the car park sign within her eyeline. Then she fastened her seatbelt and drove to Cookson House.

Once at the care home, she used the fob on her keyring to enter, then waved to the staff member in the reception area as she jogged past. She stopped for a second almost at the corridor where Anne's room was located, closed her eyes, clenched and then unclenched her fists and took a deep breath.

She pushed herself to be calm as she walked a few metres down the corridor, glancing in the communal lounge on the way. She'd expected Peter and Sam to be in Anne's room, but they were in the lounge alone, sitting adjacent to one another. Peter had his head down and one hand on his forehead as Sam rested his hand on his father's shoulder. Peter's shoulders were moving slightly, and she knew he was crying. She stood back for a second, hand against the door frame, wondering if she should turn back and leave. She didn't want to impose on them, especially not in such an emotional moment.

Sam looked up, facing the door where she stood. She offered a sad smile. He wordlessly beckoned her in with his hand. She walked into the lounge, glancing down at the burgundy floral-patterned Axminster carpet that swirled into a shapeless blob in her vision. Peter didn't look up until she was right by his side, and when he did, his eyes were pleading and red with painful tears. He held out his hand, needing comfort from his neighbour who had become so much more.

May took Peter's hand as he leaned into her and sobbed. She placed her free hand around his shoulder and tried to comfort him as he repeated, 'She's gone. My Anne's gone.' For almost two hours, the three sat in the communal lounge, undisturbed.

Peter looked out the window at the darkness that now coloured the sky outside. The winter sun had been shining when May arrived. 'I knew, but I was never ready. Never ready to say goodbye.'

'I'll get us another cup of tea, Dad. May? Do you want one?' Sam asked, the usual colour in his face drained.

'Go help him, pet. I'm okay.' Peter nodded, bringing a tissue to his eye.

May and Sam left for the staff kitchen and walked there silently as May wrung her hands, feeling useless at being unable to lessen their pain. They quietly opened the door to the kitchen, but no one else was using it. Once inside, Sam turned to May and began to sob.

In those next few days, as the rainfall of grief continued to fill the puddle they all stood in, May promised herself that she would always remember the light that had never gone out in Anne's eyes despite the disease that consumed her.

Chapter 43

December

Amongst all the happiness, excitement and future to look forward to—Scarlett and Ethan were now only a forty-minute drive away and were impatiently waiting for their baby girl's arrival, whom they'd already named Penelope—Anne's death was another example that life can throw you a grenade every now and then.

A few weeks before the twenty-fifth of December, on the correct date, May drove to her parents' home, with Peter as a passenger. On the odd day, he had colour in his cheeks and the spring of a baby lamb in his step; most days, his eyes carried a suitcase of worries and a raincloud hovered over him. Sometimes they went for a walk to the park together, often in silence, both reflecting on their grief but still having that supportive company and a hug at the end of it before they'd walk their separate paths to their flats. Despite being May's former nemesis, hugs had become a medicine to her in grief.

May pulled up to the house and turned off the car engine. Getting out of the car, Peter waved to Sam, who was now officially a tenant there. Rushing from the lounge window, from where he had spotted his dad and May, Sam soon opened the front door, with a smile as wide as the door frame.

May inhaled as she took her shoes off. The house now had a Sam smell, but she could still smell the homely house smell from when her parents had been there. As if decades of cooking, laundry powder, cleaning products and aftershave and perfume had soaked into the foundations of the house through the skirting boards and the ceiling. And that even if they were painted or replaced, the house would forever hold the smells of their lives together.

She closed her eyes and smiled, taking a moment as Peter followed Sam into the kitchen. It still felt like home, even with new people in the house. *Youse would have loved Sam and Peter.* She opened her eyes and walked through to the lounge as Sam came back from the kitchen, his face beaming.

'I've made cake. Wait here,' he announced, rushing back into the kitchen from where she could hear cupboard doors opening and shutting as Peter made hot drinks.

Left in the lounge alone, May sat on the beige sofa and stared at the bay window, where the tree would stand. Sam had added a few ornaments and photos to the room. She glanced at the fireplace, at the hearth, where the wedding photo of Fran and Victor sat, as it always had throughout her life. On the other side, in a similar frame, sat a photo of Anne and Peter. She sighed and smiled just as Sam walked back in, shoulders back, proudly presenting three slices of cake in one hand and a teapot in the other, followed by Peter with a tray of cups, milk and sugar.

'Ta-dah,' Sam exclaimed as May began laughing. He promptly gave her a slightly bigger piece of Christmas cake than he served to his dad and himself.

After pouring the tea, Peter quickly placed a forkful of cake in his mouth. He raised his eyebrows and looked away from Sam and May, coughing as he did, then took a gulp of his drink. 'Went down the wrong way,' he said, hand to his mouth.

May wasn't the greatest fan of Christmas cake, but given it was seasonal, she was more than happy to try it despite preferring lemon, red velvet or carrot cake. She picked it up, took a bite and forced a smile. *Crikey, this is awful,* she thought, trying not to cough it out as Peter almost had.

'Mmmmm.' She nodded, looking lovingly at Sam, who was sitting and waiting for praise like a kid who had brought home a glowing school report.

She looked at what now felt like an enormous slice of earth to eat through. It tasted how she imagined brandy-soaked soil and grit to taste. She politely nibbled as he shovelled the soil cake into his mouth.

She put her plate, half the cake left, on the coffee table and rubbed her stomach. 'Damn, I'm so full.' *As long as Sam enjoys it.* He didn't seem to catch her lie, which she was glad about. It was the first cake he'd baked, so hopefully he'd improve or never bake again.

She took his hand. 'Let's get the Christmas tree down.'

Sam helped May get the McClelland Christmas tree down from the loft. They sat on the lounge floor in silence, whilst Peter sat on the sofa where her dad had always rested. May and Sam remained silent for a moment, staring at the box with the tree inside.

May felt Sam's hand gently rub her shoulder. She turned to him, and he kissed her forehead.

Summoning as much enthusiasm as she could, she said, 'Okay, let's get this tree ready.'

'Can I help, pet?' Peter asked, sipping from his cup.

'Yes, you can stay there and make sure it looks alright from a distance.' May smiled at him, knowing Peter could never give the running commentary her dad had but appreciating him there, helping in ways she didn't think she could articulate.

He nodded and tapped his knee.

Sam and May took the tree out of its box, slotting the sections into the right places and straightening the branches out. This had always been her least favourite part and usually when Victor would say the tree was wonky, like it had soaked up too much sherry.

She bit the inside of her lip and leaned to her side to pull the plastic box of baubles closer. Opening the lid, she slid the box in between Sam and herself. She could almost hear her parents as she looked at the baubles, each with a memory.

Sam wrapped an arm around her. 'Shall I get them out and you can decide where they go?'

She nodded.

Sam began lifting baubles out, inspecting some more than others and passing them to May, who slowly found a place for each.

'Aw, look at this one, Dad.' Sam turned to Peter, holding a bauble that spun as the string hung from his fingers. It was a polystyrene-ball snowman that May had made at school. Its nose was bent out of shape after years of use, it was losing a black felt button and two coals for its smile were gone, making it look as though it had missing teeth.

The three began laughing.

'I was never great at art,' May said.

'Well, I think it's brilliant.' Sam handed her the snowman, and she hung it next to a bauble from her mam's childhood.

As May hung the baubles, she could almost hear her dad laughing at *Only Fools and Horses* on the TV and shouting orders whilst she and Mam laughed and pulled faces at him. But for her, although it was important to never forget, it was also now important to create new memories and traditions, like windows opening on an advent calendar—a new sight, a new experience. The decorating continued, with a few pauses as she wiped away silent tears.

She reached for a brightly coloured ceramic bauble. 'This was one we got on holiday in Mykonos.' She turned it over in her hand and moved to the sofa to show Peter. 'They had the most beautiful knick-knacks in the shops that are usually full of tat.'

'Now that is pretty, and I guess it has some nice memories for you, May?'

Taking the bauble back from Peter, she looked down at it resting in the palm of her hand. 'The best memories, and ones I know I'm lucky to have.' She placed the bauble towards the top of the tree, in the centre.

'Erm, I have something else for you, just a second.' Sam got up and dashed back into the kitchen.

May prayed he wouldn't come back with more alcohol-soaked soil cake or some other creation.

He returned, hands behind his back. 'Close your eyes and put out your hands.'

'Sam, you know I don't do surprises.'

'Fine, but I think you'll like this one.' He placed the present in her open palms—two baubles. Standing very still, watching her every move, he waited for a response as Peter craned out of his seat to also watch.

He had made baubles with photos of her parents inside. One was a photo of Fran and Victor and a baby May in her mother's arms. The other was of her parents on holiday that May had taken, heads touching, smiles wide.

She put a finger through the ribbon hooks of each bauble and held them up. She sobbed happy and sad tears. 'Thank you, Sam, that's so thoughtful.'

'Dad helped as well.'

'And thank you too, Peter. You're both so kind, so like family.'

Peter's eyes were filling with water.

'We could do some of you, Peter, with Sam and Anne? Also Gina and Lydia? All of you together, and hang them on the tree as well?' She touched Peter's arm tenderly.

'I'd like that, May. Thank you.'

Once May hung the gifted baubles of her family up, they stood side by side, facing the tree.

Peter got up and joined them, hand on Sam's shoulder. 'You've done a sterling job, May. And, Sam, you've done well as assistant.' Peter laughed. 'I'll take these cups through and give them a wash.' He gathered the empty cups on the tray and walked to the kitchen.

'How do you think Alexander will be with the tree next year?' Sam asked May.

May looked at Sam's grinning face and shook her head, laughing. 'Is that a hint?'

He stared at the tree, as if imagining what that would be like. 'Well, if things carry on the way they are, I don't see why it wouldn't be a possibility.'

'Maybe we can find out sooner?' she said, kissing his cheek.

The pair had taken their relationship slowly as May worked through her fear of abandonment and self-esteem issues with Sandra, and one thing she'd had to learn was that she owed it to her future self and the memory of her parents to live her life to the fullest, push herself and take chances.

Sam's attention snapped to her, his hand reaching for hers. 'May McClelland, are you asking to move in with me?'

'Not quite.' She snorted and playfully punched his arm. 'I just wondered if I could stay here for a few weeks whilst this is up?' She pointed to the tree. 'But obviously I'm a package deal now.'

He squeezed her hand. 'I think having you both here would be just perfect.'

May thought back to the wish she had made as she blew out the candle on her birthday cake, the wish she'd so desperately willed to come true as the flame died and the air filled with the whooping and cheering of Peter and Sam. Her wish to be happy. And although she'd lost and knew grief was far from a fleeting feeling, her eyes were now also open to possibilities and positive emotions. And within her, mingled with a range of other emotions, she couldn't deny that she truly was happy.

Acknowledgements

Thank you for reading The 31 Days of May.

The idea of the book developed through my belief that everyone, at some point in life, has felt the need to fit in and feel accepted. Standing on the outside, looking in—not quite fitting, through lack of self-belief, societal expectations, and stereotypes.

Also, none of us are immune from tragedy and trauma, and at times in life, we can feel we're in a world that doesn't understand us, feeling alone (even when we actually aren't). Poor mental health and loneliness can impact everyone, regardless of age, but sometimes we can find hope and friendship in the unlikeliest of places.

As with all my writing, some characters in The 31 Days of May are loosely based on real-life people and/or situations. Sadly, many people have felt and feel like May. Asking for help can be the hardest thing but I hope people struggling can reach out to someone, and access the many services we are lucky to have in the UK and beyond that which aim to support well-being.

My wish is that The 31 Days of May has left you with something to think about. I'm sorry if it made you cry—I cried a lot writing it! However, it also has hope, and without that, we have nothing. Even in the darkest of times, there is light—sometimes we just need help finding it.

Thank you to Cass and the team at Cahill Davis Publishing for believing in my work and helping me get it into the world. Thank you to Paul as always, for being my brightest light and biggest champion. Big thanks to my sister Joanne, and Caroline, for reading The 31 Days of May in its early development. Additional thanks to all the people, family, friends, old and new, who always ask about my books and support everything I do—it means more than you'll ever know.

If you enjoyed The 31 Days of May, please give it a review online if you can. Reviews are the ultimate thanks to authors and the team who spend countless hours creating a story and book. Two minutes of your time reviewing makes authors smile all week.

You can also follow me on social media via:
Instagram: @helen.aitchison_writes
X: @aitchisonwrites
Facebook: Helen Aitchison Writes
www.helenaitchisonwrites.com

There are a number of excellent services, websites, and resources available if any of the issues in this book have impacted on you. These include:

www.thecalmzone.net
www.mind.org.uk
www.everyturn.org
www.samaritans.org
www.alzheimers.org.uk
www.dementiauk.org
www.ageuk.org.uk
www.s4nd.org
www.autism.org.uk